CLOSE ENOUGH
TO TOUCH

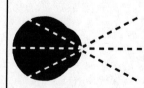

This Large Print Book carries the
Seal of Approval of N.A.V.H.

CLOSE ENOUGH
TO TOUCH

COLLEEN OAKLEY

THORNDIKE PRESS
A part of Gale, Cengage Learning

GALE
CENGAGE Learning·

Farmington Hills, Mich • San Francisco • New York • Waterville, Maine
Meriden, Conn • Mason, Ohio • Chicago

LIBRARY OF CONGRESS CATALOGING-IN-PUBLICATION DATA

Names: Oakley, Colleen, author.
Title: Close enough to touch / by Colleen Oakley.
Description: Large print edition. | Waterville, Maine : Thorndike Press, a part of
   Gale, Cengage Learning, 2017. | Series: Thorndike Press large print basic
Identifiers: LCCN 2017007392| ISBN 9781432838829 (hardcover) | ISBN 1432838822
   (hardcover)
Subjects: LCSH: Large type books. | GSAFD: Love stories.
Classification: LCC PS3615.A345 C58 2017b | DDC 813/.6—dc23
LC record available at https://lccn.loc.gov/2017007392

Published in 2017 by arrangement with Gallery Books, an imprint of Simon & Schuster, Inc.

Printed in the United States of America
1 2 3 4 5 6 7 21 20 19 18 17

For my big sister, Megan, for everything.

I don't want learning, or dignity, or respectability. I want this music, and this dawn, and the warmth of your cheek against mine.

— Rumi

■ ■ ■ ■

Part I

■ ■ ■ ■

You can keep as quiet as you like, but
one of these days somebody is going to
find you.
Haruki Murakami, *1Q84*

(Twenty Years Ago)

THE NEW YORK TIMES

THE GIRL WHO CAN'T BE TOUCHED
by William Colton

At first glance, Jubilee Jenkins is your run-of-the-mill third grader. She can name all three Powerpuff Girls gracing the front of her tiny T-shirt (and will, when prompted), and she purposefully mismatches her socks, as is apparently de rigueur at Griffin Elementary. Colorful scrunchies secure her wispy russet hair away from her face.

And Jenkins *is* like a lot of other American third graders in that she has an allergy. According to reports by the World Allergy Organization, allergies and asthma in children have been on the rise since the mid-1980s, including food allergies, which is a growing concern

11

to experts.

But Jenkins isn't allergic to peanut butter. Or bee stings. Or pet dander. Or any of the other most common allergens.

Jubilee Jenkins is allergic to other people.

Born in 1989 to single mother Victoria Jenkins, Jubilee was a typical infant. "She was perfectly healthy. Slept through the night at seven weeks, walked at ten months," says the elder Jenkins. "It wasn't until she was three that we started having issues."

That's when Ms. Jenkins, who had just been promoted to manager at Belk in Fountain City, TN, began noticing rashes on Jubilee's skin. But it wasn't just a few bumps.

"It was awful — these huge raised welts, hives that itched her like crazy, long scaly patches of skin all over her arms and face," says Jenkins. "She used to scream bloody murder from the pain of it." In the space of six months, Ms. Jenkins made more than 20 visits to their family doctor, as well as the hospital emergency room — to no avail. Jubilee also had to be revived by an EpiPen three times for anaphylaxis. Physicians were perplexed.

They remained that way for the next three years, as Jubilee was subjected to every allergy test available in the twentieth century.

"Her little arms were like pincushions," says

Jenkins. "And we tried everything at home, too — changing detergents, keeping food diaries, removing all the carpet from our house, repainting. I even quit smoking!"

It wasn't until they met Dr. Gregory Benefield, an allergist and then associate professor at Emory University in Atlanta, that they finally started to get some answers. (continued on page 19B)

ONE

JUBILEE

One time, a boy kissed me and I almost died.

I realize that can easily be dismissed as a melodramatic teenagerism, said in a high-pitched voice bookended by squeals. But I'm not a teenager. And I mean it in the most literal sense. The basic sequence of events went like this:

A boy kissed me.

My lips started tingling.

My tongue swelled to fill my mouth.

My throat closed; I couldn't breathe.

Everything went black.

It's humiliating enough to pass out just after experiencing your first kiss, but even more so when you find out that the boy kissed you on a dare. A bet. That your lips are so inherently unkissable, it took $50 to persuade him to put his mouth on yours.

And here's the kicker: I knew it could kill

me. At least, in theory.

When I was six, I was diagnosed with type IV contact dermatitis to foreign human skin cells. That's medical terminology for: I'm allergic to other people. Yes, *people*. And yes, it's rare, as in: I'm only one of a handful of people in the history of the world who has had it. Basically, I explode in welts and hives when someone else's skin touches mine. The doctor who finally diagnosed me also theorized that my severe reactions — the anaphylactic episodes I'd experienced — were either from my body over-reacting to prolonged skin contact, or oral contact, like drinking after someone and getting their saliva in my mouth. *No more sharing food, drinks. No hugs. No touching. No kissing. You could die,* he said. But I was a sweaty-palmed, weak-kneed seventeen-year-old girl inches away from the lips of Donovan Kingsley, and consequences weren't the first thing on my mind — even if the consequences were deadly. In the moment — the actual breathless seconds of his lips on mine — I daresay it almost seemed worth it.

Until I found out about the bet.

When I got home from the hospital, I went directly to my room. And I didn't come out, even though there were still two weeks left in my senior year. My diploma was mailed

16

to me later that summer.

Three months later, my mom got married to Lenny, a gas-station-chain owner from Long Island. She packed exactly one suitcase and left.

That was nine years ago. And I haven't left my house since.

I didn't wake up one morning and think: *"I'm going to become a recluse."* I don't even like the word "recluse." It reminds me of that deadly spider just lying in wait to sink its venom into the next creature that crosses its path.

It's just that after my first-kiss near-death experience, I — understandably, I think — didn't want to leave my house, for fear of running into anyone from school. So I didn't. I spent that summer in my room, listening to Coldplay on repeat and reading. I read a lot.

Mom used to make fun of me for it. "Your nose is always stuck in a book," she'd say, rolling her eyes. It wasn't just books, though. I'd read magazines, newspapers, pamphlets, anything that was lying around. And I'd retain most of the information, without really trying.

Mom liked that part. She'd have me recite on cue — to friends (which she didn't have

17

many of) and to boyfriends (which she had too many of) — weird knowledge that I had collected over time. Like the fact that superb fairy wrens are the least faithful species of bird in the world, or that the original pronunciation of Dr. Seuss's name rhymed with "Joyce," or that Leonardo da Vinci invented the first machine gun (which shouldn't really surprise anyone, since he invented thousands of things).

Then she'd beam and shrug her shoulders and give a smile and say, "I don't know where she came from." And I'd always wonder if that maybe was a little bit true, because every time I got the nerve to ask about my father — like, what his name was, for instance — she'd snap and say something like "What's it matter? He's not here, is he?"

Basically, I was a freak show growing up. And not just because I didn't know who my father was or because I could recite random facts. I'm pretty sure neither of those are unique characteristics. It was because of my *condition*, which is how people referred to it: a *condition*. And my *condition* was the reason my desk in elementary school had to be at least eight feet away from the others. And why I had to sit on a bench by myself at recess and watch while kids created trains out of their bodies on the slide and played red rover and swung effortlessly on monkey bars. And why my body was clad in long sleeves and pants and mittens — cloth covering every square inch of skin on the off chance that the kids I was kept so far away from accidentally broke the boundaries of my personal bubble. And why I used to stare openmouthed at mothers who would squeeze their children's tiny bodies with abandon at pickup, trying to remember what that felt like.

Anyway, combine all the facts — my *condition,* the boy-kissing-me-and-my-almost-dying incident, my mother leaving — and voilà! It's the perfect recipe for becoming a recluse.

Or maybe it's none of those things. Maybe I just like being alone.

Regardless, here we are.

And now, I fear that I've become the Boo Radley of my neighborhood. I'm not pale or sickly looking, but I'm afraid the kids on the street have started to wonder about me. Maybe I stare out the window too much when they're riding their scooters. I ordered blue panel curtains and hung them on each window a few months ago, and now I try to stand behind them and peek out, but I'm worried that looks even more creepy, when

I'm spotted. I can't help it. I like watching them play, which I guess does sound creepy when I put it like that. But I enjoy seeing them have fun, bearing witness to a normal childhood.

Once, a kid looked directly into my eyes and then turned to his friend and said something. They both laughed. I couldn't hear them so I pretended he said something like, "Look, Jimmy, it's that nice, pretty lady again." But I'm afraid it was more like, "Look, Jimmy, it's that crazy lady who eats cats." For the record, I don't. Eat cats. But Boo Radley was a nice man, and that's what everybody said about him.

The phone is ringing. I look up from my book and pretend to contemplate not answering it. But I know I will. Even though it means getting up from the worn indent of my velvet easy chair and walking the seventeen paces (yes, I've counted) into the kitchen to pick up the mustard-yellow receiver of my landline, since I don't own a cell phone. Even though it's probably one of the telemarketers who call on a regular basis or my mother, who only calls three or four times a year. Even though I'm at the part in my book where the detective and the killer are finally in the same church after playing cat and mouse for the last 274 pages. I'll answer it for the same reason I always answer the phone: I like hearing someone else's voice. Or maybe I like hearing my own.

Riiiiiiiinnnnng!

Stand up.

Book down.

Seventeen paces.

"Hello?"

"Jubilee?"

It's a man's voice that I don't recognize and I wonder what he's selling. A time-share? A new Internet service with eight-times-faster downloads? Or maybe he's taking a survey. Once I talked to someone for forty-five minutes about my favorite ice-cream flavors.

"Yes?"

"It's Lenny."

Lenny. My mother's husband. I only met him once — years ago, in the five months he and my mother were dating before she moved out to Long Island. The thing I remember most about him: he had a mustache and pet it often, as if it were a loyal dog attached to his face. He was also formal to the point of being awkward. I remember feeling like I should bow to him, even though he was short. Like he was royalty or something.

"OK."

He clears his throat. "How are you?"

My mind is racing. I'm fairly certain this isn't a social call since Lenny has never called me before.

"I'm OK."

He clears his throat again. "Well, I'm just going to say it. Victoria — Vicki —" His voice breaks and he tries to disguise it with a little cough, which turns into a full-on fit. I hold the receiver with both hands to my ear, listening to him hack. I wonder if he still has a mustache.

The coughing spell over, Lenny inhales the silence. And then: "Your mother died."

I let the sentence crawl into my ear and sit there, like a bullet a magician has caught with his teeth. I don't want it to go any farther.

Still holding the receiver, I put my back against the wallpaper covered in cheerful pairs of red cherries and inch my butt down until I'm sitting on the cracked and tattered linoleum, and I think about the last time I saw my mother.

She was wearing a two-sizes-too-small mauve sweater set and pearls. It was three months after the Boy Kissed Me and I Almost Died, and as I mentioned, I had

22

spent the summer mostly in my room. But I also spent a considerable amount of time shooting daggers at my mother whenever I passed by her in the hallway, seeing as how the whole incident would never have happened if she hadn't moved us from Fountain City, Tennessee, to Lincoln, New Jersey, three years earlier.

But honestly, that was the least of her sins as a mother. It was just the most recent and most tangible to be angry with her for.

"It's the new me," she said, twirling at the bottom of the stairs. The movement caused the cloying scent of her vanilla body spray to waft through the air.

I was sitting in the velvet armchair rereading *Northanger Abbey* and eating Thin Mint cookies from a plastic sleeve.

"Doesn't it just scream millionaire's wife?"

It didn't. It screamed slutty June Cleaver. I looked back down at my book.

I heard the familiar crinkling of cellophane as she dug in her back pocket for her pack of cigarettes, and the click of the lighter.

"I'm leaving in a few hours, you know." She exhaled and slid onto a couch cushion across from me.

I looked up and she gestured toward the door at the one suitcase she had packed. ("That's all you're taking?" I had asked that morning. "What else would I need?" she said. "Lenny's got everything." And then she giggled, which was just as strange as her wearing pearls and a sweater set and twirling.)

"I know," I said. Our eyes met, and I thought of the night before, as I lay in bed and heard the door to my room softly creak open. I knew it was her, but I remained still, pretending to sleep. She stood there for a long time — so long that I think I drifted off before she left. And I didn't know if it was my imagination, or if I really did hear her sniffling. Crying. Now I wondered if maybe there was something she was trying to muster up the courage to say, some profound mother-daughter moment. Or at least an acknowledgment of her poor mothering skills where we'd laugh and say something banal like "Well, at least we survived, right?"

But sitting on the couch, she just inhaled her cigarette again and said: "So, I'm just saying, you don't have to be so bitchy."

Oh.

I wasn't sure how to respond to that, so I took another cookie out of the sleeve and put it in my mouth and tried not to think about how much I hated my mother. And how hating her made me feel so guilty that

I hated myself.

She sighed, blowing out smoke. "Sure you don't want to come with me?" she said, even though she knew the answer. To be fair, she had asked multiple times over the past few weeks in different ways. *Lenny has plenty of space. You could probably have a whole guesthouse to yourself. Won't you be lonely here all by yourself?* I laughed at that last one — maybe it was some innate biology of being a teenager, but I couldn't wait to be away from my mother.

"I'm sure," I said, flipping a page.

We spent the last hour we'd ever spend together in silence — her chain-smoking, me pretending to be lost in my book. And then when the doorbell rang, announcing the arrival of her driver, she jumped up, patted her hair, and looked at me one last time. "Off I go," she said.

I nodded. I wanted to tell her that she looked nice, but the words got caught in my throat.

She picked up her suitcase and left, the door easing shut behind her.

And there I sat, a book in my lap and an empty plastic cookie sleeve beside me. Half a cigarette was still smoldering in the ashtray on the coffee table, and I had a strong urge to pick it up. Put my lips to it

— even though I knew it could kill me. Inhale my mother one last time.

But I didn't. I just watched it burn.

And now, nine years later, my mother is dead.

The news isn't out of nowhere, in the sense that about ten months ago, she mentioned that a suspicious scab on her scalp that refused to heal had been determined to be melanoma. She laugh-coughed and said, "Always thought it would be my lungs that got me."

But Mom had a tendency to be overdramatic — like the time she got a mosquito bite, became convinced she had West Nile, and lay supine on the couch for three days — and I couldn't be certain whether her pronouncement in subsequent months that she was dying was an actual diagnosis from a doctor or one of her elaborate schemes for attention.

Turns out, it was the former.

"The funeral is on Thursday," Lenny says. "Would you like me to send a driver?"

The funeral. In Long Island. It feels as though a giant fist has reached into my chest and started squeezing. Tighter and tighter until there's no air left at all. Is this what the beginning of grief feels like? Am I already grieving her? Or is it the thought of

26

leaving the house that compresses my vital organs? I don't know.

What I do know is that I don't want to go — that I haven't wanted to go *anywhere* for nine years — but saying it out loud would make me a terrible person. Who doesn't go to their own mother's funeral?

I also know it's possible Mom's Pontiac that's been sitting in the driveway for nine years wouldn't make the trip.

I gulp for air, hoping Lenny can't hear the effort it's taking me to breathe.

Finally, I answer: "You don't need to send a driver," I say. "I'll figure it out."

There's a beat of silence.

"It starts at ten a.m. I'll e-mail you the address," Lenny says. And then I sense a shift in the air between us — a steeling of his voice, as though he's running a board meeting and not discussing his dead wife with the stepdaughter he never claimed. "I know it may be an inappropriate time to discuss this, but I wanted to let you know your mother has left you the house, free and clear — I've paid off the balance of your mortgage and I'll be transferring the deed — as well as her car, if you still have it. But, well, the checks she was sending you . . . I thought I should tell you as soon as possible that I won't be continuing that specific tradition, so you'll need to make other, ah . . . arrangements."

My cheeks redden at the mention of my freeloading, and I have the urge to hang up the phone. I feel like a loser. Like those thirty-year-old men who live in the basement of their parents' house, their mothers still washing their drawers and serving them grilled cheese with the crusts cut off. And I guess in a way, I am.

The first check arrived a week after she left.

I set it on the kitchen table and stared at it for three days every time I passed it. I had every intention of throwing it away. Maybe Mom wanted to live off Lenny's money for the rest of her life, but I wasn't interested.

And then the electricity bill came. And then the water. And then the mortgage.

I cashed the check.

I was eighteen and jobless and still trying to figure out what I was going to do with my life. Surely it involved some sort of employment and college education. So I swore to myself this would be the only time. That I wouldn't take any more money.

When the next check came, three weeks later, I still didn't have a job, but I didn't feel like leaving the house to cash it, so I thought that would be the end of it. But on a break from an intense game of Bejeweled on the computer, I did a quick online search and learned that I could just mail the check into the bank and the money would magically show up in my account.

And then, as I returned to clicking on colorful gemstones and watching them satisfyingly disappear, I wondered what else I could do without leaving home.

Turns out, a lot.

It became sort of a game — a challenge to see what I could accomplish while sitting in my pajamas.

Groceries? Fresh Direct delivers.

College? I got an English degree in eighteen months from one of those online outfits. I'm not sure how legit it is, but the piece of paper they sent me is real enough. I wanted to keep going, get a master's, maybe a PhD, but $400 per credit hour was depleting my already stretched budget, so I started taking a handful of the classes Harvard offers for free online every semester. *Free.* Makes you wonder why all those geniuses are paying hundreds of thousands of dollars for their Ivy League education.

Dentist? Floss regularly and brush after every meal. I haven't had so much as a toothache, and I chalk it up to my good dental habits. And I've started to think that maybe dentistry is a racket.

When a neighbor left a note on my door alerting me that my grass was reaching unmanageable heights and he would appreciate my maintaining my lawn for the "integrity" of the neighborhood? I called a landscaping service to come once a month and left a check under the porch mat.

The trash presented a more difficult challenge. I couldn't figure out a way to get it to the curb without actually going outside. It's not that I couldn't do that, of course, but now I was determined to not have to. To figure out this last piece of the puzzle. I'm not proud of it, but I called the city garbage service and told them I was disabled. They said if I could get my trash into the bin beside my back door, the workers would come around and get it every Thursday morning. And I felt a little buzz of pride at my deceitful cleverness.

Six months passed. Then a year. And there were times when I would stop and wonder if this was it. If I would live my life out this way, never seeing another soul in person again. But mostly, I just woke up every morning and lived my life like everyone else does — not thinking about the big picture, just doing my work for class, making din-

30

ner, watching the news, then getting up and doing it all over again. In that way, I didn't think I was really different from anyone else.

Though my mother called sporadically over the years, to complain about the weather, a rude waiter, a bad ending to a TV series, to brag about one of the many trips she and Lenny were taking or to invite me for a holiday — even though she knew I wouldn't come — we never discussed the money she was sending me. I was ashamed of taking it, but I had also convinced myself that I somehow deserved it. That she owed me for being kind of a selfish, crappy mother.

But I never meant for it to go on this long.

"I know you have your *condition*," Lenny said, "but it's something we never quite saw eye t—"

"I understand," I say, the humiliation burning brighter with each second. But there's a flare of anger mixed in — anger that my mom didn't leave me any money on top of the house and car (even as I recognize how ungrateful that is), although I guess technically it's Lenny's money. Or maybe I'm angry at myself for becoming so dependent on those monthly checks. Or maybe it has nothing to do with the money. Maybe I'm mad that I didn't take her up

31

on her invitation to visit even once. Or invite her to visit me. Funny how when someone dies you momentarily forget all their faults, like how just talking to her on the phone was so emotionally draining, I didn't ever want to see her in person. But now . . . now it's too late.

"Well, then," Lenny says.

There's nothing left for us to say, so I wait for his good-bye. But then it's silent for so long I wonder if maybe he already hung up and I somehow missed it.

"Lenny?" I say, at the exact moment he speaks.

"Jubilee, your mom really . . . ," he says. His voice falters again. "Well, you know."

I don't know. My mom really what? Liked tight blouses? Smoked far too many cigarettes? Was impossible to live with? I hold on to the phone long after he's hung up, hoping I'll hear what he was going to say. That it somehow got caught in the ether between us and will materialize at any second. When I accept that it won't, I let the receiver drop onto the floor beside me.

Minutes pass. Or maybe hours. But I don't move — even when a staccato of beeps blares from the receiver, the phone insisting on being hung up.

My mother is dead.

I look around the kitchen, checking for subtle differences — comparing the before and after. If I can find one, then it's evidence that maybe I've entered some alternate universe. That maybe mom is still alive in the other, real one. Or maybe I've read *1Q84* too many times.

I take a deep breath, and tears spring to my eyes. I'm not prone to outward displays of emotion, but today I just sit and let them fall.

There are upsides to being a recluse. Like, it only takes me six minutes to wash the one plate, mug, fork that I use every day. (Yes, I've timed it.) And I don't ever have to make small talk. I don't have to nod and smile when someone says "Heard it might rain today," or mumble something inane back like "The grass sure could use it, huh?" Really, I don't have to worry about the weather, period. It's raining? Who cares? I'm not going out in it.

But there are downsides, too. Like, late at night when I'm lying in bed listening to the dead-quiet of the street and wondering if maybe, just maybe, I'm the only person left on Earth. Or if there was a civil war or a super-flu or a zombie apocalypse and nobody remembered to tell me, because nobody remembers I'm here. On those nights, I would think about my mom. She'd call me. She'd tell me. She'd remember. And a wave of comfort would wash over me.

But now, she's gone. And I'm lying in bed, listening to the night air and wondering: *Who's going to remember me now?*

Thursday begins like a normal day: I go downstairs and make two sunny-side-up eggs with toast (cut into tiny bite-size pieces after a choking incident four years ago) and eat it while reading the news online. But then, instead of clicking on the next lecture in my Harvard class (this week: "Shakespeare After All: The Later Plays"), I have to face that this day is not a normal day.

I will be leaving the house.

My heartbeat revs at the thought, so I try to distract myself with a more immediate problem: I have nothing to wear to my mother's funeral. The only black things I own are a pair of sweatpants and a matching hoodie. Not exactly suitable funeral attire.

Upstairs, I walk down the hall to my mom's room and stand in the doorway. For nine years, I've left her room exactly as it was when she walked out the door. Not in a creepy Miss Havisham kind of way. There's

34

no uneaten wedding cake on a table or anything. I told myself it's because I just didn't know what to do with her stuff, but part of me liked having her stuff where it's always been. Like maybe she'd come back for it one day.

Except now, I guess, she won't.

At my mom's closet, I stand staring at her collection of women's skirt suits circa the nineties from her days as a department store retail clerk. I remember trying on her clothes as a child when she was at work, letting the garments swim around me, inhaling her sugary scent. I'd even get in her bed, wrapping myself up in her blankets, pretending they were her arms. It was against the rules — the doctors warned that even though it appeared I only reacted to skin-on-skin contact, I had to still be careful around things that had prolonged contact with other people, like bedsheets and towels. *Allergies are tricky,* they said. But I took the risk, and fortunately never reacted. It was my little act of rebellion, but it was something else, too — the only way I could feel close to her. I pull a black suit jacket off its wire hanger and shrug it on over the white tank top I slept in.

I turn and look in the ornate mirror hung over Mom's dresser, and I scrutinize myself for the first time in years. The realization that other people will be looking at me — seeing what I see in the reflection — churns my stomach. I haven't had a proper haircut in years, relying on a few snips here and there with my nail scissors, and it shows. My hair's never been obedient, but it's grown especially unruly and wild in its freedom, brown curls crawling every which way from the crown of my head to my elbows. I try to smooth them down with the palm of my hand, to no avail.

Then I remember the suit I'm wearing and my eyes are drawn to the padded shoulders. It's as if someone is asking me a question and I'm shrugging to indicate I don't know the answer. The rest of the suit is slightly ill fitting. My mom was a little slip of a thing, aside from her large breasts. While I'm not much bigger, the sleeves are a tad too short, the skirt too snug around the waist. It will have to do.

As I bend down to look in the bottom of her closet for a pair of shoes, I swear I catch a whiff of vanilla body spray and my stomach lurches. I sit down on my butt, pull the lapel of the jacket up to my nose, and inhale.

But all I smell is musty fabric.

Downstairs, I pick up my handbag from the

side table near the door. I rifle through it, eyeing the two bright yellow EpiPens clustered at the bottom. They expired years ago, but I convince myself they'll still work in an emergency. And then I pick up my gloves. I wonder if I should put them on. I always found it kind of overkill as a child — the yellow knit gloves I wore in elementary school, graduating to more adultlike, but just as weird, leather gloves in high school. It's not as if I was going out of my way to touch people — or them me. It's not that hard to keep your hands to yourself, especially when you're treated like a pariah. But then I think of all the ways people can make contact without even thinking about it: exchanging money at cash registers; handshakes; someone in a hurry pushing past you, their arm brushing yours.

I slip the gloves on.

Then, before I can change my mind, I snatch my keys off the table beside the front door, turn the handle, and step over the threshold.

The brightness of the blue September sky assaults my eyes and I squint, raising a hand to block the rays. It's 7:34 a.m. and I'm outside. On the front porch. Though I've hurriedly opened the door under the cover of night to bring in packages left by the postman and my weekly grocery delivery, I can't remember the last time I stood here. In broad daylight.

Blood rushes to my head and I clutch the door frame, dizzy. I feel exposed. As if a thousand eyes are on me. The air around me is too loose, shifty. As if a current could just pick me up and fling me unwilling into the world.

I will my foot to move. To step forward.

But it won't. It's as if I'm standing precariously on the edge of a cliff and one step will send me into the great abyss. The world will swallow me whole.

And that's when I hear it.

The metal clanging and squeaking of the garbage truck turning onto the street.

I freeze.

It's Thursday. Trash day.

My heart beats wildly against my chest, as if it's trying to burst out of my body.

I search for the knob behind me, turn it, and step back inside, shutting the door firmly behind me.

Then I lean against it and concentrate on slowing my breath, so the rhythm of my heart can return to normal.

Normal.

Normal.

I glance at my gloved hands and snicker.

And then a full burst of laughter escapes my lips and I reach up to my mouth with leather-clad fingers to suppress the sound.

What was I thinking? That I could just leave the house and go to my mother's funeral like a normal person?

If I were normal, I would wave to the garbagemen. Or say hi. Or just ignore them completely and get in the car, as I'm sure other people do a hundred times a year without even thinking about it.

My shoulders begin shaking as my laughter mutates into crying.

I'm not going to my mother's funeral. Lenny will wonder where I am. Anything my mom's told him over the years about my being a bad daughter will be confirmed.

And while all of that is troublesome, another thought floats on the periphery of my brain, waiting to be let in. A terrifying thought. A thought that I realize maybe I've known deep down but haven't wanted to admit to myself. But it's hard to deny it when I'm leaning against the front door inside my house, unable to slow my heart or stem my tears or stop my body from shaking.

And that thought is: *Maybe there's another reason I haven't left my house in nine years.*

Maybe it's because I can't.

Two

ERIC

The fish is dying.

I don't think it is dead yet, because when I gently poke at it with the eraser end of a pencil, it flaps its fins and swims erratically around the small glass bowl for about ten seconds until it appears to give up and float to the top of the water again. It's not belly-up, though, and isn't that the telltale sign?

My eyes dart around the boxy apartment as if the solution to save this fish's life will present itself. But the beige walls, of course, are bare. The rest of the small living room only contains my couch, a glass coffee table, and a few boxes with LIVING ROOM written in black marker on the side. The pencil appears to be my only hope.

I poke at the fish again and look over my shoulder as if a PETA representative is going to be standing there shaking a finger in my face. I'm sure this is tantamount to animal abuse, but this fish needs to live. At least for the next fifteen minutes. And the pencil is my only hope.

The fish finishes its bizarre dance and resumes floating.

Jesus Christ.

"What are you doing?" The small voice gives me a start.

"Nothing," I say, jabbing the fish one more time and then setting the pencil down. "Feeding Squidboy."

"I already fed him. Last night. I feed him every night."

I turn to face Aja's large, dark, knowing eyes behind his wire-rimmed glasses and marvel — not for the first time — at how he can so often make me feel like I'm the child and he the adult. Even though he looks exactly like his dad, Dinesh — acorn skin, silky black hair, lashes long enough to be a mascara ad — he's the complete op-posite of him personality-wise. Where Dinesh was impulsive, charming, person-able, Aja is cautious, quiet, introverted. More like me, I guess.

"I know," I say, using my body to block his view of the small glass bowl. Aja's life has been turned upside down enough in the past two years — from his parents' death, to my adopting him, to my now moving

41

from the only town he's ever known in New Hampshire to Lincoln, New Jersey. If I can shield him from his dying fish, at least for today, I'm going to do it. "But he looked hungry. And I am, too. Let's go get breakfast."

Suspicion doesn't leave Aja's eyes, but he turns and plods toward the kitchen, hands in his pockets, shoulders slightly hunched, making his already slim ten-year-old frame appear even tinier.

"Ready for your first day of school?" I ask, heading toward the sink to rinse out yesterday's coffee mug with hot water. Maybe today will be the day I find the extra mugs in an errant box, as I've unpacked all the boxes marked KITCHEN, and they were not there. Moving is the only time that I'm able to suspend my belief in the laws of nature and understand that some other dynamic force is at work. Black magic? Teleportation? It's the only explanation for how things get lost. The coffee mugs should be in the kitchen boxes. Where I packed them. And yet . . .

I grab the coffeepot handle and pour the dark brown liquid into my mug. I shouldn't have made an entire pot, as, after seeing some news segment on the dire health consequences of too much coffee, I promised myself that the new me in New Jersey would only have one cup a day. I can't remember what the consequences are now, but they probably involve cancer and death. Which seems to be the end result of every health study these days. I turn back to Aja, realizing he didn't respond to my question.

"Bud?"

He's carefully measuring one cup of Rice Chex to pour into his bowl, as the serving size suggests. I know he'll measure the half cup of milk next.

When he's done with his precise breakfast preparation, he picks up a spoon.

I try again. "Aja?"

I realize I sound a bit desperate, but that's mainly because I am. Because even though I'm now four full states away I can still hear her voice as though she's speaking directly in my ear.

You don't know how to talk to your own fucking child.

And that's one of the nicest things Stephanie has said to me since our divorce. When we were married, she always complained I wasn't good at picking up on social cues or implications or the meaning behind words and actions (and maybe she was right; is it too much to ask people to just say what they mean?), but I had no problem picking up

43

on the implication of what she was telling me that night.

You're not a good father.

I didn't argue with her. It's hard to be a good father when you only see your daughter every other weekend and the entire time her ears are plugged up with those white buds, her fingers moving at light speed, typing god knows what to god knows who on her phone. I would sometimes try to glance over Ellie's shoulder to make sure she wasn't sexting, as I had read an article about that in the *Washington Post.* She may well have been and I wouldn't have known it, because all I saw were a bunch of uppercase letters that didn't make words. It was like code, and I puffed up a bit wondering if maybe she'd have a future writing HTML in Silicon Valley.

Anyway, when Ellie and I had our massive falling-out four months ago, I picked up on another implication, without Stephanie's saying a word — which I fought the urge to point out to her because I thought she would have been impressed by my progress: it was all my fault.

I should have tried harder. I should have been there more. I should have somehow made my fourteen-year-old daughter take those earbuds out and have a real, live conversation with me. Because now she won't even speak to me. Not even via coded text.

And maybe that's why I'm so desperate to have Aja respond to every single one of my questions. I've only officially been his father for two years — *Two years? Has Dinesh been gone that long?* — but I know the parent-child connection is so very fragile, like a soap bubble, and it doesn't take much to break it.

"Eric?" Aja keeps his eyes trained on the Rice Chex box.

"Yeah, bud?" I say, hating the overeagerness in my voice.

"Did you find a wheelchair yet?"

I take a long sip of my coffee, not wanting to get into this conversation so early in the morning. Or ever. Aja got in his head last week that he wanted to be Professor X from the X-Men for Halloween (which, it should be pointed out, is nearly two months away. Aja likes to plan ahead). I readily agreed, without realizing the costume required a wheelchair. I told Aja I wasn't sure it was appropriate, seeing as how he doesn't have a disability and it could be offensive to people who actually do. "But Professor X does," he said matter-of-factly. I let it drop, too overwhelmed by the move to argue

45

about it.

"Not yet," I say, and before he can ask a follow-up question, I close the gap between us with a few steps and bend at the waist so I'm eye level with him, all four of our eyes now trained on the cereal box.

"Any luck today?" I ask. It's the exact opposite of what I was told to do by the therapist I took Aja to after his parents died. *Don't feed into his delusions,* she said in her obnoxiously nasal tone. But it seemed over-reactionary. Or maybe it was that drug, that Risperdal they gave him that made him so drowsy, he slept seventeen hours a day and barely ate, that felt overreactionary. I stopped giving him the pills and didn't go back. Aja has an imagination. So what? What's the harm in that?

He shakes his head. "I can't even get a little spark, much less a flame."

"A flame?" I'm a little alarmed at this. "I thought you were just trying to move it with your mind."

"No, this week I'm working on the advanced levels, specifically telekinetic destruction." He glances at me. "That means blowing things up."

Oh. I scratch the side of my cheek and straighten up and glance around the small kitchen. My eyes land on the phone book that was on the counter when we moved in. I wonder who uses phone books anymore. And then I wonder where I put that therapist's number.

Maybe it's with the coffee mugs.

While Aja is brushing his teeth and finishing getting ready for school, I check back in on Squidboy. He is now decidedly belly-up. Giving him the benefit of the doubt, I poke him with the pencil anyway, but nothing happens. I sigh. Maybe Aja won't look at his bowl before we leave. Then I'll have time to go to the pet store, pick out a Squidboy replica, and hope he doesn't notice that either.

My phone buzzes in my pocket. I set the pencil on the shelf next to the fishbowl and retrieve my cell.

"Hey, Connie," I greet my sister. She's the reason I moved to this quiet borough just eight miles away from the Manhattan skyline. New York itself was out of the question due to the outrageous rent and even worse public schools, but I would have probably chosen a more popular — and populated — city like Hoboken or Elizabeth if Connie hadn't been living in Lincoln for the past eight years. *It's like a throwback to a different time,* she said. *The downtown is so quaint, with cute little shops and gorgeous views of the river. And the schools are really good.* I couldn't care less about the river, but she had me at the schools — and the fact that she would be a few miles away and could jump in and help with Aja if I needed it.

"First day of school," she says, skipping the greetings and jumping directly into the conversation in her lawyerly fashion. Yes, my parents raised an accountant and attorney, and though they often tell us at our WASP-y holiday gatherings how proud they are of us, I sometimes wonder if they're not a little disappointed by how boring their children turned out. "Is he ready?"

I glance down the hall. He's still in the bathroom. "Just about. Although I think he may have a potentially dangerous new interest in blowing things up."

"Don't all boys?"

I try to recall a fascination with explosives from my own childhood. "I don't think I ever did."

She snorts. "No, I think you'd qualify as the outlier in the risk-taking department."

"Oh, I would?" I say. "Hey, speaking of — how was your skydiving trip last weekend? And the rattlesnake farm? Did you handle a lot of them?"

"Ha-ha. Very funny."

"Just saying. Pot, kettle. All that."

"Yeah, but we're not talking about me."

"No," I say. "We never do seem to talk about you, lately." I look for my coffee on the shelf next to Squidboy's bowl and realize I left it in the kitchen.

"Well, my life isn't the one that's imploded on itself."

"Thanks. That's very helpful."

"No problem," she says. "But seriously — how are you holding up?"

"Fine," I say, walking into the kitchen and setting my sights on my mug on the table. I drain the last few gulps and reach for the pot on the counter to pour a second cup. (I'll stop at two today. Surely cutting back slowly is a better way to break a habit than cold turkey.) "I can't find my other coffee mugs," I tell Connie. And then I laugh.

As if the disappearing coffee mugs are the most severe of my problems. I moved four states away from my ex-wife and my daughter who's not speaking to me. I uprooted my son — who, admittedly, doesn't handle change well — from the only town he's ever known, the only friends he's ever known, the city where his parents are *buried* for Christ's sake, and am starting him in a brand-new school with kids he doesn't know. Oh, and he's into blowing things up.

And the fish is dead.

"It's only for six months," Connie says, ignoring my coffee mug comment and shooting right to the heart of the matter, like she always does. "You did the right thing."

The right thing. It's like a slippery salmon I've been trying to catch from a stream with my bare hands for my entire life. *The right thing* is why Stephanie and I got married directly out of high school when we found out she was pregnant with Ellie. *The right thing* is why I adopted Aja when Dinesh and Kate died in a commuter-plane crash, even though Stephanie was against it. *The right thing* is why I let Ellie live with her mother after the divorce, even though no part of me wanted to be without her for even a day.

But moving to Lincoln, New Jersey, so I can work in my firm's New York office filling in for the senior financial analyst during her maternity leave — even though I told myself it would not only put me one step closer to making partner, but it would be nice to have a fresh start, be an adventure for Aja, and put us closer to my sister — is starting to feel a little bit selfish, and a lot like running away, and not even remotely like *the right thing* for anybody but me.

50

"Ellie," I say, immediately visualizing her upturned nose, the wispy caramel curls that frame her round face, her doll-like eyes. But no. I'm picturing her as a child. Not as the fourteen-year-old she is now, her thinned-out face revealing defined cheekbones, her locks trained to lie flat — all hints of curl erased from existence with a metal iron, as is apparently the style. When did she become this person, this young *woman*? And how did I miss it?

I don't realize I've said her name out loud until Connie's voice softens.

"Oh, Eric," she says. "I don't think it much matters to Ellie right now where you live."

And though I know it's true, I can't explain why hearing it hurts quite so much.

The September morning is still and muggy, feeling more like the thick air of August than the crisp leaf-turning weather associated with back-to-school. As we pull into the Lincoln Elementary School car drop-off line, I swallow all of the hokey clichéd advice that my dad arbitrarily said over the years. *Knock 'em dead, tiger. Never let them see you sweat. Be yourself.*

I'm not sure which phrase would be most appropriate, anyway. Certainly not *Be your-*

self. I love him, but if I'm being objective, I have to admit that sometimes when Aja's himself, he can come across as a little patronizing and antisocial, and, well, weird — which isn't the best foot forward with fifth-grade boys you want to befriend.

My palms get sweaty as the car inches up, closer to where Aja will get out. I glance over at him. He's sitting stone still, his eyes trained straight ahead.

"I'll pick you up today," I say, just to break the silence, even though we talked about it all last night. "But you'll be riding the bus home starting next week."

He doesn't acknowledge me, and I know it's because he hates when I repeat instructions.

The carpool line attendant — a grandmotherly woman with crinkly eyes and an orange sash draped over her large belly — opens the door of the car in front of us, and a man steps out of the backseat, slinging a backpack on his shoulder. A slight panic sets in — am I supposed to be walking Aja in? They didn't mention that in any of the information packets.

The man shuts the door, and I wonder where the kid is. And then my eyes bulge as I get a glimpse of the "man's" cherubic face. He's just a child. A huge, gargantuan child.

Is this what fifth graders look like nowadays? I glance back at Aja, who looks even tinier in his bucket seat. Fragile. I wonder if it's too late to jerk the wheel and peel out of the parking lot. Possibly drive all the way back to New Hampshire.

I wonder if Aja is thinking the same thing.

"Hey, Eric?" he says in a small voice, and my heart breaks a little.

"Yeah, bud?"

He turns to me with his big eyes, and I steel myself with all the confidence I don't feel, to assure him that this is *the right thing.* That he'll have a great day. That the hulking fifth grader who probably lords over children like Aja on the playground stealing their lunch money and giving them wedgies is actually going to be a nice kid who'll bond with him over their mutual love of the X-Men.

"Can we get a dog?"

"What?" I say, tearing my eyes away from the frightening man-child who's now shaking hands with the principal on his way toward the entrance. They're almost the same height. I shudder and hope that Aja doesn't notice.

"A dog. Can we get one?"

"What? No." I pull the car up to the curb in front of the school's entrance and put it in park. The carpool attendant reaches for the handle to open Aja's door, but it's locked.

"You promised," he says, ignoring the attendant looking expectantly in his window.

"When? Unlock your door."

"You said when the fish died, we could get a dog," he says. "And the fish is dead."

"He is?" I say, hoping I sound surprised. I tap the "unlock" button on my door panel, and the elderly woman tries the handle again, but Aja promptly pushes the lock back into the down position.

I give her a forced smile and hold up one finger.

"Yeah. I don't know how you didn't notice that when you were feeding him this morning."

"Huh," I say.

The driver behind us leans on the horn. I glance in the rearview and see a mother glaring back at me. My heart starts thudding. "We'll talk about this later. You gotta go into school."

Aja adjusts his glasses and crosses his arms. "Not until you say we can get a dog."

The horn blares again.

"Aja! We don't have time for this."

I press the unlock button again. Aja relocks it. The attendant looks perplexed, as if

54

she's never encountered a child who won't get out of the car before. I look past her and see the principal start to walk toward the car. A bead of sweat runs down my forehead.

And then I remember the wheelchair, and I'm struck with inspiration. Or at least another bargaining chip.

"How about I find the wheelchair and I'll think about getting the dog?"

Beep-beep-BEEEEEEEEEEEEEEEE-EEEEEEP. I resist the urge to roll down the window and scream for the driver to keep her pants on by gripping the steering wheel so tightly all the blood leaves my fingers.

Aja's face lights up and I think I've won. But then he crosses his arms again and settles his butt more firmly in his seat. "The wheelchair *and* the dog," he says over the sound of the horn that is now just a constant tone. I had no idea suburban carpool lines were so aggressive.

"Aja! Get. Out. Of. The. Car." My teeth are so clenched it's like my jaw has been wired shut.

He doesn't budge — just looks at me, uncaring that an entire line of carpool parents are cursing us. I know that I shouldn't budge, either. That a good parent would stand his ground, not reward such manipulative behavior by letting the child get his way.

Other horns join in. *BEEEEEEEEEEEE-EEEEEEEEEEEEEEEEEEEEEEEEEEEEEE-EEEEEEEEP!*

But screw parenting — all I want in life right now is for that goddamn horn to stop blaring.

"Fine!" I say. "The wheelchair and the fucking dog!" At the same time Aja pops up the door lock and swings the car door open, letting the F-word fly loud and free into the school-zone air.

The principal stops in his tracks and the attendant's gray, squirrely eyebrows jump halfway up her forehead.

The horn is quiet, the air is still, and everyone congregated in the school entrance is staring at me. Aja, unruffled, hops out of the car and hooks his backpack over his shoulder, striding toward the front door.

I take a deep breath, my face bright red with embarrassment. "Knock 'em dead, tiger!" I yell at Aja's back. Then I reach over and grab the handle, slamming the door shut, and throw the gearshift into drive.

Back home, I pour a third cup of coffee and sit down at the kitchen table where Aja attempted to ignite the Rice Chex box just an hour earlier. In exhaustion — though it's not even eight thirty — I rub my jawline with my hand, against the grain, already feeling the stubble emerge from my pores. My five o'clock shadow appears around noon, and I have yet to find a razor to combat that no matter how "cutting-edge" the shaving technology claims to be. (And really? Razor technology? Who's inventing these things — NASA scientists?) Work doesn't start until next week, but I almost want to go into the office, so I can at least feel competent at something.

Based on the morning's events, parenting isn't going to be that thing today.

And because things on that score can't get much worse, I pull out my phone and tap out a text message to Ellie. She hasn't responded in more than four months, but that doesn't keep me from trying.

Just accidentally dropped the F-bomb, shocking Aja's new principal and a grand-motherly crossing guard. Thought that might amuse you. Love you, sweet cheeks. Dad

I know I don't need to sign texts — Ellie taught me that two years ago when she looked over my shoulder at a message I was sending and had ended with *Eric.* "Daaa-aad," she said, in that new *You're the stupidest person on earth* way she had begun drawing out my name. "You know that when you send a text, your contact info automatically pops up? Everyone knows it's from you?" This was also around the time she started ending every sentence with an upward lilt, as if every statement were, somehow, also a question. I soon learned from listening to her friends speak that this was typical adolescent-girl linguistics, and I wondered if they were handed an instruction book when they got to middle school on how to talk and dress and patronize their parents.

Anyway, I did not know about the redundancy of signing texts and was happy for the lesson — even if its delivery was a touch condescending.

But I still sign my texts to Ellie because now I like picturing her rolling her eyes at her dad's buffoonery. I hope it might even make her giggle a little. And maybe I also like reminding her that that's who I am. Her dad. Even if she doesn't want to talk to me.

I hit "send." And then I pour another cup of coffee.

Tomorrow. I'll start cutting back on coffee tomorrow.

THREE

JUBILEE

The mailman is late.

I'm trying to pay attention to the Jack the Ripper special on PBS, but my eyes keep roving to the clock on the wall. It's 1:17. The mail comes every day between 12:00 and 12:30.

And I'm worried about him. The mailman. Even though I've never once talked to him. And I don't even know his real name. I call him Earl, because one time I heard him through the door, belting out in his baritone: "Duke, Duke, Duke . . . Duke of Earl, Earl, Earl."

Maybe he witnessed a purse-snatching and chased the would-be robber down on foot, tackling him to the ground to retrieve a stranger's bag. That seems like something Earl would do — he has that kind of face. Decent. Good.

But what if it's something worse? Like a

stroke? Or a blood clot that traveled up his leg and went straight to his heart? He could be lying helpless on the street right now, under the vibrant blue sky, envelopes and packages spread beneath him like flotsam haphazardly floating in the sea.

Just as I begin to panic, I hear it. The un-oiled hinge of the metal mail slot on my front door eeking open and the cascade of envelopes and advertisements as they slide through and fall to the floor below.

I jump up from the couch; tiptoe up to the door, careful not to slip on the slick coupon circulars that now paper the foyer; and peek through the peephole at Earl's backside as he walks away.

I'm so elated to see him, alive and breathing in his blue shorts and knee-high socks that end in those unflattering medical-looking walking shoes, his mail bag slung over his left shoulder and crossing his body to fall on his right hip, that part of me wants to rush out the door and throw my arms around him.

But obviously I wouldn't do that.

As I bend down to gather up the mail, I see them: the red stamps screaming at me from the envelopes.

PAST DUE

LATE NOTICE
SEND PAYMENT

I knew they would come. Of course I knew. Lenny was true to his promise and though he did mail the deed to the house, and a final mortgage statement marked "paid," he has not sent one check since my mother died six weeks ago — so I haven't paid one bill, hoarding the little money I had left for daily necessities like food. I've spent most of my days researching jobs I could do without leaving home. I applied to be a virtual assistant, an online tutor, and even a phone answerer for an off-hours call center, though I wasn't thrilled with the idea of being awake at three a.m. But I didn't get as much as a call back. Maybe because in the "experience" section of the applications, I wrote "none," but do you really need job experience to answer phones?

And now, I'm staring at letter after letter announcing that my electricity will be cut off, and the water, even my Internet.

And how would I look for a job then? Or order groceries? Or *survive*?

I need money.

For that, I need to get a job.

For that, I apparently need to leave the house.

And at that thought, the giant fist that first clenched my heart six weeks ago is back, and it becomes difficult to breathe.

I hate when people self-diagnose. I watched my mom do it for years — she had everything from rabies (even though she'd never been bitten by an animal) to Creutzfeldt-Jakob disease to syphilis (although, in retrospect, that diagnosis wouldn't have been exactly surprising). But after conducting a pretty thorough Google search, I think it's safe to say I'm suffering from an anxiety disorder, which may or may not be agoraphobia. (Other fact I learned in my search: Emily Dickinson didn't leave her house for most of the last fifteen years of her life — and she only wore white, and made friends and visitors talk to her through her front door, which makes me feel a little better about my situation. At least I'm not *crazy*.)

What I don't understand is why no one else finds it ironic that the recommended treatment for agoraphobia is to *leave your house and seek the counsel of a therapist*.

I know I *need* to leave my house, but knowing something and putting it into action are often two different things.

Fortunately, my Google sleuthing yesterday also produced the Emotional Freedom

Technique, or EFT, which *uses psychologi-cal acupressure to remove emotional blocks that you may be experiencing,* according to the website.

That's why this morning I stand at my front door gently tapping the top of my skull with my fingertips. Then, I move on to:

my eyebrows
the sides of my eyes
under my eyes
my chin
my collarbone
my armpits
my wrists

I glance back at the paper I printed out yesterday. Shoot. I forgot to do under the nose before tapping my chin. I begin the process over again, tap all the requisite body parts, and then look back to the instruc-tions.

While you're tapping, say this phrase out loud (fill in the blank).
Even though I have this _____, I deeply and completely accept myself.

While I'm tapping? I've already done the tapping twice. I don't want to do it a third time. I crumple the paper and throw it to the floor in anger. It hits the hardwood with an unsatisfyingly light scraping sound. So I stomp on it, crushing it under my heel.

Then I stand at the door, staring out the single glass panel set in the wood. It's an overcast day and the world has a grayish tint, as if the clouds are shedding bits of themselves into the air like a shaggy wool sweater.

It's Saturday, so there's no chance of running into the garbage truck, which loosens the giant fist squeezing my chest just a smidge. But what if a neighbor comes out to get their paper? Or walk their dog? Or what if Earl comes early?

The fist curls tighter.

Maybe I am as crazy as Emily Dickinson.

I take a deep breath. I have to get out of the house. I have to get a job.

I take another deep breath, shake out my hands, and start tapping the top of my skull again with my middle fingers.

"Even though I have this fear of speaking to the garbagemen, I deeply and completely accept myself," I whisper.

Then, my eyebrows.

"Even though I don't want to run into my neighbors, I deeply and completely accept myself."

I repeat the phrase, remembering under my nose this time, and move all the way down to my wrists.

Then I open the door and step out onto my porch.

I steel my body and turn my head, scanning the street from right to left. No neighbors. No dogs on leashes. No mailman.

Still, my heartbeat revs to that now-familiar galloping pace.

And then, a fat raindrop falls out of the sky and onto my head. From the looks of the foreboding clouds above, it's the first of many. And I don't have an umbrella with me.

My hand never left the front door knob, so it's easy to turn it to the left, push the door inward, and step back into the dry cocoon of my home. The dead bolt makes a satisfying *click* as I turn it into place.

I'm both defeated and relieved. And then I feel defeated for feeling relieved.

"I'll go tomorrow," I say out loud, thinking of my sixth-grade math teacher, Mr. Walcott, who had a multitude of catchphrases he'd repeat ad nauseam, including "A promise spoken can't be broken."

But even back then, I knew that was a lie.

I don't really believe in auras or energies or

any of that psychic stuff, which means I'm pretty sure EFT is bullshit. So I can't explain why I repeat the ritual the next morning, and every morning thereafter. But the farthest I've made it so far is my front porch.

On Friday, over my eggs and cut-up toast, I decide that today is going to be the day. I'm going to get in my car and drive away from the house. That is, if I can remember how. I only had my license for a year before my mom left and I wasn't exactly skilled at the task. I hit something more often than not: the trash can, the curb. One time I nailed a bird and in my rearview mirror I saw its partner swoop down, squawking in horror at the demise of its mate. I didn't drive for two weeks after that and can still hear the high-pitched caws if I close my eyes and try hard enough.

After breakfast, I get dressed and slowly walk back down the stairs, delaying the inevitable. At the landing, I tap my wrists a few times, pick up my handbag, slip on my gloves, and step out into the crisp October air.

When we first moved to New Jersey, my mom drove me into Manhattan for an appointment with the country's most prominent allergy expert, Dr. Mei Zhang. I'd never been to a large city before and when she dropped me off at the building's entrance, I tilted my head up, and up, and up some more, my eyes searching for where the brick met the blue sky. But before I could find it, I felt as though the sidewalk were giving out beneath me, my body swaying, my stomach dropping to my toes. I had to look away.

It's the same way I feel now, as if the world is too big. As if the space around me is never-ending like the brick of that building. It's dizzying — my vision blurs, my heartbeat thuds in my ears, my palms become slick with sweat.

I grab the iron railing in front of me to steady myself. I swallow past the hard lump in my throat, willing my eyes to focus, my head to stop swimming, my hands to stop shaking. They don't obey. I feel like I'm going to pass out. And what then? Not only will I be outside, but I'll be unconscious, vulnerable. I'll be Gulliver and the neighborhood children will descend on me like Lilliputians, clawing at me with their tiny fingers and toes, me helpless to stop them.

My heart thuds harder, but I refuse to give up.

I lower my butt onto the top step, taking deep lungfuls of air. Then I start tapping. I concentrate on the monotonous drumming of my fingertips until my heartbeat slows, my vision clears.

I glance up and down the street, scanning it for garbagemen, neighbors walking their dogs, kids on bikes. It's empty. And I realize I'm surprised that it's empty. I mean, I wasn't expecting a parade or anything, but this is a monumental event. And I think I did expect at least a few slack-jawed neighbors, holding a rake midsweep, staring at me in disbelief, their thought bubbles ranging from: *There she is. She* does *still live in there.* To: *I thought she was dead.* But I'm alone. Maybe I'm not Boo Radley. Maybe no one has thought of me at all.

I stand up on quivering legs, clutch my handbag tighter with my fist, and set my sights on my mom's Pontiac in my driveway. I can picture her behind the wheel so vividly, I have to double-check that she's not in the driver's seat.

I duck my head, somehow will my body down the three porch steps, and then make a beeline for the car. Gravel crunches beneath my heels, and I focus all my attention on the sound it makes until my thighs connect with the front bumper. The contact affords some kind of minor relief. I made it. To the car, at least.

My mom's skirt, which I'm wearing, buffs the metallic bumper with each step as I walk to the other side of the Pontiac. Streaks of rust and dirt now mar the beige fabric, but I don't care. I just want to be inside the car.

And then I am. I shut the door with a *thwack* and lean my head back on the upholstered seat, covered with years of Pepsi stains and cigarette burns — my mom never did quit smoking, like she told that reporter in that *Times* article. I used to think it was gross, but now I take comfort in the familiarity of it. And the fact that a metal box is now separating me from the outside world. I exhale.

Then, with still-trembling hands, I stick the key in the ignition and turn it.

Nothing.

I try again.

It makes a coughing sound but doesn't start up. I lean forward and check the gas gauge. The little pointer stick is below the red E. That's probably the least of its problems after sitting for so long, but it's the extent of my knowledge about cars. If it doesn't run — add gas.

I remove the key from the ignition, slip out of the car, and crunch back over the gravel driveway to the front porch. I take the steps two at a time, open the door, and

69

walk inside. I know I should Google it. The car. Figure out what's wrong with it, how to fix it, like I did when the toilet started leaking in the upstairs bathroom and I had to figure out how to replace the wax ring myself. But I decide I'll start with the gas first and then go from there. Tomorrow. Right now, I peel off my mother's skirt suit, crawl into a sweatshirt and pants, and curl up on the chair with my dog-eared copy of *Far from the Madding Crowd.*

Out of all the men my mom dated, her most short-lived relationship may have been with the triathlete who wore tight spandex pants everywhere — even when he wasn't working out. His name was something seemingly British, even though he wasn't — like Barnaby or Benedict. Considering the only thing he and my mother had in common was their preferred cut of pants, their relationship was over in a matter of weeks — before she could even try out the bike he bought for her. She tried to return it to the store, but they wouldn't take it without the receipt, so she shoved it in the storage shed behind the house, where it has sat ever since.

On Saturday, I go to the shed, half expecting the bike to not even be there anymore, although I guess it's a little foolish to think it would have somehow vanished into thin air. But there it sits, next to a metal toolbox and a half-empty bag of potting soil from the one and only time Mom decided she might like to try gardening.

After removing the cobwebs from the handlebars and spokes and filling the tires with air from the pump attached to the frame, I navigate the bike out of the shed and onto the gravel driveway. I try to ignore the now-expected physical reactions that take over my body — sprinting heart, sweating palms, blurring vision.

Mind over matter.

Mind over matter.

Mind over matter.

But my mind is apparently not more powerful than matter. And it takes me a full forty-five minutes of stopping and starting, inching myself and the bike past the Pontiac and finally onto the street. I look in both directions, and my heart lurches when I see a woman a few houses down picking a newspaper up out of her yard. I fight the urge to drop the bike and bolt. Instead, I stand there, watching her tuck the paper under her arm. Then she looks up, directly into my eyes, and lifts her hand in a little wave. I'm too stunned to move. I haven't been in contact with anyone in nine years.

In person, anyway.

That sounds pathetic, but it's not like I don't have friends. The Internet is teeming with people who just want to chat. And plenty of late nights when I couldn't sleep I would seek them out. Granted, some of them were a little creepy, like the policeman in Canyon City, Oregon, who seemed nice until our conversation quickly devolved into his fascination with S & M and he asked me to go get a brush so I could spank myself. (I did not.) But then there was the woman in the Netherlands, who knew like seventeen foreign languages and taught me the curse words in all of them. (My favorite is Bulgarian, *"Kon da ti go natrese,"* which roughly translates to: "Get fucked by a horse.")

But being online, and even on the phone, is worlds away from speaking to someone in person. And I wonder if I even remember how — where do I look? What do I do with my hands? Fortunately, the woman doesn't wait for my acknowledgment of her and just turns and walks back to her front door, as if it's just any normal day and I'm any normal neighbor. I let out a breath. Then I fix the strap of my handbag across my chest diagonally, ease myself over the seat, push off the ground with a foot, and wobble my way onto the pavement.

Whoever said "It's just like riding a bike" to convey a skill that, once learned, is never forgotten is an idiot. I learned how to ride a bike as a child and this is nothing like that. There are gears, for one. And I have no idea what to do with them. As I'm staring at the metal knobs, I hear a car coming up the street behind me. Even though I'm only creeping along — the pedals are so hard to push it's almost like they're glued in place — I panic and reach for the brake, accidentally jerking the handlebar and toppling the bike over into a bush next to someone's mailbox.

The car rolls past me, and my body freezes, willing it to continue. To not be a Good Samaritan that wants to check and see that I'm OK. It's not. I wait until the car turns the corner, exhale, then stand up, pick up the bike, readjust my shoulder bag, and get back on. After a few more tries, I'm able to keep the bike steady, and with a lucky flip of one of the knobs, the pedals miraculously become easier to push. I ride down to the end of the street. At the stop sign I turn left onto Plumcrest and then out of the neighborhood, carefully steering the bike onto the narrow shoulder.

Cars rush past me, the exhaust filling my

lungs, and I feel exposed, like I forgot to put on pants. I grip the handlebars tighter, my shoulders a steel rod of tension. I'm headed toward the Wawa that's next to the CVS, and it occurs to me that it may no longer be there. How would I know if it had closed? Or moved? Or burned down? My heart beats harder, until I round a bend and see the familiar red italic sign.

Exhaling, I pedal the bike to the front of the store and carefully extract myself from the seat. My crotch and thighs are sweaty from the short ride and my legs are shaking.

I did it. I left the house during the day. And I am at a gas station. I close my eyes and breathe in the heady, toxic air.

But now what? I glance at the glass door, where a bell heralds the exit of a man in a green ball cap and flannel shirt. He glances at me and I look down. After he passes, I leave my bike propped up by the door and enter where the man came out. I move up and down the aisles, until I spot a red plastic gas can and take it up to the counter, placing it in front of a woman with a strong overbite and cat's-eye glasses. She doesn't look at me as she grabs the handle and scans the UPC tag.

"You wanna fill this up?"

Her voice startles me. And just as I feared, I start to panic — I *don't* know where to look or what to do with my hands. I hear my mom's voice in my ear. *Just* smile. *Why do you have to look so damned serious all the time?* So I do. I put on a big grin, flashing my teeth at this woman, who's still waiting for my reply.

She fixes me with a look that I feel certain she reserves for idiots and my face starts to burn. "Want me to charge you for the gas to fill this up?" she says slowly. "Or are you just buying the can?"

I stop smiling. "Oh, uh. The gas, too."

She nods, punches a few buttons on the cash register. "Twenty-one seventy-three," she says.

I dig in my purse and fondle the $20 bill that's been in there since high school — I've had no need for cash the past decade. But since it's not enough, I let it go and grab the debit card, trying not to picture its dwindling account balance. I hand the card to her, and if she notices the gloves or thinks it's weird I'm wearing them, she doesn't say anything. She just swipes the card and hands it back to me. I quickly turn to leave with my head down.

"Your gas can!" she barks behind me.

Oh, right. I turn back, grab it with a

gloved hand, and head out to the pumps.

I did it, I think to myself. I really left my house. I even spoke to someone. And now I'm getting gas. Like a regular person. But just when I start to relax a little and congratulate myself for the day's accomplishments, I hear my name — "Jubilee?" — and everything in my body clenches again. But it sounds kind of far off and I think I must be hallucinating. Maybe the exertion from the bike — and the whole day, really — has messed with my brain.

"Jubilee?"

This time it's clear as the bell on the gas station door, and I stand perfectly still, hoping I am invisible, or that the person saying my name will think they're mistaken, that they've got the wrong person.

"Jubilee!" It's a statement this time, a confirmation.

I turn my head slightly toward the voice, my insides a jumble of screws that have all been turned a rotation too tight.

My eyes are drawn directly to the mouth that formed my name. I'd know that mouth anywhere. I used to stare at it in school — so much that at times I wondered if I might secretly be a lesbian. But in the end, I realized it wasn't my fault. She knew how to draw attention to it. Constantly licking her lips, as if she were always searching for a crumb at the corner of her mouth that was just slightly out of reach. I spent hours in the mirror trying to lick my lips like that, but I always looked like a camel whose tongue was too big for its mouth.

Now her lips are formed into a wide smile — so wide that I'm afraid her lips might crack, if it weren't for the layers of thick, gooey gloss holding them together.

Her hair, which used to shine all the way down to her mid-back, now stops just below her chin and is swingy, but other than that she looks the exact same.

Madison H. There were three Madisons in our class, so we identified them by their last initial, but Madison H. was the only one who mattered.

She nods, and I realize I've said her name out loud.

"Jubilee Jenkins," she says, never breaking her grin. She's now within spitting distance of me and my hand reflexively squeezes the handle of the pump tighter.

I watch her eyes take me in — my black sweatpants, my gloves, the gas can I'm holding limp at my side like a cumbersome handbag — and I'm sixteen again, wishing I could be more like her.

"I heard that you had . . . um . . . moved,"

she says, her eyes darting down and to the left. I wonder what the real rumors were. That I died, joined a traveling circus, entered some top secret government research program. When we moved to New Jersey and I started Lincoln High School as a freshman, the only saving grace was that I had the chance to start over — to be somebody new. Aside from the faculty and school nurse that we met with before school started, I didn't have to tell anyone at Lincoln High about my condition. So I didn't. And as far as I could tell, the teachers kept it a secret. But that didn't stop the stares and whispers and speculation in the hallways and during class.

"Nope," I manage. My voice is soft, shaky, and I'm as embarrassed by it as I am by my appearance.

She stares at me, as if waiting for something more — an explanation of what I've been doing for the past nine years — and the same panic I felt with the cashier begins to creep in: Where do I look? What do I do in the silences? What if I laugh at something that's not funny?

"Well, I'm divorced," she says with a little giggle, as if she's just told a corny knock-knock joke. "Trying to get back out there in the dating scene, but it's not so easy with three kids."

My eyes bulge, even as I direct them not to. Perfect, pretty, popular Madison H., who was probably voted most likely to be a famous reality TV star — or at least marry one — is a twenty-eight-year-old divorcée with *three* kids?

Oh, how the mighty have fallen. It's my mom's voice. I don't think I'm mean enough to take joy in other people's misfortunes — even if that person is Madison H.

"I'm sorry," I say. "About your, um" — I clear my throat, hoping that will force it to become louder, less shaky, more normal — "divorce." It doesn't.

She waves her hand at me. "Oh, it's fine. Those high school romances aren't meant to last a lifetime. Should've listened to Nana about that."

High school romance? "So . . . you mean . . . you married . . ." I search for my tongue in my mouth and try to make it form the name, but I am the very definition of speechless. Unable to speak. His name, at least.

"Donovan, yeah."

She says it so easily, so casually, as if she's telling me something irrelevant, like that she had muesli for breakfast.

I try to repeat his name, to see if it is that

79

easy. If it just rolls off the tongue.

It doesn't.

"You didn't know that?" She cocks her head. "Aren't you on Facebook?"

I shake my head no, hoping I'm giving the impression that I'm better than Facebook and not that I belonged to it for a total of three weeks and the only person who friended me was a man whose profile wasn't in English. It may have been in Russian, but I'm not sure — I'm not great at differentiating between the various Slavic languages. In short, I closed my account.

"Well, anyway . . ." She eyes me up and down — her gaze resting on my gloves for a second longer than anywhere else — and I cringe again at my appearance. "What are you up to?"

I clear my throat as my brain scrambles to answer her.

"I ran out of gas," I say. "And I need it." That was stupid. Of course I need it if I ran out. "I mean — I, um . . . I'm looking for a job."

"Get out!" she says, and she moves her hand as if she's going to tap me right in the arm with her bloodred manicured hand but then stops at the last second. I flinch anyway, and it's an awkward moment.

"Sorry," she says, her extra-wide grin re-

80

appearing, "but we're losing our assistant at the library and maybe that's something you'd be interested in?"

The *library*? Madison H. is a *librarian*? A vivid memory barrels its way into my mind — Madison H. in English lit our junior year loudly complaining that *Huckleberry Finn* was too hard to get through: "Why can't they just use *real* English?"

"So you work . . . at the library?"

"Oh God no," she says. "I'm in real estate — well, I just got my license to be a Realtor. But I'm on the board of the library. Donovan thought it would be good for me, with him being in line to be president at the bank when his dad retires, blah, blah — not that any of that matters now." She titters again. "But it's fine. It's a good experience."

I nod, the word "Donovan" striking a chord in me again, vibrating through my whole body. And then I'm lost in the tidal wave of memories his name — and seeing Madison H. — conjures.

"Jubilee?" Madison says. I blink. Her voice is quiet, subdued.

"Yeah?" I say, struggling to meet her eyes. The humiliation is so acute, so fresh, it makes me want to sprint all the way home, leaving my bike, my handbag, the gas can, everything parked in front of the glass door

81

at Wawa.

"Why are you doing that, that thing with your hands?"

I look down and see that my right fingers are methodically tapping the wrist that's attached to my hand holding the gas can. I wonder how long I've been doing it.

"No reason," I say, heat rising in my cheeks. I give my head a shake, a futile effort to rid myself of the past. "So, um, I don't have any résumés with me. Can I send you one? For the library thing?"

Her eyes brighten. "You're interested?" she says. "That's great. Don't worry about the résumé." She pulls out her cell phone from the purse hanging off her shoulder. "Just give me your number and I'll put in a word for you. I'm sure they'll call you."

I nod again and enunciate the digits that correlate with my house phone.

"Great," she says. "Well, it was really good to see —"

"Why are you doing this for me?" I know it's rude to interrupt, but the question is burning the insides of my mouth and I have to release it.

She shrugs, as if she doesn't know what I mean, but her eyes shift, betraying her. "It's a good coincidence," she says. "You're looking for a job, and I know a place that has one."

But we both know it's more than that. If you could open our brains and reveal our thoughts, I'm sure we'd both be thinking of the same moment, in the same courtyard that, try as I might, I can't ever forget — the moment when Donovan kissed me. I thought we were alone, until a gaggle of kids came charging around the corner, pushing one another and laughing and shoving money toward Donovan — payment on their bet. Madison was one of them, though I don't remember her laughing. Her face was long, serious, and the last one I saw before I passed out. And I always wondered, if she wasn't there to laugh at me like the rest of them, why was she there at all?

FOUR

ERIC

A year before our divorce, Stephanie and I went to see her priest for counseling. It wasn't my idea. When she suggested it, I countered: "How can he help us? He's never been married." But as with many of our arguments, I lost. In one of the sessions, she complained that I was too negative.

"I'm just realistic," I said. Still, wanting to do what I could to save our marriage, I took Father Joe's advice and tried putting a positive spin on things.

Sitting across from the guidance counselor and principal at Aja's new school, I catch myself doing it now. Aja went to school for six whole weeks without getting into trouble. He's not a troublemaker, per se. Or at least, he doesn't mean to be. But schools take everything so seriously these days.

"Did you hear us, Mr. Keegan?" says the guidance counselor. She introduced herself when I walked in, but now I can't remember her name. It sounded like a candy bar. Hershey? "Aja threatened to blow him up. We take threats like that very seriously here."

I sigh and rub my hand over my face. After deciding in September that curtailing my caffeine intake while simultaneously starting a new job was a bad idea, I promised myself I would try again in earnest in October. That's why this morning — two weeks into the month, but still technically October — I gave up my habit cold turkey, And now, the beginning of a monstrous headache is lurking directly behind my eyes. It's starting to feel like a poor decision. "Yes, I'm aware," I say. "But I doubt he *threatened* anyone. He's not exactly menacing. Look at him."

Aja's sitting in the chair next to me, his bony shoulders hunched over, his feet swinging below his bent knees — too short to graze the ground. He has headphones on, and he's staring intently at his iPad, tapping the screen furiously with his fingers, but his face looks so, well, *not intimidating*. I pull one of those godforsaken earbuds out of his ear and he looks up at me. "Aja, did you threaten to blow someone up?" His large eyes grow larger. He shakes his head.

I put the earbud back in, resisting the urge

to sneer at the guidance counselor.

"I threatened to blow up his book bag," Aja says loudly, unable to modulate the decibel level of his voice due to the video game sounds infiltrating his ears. He turns his attention back to the iPad.

"You *what?*"

The principal and Mrs. Hershey look at me with their overly concerned yet smug faces. Something explodes in a fiery burst on Aja's screen.

"Yahtzee!" he yells. I hope they can't see what he's playing.

He looks back up, as if he's just realized that that's what we're here for. "It didn't work, though," he says, and turns back to his game.

"Obviously, he's joking," I say, glaring at Aja. "He didn't have any explosives on him, did he?" I feel confident that he didn't, but I pause just to be sure.

The principal gives a small shake of his head, and relief floods through me.

"So, how could he possibly blow up something?"

"Mr. Keegan, we have to take every threat seriously," says the principal.

"Well, it's not exactly a threat if he didn't have any of the required materials to follow through on it. And anyway, what about *that*

86

guy?" I direct my thumb and their attention at the giant fifth-grade kid sitting on the other side of the glass window from us. "He didn't just *threaten* Aja, he assaulted him."

"Yes, well, we're dealing with Jagger. But right now, we're talking about Aja," says Mrs. Hershey.

"Jagger? His name is *Jagger*?"

She ignores me. "Given Aja's . . . er, background. I'm afraid we're going to have to take some precautionary measures."

"His background?" Here it comes.

She glances down at the top paper in the thick manila folder she's holding. "Yes." Her eyes flit to Aja. "Aja, could you step out of the room for just a minute?"

Aja doesn't hear her. I tap him gently on the arm and he pulls out an earbud. "Aja, head out into the hall. I'll be there in a minute." He pauses his game, stands, and walks to the door. "And stay away from that Jagger kid," I yell after him.

The door closes behind him and I look back at Mrs. Hershey.

"Specifically, we're concerned about the schizotypal personality disorder," she says.

I roll my eyes. "He's never been formally diagnosed with that. It shouldn't even be in his records."

The principal, who hasn't said much during this meeting, clears his throat. I look at him, waiting for him to chime in, but he doesn't.

"Look, he doesn't meet the requirements for that, that . . . *disorder* — or for the autism spectrum or grand delusions, or any other label you people have tried to stick on him in his short life. He's just a kid! A regular freakin' kid."

OK, to be fair, I know Aja's not regular. But, really, who is? That Jagger kid isn't exactly your typical fifth grader, either. And I'm not taking Aja back to some psychiatrist just so he can be drugged out of his mind again. My head is throbbing in earnest now and I massage a temple with two fingers. They really should offer coffee at these things.

"Let's calm down now," the principal says in his deep baritone. "We're just going to give everyone a few days to cool off."

"You're suspending him. That's what that means, right?" Damn it. Even though I've been at work for five weeks, I'm still the new guy trying to set an example for my team — not to mention we're slammed. There's no way I can take off.

"We think that's best for everyone right now," he says.

"How is *not* going to school the best thing

for Aja?"

He continues as if I haven't even spoken. "And then we can discuss seeking a more . . . *appropriate* behavioral monitoring plan for Aja. Perhaps he'd do better in a different classroom environment."

"If you're talking about some kind of special education, you can forget it. Aja is one of the most intelligent kids in your school. Hell, five minutes ago, he was the most intelligent person in this room. By far." I nod my head in the direction of the folder the counselor is still clutching. "Look *that* up in his chart."

I stand up and leave without so much as a good-bye and let the office door swing shut behind me. Aja's sitting in a chair on the opposite side of the room from Jagger. I glare at the giant kid as I tap Aja on the shoulder. "Come on. We're leaving."

On the walk to the car, I can almost hear Dinesh in my ear. *Well done, mate. Fuck 'em all. Let's get a pint.*

No, that's what he would have said if I had told off an annoying coworker, or Stephanie in the thick of our divorce proceedings — but the administration of his son's school? Dinesh never would have done that. He would have charmed them with his muddled British accent and smoothed things over in less time than it took me to sit down.

I don't know why he chose me to be Aja's guardian. I do, in the sense that I was the only logical person, geographically. His wife Kate's parents, with whom she wasn't all that close to begin with, still live in Liverpool, and Dinesh and Kate wanted Aja to be raised in America. And Dinesh's parents didn't let the modern metropolis of their home in London influence their belief that Dinesh should marry the Indian girl of their choosing. They stopped speaking to him soon after he informed them of his engagement to Kate.

Dinesh and I met in college, when we were put on a group project together in a business management class. I was already married to Stephanie, and I was taken, as most people were, by his devil-may-care attitude toward life in general. Maybe I was jealous of it. But I also became quickly annoyed at his propensity to debate every opinion that arose in the course of our project. We got into a blowout argument over the correct branding strategy for the fake cereal company we were managing together, and just when I thought I was going to explode in anger over his irrationality, he started laughing, chucked me in the arm, and said, "You win, mate. Let's go get a pint." It was all a game to him. Debating. Being the devil's advocate. Getting people ruffled and then just as easily smoothing things over. And getting a pint was his solution for everything.

Four years later over another beer, he told me Kate was pregnant and joked that having been the best man at his wedding, I'd inherited the role of godfather to his soon-to-be-born son, with the responsibility of stepping in if anything ever happened to him. We clinked glass mugs and I promptly forgot about it, because what would ever happen to Dinesh? He was invincible.

Until he wasn't.

"What are we having for dinner?" Aja asks me when we get in the car. For a second, I swear I can hear Dinesh's voice in his. Aja only has a trace of a British accent — a small part of his dad that he carries with him like a coin in his pocket. And he sometimes interjects words like "quite" and "actually" into his sentences, making him sound even older than he already does with his advanced vocabulary.

"Dinner? We're not talking about dinner, Aja," I say. "You're in big trouble."

"Why? I didn't do anything," he says.

"What do you mean you didn't do anything? You threatened to blow someone up!"

"Not *someone,* a book bag," he says.

"Fine, a book bag. You can't do that, Aja. And now you're suspended for three days, and I have to go to work. You've got to stop with all this telekinetic explosion stuff."

"Destruction."

"Whatever, destruction. Either way, it's got to stop."

Instead of nodding in agreement, he just stares at me with his large eyes. "But it didn't work."

"It doesn't matter. You can't *talk* about it. It's like at the airport. You can't say the word 'bomb.'" I put the car in reverse and start to back out of the parking spot.

"Why not?"

"Because bombs are dangerous," I say, putting my foot on the brake and turning to look at him. "They can hurt people. Lots of people. And when you talk about it, or say the word — especially at the airport — people get scared and think you want to hurt them."

"I wasn't trying to hurt anyone," he says.

I sigh and rub my jawline. "I know. I know, bud. You just can't say it, that's all."

I slide the gearshift into drive and press the gas. We ride in silence for a few minutes and then Aja says, "But what if I'm talking about a video game?"

"No! Aja, no. You can't talk about blowing things up. That's the rule. Period. The end. Got it?"

"OK," he says, staring straight ahead at the glove box.

That settled, I run through my mind the things I need to do when we get home. Call Connie, for starters, and see if she can take a few days off work to hang with Aja, while I'm at work. I know it's asking a lot of her, but I don't know what else to do.

When we pull into the driveway, I notice that Aja is still looking at the glove box.

"Aja?" I say.

He doesn't respond.

"Aja, we're home."

He doesn't move.

"Aja! What are you doing?"

He turns, and in a quiet voice says: "I'm not supposed to talk about it."

"Oh my god — are you trying to blow up the car?"

"No," he says. And then: "Just the glove box."

"No! No more telekinetic explosion! It's done."

"Destruction, not explosion," he says.

"Whatever! You need to go back to just

trying to *move* things with your mind. Got it?"

Nothing.

"Aja?"

He opens his mouth: "Can we still get a dog?"

FIVE

JUBILEE

As I suspected, the lack of gas wasn't the problem with the Pontiac. After I put a few gallons in the tank, it still wouldn't turn on, which is why I find myself riding my bike to my first day of work at the library. And once I get used to the cars whooshing by me, and the terrible feeling that I'm going to die at any second, I kind of start to like it. The wind. The feeling of freedom.

I pass over the Passaic River Bridge into downtown, mesmerized by the light reflecting off the water, and pedal a few more blocks to the library. A block off Main Street, the Lincoln Library is a small, squat brick building sandwiched in between a bank and an old house that now functions as a day spa. I ease off the bike and roll it into the bike rack, threading the lock I ordered online through the spokes of the bike and the metal bars of the rack. Then I stand up, straighten my skirt, and tug at the edges of my gloves. And that's when I start to panic.

I complete a round of tapping from my skull to my wrists, take a deep breath, and walk up the sidewalk to the single glass door adorned with black sticker lettering announcing the library's hours of operation. I open it and step inside.

"You must be Jubilee," a woman says when I approach the main desk in the middle of the library. She has wispy salt-and-pepper bangs and a lined face, and when she stands up, I see that she's thin everywhere except her hips — her body looks like a snake that's just swallowed a rodent.

I nod in response to her question.

"I'm Louise, the circulation manager." She sighs. "That's really just a fancy title that means 'librarian that's been here forever.' Welcome to the library."

"Oh dear, someone ripped the last three pages of this book," Louise says a few hours later, holding a copy of *If You Give a Pig a Party*. It's the third time she's said "dear" since I got here.

To me: *You didn't bring an umbrella today, dear? It's supposed to rain this afternoon.*

On the phone with someone I assumed was her daughter: *Oh, it was so* dear. *Little striped tights and yellow wings, and I can just hear her saying "bzzzzz" in that cute little voice. I can pick it up on my way home from work today.*

But she also said "shit" under her breath when she dropped a large-print volume of Ayn Rand's *Atlas Shrugged* and it landed on her toes, and I'm not sure why, but it made me smile.

"Now, when you find a ripped page like this," she says to me, "don't use regular tape to fix it. We have special tape." She opens a drawer and takes out a square orange box that says "Filmoplast" on the side. As she pulls out a length of the adhesive, she continues speaking. "For a tear this size, we wouldn't charge a fee, but if the damage was extensive — coloring on the pages, water damage, a lot of ripped pages — then you'd want to show it to somebody — me or Maryann — to assess the cost of repair or replacement."

Maryann is the library director, the woman who called me two days after I ran into Madison H. and had started to convince myself that the encounter didn't actually happen — that it was a figment of my overactive imagination, or that the library had found someone more qualified, with actual work experience. Turns out, they hadn't.

I nod, my head swimming with the numerous instructions I've already been given regarding the computer system, late fees, reshelving books, the finicky printer that has to be at least half-full of paper or it won't work properly, and how to assist *patrons,* which are not high-end library donors, as I first thought, but what they call their regular customers. She also gave me a rundown of Maryann's Commandments, rules like *Never leave the circulation desk unmanned* and *Always smile when you're greeting patrons.* But that's all nothing compared to how overwhelming the library is in general. It's not a large space — just a one-story brick building — but to me it's cavernous. And sitting behind the circulation desk, I feel like I'm on display. The Hope Diamond in the center of the room, except I'm not encased in glass. I've spent most of the morning glancing behind me, even though there are only three or four people milling around the stacks and none of them are anywhere close to the circulation desk.

"Oh, good," Louise says under her breath, rolling her eyes. "The pillow golfer is here."

I follow her line of sight and see a man wearing sweatpants and carrying a pillow with a floral case toward the computer carrels.

I look back at Louise. "Real name's Michael. Thirtysomething," she whispers. "Unemployed. Been coming in here every day for the last six months with that same pillow. He sits on it while playing some computer golf game. Guess the chair gets uncomfortable after a while. One time I swear he didn't get up to even go to the bathroom for eight hours straight." She laughs, and I turn to take him in once again, feeling a bizarre kinship with this stranger. He's probably just lonely — a feeling I'm intimately familiar with. "I don't know if Maryann mentioned to you, but we get all sorts in here. The job is really only about sixty percent books. The other forty percent is community service. Mostly mental health."

My eyes widen at this. Books, I can handle. Checking in, checking out, shelving. But people?

"Don't worry," Louise says, patting my gloved hand. I flinch at the contact and jerk my hand back. Louise looks up at me, her eyebrows slightly raised. "I know it's a lot to take in, but you'll get the hang of it. Really."

For the rest of the day, I make sure I stay at arm's distance from Louise.

Just in case.

Right before the end of my shift at four, I'm finishing up some new-employee paperwork when I get to this question in the insurance information section: *Do you have any pre-existing conditions?* I hesitate, and then check the box next to "allergies," just as Louise appears behind me, pushing a cart of reference books. "Take these to the back," she says. "Row nine forty-six, and reshelve them according to the numbers on their spines. Think you can do that, dear?"

I nod again, and realize I haven't spoken out loud once since I arrived that morning. I wonder if she thinks I'm mute.

I step out from behind the circulation desk and my legs tremble. I grab the edge of the metal cart for support. The enclosed space of the circulation desk has become my home for the day, my safe haven. But now I have to step out into the aisles. Where the people are. And who knows what might happen?

Even though I have this fear of leaving the circulation desk and walking through the library, I deeply and completely accept myself.

Though I feel a little ridiculous thinking it, the phrase does give my feet the impetus they need to start moving forward. But I still glance to my left, my right, and sometimes behind me as I make my way to the back of the library, searching for the people I could swear are drilling holes into me with their powerful lines of sight. Louise isn't. She's looking down, busying herself with tidying up the circulation desk. Her lips are moving slightly and it looks as though she's muttering to herself.

The cart has one wobbly wheel that lightly whines in protest. When I arrive at row 946, the sound mercifully stops, but instead of silence, the noise is replaced by something else. Some kind of shuffling, as if a raccoon is trapped in the stacks and trying to make its way out. A very heavy-breathing raccoon. Who giggles.

My heart pounding, I quietly pad to the next aisle and peer around the corner, not quite sure what will greet me.

And then I stop, my feet blocks of cement, unable to move forward or backward. At the end of the aisle are two bodies so entangled with each other, they are literally one. They are a jumble of hands, exposed throats, mouths. It's a Klimt painting come to life. And though I know I shouldn't be staring, I can't look away. It's so raw. And fumbling. And kind of a mess.

And it makes my throat close up and my body flush with that feeling that wakes me up in the middle of the night. That hot hunger and yearning and burning humiliation.

A small scream pierces my eardrums and I realize the two faces that were once buried in each other are now trained on me. I'm shocked by their youth. The girl has braces and flushed cheeks. The boy a smatter of pimples on his jawline.

"You perv," the boy says, his eyes burning with the testosterone coursing through his veins.

And though I know I should say something, admonish them in my adult voice, I still can't move. They uncouple, like train cars disengaging, and the girl quickly rearranges the buttons on her shirt, while the boy continues to glare at me.

I feel a presence come up behind me and then Louise's voice loudly in my ear. "Brendon! Felicia! I've told you twice now — the library is *not* the backseat of your car. Last warning. Next time I'm calling your parents."

They both drop their gazes to the ground, and Brendon grabs Felicia's hand, leading her out of the stacks.

When they squeeze by me, Brendan whispers just loud enough for me to hear: "Like what you saw?"

I flush deeper and stare at the row of reference books in front of me, concentrating on the numbers.

Then the kids are gone. Louise mutters, "Horny teenagers," and heads back to the circulation desk, and I'm left with a cartful of heavy books, waiting to be put in their rightful place.

Everyone is moving around me, going about their business, but my feet are nailed to the spot of worn carpet I'm standing on.

All I can think about is Donovan.

And the way his mouth felt when it was on mine.

Six

ERIC

Reflexively, I pick up the blue tie from my meager collection and begin to loop it around my neck. I wear the blue tie on Thursdays.

I don't have OCD or anything — I don't freak out if I can't find my blue tie on Thursdays. It's just efficient — one less decision I have to make. Kind of like why Mark Zuckerberg wears a gray T-shirt every day. I'm the Mark Zuckerberg of accounting. I sometimes use this line at parties and it always gets a perfunctory laugh that pleases me.

I finish the half-Windsor knot and fold my collar down. Then I grab my watch from the bathroom counter and secure it on my wrist. As I walk down the hall toward the kitchen past Aja's room, I hear him clacking away at his computer.

When he first came to live with me, I was

alarmed at how much time he spent on the computer, considering he was only eight at the time. Ellie, of course, was addicted to hers too, but she was nearly five years older. At eight, she spent a lot of time riding her bike with a neighbor friend and choreographing dances and obsessing over Monster High dolls. I didn't remember Dinesh mentioning that as one of the myriad things he was worried about when it came to Aja. So it was one of the first real conversations I had to have with him after he moved in and I had no idea what to say, since Stephanie had always handled most of those tough talks with Ellie. "You know there are people out there — on the Internet, I mean — that aren't always nice. You know, to kids. Well, they start out being nice, but then they're not." I replayed what I had just said in my mind. It didn't make sense even to me. "I mean not like bullies, but like . . ." I searched for words that wouldn't come. How to explain this to an eight-year-old?

"Are you talking about sexual predators?" he said, enunciating each syllable in that formal way he has. My mouth dropped open. "I know all about that. I'm not stupid."

I closed my mouth. "OK then," I said. I went to pat his leg, but then I remembered

105

Dinesh saying he didn't really liked to be touched, so I awkwardly patted the bed-spread beside his leg instead. "Good talk."

Now I feel the need to continue my due diligence and call out as I walk past his open door: "You're not talking to any sexual predators in there, are you?"

His small voice responds: "I guess I wouldn't know, would I?"

Good point.

Thank God Connie has agreed to watch him today. Not without some requisite grumbling from her: "I have a real job too, you know."

And some placating from me: "I know. And you're very good at it. Best and most underpaid lawyer this side of Passaic."

Eventually, she acquiesced. "I'm only do-ing it because I love Aja," she said. "And because I don't want him to blow up your apartment."

"Thank you."

The doorbell rings just as I'm pouring my second cup of coffee.

"Aja," I call. "Connie's here."

He doesn't respond.

I check my watch — twenty minutes until the train I need to catch — and open the door. Connie walks past me and looks at my coffee cup.

"I thought you were cutting back."

"It's my first," I lie, then I turn and call for Aja again.

"Where is the little troublemaker?" she asks, setting her purse on the lone chair in the dining room, which isn't so much a "room" as it is an extra space adjacent to the living room/foyer/den. Such is apartment living. I'm only here for six months and I thought bringing both my small kitchen table and the dining room set from my house in New Hampshire might be overkill. It's not like I'm throwing dinner parties every weekend. Or ever.

"In his room. On his computer."

"Ah."

"Aja!" I turn around and almost run smack into him. "There you are."

"Whatcha doin' in there, champ?" Connie asks.

"Talking to Iggy," he says, without looking up.

"The rapper?" she says, chuckling at her own joke.

Aja just stares at her.

"You know, that Australian girl?" Connie says. "With the large bottom?"

"Iggy's a boy," he says, adjusting his glasses.

"Or a forty-five-year-old sexual predator,"

107

I joke, even though a month ago, much to Aja's embarrassment, I popped into his room while he was Skyping one evening to make sure Iggy was, in fact, a ten-year-old kid. "Guess we'll never know, right, Aja?"

He fixes me with his serious look. "You do know. You saw him. Can I go back to my room now?"

"No," I say. "I figured out your punishment. Today, you'll be unpacking all of the boxes we have left until you find the rest of my coffee mugs."

"OK," he says. That's the weird dichotomy about Aja — he's surprisingly easygoing when he wants to be. Doesn't throw tantrums or get sullen like most other kids his age.

"OK, then," I say. I check my watch again. I have to leave. I can't miss the train into the city and risk being late. "Thanks again, Con."

"Go," she says. "We'll be fine."

"Aja, be good."

I grab my keys and wallet and start to head out the door.

"Eric?" Aja calls after me — and I know he's going to say the same thing he's said to me every morning for the past six weeks. "Don't forget to look for a wheelchair!"

That damned wheelchair.

■ ■ ■ ■

Later that night — much later, since the train stopped for an interminable fifty minutes between Secaucus and Newark, leaving me to believe, briefly, that I would never, ever make it home — I walk into the quiet apartment, lugging an adult-size wheelchair behind me. I finally found it at a Goodwill store in Harlem for $25, taking the entirety of my lunch break to call every secondhand store in the city before I found one. I felt a little guilty for buying it, possibly taking it away from someone who really needs it. But I promised myself I'd return it when Aja was done — and make a monetary donation to the nonprofit while I was at it.

Connie's reading on the couch. She stands up when she sees me.

"How was work?" she asks.

The question stops me in my tracks. It's been so long — at least the two years since the divorce and probably even many years before that — since someone asked me that at the end of the day. Since someone cared. I didn't realize how much I missed it — not Stephanie, just *someone* — until this moment.

"Good," I say. "Aja?"

"Asleep," she says. "He's a good kid."

"I know." I grin a little. He's frustrating as all get-out. But there's no denying that he is good. Genuinely better than most other humans. I lean the wheelchair up against the wall where he'll see it first thing in the morning.

"We found the coffee mugs," she says.

"You did?"

"Yep. In the box marked 'board games, poker chips, and miscellaneous,' of all places."

I look at her. "I have poker chips?"

"You do."

"Huh." I toss my wallet and keys on the side table next to the couch. "Well, thanks," I say. "I really mean it. Same time tomorrow?"

"Yeah," she says, moving to gather her things. "Oh, and we found something else."

"I hope it's the cereal bowls," I say. "I can't find those either. Aja's been eating his Rice Chex out of a ceramic tureen."

"It's a journal," she says, and then clears her throat. "Ellie's journal."

I look at her. I didn't even know Ellie kept a journal.

"How did it get into my stuff?"

110

"I don't know. Maybe she left it at your house?"

I run my fingers through my hair. "What do I do with it? Should I read it?" I'm overcome with the sudden desire to do just that. To get inside Ellie's brain, find out everything that she's been thinking. Unravel the mystery that is my teenage daughter.

"No! You can't read your daughter's journal. That's against every parenting rule. Ever."

I know she's right. She's right. But still.

"Well, I could text her and see if she wants it back, but she's not exactly speaking to me."

"Eric," Con says.

"I know, I know," I say. "I'm sure she wants it back. I'll just mail it to her."

"Eric," she says again, fixing me with her ever-changing hazel eyes that mirror my own. Right now, they're more green than brown.

"What? I won't read it. I swear," I say, crossing my heart. "Where is it?"

She stares at me a beat longer and then says: "On your dresser." She walks past me to the dining room to collect her purse from the lone chair, then turns and puts her arms around my shoulders. I stand there awkwardly as she hugs me. We're not a hugging family.

"Er, Con?"

She lets go and sighs. "I just wish you would find someone," she says. "You shouldn't be doing all this alone."

I scoff, even though I don't entirely disagree with her. "What, are you going to set me up again? That didn't work out so well."

A year after my divorce, I went on a blind date with someone Connie knew in college who lived about thirty minutes away from me. A lawyer. Corporate attorney of some kind. She was lovely — big, doe-like eyes and thick lips balanced out by a sliver of a nose and thin, stick-straight locks of hair that grazed her shoulders like blades of grass. She laughed easily at my pathetic jokes and robustly defended her stance — like any good lawyer — on the merits of corn versus flour tortillas.

I behaved jovially, like a gentleman. I laughed at the appropriate times, opened car doors, fetched her a glass of water after an athletic bout of sex later in the evening.

But alone the next morning, I stared at my face in the mirror, searching . . . for what, I didn't know. I felt numb. Or worse than numb, like I had lost a limb and was still having pain in it. I called her that afternoon and told her voice mail I had had a lovely time but didn't think I was quite ready to date again.

"You had just gone through a divorce," Connie says. "You weren't ready yet. That's normal."

I stick my hands in my pockets and shrug. "I don't know that the word 'normal' applies to me."

She smiles. "I've been trying to tell you that for years," she says, reaching for the door handle. "See you tomorrow."

When Connie's gone, I pull my cell out of my back pocket and scroll to Ellie's name. I have her journal. Surely telling her that would elicit a response. Even a threatening "Don't you dare read it or else" would be preferable to silence. And I could tell her that I wouldn't dream of betraying her privacy that way, that I'll mail it back instantly, which would maybe garner me some kind of cool-dad points in her book. But that all feels slightly manipulative, and as much as I want my daughter to speak to me again, I don't want it to be because she's being coerced to do it.

So instead I tap out a quick message:

I love you, Ellie. Dad.

Then I turn off the lamp and walk down the hall to my bedroom, stopping for a moment at Aja's door and placing my ear to it. I hear the keys clacking away at his computer, of course. I'll give him a few more minutes before lights-out.

In my room, I sit on the bed, the mattress groaning beneath me, and take my shoes off one by one, thinking about what Connie asked me: *How was your day?* Stressful. That's how my day was. How every day has been since I started this job last month. Naturally our largest client would be acquiring an S & P company now, rather than doing it before Shelly left for maternity leave or waiting until she gets back, leaving me — and the team, but really me, since I'm in charge — solely responsible for all the valuations and analyses. There's no room for error or senior management will go ballistic.

I loosen my tie and lie back on the bed, surveying my barren room and giving in to a self-pitying *What in the hell am I doing in this apartment in New Jersey* moment. The notebook on my dresser catches my eye. Ellie's journal.

Ellie. My daughter who hates me. I knew the divorce wouldn't be easy on her — is it ever easy on any kid? But I never thought we'd be here. We had a good relationship. I thought we did, anyway. Better than most. I knew exactly how to make her laugh. Corny jokes, silly faces behind Stephanie's back, a well-timed pun. We watched every episode of every season of *The Amazing Race* together — and the best moment of my life might have been when she turned to me and said, "We should do it. We could totally win."

How did we go from that — being a hypothetical team on a world-traveling reality show — to this? I glance at Ellie's journal again and then look away, as if not seeing it will make it less tempting to open it. It's not. I get up from the bed, snatch the book from the dresser, and quickly open the top drawer, throwing the book in and shutting the drawer before my hands and eyes have a chance to betray my best intentions.

Then I walk down the hall and knock on Aja's door. I hear him grunt and take that as an invitation to open it. I'm greeted with his profile, his eyes locked to the computer screen. I stand there for a minute, but he doesn't move.

"Found your wheelchair today," I say.

He grunts again.

"Hey, did you hear me? I thought you'd be really excited."

He turns to me, his eyes large and serious. "I just found out they don't do dress-up at this school, like they do at home. Mrs. Bennett said it's too much of a distraction."

I suppress a sigh. Would have been nice to know before I spent my whole lunch break tracking a wheelchair down.

"But at least you can still wear it Halloween night? Go trick-or-treating?"

"I'm too old for that."

"You are?" I try to remember when Ellie stopped. I guess it was around this age.

"Well, it's probably for the best, considering it could be really offensive —"

"I'll find somewhere to wear it." Aja cuts me off.

I rub my hand over my face. I wonder if I should continue arguing, try to make him see my point of view, but then decide it's not worth it. If he can't wear it to school or trick-or-treating, the chances are slim that he actually will find another place to wear it. It's not like he has a gaggle of new friends at school that will be inviting him to parties or anything.

"What are you doing on there?" I ask.

"Talking to Iggy," he says.

I stand there for a minute more and then say, "Just a few more minutes, then bed. It's getting late."

He doesn't respond, so I gently close the door, but before it shuts all the way, I hear him mutter something. It sounds a lot like "I hate it here."

The door latch clicks in place and I take a deep breath and close my eyes, trying to swallow the guilt that I feel and reminding myself, *It's only for six months.*

On Saturday, I'm supposed to be getting ready to take Aja to the animal shelter — even though a dog is the last thing we need right now — but I can't stop thinking about Ellie.

I read the journal. I know I shouldn't have, but when I couldn't stop thinking about it, wondering if it had some magical insight into Ellie's mind that would help me understand why she's so angry — why she won't speak to me — I got up and opened the drawer where I stashed it. Before I could convince myself that what I was doing was wrong, I reached in, picked up the spiral notebook, opened the front cover, and started reading. And here's the thing: it's not really a journal, which must be why Ellie's not freaking out about where it is. I mean, it is a journal, in that it's her thoughts written down on paper. But it must have been some kind of school assignment, because there's a grade and handwritten comment on the inside front cover: "A, Great job!" (That's my girl. Or that *was* my girl, until she started hanging out with Darcy and her grades nose-dived into the C and D territory.) And each page is devoted to a different book — presumably books that she read and then discussed her opinions of in this journal.

But still, to be fair, I texted her immediately afterward.

Found your book journal assignment. OK if I flip through it? Dad

What's that saying about how it's better to ask for forgiveness than permission? OK, so maybe this is more like asking for permission after you've already done the thing you want permission for, but same principle. Kind of. Regardless, I took her silence as approval.

I'm rereading her entry on *The Catcher in the Rye* (a book I think I read in high school but don't remember much about) when Aja appears in the doorway to my room.

I drop the journal, as if it's a porn magazine I've been caught looking at. (So, maybe even with her silent approval, I still feel a little guilty.)

"Are you ready?" he asks. "You said we were leaving for the animal shelter at nine."

"Yeah, sorry," I say, glancing back at the journal. Suddenly I have an idea. A way to try to make inroads with Ellie. "We just have to make a quick stop first."

"Where?"

"The library."

Thirty minutes later, when I reach for the handle on the door of the Lincoln County Library, I spot a sign affixed to the glass.

JOIN US NEXT SATURDAY, OCTOBER 31 HALLOWEEN STORY TIME FOR CHILDREN OF ALL AGES WEAR A COSTUME (BOOK CHARACTERS ENCOURAGED) FREE CANDY!

I glance over at Aja and he's grinning at me, his face a lit-up Christmas tree. "Told you I'd find a place to wear it," he says.

I sigh, and open the door.

Seven

Jubilee

"Don't forget to wear a Halloween costume, dear!" is the last thing Louise said to me as I was leaving on my fifth day of work.

"A costume?"

"Tomorrow's Halloween," she said. "We always dress up at the library."

I've only worn a Halloween costume once in my life. I was nine and my one and only childhood friend, Gracie Lee, and I dressed as the twins from *The Shining.* "Why on earth would you want to go as that?" Mom asked, snuffing out a cigarette on a paper plate. "It's morbid." Gracie Lee took out her bulky blue hearing aids and wore a pair of gloves to match me, even though the girls in the movie didn't wear them. But nobody really got it — maybe because we looked nothing alike in the face — and one woman even commented how "cute" we were. Gracie Lee couldn't hear her, so I told her

120

the woman said we looked creepy and she smiled. And then another memory from that Halloween bursts through. As we were sorting our loot at the end of the night, Gracie bit into a Baby Ruth, not knowing it had caramel in it. She hated caramel, so she handed me the candy bar. Before I could get it to my lips, my mom slapped it out of my hand. "Are you trying to kill yourself?" she screamed. "Do you want to die?" That night I had seen vampires and ghosts and a boy in a terrifying mask that looked like it had real blood dripping down its face, but that was the most scared I'd ever been. I was still shaking when I went to bed.

Now, staring at my mom's closet, I finger the sleeves of each suit and blouse, hoping inspiration will strike me. But so far, I can only think of Business Executive Barbie in Mom's bubblegum-pink suit that I have yet to wear, because it's bubblegum pink.

My fingers reach the end of their journey at the back of the closet and land on something soft to the touch. I pull the garment off the hanger and bring it out into the light. It's a long, white gown — not like a wedding dress, but more like something to sleep in. I have no idea why my mom owned this unflattering, way-too-much-coverage-for-her-taste getup, but it's perfect.

I'm going to be Emily Dickinson. In the latter part of her life, when she didn't leave her house and only wore white and talked to her friends and family through her front door.

I peel off my sweatshirt and flannel pants and tug the gown over my head. Like all of Mom's clothes, it doesn't fit perfectly, but it will do. I go to the bathroom and release my hair from the rubber band that's been holding it hostage on top of my head. Even though Emily Dickinson wore her hair tightly smoothed back in a conservative bun in all the portraits I've seen of her — and I've been wearing mine pulled back every day at the library — I decide to let it be loose and wild today. If she holed up in her house for years and didn't accept visitors, it stands to reason she wouldn't fix her hair. I glance in the mirror one last time and then go downstairs to get my gloves and keys.

When I walk into the library, Louise looks at me. "Oh dear, did you wake up late?"

"No," I say.

She frowns. "Why are you wearing a night-gown?"

"This is my costume." I slip my bag behind the circulation desk.

She's got on a black cap and aviator

sunglasses, so I feel rather than see her narrow her eyes at me.

"Are you that weird pop singer? That Lady Gaga or whoever?"

"No," I say. "I'm Emily Dickinson."

"The poet?"

"Yeah."

I can see she's still trying to figure it out.

"Toward the end of her life, she was kind of a hermit and only wore white."

"Huh."

She turns her body to face me, and I notice the silver handcuffs hanging from Louise's belt loop. She points to the paper she's taped to her chest. It reads: GRAMMER POLICE.

"You spelled 'grammar' wrong."

"I did?" She looks down. "Well, damn."

She rips the sign off her blouse and pulls a fresh sheet from the printer on the desk. She picks up a black Sharpie and I start wheeling a pushcart toward the door so I can pick up the returns from outside.

The library doesn't feel as cavernous as it did on the first day, but I'm still leery of leaving the circulation desk. It's like I'm testing myself each time I do it. How far can I go today? I know the answer: to the returns box outside. It's like the library — and, weirdly, the people in it — have become

123

an extension of my own house.

Three other librarians are typically working during my shifts — Maryann, the library director; Roger, the children's librarian; and Shayna, another circulation assistant — but Louise is my favorite. Maybe it's because she's the first person I met and I'm naturally more comfortable with her. Or maybe it's because she's the person I have the most contact with — Roger sits behind a desk in the children's section, Shayna's shift and mine only overlap for a few hours each day, and Maryann is often working in her office in the back or running out to a meeting. Or maybe it's because she doesn't probe. (The first thing Shayna asked me when we met: "What's with the gloves? Are you, like, perpetually cold?" I just shrugged. "Something like that.") But Louise has never mentioned my gloves or asked anything else personal about me for that matter — like if I have a boyfriend or where I went to college. She just does her job and I do mine.

At two forty-five Louise comes rushing up to me, out of breath.

"Aren't you on break?" I ask.

"I had to come back," she says. "Maryann called and Roger isn't coming in today." She gasps for air.

"Do you need to sit down?" The police hat is perched a tad lopsided on her silver bouffant and the sign on her chest is heaving.

"No, I'm fine. I'm not used to running."

I picture her in her cop getup bursting out of TeaCakes, the coffee shop where she was taking her lunch break, rushing down the sidewalk to get back to the library, and can only imagine what passersby must have thought: *There's a grammar emergency! Get out of the way!*

"You'll have to do story time for the kids."

"Me?"

"Yes, you. I need to man the circ desk."

"But I've never done that before," I say, my head spinning.

"Well, no. But surely you've read to children before, yes? Nieces? Nephews?"

I shake my head no.

She frowns. "It's easy. Roger left the three books on his desk and I think you give out candy and sing a song or something. Over in thirty minutes."

"Sing a *song*?" This is getting worse by the second.

"Yes. Run along, dear." She shoos me with her hands toward the kids' section. "The children — Oh, look! A few are coming through the door now."

125

I grab the books off Roger's desk and head to the carpet circle where one lone adult chair faces an empty floor. I sit down in the chair and look up to see the children who raced through the door now coming at me with full-fledged enthusiasm. There's a girl pirate, three princesses wearing what appears to be the exact same blue dress, and a boy in an astronaut costume.

I smile at them tentatively, but as they get closer, I see that they're not smiling back. In fact, one girl — one of the princesses — looks angry. My heart starts to gallop.

"Where's Mr. Rogers?" she asks.

I want to point out that his name is Roger, without an "s," and that his last name is Brown, and so he would therefore not technically be Mr. Rogers, who was a popular children's television show host — but now doesn't seem to be the time.

"He's sick today," I say, which I'm not even sure is true. Louise didn't say why he wasn't coming in. "So I'll be taking his place."

"Do you have candy?" she asks.

Crap. The candy. I only grabbed the books.

"I do," I say, hoping Roger left the candy at his desk somewhere.

She stares at me for a beat longer and then

nods as if I've satisfied her demands. Then she and the other two princesses sit down in a row and more children begin to trickle in and do the same.

It feels like they're coming from every direction and I want to round them up and keep them all in my line of sight. What if one of them gets too close and tries to touch me? Children are like snakes — they're unpredictable. I scoot my chair back toward the wall as far as it will go, feeling my throat close up as if I've already been touched.

I look around wildly, hoping Roger might appear, Louise will step in, the fire alarm will go off and we'll have to evacuate the building . . . anything to stop this nightmare. Instead, my eyes lock on Madison H. She's pushing a stroller and guiding two kids into the circle. My heartbeat slows a little.

She stops short as she takes me in. "Did you forget to comb your hair this morning?"

Before I can respond, the little girl holding her hand says, "Mommy, it's a *costume.*"

"Oh, right! Let's see." Madison sizes me up. "Are you that girl that crawls out of the TV in — what was that movie — *The Ring*?" She shudders. "God, that was horrifying."

"Of course she's not," her daughter says, rolling her eyes, which seems awfully adultlike for such a small child. But then, I don't know much about children. "She's Lady Gaga."

I shake my head. "No, I —"

"Lady Gaga doesn't wear pajamas," a tinny voice says, cutting me off. I think it's the pirate.

"Are you the Ghost of Christmas Past?" says another.

"I know, I know! She's Amish! Grandma took me to that village in Pennsylvania last year. They don't have dishwashers or TV."

"*Every*one has TV."

My eyes dart to where the voices are coming from, but it's hard to tell.

"She's a serial killer." The word "killer" sucks the air out of the room and everyone turns to look at a young boy sitting in a wheelchair. His dark eyes aren't looking at me — they aren't really looking at anybody.

His dad — I assume it's his dad, even though they look nothing alike, because he's standing behind him gripping the handles of the wheelchair — laughs nervously. "Why would you say that, buddy?"

"The gloves," the boy says. "Serial killers wear gloves."

Fifteen wide-eyed kids turn back to stare at me and my hands. I shift in my seat and my heart revs up again.

"What's a serial killer? Is it someone who really, really likes Cap'n Crunch?"

"Why do they wear gloves?"

"I like Cap'n Crunch!"

"Are you going to kill *us*?" a shaky voice asks.

At least two kids burst into tears.

My heart is thumping so loudly, I wonder if everyone can hear it. If I'm an Edgar Allan Poe story come to life. This is so much worse than I anticipated. I scan to my left and right looking for an escape route, but there are kids everywhere. I take a deep breath and clap my gloved hands together. I can do this.

"No one is killing anyone," I say, and offer my friendliest smile. "I am not dressed as a serial killer or Lady Gaga or an Amish person — though that was a good guess." I nod toward the fireman, who I think said the bit about Amish people and TVs. He beams.

"I'll give you guys one hint." I feel rather than see the kids lean forward. And even though they're just children, my cheeks flame up and I wish my chair would collapse and swallow me whole. I clear my throat. " *'Hope'* —" The word comes out squeaky, like a mouse tittering. I try again. " *'Hope' is the thing with feathers . . . that*

129

perches in the soul. And sings the tune without the words and never stops at all."

The poem hangs in the air and the kids just stare, silent. Finally, one pipes up.

"Are you a . . . bird?"

I glance around at their tiny faces. I guess they're a little young for Emily Dickinson. My eyes stop when I get to the dad standing behind the wheelchair. He's looking at me, but he's not just looking *at* me — his eyes are penetrating my face, as if he's almost looking through me. It's unblinking and intense. Maybe he thinks I'm a serial killer after all.

I quickly look down and pick up the first book in my lap. *Flat Stanley and the Haunted House.* "Let's get started," I say, and hold it up.

The air erupts in cheers and shouts for Flat Stanley. I've never heard of this character but apparently he's quite popular. I silently thank Roger for at least picking out the right books.

Later, when the kids clutching handfuls of candy in their tiny palms have dispersed through the stacks to find their parents — Louise found the bags Roger had stashed and brought them over, to my great relief — Madison H. pushes her stroller toward

130

me and, when she gets close enough, says in a low voice: "I still can't believe Donovan skipped out on this. The kids have been looking forward to it for weeks."

I glance at the baby snuggled in his car seat, staring up at us with wide eyes, and wonder what it would be like to hold him. To feel the wisps of his eyelashes against my cheek.

"He said he had some 'big, important meeting,' " she says, making air quotes with her fingers. "Pretty sure that's code for fucking his secretary."

I start coughing, literally choking on any words I might say in response. My eyes dart around the room again, looking to see if anyone may have overheard.

"Anyway, good to see you," she says. "We should get lunch next week."

I stare at her as if she's speaking Swahili. *Get lunch.* I wonder whether she means it or it's just something people say to be nice.

"Sammy! Hannah! Let's go." I hear, rather than see, the kids whine in protest, their voices floating from behind one of the stacks in the children's section. "Now!" Madison shouts. Then she sighs. "C'mon, we'll get mocha lattes on the way home."

Mocha lattes? Do children drink coffee now?

Yips of glee filter from the stacks and Hannah and Sammy come running out toward their mom. I maneuver around the kids and walk back toward the circulation desk. Louise looks up as I enter our workspace.

"See? That wasn't so bad, was it?" Her eyes look past me, and she lowers her voice to a whisper. "Oh dear, don't look now. This guy came in a few days ago. He and his boy seem a little . . . off." She turns around, busying herself with checking books in, and I look up — because who *doesn't* look when someone says "don't look now" — and directly into the eyes of the wheelchair dad. He's tall, but not in an imposing way. And his hair is like a spice mix of colors, mostly nutmeg and cinnamon, with a touch of salt. It sticks out haphazardly from his head, as if just begging for a mussing by a grandmotherly type. If he didn't have such an intent, serious look on his face, it would almost be charming. I train my gaze beside him on his wheelchair-bound son, struggling to push himself up to the circulation desk.

"Help me," he says to his dad. He looks so small in the large chair, and his big eyes grow even bigger with the strain. My heart melts for him instantly — even if he did call me a serial killer.

"No." The man looks away from me and back at the boy. "I told you I wasn't going to push you all day."

It's so callous, so harsh, that my mouth drops open. Maybe this is some kind of new-age tough-love parenting, but good grief. The kid is handicapped.

The dad sets a stack of books in front of me on the desk but I make no move to check them out. I'm watching the boy writhe and wrestle with the too-big wheels. Feeling eyes on him, he glances up at me and then back down.

"You should have worn glasses," he says.

"What?" I'm not even sure he's talking to me because he's not making eye contact.

"Big ones, with clear frames." The words come out a little choppy as he puffs with effort.

"Do you need help?" I ask him.

"He's fine," the man cuts in, an edge to his voice that sounds sharper than necessary.

I ignore him and keep my eyes trained on the boy.

"Dorothea Puente," he says in between huffs. He's now about four feet from the desk. "She ran a boardinghouse and killed nine of her tenants over a span of six years."

He glances back up at me and looks away again. "You're dressed like her. A younger her. But she wears glasses."

"OK, that's enough," the man says, and then turns to me. "Sorry about that."

He looks back at the boy, who now I'm thinking may not be his son after all, because not only does the kid have darker skin and silky black hair, but he talks with just a hint of an accent. He could be adopted, but the guy doesn't strike me as the warm and fuzzy adoptive type.

"Cut it out with the serial killer stuff, OK?" the man says.

"No, it's all right," I say. "I've never heard of her."

"Most people haven't," says the boy. "Female serial killers aren't as notorious as male ones based on the stereotype that all women are driven by emotions and therefore can't be psychopaths, who, by definition, lack empathy."

The man sighs.

I stare at this kid, who's now looking me directly in the eyes, and I'm not sure what to make of him. For one, he's tiny. I'm not adept at guessing the ages of kids, but he can't be more than eight, and he talks like a college graduate. And he's wearing a three-piece suit. I didn't even know they made three-piece suits for children.

"Did you know Jack the Ripper only killed five women?" I say, because he's the only serial killer I really know anything about and for some reason I want to trade obscure knowledge with this boy.

The man's eyes widen at me.

"Of course," says the boy. "Everyone knows that."

Oh. I change the subject. "Why didn't you dress up for Halloween?"

"I did," he says.

I peer at him more closely. I wonder if it's some kind of beyond-his-years play on words — he's being clever by literally "dressing up" in formal attire, rather than a costume.

"Picture me with a bald head," he says, and darts his eyes up toward the man. "I was not allowed to shave it."

I try to think of bald, well-dressed men.

"Bruce Willis?" I ask.

"Who?"

"He's an actor. He was married to Demi Moore."

"I don't know who that is, either," says the boy. "I'm Professor X."

This name means nothing to me, and I guess my face reveals that.

"From the X-Men?" he says.

"Oh, that movie," I say, now remembering seeing commercials for the blockbuster that had a woman painted in blue, a kind of fox guy with talons, and the older, bald man who — oh right! — is in a wheelchair. That must be Professor X.

His eyes get big and he looks stricken, as though I've deeply offended him. "The comic books," he says, enunciating each word, as if I'm the child and he's the adult.

"Well, it was very clever of you to choose a character that also uses a wheelchair," I say.

The man beside him inhales deeply and then lets his breath out — a long stream of air — before he says: "He's not disabled."

"Professor X?" I ask, confused.

"No, my son," he says, nodding at the boy.

"Oh." I'm not sure what to say then. I look down at the boy, who smiles up at me, and I'm struck, not only because it's the first time he's smiled, but because it lights up his entire face. I can't help but grin back at the large, protruding teeth that are occupying the place where his lips used to be.

"I didn't think it was quite . . . appropriate, but he insisted, and . . . ," the dad is mumbling, and then he cuts himself off. "It doesn't matter."

He sets his armload of books on the

136

counter in front of me as if signaling that the conversation is over and it's time to get on with the checking-out process.

I tear my eyes away from the boy and oblige, picking up the first book on the stack. It's *Breaking Dawn,* the fourth book in the Twilight series. I glance at the boy once more — surely he's too young for this book? But then again, he does seem rather precocious and he has a wealth of knowledge about serial killers. I scan it and set it aside.

Next is *The Virgin Suicides.* It's one of my favorites and I let out a small, involuntary gasp.

"Excuse me?" the dad says.

I look up at him. "Oh, nothing. Sorry. I just love this book."

He furrows his brow at me, giving me the same intent stare that unnerved me during the children's reading circle. "You do?"

I look away from him, letting out a quick "yes," and move on to the final two books: Sylvia Plath's *The Bell Jar* and Nicholas Sparks's *The Notebook.* Strange picks for both an eight-year-old boy (even if he is mature for his age) and a grown man.

After scanning them, I take his proffered keys out of his hand and scan the library card that he has on his key chain. I look at the screen and a name pops up: Eric Keegan.

I print out the receipt; stick it in the middle of the top book, which is now *The Notebook;* and heft the stack up on the counter in front of the man. "These are all due back in three weeks, Mr. Keegan," I say. "November twenty-first."

He nods and then looks down at the boy. "Let's go," he says. When the boy starts to maneuver the wheelchair with exaggerated effort, the dad sighs again. "Can't you just get up and push it? The costume event is over."

"Professor X couldn't just get up," says the boy. "And neither can I."

In a burst of energy, the boy rams the chair directly into the circulation desk, with enough force to knock over a pen jar in front of me.

"I told you to wear your glasses," the dad mumbles.

"Professor X doesn't wear glasses," the boy replies.

"Sorry," the man says to me as I busy myself picking up pencils and pens and putting them back in the overturned jar. I want to tell him it's OK, but I can't push the words out of my mouth. It feels like too much, this man with the intense gaze, this entire conversation — which might be the longest one I've had in years — this day. My fingers find my wrist and I start drumming, willing my heartbeat to step in line with the rhythm.

The man grabs the handles of the chair and helps turn the boy around, toward the exit. "There," he says. *Finally,* I think, glad to see the man isn't a complete jerk. I lift my head to watch them go, but as soon as I do, he glances back at me.

Embarrassed to have been caught studying them, I avert my gaze to the computer.

"Thanks," he says. And then after a moment, he adds: "Emily."

Shocked, I jerk my head back up at him, but he's already turned around, slowly pushing the large wheelchair and his son toward the door.

Louise comes up behind me and says under her breath, "Told you they were weird, didn't I?"

I don't respond, still a bit stunned from the whole exchange.

"Dad seems like kind of an asshole, if you ask me," she continues.

I nod slowly. He was a bit . . . stern. But then, he also knew Emily Dickinson by heart, and to be honest, I'm just not really sure what to make of that.

Eight

ERIC

My mother loved that poem, " 'Hope' Is the Thing with Feathers." A cross-stitch of it hung at the end of our hallway and even though I saw it every evening on my way to bed, it's one of those things that I stopped noticing because I was so used to its being part of the landscape.

But then I heard the opening refrain, and I remembered it. And I knew right away that that librarian was dressed as Emily Dickinson.

Doesn't really explain her wild hair, though.

Or the gloves.

Or why, when I looked at her, I couldn't stop looking at her, as if her face were a magnet and my eyes were made of steel. Maybe it was because she had this strange quality about her — almost feral. Like a back-alley cat that jumps at sudden move-

141

ments and runs in the opposite direction of people. To be honest, she looked a little like a mental institution patient in that getup.

But later that night, as I crack open *Breaking Dawn* and her face flashes in my mind for the third time, unbidden, I have to admit — she is quite possibly the most beautiful insane woman I've ever seen.

PART II

I dwell in possibility.

Emily Dickinson

(Twenty Years Ago)

THE NEW YORK TIMES

(continued from page 3B) Back in 1947, 42 years before Jubilee Jenkins was born, a scientist named Dr. Frank Simon conducted a small study to discover if human dander could be the cause of some cases of eczema — particularly infant eczema. His results were positive. Five patients developed atopic dermatitis when they came into contact with the skin cells of other people. The study, published in the *Journal of Investigative Dermatology,* attracted little notice, seeing as how atopic dermatitis was a mild skin reaction and was known to be caused by any number of environmental allergens — now, thanks to Dr. Simon, other human skin cells included.

But Dr. Simon's work did not go unnoticed by Dr. Gregory Benefield, an allergy expert who received his undergraduate degree at Johns Hopkins in 1967 and did his graduate work and residency at Mount Sinai.

"He's the first person I thought of when I reviewed Jubilee's medical file," he says, his voice a deep and serious baritone.

In fact, everything about Dr. Benefield is serious — from his crisp bow tie and thick-rimmed bifocals to his dark eyes that only lit up when I first mentioned Jubilee's name.

"Ah, yes." He smiled. "My little walking medical mystery."

Though Dr. Benefield had never come across a case of a person being so severely allergic to other humans before (and in fact, there are only three other documented cases of it — none in the United States), he had a hunch about what the cause must be.

"I recalled Dr. Simon's work from my graduate studies," he says. "And every doctor before me — and there had been many — had ruled out nearly every other possibility. I just thought, "What if?" I ran a few simple tests — experiments really. We kept her in an isolation ward for a week, and her symptoms cleared up. Then I touched her arm to see what would happen. Sure enough, an hour later, a rash. It appeared to be the cause of her condition."

Her condition that, after a few more tests,

finally had a diagnosis — an allergy to humans.

"It's the most fascinating thing, genetically speaking," says Dr. Benefield. "When you're allergic to something, like a food protein for instance, your body mistakes it for an invader and attacks it with a release of antibodies and histamines. It's an understandable mistake to an extent — it's a foreign protein, just not a dangerous one. But for a human body to attack other *human* proteins would mean that the affected person doesn't have at least one of those proteins — those very building blocks that make us human. Technically speaking, does that make her *not* human?"

A mind-boggling proposition for sure, and not one that Dr. Benefield means literally, he assures me. "There is obviously some genetic mutation in her DNA — a variation causing her to be absent one or more human proteins." It's estimated the human body is made up of more than two million proteins. "She would be a fascinating candidate for genetic sequencing."

He's not the only one who thinks so. Since Jubilee's unique condition has been publicized, Ms. Jenkins has received numerous phone calls and requests from researchers all over the country — and in some instances, internationally — to study the young girl's condition.

But could further testing, or genetic sequencing, lead to a cure?

"Perhaps in the future," says Dr. Benefield. "There is still much we don't know about allergies, particularly how to heal someone of their condition. Studies are ongoing, but our best practices at the moment are symptom management — in Jubilee's case, keeping her away from any skin-to-skin human contact — and the hope that children will outgrow their allergies with age."

Does that happen often? I ask.

"It happens," he says. "Though typically not with very severe allergies."

Like Jubilee's?

"Like Jubilee's." **(continued on page 26E)**

NINE

ERIC

"Aja! The dog needs breakfast," I yell as I grab the coffeepot and start to pour my first cup of the morning. I gave up on quitting — especially since we brought this mutt home from the animal shelter two weeks ago. Aja couldn't think of a name, so we've been calling it The Dog, though The Puppy would be more accurate, as it's been waking me multiple times every night, needing to go out, wanting to play, or whining for no discernible reason at all, bringing back memories of Ellie's sleepless first year of life.

I walk down the hall, The Dog at my heels. "Aja!" I say, giving his door a firm knock with my knuckle as I pass by. In my bedroom, I set my coffee mug on my nightstand and pick up *The Virgin Suicides* from where I left it last night. I flip through it, skimming a couple of paragraphs here and there, hoping something might jump out at me that I missed the first two times I read it this week.

Those vampire books? I breezed right through and sent Ellie a text:

Read Twilight. Team Jacob all the way. Dad

I was glad she was, too — according to her journal, she found him to be "soooo much hawter than Edward" — because that vampire seemed to have some serious control issues.

But this book? I can't understand why Ellie wrote: "This Eugenides guy gets it. He just really gets it." I think of her words and look back at the book: what exactly does he get?

I'm tempted to have Aja read it because I'm fairly certain he's smarter than me, but I don't think the material (boys spying on girls with binoculars, sex under bleachers, virgins impaling themselves on fence posts) was appropriate for Ellie to be reading, much less a ten-year-old boy.

"No!" I shout. The Dog has squatted on the carpet in front of me and is releasing a stream of urine onto it, while his dewy black eyes stare up at me, as if to say, *I told you I needed to go out.* I sigh, and realize Aja still hasn't responded to me. I'm reaching down to scoop The Dog up when a loud crash jerks my head up in the direction of the living room.

"Aja?"

Silence. I run down the hall toward the noise, panicked that I've forgotten some Art of Safe Parenting rule — something Stephanie would have innately known, like maybe I should have secured the flat-screen to the TV stand with bolts. I have visions of Aja sprawled beneath it, crushed by forty-eight inches of LCD technology.

But when I get there, Aja is standing upright, looking not at the TV, but at the glass coffee table, which no longer resembles a coffee table. It's shattered, likely by the hammer that — for inexplicable reasons — is sticking up from the center of it.

"Aja!" I yell, brought up short by the sight, my heart still hammering from my sprint down the hallway. "What *happened?*"

My eyes scan the large plates of sharp-edged glass at his bare feet, surrounded by thousands of tiny glittering shards lighting up the carpet. The Dog, who followed me from the bedroom, is dancing around the mess and barking. I grab his collar to still him and then look to Aja for an explanation

151

of what I'm seeing.

His head hangs on his shoulders, eyes trained to the ground, and he's standing so still, I have the fleeting horrific thought that a shard has somehow struck him directly in the heart and killed him where he stands.

"Aja!" I say again, but then realize that I don't want him to move, seeing as how any step he'd take in any direction would certainly embed glass in the soles of his feet.

"Don't move." I feel a little ridiculous when the words come out — it's like giving an imperative to a marble statue. I walk The Dog to his crate in the corner of the living room, secure him inside, and then go back over to Aja, trying but unable to avoid the glass crunching beneath my tennis shoes.

"Aja," I say again when I'm hovering over him, staring down at the crown of his head, where black hair sticks out at various angles and on either side the bent legs of his glasses are clinging to the tops of his delicate ears. This close, I notice that his body is trembling ever so slightly, as if a vibration of the earth is happening just in the spot below his feet.

I bend my knees until my chest is level with his head and put my arms around his tiny frame, easily hefting him up in the air. His body, arms rigid at his sides, is as stick-

152

straight as a pencil — and nearly feels as light.

When I set him gently down in the kitchen, we both stand there not touching or speaking and I wonder if maybe he's traumatized or in shock. I search my brain for the first-aid treatments I learned in Boy Scouts. Did we cover shock?

As I'm deciding between slapping him across the face (seems harsh, but I have a flash of a scene from a movie where it works) and throwing a cold cup of water at him (ditto), Aja speaks. Or at least, I think he spoke.

"What?" I bend down a little, trying to see his face, if I can make out the words his mouth is forming.

"I'm sorry," Aja says, so quietly it takes me a minute to register the phrase.

Before I can respond, Aja takes off, running out of the kitchen and down the hallway. His bedroom door slams shut and the noise reverberates in my ears.

And I'm left there, feet glued to the linoleum tiles, looking back into the living room at the big sparkly mess and wondering what the hell just happened.

After picking up the large shards, then sweeping and vacuuming the leftover bits, I get on my hands and knees to look under the sofa and make sure I got it all, but before I can even look I feel a sharp stab in my palm. I lift it up to look and a long sliver of glass glints back at me, a bead of red blood already asserting itself on the squishy pad beneath my fingers.

I swear under my breath: "Shit." The pain is concentrated and intense and I know it's going to hurt even more when I pull it out. Though I've kept it at bay ever since Aja ran to his room obviously traumatized, anger wells up from somewhere deep. Intuition tells me Aja put that hammer through the glass on purpose, but I have no idea why. What was he possibly thinking? I hold my hand steady down the hall, so the blood now pooling in my palm doesn't drip onto the carpet. At Aja's door, I pause. I lean my head closer, my ear almost touching the door, and I hear the faint clack of the keys on the keyboard. I sigh and continue to my room in search of the first-aid kit under the sink in my bathroom, my foot stepping squarely onto the wet spot left by The Dog.

Double shit.

After bandaging my hand and cleaning the dog piss out of the carpet, I know I should go talk to Aja, but I pick up my cell and dial Connie instead.

"Good lord, Eric," she says after my brief recap of the incident. "And he didn't tell you what happened?"

"No."

"Did you *ask*?"

"Of course I did," I say, thinking back. Didn't I? "I think I did. I don't know, he just seemed so traumatized or something."

"Where is he now?"

"In his room."

"You've got to go talk to him and let him know that accidents happen. He probably feels terrible."

I open my mouth to tell her I don't think it was an accident, but I realize how awful that sounds, so I change the subject.

"Have you read *The Virgin Suicides*?"

"What?"

"The book — *The Virgin Suicides*. Have you read it?"

"Uh . . . I don't think so. Why?"

"Just wondering."

"Eric, seriously. Go talk to him."

"OK, OK," I say.

I throw my phone on the bed, rub my good hand over my stubbly cheek, and a stench wafts up from my armpit. I'll talk to him after I shower.

Fifteen minutes later, when I walk into the hall with my still-damp hair, the first thing I notice is Aja's wide-open door.

"Aja?"

I peer into the room. It's empty. "Aja?" I yell out again. Silence.

I wonder if he took The Dog out for a walk. I head to living room and my eyes dart to the crate in the dining room — where The Dog is lying, head on his paws, looking up at me with sorrowful eyes. My heart starts to beat a little faster.

"Aja!" I yell, even though it's a futile attempt. I know I won't be getting a response. A glance in the kitchen confirms what the newly formed pit in my stomach is trying to tell me. Aja's gone.

I run out the front door and down the concrete steps to the parking lot, calling his name with even more urgency. The bright blue sky forces me to squint and the hairs on my arm react to the unexpected cold air — wasn't it sixty-five earlier this week? — as I scan the cars, the sidewalk, the road. A hunched balding man in an overcoat two apartment buildings down from me is walking a puff of a dog that looks like a Pomeranian. The guy's staring at me, open-mouthed, and I glance down at myself, taking in what he sees: a barefoot guy clad in a robe, breathing heavily and shouting.

"Have you seen a boy?" I ask, staring back at him. "He's ten, but small for his age. Looks about seven?"

He puts his hand up to his ear, which even from this distance I can see is sprouting a handful of long white hairs. "Ten, you say?" His voice is gruff.

I nod.

He sets his lips in a line and shakes his head, while his dog lifts its leg and pees on a car tire.

As I turn to go back inside and get my car keys, I wonder: am I overreacting? When I was ten, I would stay outside for hours with my buddies. I try to remember what we were even doing. I have a vague memory of throwing rocks at stuff. Well, my friends were throwing rocks. I was most likely studying them.

But Aja doesn't have any friends. And he's never shown the slightest interest in going outside — he's always on that blasted computer.

The computer!

I rush into his room and swipe the mouse to wake up the screen, praying he followed my rule about not leaving it password-protected. A chat room fills the monitor and relief floods me. He's a good kid.

I scan the missives.

ProfX729: Didn't wrk.
IggyCanFly: What'd u try?
ProfX729: Hammer. Annihilated coffee table.
IggyCanFly: W@?! D00000000000d. Bet ur dad's P'd.
ProfX729: Nt my dad.
IggyCanFly: Rght. Sry.
ProfX729: Think I ne2h sth bigger. More ke.
IggyCanFly: Like w@ — a car? ;)
ProfX729: Maybe.
IggyCanFly: D00d, jk. C the winky face? ^ ^
ProfX729: Got an idea. MTF.
IggyCanFly: Wait. Not a car, K? 2 yng 2 drive.
IggyCanFly: D00d, u there?
IggyCanFly: D00d?

I only understand every third word, but two things are clear: 1) Aja did throw the hammer into the coffee table on purpose. 2) He's left to go try whatever he was trying with something else. Something bigger. Something that may or may not be a car. And the panic that's rising with every second, flooding my body with alarm, is telling me that whatever it is he's doing, it's something dangerous.

And the only question that remains is: *can I find him in time?*

TEN

JUBILEE

"Well, this is a first," Louise says.

I look up from the returns I'm scanning.

"Found this in the stacks," she says, holding up a flip-flop.

"Shoes?" I ask.

"Just the one," she says. "I've found a lot of strange things here before — I keep a box in the back — but never one shoe." She walks around the circulation desk. "You'd think someone would notice if they walked in with two sandals and walked out with one."

Roger appears over Louise's shoulder. "In the stacks?" he asks, nodding at the shoe.

They're both behind the circulation desk now and the hairs on the back of my neck start to stand at attention. The area is feeling just a little too crowded. I start to tap my left wrist.

"Yep," Louise says. "Might be the weirdest thing yet."

"I don't know," says Roger. "That naked American Girl doll with the pins stuck in its eyes — remember? That was pretty creepy."

"Oh dear, yes. That was strange."

"A librarian friend of mine in the city? Found one of those house-arrest ankle bracelets, cut clean through," Roger says.

"Oh my! Can you imagine?"

Roger and Louise laugh and keep talking, but with a lowered pitch, which is how I know a patron is approaching. I look up, hoping it's not someone asking me how to use the Internet again. That was an anxiety-ridden experience. My eyes lock on Madison H. I'm surprised to see her, since she was just in a week ago, and she doesn't strike me as someone who comes to the library that often — even if she is on the board.

"Hi," she says, smiling, her thick lip gloss shining like a just-licked lollipop.

"Hi," I say, staring at her. I look in her hands for books, but she's not carrying any. "Um . . . can I help you?"

"Oh, well I thought we had talked about grabbing lunch last week. I was in the area — do you still want to?"

Huh. I guess she did mean it when she asked on Halloween. I glance at the clock

— it's 12:10 — and I technically could take a break right now, if I wanted. I look back at her expectant face.

"I'm sorry, have you already eaten? I probably should have called first."

"No, no," I say, turning my attention to my computer screen. "Um . . . let me just finish checking in these books and, um . . . I'll be ready to go."

Madison navigates her car into the parking space in front of TeaCakes. It's only a few blocks from the library, but she said she'd drive because the weather has taken a sharp turn toward cold the past few days.

She moves the gearshift to park, while I peer at the storefront — the large expanse of window, where people on the other side are eating and talking and gesturing with their hands. But when I imagine that Madison and I will soon be sitting at one of those tables, the giant fist starts squeezing and tightening my chest, and my body freezes, limb by limb. I can't get out of the car. And I know no amount of tapping is going to change that.

So I sit there staring dumbly — at the eating, gesturing people who make being human look so easy. I kind of hate them. Not in such a way that I'd wish anything bad would happen to them, but just in the way that you hate the pretty, popular girl at school. Like the way I kind of hated Madison H.

"You coming in?" she says.

I stare at her, my face filling with heat. "No," I say, my dry throat expelling the word like a stuck crumb.

"No?" She tilts her head.

My brain races to find an excuse, something plausible as to why I can't leave the car, and then I look down and land on one.

"I forgot my coat." It's true — I left it in the back room of the library in my shock and confusion at Madison's asking me to lunch — but I know it's a feeble justification, considering I walked to Madison's car without it, and TeaCakes is only a few yards in front of us.

Her eyes fix on me for a beat and I wonder if she's going to start laughing. Or if she'll just drive me back to the library, patting herself on the back for attempting to be friends with me, but c'est la vie, I ended up being too weird, and, well, she tried.

She squints, looks toward the café and then back at me. I hold my breath. "Do you want to eat in the car? I could just run in and get some sandwiches to go."

I try to hide my surprise and nod. "That

would work."

Ten minutes later, Madison is back in the car, presenting me with a sandwich wrapped in wax paper. I reach for it with my gloved hand.

"Do you like tuna? I should have asked. I also have chicken salad."

"This is fine," I say.

While we eat, she tells me about Hannah punching a boy who pushed her off a swing. "I mean square in the chest," she says, laughing. "I know I'm supposed to be upset, and of course I pretended I was in front of the other mother, but really I'm proud of her. I like that she won't let anybody mess with her."

I nod and turn a vent away from me, as it's getting unnaturally warm in the car now.

We chew our sandwiches in silence for a few minutes.

"It's not because you forgot your coat, is it?"

"What?"

"Why you wouldn't go inside?"

I don't say anything, concentrating on the last two bites of my tuna sandwich. I actually don't like tuna — or maybe it's just that it doesn't taste right without pickle relish in it, the way I grew up eating it. I swallow. How do I explain — not just my condition, but my illogical fear of new places, new people? It sounds ridiculous to say it out loud, so I just give my head a small shake.

"Is it . . . are you . . ." She stutters over her words, and I realize it's the first time I've seen Madison H. falter. "I mean, there were rumors at school, but I wasn't ever sure which ones were true."

I stare at her, unsure what to say. "What were the rumors?"

"I think the most common one was that your skin was completely burned from the neck down in a house fire when you were little. Hence the gloves." She gestures to my hands. "Some said you were an alien, but most people didn't believe that. Hmm . . . let's see. I think someone said you were Mormon? And that's why you couldn't show any skin. Is that the Mormons? Or Muslims. I don't remember. But then, you didn't cover up your face, and that's what was most confusing to people, I guess. And then after Donovan . . . well, you know."

At the mention of his name, my face catches fire. I know immediately she's referring to the Incident and part of me wants to bolt from the car. Oh, the irony that I can't.

"He said you were allergic. To people."

She peers at me as if trying to suss out

the truth of it from the expression on my face. "I don't think anyone really believed him, but I did." She pauses and then scoffs. "God, I believed anything he said back then. But there was something about that explanation — as crazy as it sounded — that seemed particularly true. Or I just thought he was too dumb to make something like that up."

She looks at me again, and I wait for the feeling. The one I used to get in high school, like I was a curiosity. Something on display, like the two-headed snake floating in formaldehyde in the biology classroom. But it doesn't come.

I stuff the last bite of sandwich in my mouth under her watchful gaze and chew it slowly, while crumpling the wax paper into a ball in my hand. I swallow, then turn to meet her eyes. "It's true."

"What Donovan said?"

"No, the alien thing."

She laughs, and a warmth spreads through my belly, different from the warmth that was occupying my face. I like hearing her laugh and knowing that I caused it. It's like the satisfaction of planting a seed and then harvesting a tomato. But better.

"So, seriously. What's it mean? You can't, like, touch people?"

I get such a spectacular sense of déjà vu, my head feels as if it's swimming backward through time and I'm sitting on a rock in the courtyard of my high school staring into Donovan's questioning eyes instead of Madison's.

My stomach lurches.

I will myself back to the present.

"Yeah, that's the gist of it," I say.

Madison's eyes grow wide.

"So you could *die* from being touched?"

I shrug. "Hypothetically. Mostly, I just get a bad rash. I did have anaphylactic shock a few times as a kid, but it was before I was diagnosed, so they don't know if it was too much skin-to-skin contact that overwhelmed my system, or if I somehow ingested skin cells, like sharing an apple with my mom or something." I pause. "And then, of course, what happened with Donovan." I expect her to say something then, but she remains silent, so I keep talking. "The problem is, allergies are unpredictable. There's this girl who was allergic to milk, so her parents made sure she never drank it. Then one morning at breakfast, a gallon of it got knocked over and some milk splashed on her arm, and she went into anaphylactic shock and died. Just like that. Her parents couldn't get her to the hospital in time."

"Jesus."

I know a ton of these horror stories. My mom used to tell them to me like other parents read bedtime tales to their children. They were meant to be cautionary, but all they did was terrify me.

After another few minutes of silence, she says: "I wish Donovan had that. An allergy to people."

I raise my eyebrows at her. Who would wish this on anyone?

"He cheated on me when we were married," she says. "A lot, I think."

Oh. "I'm sorry."

"Me, too." She shrugs, then turns her attention back to me. "Did you really almost die?"

I nod my head.

"Geez," she says. We sit in the still of the car while this sinks in. "Wait, but then what? You didn't come back to school. You weren't at graduation. It's like you just dropped off the face of the earth. Some people said you *did* die, but I knew it would have been in the paper." She pauses. "Where did you go?"

My lips part as she talks, then grow dry from my slow breaths. I can't believe she noticed that I wasn't at school. At graduation. People did stare at me in high school — like I was a curiosity — but I didn't think anyone ever *noticed* me. It's a strange feeling, to be seen but invisible at the same time. I always felt a little like an apparition. There, but not there. Until Donovan kissed me, anyway. Afterward, I just felt foolish.

And then I wonder: did she look for me in the paper? For my death? I shiver at the morbidity. Madison is staring at me, waiting, her mascara-clumped lashes fanning out from her round eyes like peacock feathers.

"I didn't really go anywhere," I say. "I just sort of stayed in my house."

"What — for a couple of months?"

I hedge, my shoulder blades tensing. "A little longer."

"How long?"

I hesitate again. "Nine years."

Her eyes fly open. "Nine? But, I mean, you went out, right? Didn't you have to work? I just don't understand why nobody has seen you. Why *I* haven't seen you. Or heard about you. This isn't exactly a huge town."

A Walcott-ism from my sixth-grade teacher enters my mind: "In for a penny, in for a pound." I take a deep breath and decide I might as well go all in with Madison H. "I didn't leave my house at all. Ever. For anything. I've been a bit of a hermit, a recluse. Whatever you want to call it. And then, I sort of got a little agoraphobic, I guess, and *couldn't* leave my house. For anything. But by then, I had to. I had no money and I needed to work. But I still don't like being out" — I gesture toward the tea shop in front of us — "like this. With other people. The library's been hard enough."

I keep my eyes trained on my lap waiting for her reaction, but out of the corner of my eye Madison is a statue. She's silent for so long, I wonder if she heard me at all. Or if time is somehow being manipulated and what seems like minutes for me is just seconds for her. I turn my head a smidge toward her to check and that's when she speaks.

"So," she says. "You don't, like, go to Starbucks? Or the movies? Or to get your hair done?"

I raise my eyebrows at her. "Does it look like I get my hair done?"

She smiles.

"Anyway, I couldn't get my hair done if I wanted to. Can't be touched, remember?"

"Oh my god — so you've never had a manicure?" She glances at her own shiny talons, painted a shimmery purplish color today.

"Nope."

"Or a massage?"

"Un-uh." I shake my head.

And then her eyes get big and she holds out her hand as if to stop me, even though I'm not doing anything. "Wait. Oh my god. You've never had *sex.*"

She whispers the word "sex," which strikes me as funny, considering she nearly shouted the word "fucking" in a library not a few days earlier. I'm perplexed by how she decides when to be discreet.

I shake my head no.

She gasps and her hand moves to her chest, her manicured fingers splayed over her heart, as if to make sure it's still beating. "Don't you *want* to?"

I consider this question as if no one's ever asked me it before. Mainly because no one's ever asked me it before.

"I don't know," I say.

But then, I think back to those teenagers secretly devouring each other between the stacks at the library, and my body gets all tingly, and I wonder if, maybe, that's not true.

Pedaling home, the biting wind whips through my coat, as if I don't even have one on. I make a mental note to look into thermal underwear, and some kind of face mask, seeing as how I can't feel my nose. And maybe a headlight? Do they make those for bikes? At five thirty p.m., it's still light out now, but I know it's only a matter of time before that changes. As I approach the Passaic River Bridge, I'm wondering when the first snow will come, and what I'll do about getting to work then, when I notice a figure standing just underneath the bridge, on one of the support beams. I slow down and squint, while two cars pass in quick succession. It looks like a young boy, but I can't understand how he got there — or what he's doing. And suddenly, he's airborne — body flat out, like a skydiver without the parachute, and then he hits the water with a slap that I know even from my vantage point must have hurt like the dickens. I gasp and look around for other kids. Maybe he's on a dare? But I don't see another soul. The cars that drove past me are already on the bridge headed away, and it doesn't appear that they noticed the boy. I look back in the river, where I see his arms flailing, his eyes wide in panic, and his mouth opening and closing like a fish's, searching for air as he surfaces. *Come on,* I silently urge him. *Swim to the side.* But his little body stays in the middle, the slow-moving current steadily whisking him downstream.

And then he goes under.

I stand there staring at the murky water, too stunned to move. It feels like I'm in a movie or maybe my mind is playing some bizarre trick on me. I look around again for someone — anyone — who can help, but I'm alone. My mouth dry, I look back at the water, in time to see the dome of his black-haired head break the surface, bobbing like a buoy. And I know I have to do something.

I drop my bike on the shoulder and stumble down the grassy embankment, keeping my eyes trained on his floating head, while throwing off my coat. When I reach the river, I run parallel with it until I'm past the boy, then jump in, bravado pumping through my veins like I'm a goddamn superhero — until my body hits the icy water, stealing my breath. I let out an involuntary scream and start flailing my arms, mimicking the boy's own reaction when he fell in. Then I put my feet down and realize, with some relief — especially since I haven't been swimming in more than ten years — I'm able to touch bottom. I stand up, the cold water grazing my chest, and, training my eyes on the boy again, start pumping my legs toward the middle of the river. With growing alarm, I watch his body coming faster — the current must have picked up — and I'm not sure that I'll reach the interception point in time. I pump my legs harder, using my gloved hands to propel my body even faster through the water. Then, at the last possible second, I launch myself forward, stretching out my fingertips as far as they will go and grasping on to the wet material of his sweater. I get a clump of it in my hand and start pulling him toward me — surprised at how light his waterlogged body feels — while searching for purchase with my feet again in the silty earth. His head now out of the water, the boy sputters, expelling a surge of water from his lips, but then his head rolls over to one side, lifeless.

The return to the shore seems illogically faster — perhaps propelled by my eagerness to get out of the cold water, or my panic at his motionless form. Grunting, I push his tiny body onto the muddy bank and pull myself out after him.

Shivering — and my heart galloping at what feels like the same pace as my chattering teeth — I crouch over him. "Hey," I say, poking him in the arm with a gloved finger. He doesn't respond. I know the next logical step is CPR. I've seen it in a thousand medical dramas, but it always looks so intuitive — like it's an inherent skill encoded in your DNA. I wait for my body to take over, to do what needs to be done, but the only thing my gut is screaming at me right now is that if I don't do something immediately, this boy will die. Looking at his blue lips, I wonder for an instant if he already has. I tentatively put my palms on his chest and push, but I have no idea if I'm in the right spot or applying the correct amount of force. After ten or so pumps, I hesitate. I know what I need to do next. I also know that it could kill me.

Shit. Shit. Shit. I tilt his head up with a gloved hand and cover his nose and mouth with mine. I exhale into his lungs. Once. Twice. And then go back to pumping on his chest, while my lips begin that all-too-familiar tingling. I hear a shout and look up. A few cars have pulled to a stop right before the bridge and a man is getting out of one of them, waving his cell phone in the air. Relief floods through my numb body. I open my mouth to yell at the man to call an ambulance, but my throat is suddenly too tight to expel the air. I wheeze, trying to inhale, while still pumping away on the boy. My vision starts to blur, dark spots floating in at the edges, as I look up at the boy's face to see if my ministrations are making any difference — and that's when I realize I recognize him. I've seen this boy before. The phrase "serial killer," of all things, floats in my mind, unbidden.

The man from the car is suddenly beside me and I stumble back, watching as he immediately takes over pumping on the boy's chest. Clutching my own throat, silently begging my airway to open, I fall down on the grass. I hear coughing, but I'm not sure if it's my own or the boy's. Somewhere beyond that is the siren of an ambulance in the distance. My whole body feels warm and I let it sink farther into the ground, while the panic over not being able to breathe strangely begins to subside.

And then everything goes black.

ELEVEN

ERIC

Whoever created these little hospital chairs that fold out into sleeping cots should be executed. After lying on it for five hours, the muscles of my back have now constricted into a long string of knots, like that rope we used to climb up in gym class. I'm amazed the chairs haven't gone through any major improvements in the fourteen years since I last slept on one, when Ellie was born. My heart seizes as I think of her scrunched-up face, the tiny mews emanating from her puckered lips. That night, I couldn't sleep, not because of the uncomfortable chair, but in the event something happened with Ellie — what if she suddenly stopped breathing, or rolled over, or somehow managed to wrangle her way out of the straitjacket swaddle, up and over that terrible plastic encasement that was supposed to stand for a crib, and onto the floor? I lay

177

awake for the entire night, listening to her every tiny breath and whimper, wondering how I would ever rest again. Now I peer through the darkness at Aja's peaceful face, as if to remind myself that it's this child I'm keeping vigil for.

His chest rises and falls with sleep, and I review the day's events in my mind: driving all over the city with Connie searching for Aja, the relief and alarm flooding me instantaneously when I got the phone call alerting us to his location at St. Vincent's Hospital following a near-drowning incident, the doctor telling us he was a "very lucky little boy" and would only need to be kept overnight for observation.

I'm trying to stay focused, on the hard lumps of the chair digging into my spine and hips, on the methodical beeping of Aja's heart-rate monitor, on the footsteps of the janitor in the hallway, the swish of his mop sliding back and forth across the linoleum tile, on the streetlights peeking in through the gaps between the shoddy plastic blinds — on anything but the fact that Aja almost died. That I'm spectacularly failing at parenting with not just one but two children. That I would give anything for Ellie to start speaking to me again — if only to counteract some of my guilt over the current situation with Aja. In a moment of hopefulness, I wonder if maybe she tried to text during the evening while I was dealing with Aja. I sit up and dig my cell out of my pocket. The screen announces the time in glowing numbers — 3:14 a.m. — but nothing else.

My fingers twitch over the keys, wanting to text her, but I know it's much too late.

The next morning, the first thing I see when I open my eyes is Aja sitting up and licking chocolate pudding off a spoon. I blink, shocked that I actually fell asleep at some point.

"Hey, tiger," I say, groaning as I try to maneuver my stiff body into a sitting position. Forgetting my hand injury, I push up on my bandaged palm and wince at the sharp pain.

"Hi," he says, keeping his eyes trained on the pudding cup.

"How you feeling?"

"Good."

I was bursting with questions by the time Connie dropped me off at the hospital last night before she went to get The Dog, but Aja was already asleep, his tiny body worn from exhaustion. Now that he's awake, in the morning light, I have no idea what to say to him. Do I yell at him? Ground him? Hug him? Ask him what the hell he was thinking? I'm a jumble of emotions, the foremost being the familiar fear that I'll say the wrong thing. That I'll push him even further away from me. I made that mistake with Ellie, and I can't afford to make it again.

I glance at the nurses' white dry-erase board on the wall. It just says: *Tricia — Ext. 2743.* I look back at Aja.

"So. How was your swim?"

He stills the spoon on his tongue, midlick, and appears to ponder the question. Then he sets it down on his tray.

"Cold."

I nod, running my hand over the coarse hairs on my face. "Aja, you gotta help me out here, buddy. What were you —"

"Where's the librarian?" he asks, training his eyes on me.

"What?"

"The librarian. They took her away."

The doctor said Aja was awake and alert when he arrived at the hospital, leaving little concern for any lasting neurological damage, but we haven't been to the library in a week and I wonder if he's having some kind of memory lapse. I glance back at Tricia's number.

"Do you know what today is?" I ask, my brows knitting together.

Aja thinks about it. "Sunday."

"Who's the president?"

Aja looks at me with his liquid brown eyes. "Do you *not* know?"

A light rap at the door precedes a nurse opening it and walking in. "Good morning," she trills. "And how is our patient this morning?"

She's looking at a clipboard in her hand, so I'm not sure if she's talking to me or Aja. Neither one of us responds. She looks up. "Let's get that blood pressure, mmm?"

She lays the chart on the foot of the bed and wraps the cuff around Aja's thin arm. Afterward she takes his temperature and listens to his chest with a stethoscope. Then she scrawls on the paper she came in with. "Dr. Reed will be by on rounds in the next hour or so, K?"

"Tricia?"

"Oh, nope." She goes over to the board and wipes the name clean with her marker. "She was the night nurse. I'm Carolyn."

"Oh. Sorry," I say, and then nod in Aja's direction. "How is he?"

She looks down at the chart, as if she's already forgotten. "His vitals are great," she says. "I imagine he'll be able to go home sometime this afternoon." She clutches the chart to her chest. "Any other questions?" she asks, and turns to Aja. "Do you need anything?"

"My glasses," Aja says. "I can't see anything."

The nurse smiles and walks over to the counter where Aja's glasses are sitting. She picks them up and hands them to him.

"And where's the woman? The librarian?" he asks as he slides the hooks over his ears.

Well, here we go. I cover my face with my hands.

"The one who saved you?" My head shoots up.

Aja nods.

"She's recovering on the fourth floor," she says. "She had some, ah . . . complications."

"Wait, what happened?" I realize I was so solely focused on Aja's health last night that I don't even know what really happened to him. I know he somehow fell in the river and some passersby spotted him and called 911. I didn't think to ask anything else. *Just like a man,* I can hear Stephanie's voice saying in my head.

"A woman riding by on a bicycle spotted your son and dove in after him. She performed CPR until someone called the ambulance."

"It was that librarian. From the other day," Aja chimes in, shooting me a blank expression that I take to mean *I told you so.*

My mouth feels dry and I'm strangely aware of my heart beating in my chest. Emily. I'm sure it's not her real name, but it's the only one I know her as. I have a sudden image of her swan-diving into the Passaic in her long white nightgown. I look at the nurse. "You said something about complications, though. Is she OK?"

"I'm sorry, I'm not really supposed to say."

I can't believe that woman — that timid wisp of a woman who was just reciting poetry and checking out our library books — saved Aja's life. I feel indebted to her. And I need to make sure she's OK. "Can I see her?"

The nurse pauses. "I'll have to ask her. I'll let you know." She glances back at the chart. "Oh, and the social worker will be by later today."

"Social worker?" I ask.

"Just standard protocol," she says, but she doesn't meet my gaze.

After she's gone, I push the librarian from my mind and turn my attention back to Aja. "So. Are you going to tell me why you were on that bridge?"

He stares at the empty pudding cup as if

willing it to refill with his mind. Hell, maybe that's exactly what he's trying.

"OK," I say. "Why don't we start with the coffee table?"

He doesn't move.

"That wasn't an accident, was it?"

He remains statuesque.

"Aja," I say. "Look at me." I can't keep the desperation out of my voice and maybe that's what drags his eyes upward until they lock with mine. "Talk to me."

He opens his mouth and mumbles something.

"What?" I lean forward in my chair to try to hear him better.

"Kinetic energy."

I remember the term from physics class but am baffled as to why he's said it. "What about it?"

"I was trying to harness it," he says.

"O-kaaaay," I say, studying his tiny body and face.

He sighs and sits up a little. "You know Newton's first law?"

"I think so," I say.

"An object at rest stays at rest unless an external force acts upon it."

"OK."

"I've been trying to move objects at rest." He stares at me from behind his glasses with

184

his large eyes, as if this explains it all.

"With your mind," I say.

"Right." He leans back against the pillow, pushing the wheeled table holding his breakfast tray and empty pudding cup away from him, and I realize he's done talking.

"Um. I'm going to need a little bit more," I say. He gives me a look so similar to one of Ellie's *You're such an idiot, Dad* faces that it nearly breaks me in half. Does it start this young?

Aja sighs. "I realized all this time I've been trying to convert an object's potential energy, when it makes so much more sense to try and manipulate its kinetic energy. If an object is already moving, shouldn't it be easier to move it? Like a car that won't start — it can take a few people to push it, but then once it's rolling, one person can easily keep it going."

I consider this and what he's saying does make sense, but I'm still not sure what it has to do with my broken coffee table and his near-drowning incident. "OK," I say, nodding. And then it's like the sun has broken through the clouds and I can see everything clearly. "Wait. You *threw* the hammer so it would have kinetic energy, so it would be easier to move with your mind?"

"I didn't *throw* it," he says. "I just kind of

185

dropped it. I was using gravity as the work — the external force to change potential energy into kinetic. There's a formula —"

"I don't care about the *formula*." I nearly spit the word. "Why the *coffee table*, though? Why not just drop it on the carpet?"

"I did! I started with the carpet, trying to stop it from falling with my mind, or at least change the trajectory, but it wasn't working. I thought if there was a bigger consequence, something I really wanted to not happen, then my brain would be more powerful, try harder or something."

I stare at him, incredulous.

"It didn't," he adds.

"No, it didn't." I sit up, my mind reeling, and I remember the online chat I read about his wanting to try something bigger — maybe a car. "So what were you trying to drop in the river?"

He looks down at the hospital sheets covering his tiny legs, which is when it hits me out of nowhere.

"Oh my god. You were trying to drop *yourself* in the river." I really can't believe that he would throw himself into a raging body of water on purpose, but the instant I see his face, I know that it's true. "Aja — you don't even know how to swim!"

His voice is small. "I thought it would

be . . . more motivating."

"To help you *levitate*?"

And I realize *that* was the big idea, the thing he was talking to his friend about online.

He studies the corner where the ceiling meets this wall, as if it's the most fascinating thing he's ever seen, and I know that he's done talking.

We sit there, me staring at him, him staring at the ceiling, while I try to suss out the conflicting emotions in my brain. But the overriding one is fear — that maybe his imagination isn't as harmless as I've thought. That I've been dismissing too much. That I haven't wanted to see what was right in front of me. That maybe Stephanie and the one-time therapist and the school counselor might all be right — maybe Aja does need help.

Her hair looks very similar to the way it did the day I first saw her in the library — long, disheveled chestnut-colored strands, like tangled vines growing out of her head and engulfing the pillow behind her. It occurs to me that maybe this is just the way that she wears it, not part of a costume or the by-product of some heroic mission.

But her face — her face is different. She's

pale — paler than I remember — and she has dark circles under her eyes like she hasn't slept in a week. Angry red welts surround her lips and one is crawling up her cheek. I cover my mouth with my hand, hoping to conceal my surprise at her appearance.

She sits up a little when she sees me, that same startled look in her eyes — and I realize even though she told the nurse I could visit, I'm still a strange man in her room.

We stare at each other in silence for a few beats, until I recover enough to speak.

"Thank you," I say. "You know, for . . ." It occurs to me that I'm not exactly sure what her role in saving Aja's life was. I clear my throat.

"It's OK," she says, but the words come out hoarse, as if she's just smoked an entire pack of cigarettes. "It's nothing. I was on my way home from work. Right place, right time, I guess."

"Well, no, it's not nothing," I say, thinking: *Look at you.* Instead, I say: "You *are* in the hospital."

She shrugs and then starts coughing, but it comes out more like a wheezing sound that makes my own throat itch.

I notice she has a similar heart monitor to the one that's hooked up to Aja.

She must have almost drowned in rescuing him — I want to ask, but it feels too personal, somehow. And then it occurs to me that I still don't know her name.

"I'm Eric, by the way."

She nods and then has just opened her mouth to respond when the door bursts open.

"Jubilee Jenkins," says a booming voice. A man in a white coat and glasses enters the room behind his voice. He's hefty, like he once was a high school linebacker and never stopped eating like one. I step out of his way, but he barely glances at me, his eyes trained on Emily, whose name is apparently Jubilee.

"I wasn't sure I'd ever see you again," he says. "Wish it was under better circumstances, of course. How long has it been? Five, six years?"

"Nine," Jubilee says.

"Nine! Holy cow. Where does the time go?" he says. "Never forgot you, though. You've been the topic of many a dinner conversation. I mean, not your name, of course, patient confidentiality and all that." He clears his throat. "Anyway, you're lucky that EMT noticed your swollen lips and gave you the Epi. He's worked enough anaphylaxis cases to know, I guess. You

189

really should be wearing one of those allergy bracelets, though — do you have one? I can see about getting you one, if you don't." He looks down at the chart he's holding in his hand, shakes his head, and lets out a long whistle. "Man, you really are lucky. So, how are we feeling?"

Jubilee's eyes are big and she looks as bewildered by this man as I feel. I didn't think he'd ever stop talking. And what was that about an allergy? Was she stung by a bee or something while she was trying to save Aja?

"I'm OK," Jubilee says, and I can't tell if I imagine it or if her eyes flit over to me for a second. "When can I go home?"

"Well, your heart's pumping fine, but I don't like that lingering wheeze you've got there," he says. "You're not really out of the woods yet. Anaphylaxis can reoccur up to seventy-two hours after the event — and yours was pretty severe. According to the EMT's report, you were already unconscious when they got to you."

She gives a slight nod.

"I mean, if you have someone to look out for you, I'd be more inclined to release you." He looks up at me, as if he's finally noticed me standing there. "Are you family?"

I start to shake my head no, just as Jubilee says: "Yes."

The desperation in her eyes is so fierce, I immediately change the direction of my head to an up-and-down motion. "I am," I say. "Her . . . cousin?"

She bobs her head, mimicking mine. "He is. He can look after me."

"Ohhh-kay," says the doctor, then walks closer to Jubilee. "Listen, who's your allergist? I checked with Dr. McCafferty's nurse and he doesn't have you on file."

She shakes her head no.

"Someone else?"

She gives her head another small shake.

"Jubilee! You need to be working with somebody. There have been so many advances with allergies the past few years. Maybe you could work on getting this thing under control somehow. Where do you get your scrip for EpiPens? Don't tell me from some quack online."

"I don't —" she starts, her voice cracking. "My Epis are expired."

The doctor has a visceral reaction and I think he might come out of his skin. "You don't have *Epis*? Jesus! I'd rather you said you were getting them online."

She doesn't respond.

The doctor stares at her for a beat and

then looks at his watch. "Jubilee, at the very, *very* least, you need to get Epis and a bracelet. The very least." He fixes her with a look. "I'm serious. I don't want to see you in here again." He pauses, as if for dramatic effect. "I can't imagine you'd be this lucky a second time."

It works. On me, anyway.

And then he's gone, and I'm left standing there, eyes locked with Jubilee's, the air heavy between us. There are so many questions, but I know the answers are none of my business, so I just wait, hoping maybe she'll speak first. She doesn't. The only sound I can hear is my heart thumping like a dog's tail in exuberant greeting. I wonder why it's doing that. I wonder if she can hear it, too.

"Well, cousin," I say, smiling in an attempt to smooth over the awkwardness. "Can I give you a ride home?"

When I get back to Aja's room, there's a woman standing outside the door. Clad in casual black slacks, a gray blouse, and slip-on shoes, she resembles other visitors I've passed in the hallway, save for the official-looking lanyard draped around her neck and the briefcase she's carrying. Regardless, I don't recognize her, so my first thought is that she's got the wrong room.

"Excuse me," I say as I brush past her and reach for the door handle.

"Mr. Keegan?" she asks.

I stop. "Yes?"

"Latoya Halliday, medical social worker here on staff," she says, sticking her hand out toward me.

Oh, right, the nurse mentioned this. "Come on in," I say, giving her proffered hand a gentle squeeze and then reaching back to the doorknob. "We'll see if he's up."

"Oh no, I was hoping to talk to you," she says. "Privately. I've already spoken to Aja."

I take a step back. "You did?" I ask. "I mean, that's legal, without me being there?"

"Standard procedure," she says, echoing what the nurse said earlier.

I narrow my eyes. "Standard procedure for what, exactly?" I ask. "Do you visit every child that gets admitted to the ER?"

"No," she says, shifting her eyes to the door and then back at me. "Just when it's deemed necessary."

"Deemed necessary by whom?" I feel like I'm missing something, like I'm not getting to the root of the issue with my questioning, but I'm caught off guard and my mind is swirling.

"Why don't we go have a seat, Mr. Keegan?" She nods toward a bench in the hallway.

Without much choice in the matter, I follow her like a puppy on a string. When we're settled, she looks directly at me, and I sense a shift in her tone. "Our concern is that Aja's fall wasn't an accident."

As her eyes search mine, I realize immediately what she's inferring.

"Oh no, no. He wasn't trying to kill himself." And then I stop. I'm not sure how to explain what he *was* doing.

She presses her lips together and her face mutates into a canvas of concern.

"I understand this is difficult, but if you could just answer a few questions for me . . ." She looks around, as if expecting someone to materialize in the hallway. "Is there a Mrs. Keegan? Is Aja's mother . . . involved?"

"No," I say. "His parents died a few years ago and I adopted him. I'm . . . um . . . divorced." Even though it's common, I hate saying it out loud. It's like announcing I've failed. That I'm a failure. "Wait — this is all in his file. Don't you have it?"

"In New Jersey? There was nothing on him."

"Oh, right. We just moved here."

She gives a curt nod and then gets back

to the matter at hand. "Have you noticed any depressive or strange behavior from Aja in recent weeks?"

I knead my jawline, last night's lack of sleep finally catching up with me. "How so?" I ask.

"Spending an abnormal amount of time in his room and/or bed, withdrawing from friends, withdrawing from you, idealization of things that could harm him, like guns, explosives —"

I nearly choke on a bubble of laughter and begin clearing my throat to disguise it. The woman looks at me funny.

My phone rings and I finagle it out of my pocket. It's Stephanie. My ex-wife rarely calls, but it will have to wait. I silence it.

"Nothing out of the ordinary from his usual behavior," I say, composing myself. "Look, I'm afraid this has all been a big misunderstanding."

"And I'm afraid you don't understand the seriousness of what your son is going through," she says, an edge to her voice. "Is there a history of mental illness in his family?"

"No," I say firmly. Then I pause. The truth is, I don't know anything about Dinesh's and Kate's parents and grandparents beyond the little they told me about them.

"Trouble at school? Any bullying?"

I hesitate, thinking about his three-day suspension and Jagger, that hulk of a fifth grader. "A minor misunderstanding. Once."

The phone buzzes in my hand. Stephanie again. "I'm sorry," I say. "Let me just . . . real quick —" I slide my finger over the screen and put it up to my ear.

"Stephanie, sorry, I'm in the middle of some —"

"It's Ellie."

My heart drops as I stand up. I look at the social worker and hold up my finger. "Can you give me just one minute? I'm sorry. I've gotta —" I walk off down the hall without waiting for a reply. "What's wrong? Is she OK?"

"She's fine. I just thought you should know . . . well, she got suspended."

"From *school*?"

"Well, yeah, Eric, where else would she get suspended from?"

I ignore her sarcasm. "What for?"

Stephanie pauses. "She was caught smoking on school grounds."

"Cigarettes?" I hiss, glancing at Latoya. She's staring at me intently. I turn my back to her.

"Not exactly."

"Pot?"

196

"Yeah."

"*Jesus*, Stephanie!"

"Calm down, Eric! It's just a little weed. It's not *heroin.*"

"Not today, it's not."

"Oh, don't start with that gateway-drug crap. *We* smoked weed. It's just something kids do." I can't believe she's being so nonchalant about it.

"Not at fourteen!"

"Yes, at fourteen. We were seventeen. Not much difference. Look, I admit it was a bad choice, and I told her as much, but I don't think we need to get apoplectic here."

"No, I'm sure you don't," I say. "Put her on the phone."

"No. She doesn't want to talk to you," she says. "And even if she did, she's not here."

I clench my teeth and speak in a low voice so Latoya can't hear me. "She got suspended from school for drugs and you let her leave the house? What kind of mother are you?" As soon as it comes out, I know I shouldn't have said it. I close my eyes and wait for the tsunami that's coming.

"What kind of mother am *I*? Are you serious right now? I'm the kind of mother that's *here,* which isn't something that can be said for you, is it?"

I pinch the bridge of my nose with my free

hand, recognizing the irony. No, I'm not there. I'm with my other child, who is currently in the hospital. "It's only six months — and you agreed I should take it. That it would be the best thing," I say wearily. "Look, let's not — We promised we wouldn't do this."

"Yeah, well, we promised a lot of things to each other, didn't we?" And then I hear a click as she ends the call.

I clutch the phone tighter, and resist the urge to chuck it down the hall and see it shatter into a hundred pieces. I hate when she does that — gets all pious about our divorce, as if she didn't want it as much, if not more, than me. I take a deep breath and remember where I am. I compose my face and turn around to Latoya, who's still sitting on the bench, wearing a worried expression.

"Where were we?" I ask, walking toward her.

She tilts her head skeptically, as if she wants to ask about the phone call, but then thankfully looks back down at her notes. "We're concerned about your son's emotional —"

"What exactly did he say to you?" I ask, cutting her off.

She lowers her eyes. "Well, not much,"

she admits. "I asked him the standard questions: if he wanted to harm himself, if he had thought about it before, if he ever thought about harming others. He mostly ignored me."

I nod, a little absurdly grateful that it's not just me he ignores.

"But when I asked him if he meant to jump off that bridge, he said yes."

I clear my throat. "I don't think he meant that he was trying to commit suicide," I say, and then pause, trying to figure out how to explain this. "He's become quite interested in the idea of . . . mental powers recently. Telepathy, telekinesis, X-Men type stuff. I think what he was trying to do, last night — as ridiculous as it may sound — is levitate over the river." I add a lame chuckle, trying to convey a *Kids will be kids, eh?* kind of tone, but the woman doesn't smile.

She purses her lips and sits back. "I see," she says. "You know those kind of delusions can be indicative of a larger psychiatric issue."

"I know," I say. "He's been to counseling. A few times, anyway, and they were unable to commit to a diagnosis."

"You also know that he may not be telling you the complete truth? I'm not saying your son's a liar — not at all. But children aren't always forthcoming with their parents."

Ellie's face flashes in my mind. "Tell me about it," I say.

"And we can't gloss over the real possibility that it was an attempted suicide," she says.

I open my mouth to argue, but I've lost the will. I know Aja wasn't trying to kill himself, but I also know what he was trying to do isn't much better. We sit in silence for a few beats and then she picks up the briefcase beside her and opens it. She shuffles through the papers until she comes to the one she's looking for. "OK, well, this is what I'd like to do, Mr. Keegan. Given the circumstances, I don't think a psychiatric transfer for Aja is necessary at this point, but I would like to refer you to a number of pediatric mental health professionals — these are broken out by network. You'll need to make an appointment within the week, and then that doctor will advise you on a further treatment plan." She hands me a piece of a paper with a list of doctors' names and telephone numbers. "I also think he's in need of around-the-clock supervision. Do you work, Mr. Keegan?"

"Yes," I say.

"Who brings Aja to school?"

"I do. I drop him off and then go to the

train station."

"Who watches Aja after school?"

"No one," I admit, thinking of our routine the last few weeks. "He rides the bus, and I call to make sure he got in OK. Then he plays computer games and does homework until I get home. It's only a couple of hours. I know it's not ideal, but —"

"You'll need to make other arrangements. He really should not be left alone, in case he decides to act again on these beliefs," she says. "I'll be drawing up a form that you'll need to sign, stating that you agree with these requirements, before Aja can be released from the hospital. I'll transfer the case to the Department of Children and Families, who will be performing follow-ups in the form of phone calls and a home visit to make sure you are adhering to these guidelines. Failure to do so could result in Aja being removed from your care." She sounds like a typewriter moving at eighty words per minute — monotonous and perfunctory.

"Wait — slow down. Removed from my —You're going to take him away from me?" Anger and fear are humming through my veins. I stand up so they have more room to circulate.

She puts her hand up. "Calm down, Mr.

Keegan," she says, her voice softer, as if she's trying to soothe me with the tone. "I just need to make you aware of the standard procedures. If you follow these mandates, it's very unlikely that will happen."

"You're damn right it won't happen," I say.

The woman sits patiently, waiting out my frustration. It reminds me of how I dealt with Ellie's toddler temper tantrums, and I realize that I'm currently the child in that scenario. I close my mouth. After a few more moments of silence, she speaks. "Listen, we all want what's best for Aja here," she says, putting her hand on my arm. It's the first time she's touched me, and it's such a gentle gesture that I alarmingly feel an excess of water pooling on my corneas. I turn my head and open my eyes wide in the hopes of drying them out. "Whether he was trying to kill himself or not — he almost did," she says. "And we need to make sure it doesn't happen again."

My shoulders sag under the weight of what she's said. I know she's right. I know I should have listened to Stephanie about Ellie and to Aja's last therapist and to the school counselor all along. I know that I've failed at one more thing as a father. But what I also know, more than any of these things, is this one fact: I won't lose Aja, too.

TWELVE

JUBILEE

I've never worn a man's clothes before. It feels oddly intimate — all the more so because Eric's sweatshirt doesn't smell like a freshly laundered shirt. It smells kind of woodsy — sweet and piney at the same time. Like him, I guess.

I panicked when Dr. Houschka said he wouldn't let me go unless I had someone to care for me. If I had to stay in that hospital, in that strange room with those strangers coming in and out, a second more, I felt sure I would die. And that serious man from the library — Eric Keegan — was standing there and it just came out of my mouth.

I'm actually surprised he went along with it. Everything about him seems so uptight — not just the way he stands, his spine rigid, his shoulders tense and square, but the intensity in his eyes, the way his lips

204

remain straight and parallel, like an equals sign.

But then they turned up, just a little, when he offered to give me a ride home, and he surprised me again.

Now, sitting beside Eric in the passenger seat of his car, all traces of any joviality are gone and he's gripping the wheel, still and stony as a statue — Atlas holding the weight of the world on his shoulders.

Granted, his son did almost die. But he didn't. And even though I told Eric it was nothing, I would think he'd be just a little bit more warm, more grateful to me, instead of acting so indifferent.

Maybe he is kind of an asshole, like Louise suggested.

But then, he's also kind of polite.

Like how he didn't pepper me with any questions about why I was in the hospital or what was wrong with my face after Dr. Houschka left my room.

And how he brought me the extra clothes he had in his car — his Wharton sweatshirt and a pair of gym pants — since my clothes were so wet and muddy from the day before they had to be thrown out.

And how he wouldn't hear of it when I offered to sit in the back so his son, whom he introduced as Aja, could have the front seat.

Whatever. Doesn't really matter to me who this guy is, except that he's the way I'm finally getting home. After the unexpected events of the past twenty-four hours — and lying wide awake in a hospital room for the entire night — all I can think about is getting inside the front door of my house. Being alone. Safe.

On the way there, I break the overwhelming silence a few times with one-word or two-word directions: "Right, here." "Left." And when Eric pulls into my driveway, it takes everything in me not to jump out of the car before it comes to a complete stop and race inside, throwing the dead bolt behind me with a satisfying *click*.

But I know that would be rude.

"Thank you for the ride," I say as I open the car door, each word still an effort to expel from my sore throat.

He pulls up the parking brake between us and turns the key, cutting the engine. "I'll get your bike," he says, opening his door, too.

I open my mouth to protest, but when I stand up, I'm so overcome with exhaustion, lifting the bike myself seems an impossible task. Plus, the sweatpants I'm wearing are threatening to fall to my ankles at any second, even though I pulled the string as tightly as I could and knotted it. I sling my bag over my shoulder and grab a fistful of the pants' elastic band to be safe.

"Where do you want it?" Eric says from behind the open trunk.

"Just inside the gate is fine," I say, gesturing to the end of the driveway beside the house with my free hand.

Instead of wheeling it like I would, he hefts it up by the frame with one fist and does as directed, while I make my way to the porch. When I get to the front door, I turn to give a quick wave, but am startled when I see that he's right behind me at the foot of the steps. He shoves a hand in his pocket and scratches the back of his head, his stance as awkward as I feel. I stare at him, my hand on the knob, my body itching to get inside.

He nods as if to seal our agreement. "Well, um . . . are you going to be all right?" he asks, glancing back at Aja once more. "Maybe we should stick around . . . you know, the doctor said . . ."

"I'm fine," I say, panic rising at the thought of him — of anyone — coming inside my house. "I'll be fine. Thank you, though. Thank you for, um . . . everything."

207

"No, god," he says. "Thank *you.*" He fishes in his back pocket with his right hand and produces a wallet. My eyes widen in alarm. Is he going to give me money? Like a reward for saving his kid? Or — and this is more likely, remembering my reflection in the hospital mirror — maybe I just look that destitute.

He unfolds the leather flap and pulls something out of it, then pushes it toward me. My shoulders relax when I see it's just a business card. "Take my number," he says. "Please. Just in case."

I take my hand off the doorknob and grab the edge of the card, taking care not to touch his fingertips with mine. My gloves, still damp from the ordeal, are sitting in the bottom of my bag.

"K," I say, dropping the card in my bag and clumsily fishing my keys out of it with one hand — the other is still holding up my pants. "Well, um . . . bye." I lift my hand with the keys in a little wave and turn to go in the house without waiting for a response.

"Hey, wait," he says. I stop, fighting the urge to scream in frustration or desperation — I'm not sure which — and turn my head back in his direction.

"Yeah?"

"This is completely random, I know. But

didn't you say *The Virgin Suicides* was your favorite book?"

I pause. "One of them," I say.

"Why?" he asks. "I mean, what's so great about it?"

I narrow my eyes at him, this out-of-the-blue question reminding me of his bizarre book choices at the library.

"I don't know," I say, not wanting to prolong the conversation. But I do know. I remember exactly how I felt when I entered the lives of the Lisbon sisters. Like somebody understood.

"But you do know. You must," he says. "If it's a favorite."

I stare at him, willing him to read my body language, which is screaming, *Let me go inside!* But he just stares back at me, waiting. I take a deep breath and use the momentary pause to examine his face. *Good-looking.* That's the other thing Louise called him — and he is, in that his face is striking. It entreats exploration. *Good bone structure.* That's what Mom would have said. I always thought that was funny, because if you've ever seen a human skull, the bone placement is pretty universal. What I'm drawn to, what I can't seem to stop staring at, is his eyes. They're green, like two olives dropped into the center of his face, polished to a glossy shine. And they're intense, yes, but there's also a kindness about them. They're a contradiction, similar to Eric himself. And I find it difficult to look away.

I realize he's still waiting for me to answer. That he's not going to leave until I respond. I clear my throat. "It's just so real," I say. "I read it as a teenager — and it captured . . . I don't know, everything. The loneliness. The way we idolize other people's lives. The desire to be accepted. To be noticed."

He stares at me, his mouth slightly ajar, and I start to feel exposed, like he can see through me, somehow. I break his gaze and pretend to study the rocks at his feet. "Um . . . for me, anyway. That's what I liked."

He still doesn't respond and I feel the heat rise in my cheeks again. "Well, I really better get inside," I say, and shuffle back toward the door.

"OK," he says from behind me. And then: "Bye, Jubilee." It's the first time he's said my name and I fumble the keys in my hand, dropping them on the porch. I quickly bend down to pick them up, taking care not to let go of the sweatpants' waistband, conscious of how ridiculous I must look.

I straighten up, fit the key in the lock, and turn it, twisting the handle with relief. I scoot in and close the door behind me, turning the lock with a swift flick of my wrist. I lean back against the door, dropping my bag onto the ground at my feet next to the pile of mail that's landed there in my absence and sigh, looking around. My house.

I'm in my house. Lying in the hospital bed, I fantasized about all the things I wished I were doing at home — lying in my own bed, for starters, reading a book in my comfy corner chair, making eggs and toast, mopping the floors, watching the next lecture in my Harvard series.

So it surprises even me that the first thing I do isn't to go upstairs and change. I walk over to the window and gently push the curtain to one side and watch as Eric slides into the front seat of his car. I stare at his face as he turns to say something to Aja, who's still in the backseat, and watch as he slowly eases the car in reverse out of the driveway. I picture myself in the passenger seat beside him. What I must have looked like there — what *we* looked like to people driving beside us.

That night, I can't sleep. Dr. Houschka's words keep replaying in my mind: *Maybe you could get this thing under control.* It's the reason Mom moved us from the only home I've ever known in Tennessee to New Jersey in high school, so we could be closer to Dr. Zhang and get this *thing* under control. (Although to be honest, I also think she'd run out of men to date in our small town of Fountain City.)

But after the first appointment, I refused to go back. It was clear there wasn't going to be some magic cure, and besides, I didn't like the way Dr. Zhang was looking at me, that glint in her eye. She wanted to *study* me, like I was some kind of alien species. I wasn't interested in being her guinea pig. Mom encouraged me to give her another chance, but she didn't — couldn't — force me to go.

I'm still not interested in being a lab rat, but I know Houschka's right about one thing — I don't want to end up in the hospital again any more than he wants to see me there. And I can't exactly stay holed up in my house. I have a job now. A job that I need. And what if he's right about the rest of it? What if they do know a lot more about allergies now? Whoever *they* are. What if there is something that can be done?

I get out of bed and creep downstairs, not wanting to interrupt the silence with the creaking of the hardwoods. In the study, I

212

slide into the desk chair and shake the mouse of the computer. The screen glows to life and nearly blinds me. When my eyes adjust, I type "Dr. Mei Zhang" into Google. Her picture immediately pops up under the heading *George Watkins University Allergy & Immunology.* I shudder, remembering the way I felt underneath her gaze. As if I were a frog in science class and she was gleefully holding a scalpel. But maybe that was just an irrational childhood fear, like imagining monsters under the bed. I click the link, grab a pen and piece of scrap paper from where they lie on the desk, and jot down the phone number and email correlated with Zhang's name. I stare at it, by the glow of my monitor, and a feeling washes over me. An emotion so foreign, I can't immediately identify it.

Possibility.

It feels so naive, the hope I used to carry around like Linus's blanket, imagining a new life — a life without this debilitating allergy — was waiting just ahead. But there it is, blossoming in my belly, and I can't dampen it. Not immediately. I mean, I don't plan on running around giving CPR to strangers all the time, but what if I could work at the library without my gloves, or shake hands with people — or I don't know, take a business card from someone and let my fingers graze his, like a normal person? Or maybe that isn't normal — to think about touching a near stranger's fingers with your own.

In the dark, I peer down at the Wharton sweatshirt I'm still wearing — that I just didn't really want to take off — and wonder if maybe that's not normal either.

Anyway, I remind myself, Dr. Houschka said "under control"; he didn't say "cured." That's because there is no cure. *There is no cure.* I say it aloud so that it sinks in. I will always wear gloves. There is no new life waiting just around the corner.

I stare at the phone number on the piece of paper one last time, before I crumple it up, drop it in the wastebasket beside the desk, and go back upstairs to bed.

In the morning, I wake with a start, my hair sticking to my face, my pillow damp with sweat. I was having a nightmare. About Eric's hands. His fingers were swollen, cartoonishly large, and they were touching mine — engulfing them, really — the pads of his bulging thumbs rubbing my knuckles. I was trying to tell him to stop, that I can't be touched, but I felt as though I were underwater, that my mouth wouldn't obey my brain, that my words were being stolen right out of the air, unable to fulfill their duty of being heard. The harder it was to move my mouth, the harder I tried, until I was paralyzed in fear and panic consumed every nerve in my body.

I sit up, trying to slow my galloping heart. But as I take deep breaths, replaying the scene in my mind, I can almost feel the rough warmth of his fingers on my skin. Or what I imagine it would feel like — I haven't been touched in so long. Not since right before Dr. Benefield put me in that plastic isolation room when I was six. Right before he diagnosed me and my entire world shifted. For months and years afterward, I tried so hard to remember that last interaction with my mother. The last time she touched me. Did she clasp my face? Kiss the top of my head? Wrap her arms around my tiny frame and squeeze me tight? I'm sure she said something soothing like, "It's only a week. I'll be right out here, baby." But the words don't matter. If only I had known it was the last time I would be touched, the last time that I would feel the palm of her hand on my arm, her breath on my face, I would have held on a little longer. Imprinted the feeling of her fingertips on my skin. I would have made sure to remember.

But I didn't. And now, sitting in my bed, trying to recall the touch of Eric in my dream — to really feel it on my skin — it's the same fruitless effort I expended for years trying to recall my mother's last touch. And then, as my heartbeat slows, I begin to wonder if it really was a nightmare. I wonder if my heart's racing because I was terrified — or because it was so wonderful.

"Did you have a good weekend, dear?" Louise asks when I walk behind the circulation desk Monday morning. She turns to look at me and gasps.

"Oh, *dear*," she says, covering her mouth with her hand. The rash around my mouth had lessened when I looked in the mirror this morning, but some red splotches were lingering and my lips were still a bit bruised and swollen. I found a tube of lipstick in my mom's dresser, but it only accentuated the problem, so I wiped it off.

"What *happened*?" Louise asks.

My shoulders tense and I silently chastise myself for not preparing a response. I was hoping no one would notice. "Allergic reaction," I say. When that doesn't seem to satisfy her, I add: "New lipstick," because

216

it's the first thing that pops in my mind.

"What brand? Remind me never to get *that* one."

"I don't remember," I say feebly as Roger approaches the circulation desk, holding a coffee mug.

"Morning, ladi— Whoa," he says, staring at me.

"It's just an allergic reaction," Louise says, waving him off. "And it's no wonder, really. You know what they put in lipstick? Crushed-up bugs. Bugs! And lead, I think, if I'm remembering right. Read some article about it a few weeks ago."

I eye a pile of returns on the desk and start scanning them back in, as Louise and Roger's conversation is devolving into a discussion of weird things in food, like yoga mat particles in sandwich bread. I tune them out, so I'm not sure if I've heard correctly when about five minutes later, Louise says: "It doesn't matter, we're all going to be fired anyway."

My head snaps toward her. "What?"

She looks at me. "Oh, you didn't hear? Maryann's in another big fight with the city, trying to keep them from cutting our funding *again*. We used to have four circulation assistants — can you believe it? But that idiot Frank Stafford, city council's finance chair, keeps funneling money to the rec center, because his son plays peewee football and he's convinced he's going to be the next Ted Brady — that's a quarterback, right?"

"I think it's Tom," Roger says.

"Ted, Tom," she says, waving her hand. "Anyway, she's been trying to prove how needed we are in the community, but the circ numbers are down and the few programs we do have are so poorly attended —"

"Could we really be fired?" I cut her off.

"Oh dear," she says, and reaches out to pat my gloved hand. I move it away from her. "I didn't mean to alarm you." She sighs. "But I don't really know how we'll even keep the doors open and lights on if they cut the budget any more. It's bare-bones as it is."

I stare at her, my mind reeling. This job essentially fell into my lap and I can't lose it. I need the money. And against all odds, I'm mostly comfortable here. I can't imagine looking for something else, going into all those strange buildings, talking to new people. At just the thought of it, a vise threatens to clamp down on my heart and stop it once and for all.

When I come out of the break room at four,

I'm surprised to see Madison H. standing there, baby on her hip. I wonder why she's at the library so often when she never seems to check out any books. Maybe it has something to do with being on the board.

"Jubilee!" she says when she sees me, her eyes betraying her horror. I lift my gloved hand to my mouth, willing the redness to just disappear already. "What happened?"

"Long story," I say, sliding into my chair.

She shifts the baby to her other hip and looks at me pointedly. I sigh and glance behind me, making sure Maryann and Louise are still in the back room. Then I give her the abridged version of the weekend, ending with Dr. Houschka's visit.

She stares at me openmouthed. "Jesus, I leave you alone for two days and you go and almost kill yourself."

"That's dramatic," I say.

"Well have you made an appointment?"

"With who?"

"An allergist. To get that bracelet thing. And EpiPens. You should be carrying EpiPens! My nephew has a peanut butter allergy and doesn't leave the house without one."

"I don't need an EpiPen. Or a bracelet. It's not like I'm going around giving people CPR left and right," I say, reiterating my in-ner thoughts from last night.

"Well what if there was another kind of emergency?"

"Like what?"

She thinks for a minute and glances down at her baby. "What if a kid drooled on you?"

"I'd get a rash," I say, trying to make it sound like no big deal. But I shudder at the possibility, thinking of the girl who almost died from a drop of milk on her skin. And then my stomach starts to tingle and itch right near my belly button as if I've conjured a rash just by saying the word aloud. The mind is a funny and powerful thing. I start to scratch it through the material of my shirt. "And then I'd stay away from that kid."

"What if he bit you?"

My eyes grow wide. "Why would a kid bite me?"

She shrugs. "Why do kids do anything? Hannah found a jar of honey and smeared it all over Molly's face and hair last week when I was in the bathroom. Looked like she had a spa mask on. Do you know how hard that was to clean up?"

I stare at her, trying to decide if I should continue her little game. "I don't think a kid is going to bite me."

She sighs. "Look, I'm not taking you out

until you get an EpiPen, OK?"

I look up at her, confused. "Take me out *where*?"

"On an adventure," she says, a self-assured smile on her face. Although, I'm not sure that she has any other kind of smile. I think Madison H. came crawling out of her mother's womb annoyingly confident. "That's what I came to tell you. I'm going to be your official guide to all of the things you've missed the past nine years."

I stare at her openly now, my mouth an oval of disbelief. "You've got to be kidding me."

"Nope."

"That's ridiculous."

"No, it's not," she says, shifting the baby again to her other hip. "It'll be fun."

"What if I don't want to?"

"Oh, c'mon," she says, pushing out her bottom lip in a pretend pout. "You do. You want to. At least give me one night. If you have a terrible time, we'll never do it again. Scout's honor."

"You were a Girl Scout?" I ask, itching my stomach again. I must have gotten a bug bite or something.

"No," she says. "Is that what that means?"

I snort and shake my head. Then I change the subject. "Hey, has the library board met this month?"

She squawks: "Ha!" The baby jumps in her arms, startled. "No," she says, calmer. "We meet like once a year. Why?"

"There's a problem with funding. The city wants to cut it."

"What else is new?"

"Oh. Well is there something that you guys can do about it?"

"Not really," she says. "The board's kind of a joke. We mostly get together to gossip and eat Enid's rum cake. We don't really have any power. Not like the city council."

"Huh," I say, while my heart revs underneath my blouse. Somebody must be able to do *something.* I can't lose this job. I won't. I need the money.

She jostles the baby back to the original hip. "So you'll go?"

I give her one last hard stare and then throw my hands up in a gesture of defeat. "Why not?" I say, pushing down the real question burning deep inside my gut: *why?* Why does Madison H., the most popular girl from school, suddenly want to be my friend? Doesn't she have better things to do with her time? Why does she care so much?

But later, as I'm arranging a display on books about Native Americans to correlate with Thanksgiving, I chide myself for such childish thoughts. I'm not in high school anymore. We're adults. She's being kind. I should stop questioning her so much and just accept it for what it is. Besides, I have to admit, it's kind of nice to have a friend.

I stand up the final book, *Black Elk Speaks,* on the end of the row, and absentmindedly scratch my belly again. It's burning a little now, and I wonder if all my scratching over my phantom rash has somehow irritated the skin. I yank up my blouse to examine it, an audible gasp escaping my lips when I see my bare skin — angry boils and red bumps are burning a path from my belly button down toward my hip. But I don't understand — why would a rash spring up on my stomach? No one has touched me there. I take a deep breath. It's probably just a . . . just a . . . rash. From something else. Laundry detergent — isn't that what people always say? But I haven't changed my laundry detergent. And I've seen this reaction enough in my life to know exactly what it is.

What terrifies me is I have no idea how it got there.

THIRTEEN

ERIC

Seven voice mails. One hundred forty-two emails. Twenty-three text messages. (None from Ellie.) This is the shitstorm I'm trying to weed through as I sit at my kitchen table at 5:30 Wednesday evening, while a boxful of spiral pasta boils on the stove.

Little-known fact — if your child is thought to have possibly attempted suicide, they won't let him return to school until he's been deemed by a professional to no longer be a risk to himself or others. And that professional may not have an opening until Thursday. And since he must be supervised at all times, and I had no way of finding a babysitter on such short notice, here we are.

But it's not Aja's fault I have so much to catch up on. Instead of working from home all week, as I told my boss I would do, I've spent all three days with my nose stuck in a book. All of Monday morning and most of the afternoon was dedicated to rereading *The Virgin Suicides*. It was like some light had clicked on, and I know it was Jubilee that threw the switch. Sentences started to jump out at me, as if they were written just for me.

Like: *At that moment Mr. Lisbon had the feeling that he didn't know who she was, that children were only strangers you agreed to live with.*

And I wondered if this Jeffrey Eugenides really *is* a genius. Or maybe just a dad. After Stephanie's news, I tried to call Ellie a few times to talk about her suspension, but she never picked up. I contemplated sending her a text about it but was afraid I would push her further away. Instead, I texted her another one of my favorite lines from the book. The response of Cecilia, who, when asked by her doctor why she attempted suicide when she's too young to know how bad life gets, said: *"Obviously, Doctor, you've never been a thirteen-year-old girl."*

Ha! I wrote after the quote. *Zinger! Love, Dad.*

Now I'm in the middle of *The Bell Jar*. Ellie wrote in her journal that she wanted to be a magazine editor in New York, which surprised me. I didn't even know she liked to write. Or read magazines. But the thing that's concerned me the most is how she said she "totally relates" to Esther, the main character, who's clearly going through some kind of manic depression.

I click off my email and find myself thinking about Jubilee. What she would say about the book. About Esther. About Ellie.

"Pot's boiling over." I look up and see Aja standing at the door. Then I glance back at the stove.

"Damn it!" I jump up and grab the pot handle to move it off the burner without thinking. The shock of the heat in my palm mixed with my dumb clumsiness somehow ends up with the entire pot crashing to the floor, a cascade of boiling water and pasta dispersing all over the linoleum. Miraculously, I've stayed out of the spray, but my shoes are already soaking up the hot starchy liquid and my feet start burning.

"You all right?" I ask over my shoulder.

Aja just stands there, arms crossed. "Pasta's ruined."

I sigh. "Yep." I slosh toward where he stands so I can get out of my waterlogged socks and shoes. "Want pizza?"

"Chili dogs." No one delivers chili dogs and I open my mouth to say this, but we've been shut in this house all day, and I think it might be nice to get out for a little bit.

"Great," I say. "Let me get this mess cleaned up and we'll go."

As we're pulling out of the drive-through twenty minutes later, I should turn left to go home, but I turn right instead.

I want to see her. Jubilee.

It's the courteous thing to do. Check in on her. Make sure she's doing OK.

I wolf down a hot dog on the way and when we pull into the parking lot, I glance in the rearview mirror to see if I have any lingering bread stuck in my teeth.

"What are we doing here?" Aja asks between bites.

I look over at him. "I've got to renew my books."

"You don't have any books."

Shit. He's right. "I think they can just do it on the computers."

He pulls a crinkle fry from the bag on his lap. "Can I stay in the car?"

I hesitate. I don't really want to leave him alone, after everything that's happened, but it's a library parking lot, I reason, and I'll be able to see him through the window. "I guess," I say, and then: "But just eat. No telekinetic stuff or destruction or anything, got it?"

227

He nods, and I wonder how many other people need to give that directive to their children before leaving them alone for five minutes.

I avert my gaze from Aja and direct it through the front windshield of the car. From my vantage point in the parking lot, I have a direct line of sight to the brightly lit innards of the library. And Jubilee. She's standing at the checkout counter, her face partially obscured by the wild vines of her hair. I don't know why I'm so drawn to her. She's beautiful, yes, but it's more than that. There's something different about her — how she's guarded yet completely vulnerable at the same time. She's like a Rubik's Cube that I find myself eager to sort into a pattern that makes sense. Or maybe I'm eager to sort out why I keep thinking of her. I don't know. I've never met anyone quite like her. And I was never good at Rubik's Cubes.

My stomach gurgles. I take a swig of the water that came with my meal to try to settle it. I shouldn't have eaten so fast.

Walking in, I notice that the library is mostly empty, save for a man at a computer carrel sitting on a pillow playing what looks like a golf video game on the screen. I wonder if he just had surgery or something.

"Slow night," I say when I get within a few yards of the circulation desk and Jubilee.

She starts and looks up at me, her eyes wide. I never really noticed them before, beyond the fact that they're brown. But under the fluorescent light of the library they look like chocolate that's been flecked with caramel.

"I'm sorry. I didn't mean to scare you."

She relaxes her expression. "It's OK," she says. "It was just so quiet in here. I didn't hear you come in."

We stare at each other for a few beats and I study her face up close. Her lips and cheek look a little better, not as red or swollen. I tear my gaze away from her mouth and run it down her neck, over her ill-fitting suit jacket, to her hands, which are cased in leather gloves. The same gloves she had on for Halloween. I eye them for a beat.

"Um . . . can I help you?" She glances up at the wall beside us and I follow her gaze. A clock. Its hands point to 6:55.

"Yes, I'm sorry." I draw my eyes back to her face. "I, um, need to renew my books."

She glances at my empty hands and then narrows her eyes. "Didn't you just check them out? On Halloween?"

"I did," I say.

"You get three weeks. It's only been" — she calculates the numbers in her head — "eleven days."

"Oh." I rap my knuckles lightly on the counter. "Right. Good, good. Then they're not late."

I came with the intention of asking her about *The Bell Jar* but now find that I'm not sure how to say it. Or maybe that I don't want the conversation to be over so quickly. "How are you feeling?" I ask, at the exact same time she says: "Are you taking a class or something?"

We both laugh.

"You first," I say.

She repeats her question.

I tilt my head. "What do you mean?"

"I don't know — are you taking a class in modern literature? I've just been trying to figure out why you're so interested in *The Virgin Suicides.* You're not exactly the demographic."

"No? You mean, you don't have middle-aged men checking out young adult books all the time?"

"You're hardly middle-aged," she says, then looks down. She's doing that thing again, where she's bold and forward and then suddenly timid, self-conscious. It's like a dance and I don't know the steps.

"It's for my daughter," I say.

She crinkles her brow. "Daughter?"

"Yeah. Ellie. She's fourteen. Lives in New Hampshire with her mother." And then I add: "My ex."

She crinkles her brow. "So . . . are you guys in a father-daughter book club or something?"

I offer a grin, but I know it's a sad imposter. How do I explain what I'm doing? What *am* I doing? "Something like that," I say. "I'm just, I don't know, reading some of the books she's read, trying to relate to her, I guess. Trying to understand her better."

She glances up at the clock again.

"Sorry, is it — What time does the library close?"

"Seven," she says. "But it's OK. Michael's still here."

She nods toward the man with the pillow. I glance over at him and then back at her and decide I should get to the point. "So, you've read *The Bell Jar,* right?"

"Of course," she says, as if everyone on earth has read it, when I only just heard of it from Ellie's notebook.

"If someone really identifies with Esther — do you think that's concerning? Like, maybe they're — I don't know — suicidal or something?"

231

"Are we talking about your daughter?"

"Yeah."

She purses her mouth as if really thinking it over, or maybe she's just trying to remember details of the book, and I notice she has a slight underbite, forcing her top lip to protrude like the brim of a tiny hat. I stare at it, unable to look away. Finally, she says: "I think it's more concerning if a teenage girl doesn't relate to Esther."

"Really?" I say, dragging my eyes up to meet hers. "Why?"

"Well, she's flailing, right? She feels trapped, insecure, unsure of herself and her place in the world. Even when she has this glamorous internship that other girls would kill for, she feels like an imposter."

"And that's a good thing? Low self-esteem?"

She tucks her tiny bottom lip under her teeth. "Better than the alternative."

"What's that?"

"You were in high school once — is there anything worse than an arrogant teenager?"

I laugh, and then get a little pang thinking of Ellie struggling with these big life issues, wondering where she fits in.

"But then again," says Jubilee, "that book is partly autobiographical and Sylvia Plath did kill herself a month after it came out.

So, what do I know?"

I stare at her deadpan face, until she cracks a small grin. "Thanks," I say with a soft chuckle, trying to conceal my surprise at her wit. "Very helpful."

She glances over at the computer carrels. I follow her gaze and see that Michael has just turned off the computer screen and is now on his feet, stretching. I watch as he picks up his pillow and slowly makes his way to the door.

"What do you have to do to close up?" I ask.

"Not much," she says. "Just turn off the lights. Lock up."

"Can I walk you out?" It just falls out of my mouth, but then, when her eyes drop to the desk, I worry that it's too forward.

"Um . . ."

"Sorry, it's my grandmother."

"What?" she asks, looking at me in confusion.

"I know it's the modern era," I explain, rubbing my jaw, "but I'm pretty sure she would rise up from her grave and kill me if I didn't at least offer."

"Um . . . OK," she says, the right side of her mouth turning up. "Let me just get my coat."

Outside, I glance at the front seat of the

car, where Aja is sucking soda from his straw. The night air has ushered in even colder temps, and I hope he's not too chilly sitting there. Sticking my hands in my coat pockets to try to keep them warm, I turn back to where Jubilee is fumbling with the keys and lock. When she's done, I clear my throat. I glance out into the parking lot, lit by the street lamp overhead, and that's when I realize my car is the only one there. "Where *is* your car?"

"Oh, um. I ride my bike to work."

I know she was on her bike when she saved Aja, and it was cold that day, but not *this* cold. "You a hard-core environmentalist or something?"

"No," she says, and then pauses, considering. "I mean, I do turn off the water when I brush my teeth."

My lips spread into a smile. "So, why do you ride your bike to work in this weather? Didn't I see a car in your driveway yesterday?"

She nods. "It won't start. I hoped maybe it was just out of gas, but that's not it."

"Can I help you with it?" It's out of my mouth before I can think. But she saved Aja's life and it's the least I can offer her.

"You want to buy me a new car?"

A loud clap of laughter bursts from my

mouth, like a cannon shot from its barrel. The sound slices through the air. She grins at me, and it feels like something has been broken between us. The weird awkwardness that seemed to hang between us like a fog — in the hospital, standing in front of her house, just now in the library — it's gone. My hands don't feel cold anymore.

"Ah, no," I say. "Not exactly. But I could take a look at it for you. See what the trouble is."

"You know about fixing cars?"

I shrug. "A little."

She chews her lip as she considers this and I try not to stare. I fail.

After what feels like two full minutes of silence, her eyes meet mine again. "OK," she says.

"OK," I say. "Saturday?"

"OK," she repeats.

I glance over at Aja and he's just staring through the windshield now, his dinner long eaten. I know I need to go, to get him home, but strangely I find myself not wanting to leave Jubilee's side.

I turn back to her. "Well, can I give you a ride? It really is freezing tonight. Literally. The clock on the bank said thirty-one degrees."

"No, I'm fine," she says. "I'm used to it."

I push one more time. "Are you sure?"

"Really. It's not necessary," she says. "But thank you."

"OK," I say, accepting defeat. "Well, good night, Jubilee."

"Night," she says.

I slide into the front seat and watch as Jubilee swings a leg over her bike and navigates it out of the parking lot and down the silent street, a tiny dark mass under the light of the lampposts. I notice she doesn't have any reflectors on the bike, and I have the sudden urge to follow her. To keep her safe. I watch until she's pedaled out of sight, and then I lean back against the headrest and exhale.

I lied. I don't know anything about fixing cars.

My dad was a real do-it-yourselfer. He always had some kind of dirt and grime under his fingernails and spent full weekend days in the garage doing god only knows what. Connie joined him when she was old enough and they'd dissect car issues over dinner like they were discussing life-and-death medical procedures. He tried to teach me how to change the oil once, but I just couldn't understand the point when there was a Jiffy Lube not even two miles from our house.

I don't know why I offered to look at it, except I had this overwhelming desire to *do* something for Jubilee. For this woman who, in such a short time, has done so much for me. Like jump into cold, rushing water and pull my son to safety. The least I could do is try to fix her car. That's what I've been telling myself, anyway.

Sitting in the therapist's waiting room while Aja finishes with his appointment on Thursday afternoon, I punch out a text to Ellie:

I didn't know you wanted to work in magazines. Dad.

Then I Google: *Car won't start.* The first entry that pops up is car troubleshooting for dummies. Instead of being offended, I'm grateful. Maybe I'll actually understand some of the terminology. But after scanning the first few paragraphs, I realize it's hopeless and click off my phone. I stand up to help myself to a Styrofoam cupful of what I'm sure is cold coffee sitting in the glass pot of a brewing machine on a table cluttered with magazines. As I take a swig of the tepid sludge, the thick wooden door in front of me swings open and Aja emerges. I arrange my face into a welcoming smile. "How'd it go, bud?" My voice is laden with forced cheer, as if he's just played a basketball game instead of spending an hour in therapy.

He shrugs without glancing my way and reaches for the iPad he left on the chair beside me. He sits down and slips the earbuds in as the therapist, who introduced herself as Janet when we arrived, appears in the doorway Aja just came out of. "Mr. Keegan? Want to come in for a chat?"

"I'll be right back," I say to Aja, who's already absorbed in the world on his screen. He doesn't acknowledge me. Embarrassed, I glance up at Janet, who offers me a consolatory smile.

In her office, I sit down in the chair across from her desk. A picture of three towheaded children, all straight-teeth smiles and matching white and khaki outfits on a sandy beach, stares back at me. "Yours?" I ask.

She nods, and I have to keep myself from rolling my eyes. I wonder if it ever occurred to her how obnoxious it is to view her perfect family on display while you're there to discuss your family's imperfections. Maybe it's her form of credentials. *Look, my children can stand in a row and smile at the same time in unwrinkled, coordinating outfits!*

238

Your family can be as well-adjusted as mine, once we figure out this suicidal/ delusional-thinking stuff!

"They're all grown up now," she says. "Hard to believe."

"Mmm." I peer at her more closely. On first glance I thought she was late thirties tops, but now I can see a thin line of gray peeking out at the root of her blond locks, pulled tightly back in a bun. And her face is a little too taut. On closer inspection, she just looks well preserved.

"Well, you've obviously got a very intelligent child there," she says, sliding into her large leather chair.

I would normally say thank you, but I'm too stressed — about work, about Aja, about life — to deal in niceties. I cut to the chase. "Do you think he's suicidal?"

Her eyes widen for a moment and then she gives a quick shake of her head, as if she understands that I just want to get on with it. "No," she says. "I don't."

"Great." I clasp my hands together in front of me. "Did you sign the required paperwork? I need it for his school."

She picks out a piece of paper from the stack in front of her and slides it across the desk toward me.

"I'd like to see Aja once a week."

"For this delusion stuff?" I say. "That's fine. I'll figure it out with work." I pick up my phone and the paper she gave me off the desk and start to stand.

"No," she says.

I freeze, my body not yet completely unfolded, and look at her. "No? No, what?"

"I don't want to see him for the delusions — although his acting on them is concerning. And I disagree with his previous counselor's assessment. I think he may be on the spectrum," she says. "But right now, what I'd like to see him for is his grief."

Gravity pulls me back down into the chair and my eyebrows follow suit. "His grief?" I try to recall Aja crying or behaving sadly. I can't. I don't even think he cried at the funeral, although my memory of that time is spotty at best, considering I was in the middle of a huge audit, working sixteen-hour days, my best friend had died, and I'd learned I was going to be doubling the number of children I had overnight. "I don't . . . I'm not sure . . . His parents died more than two years ago. Did he tell you that?"

"No — he didn't actually say much at all. I read it in his file," she says. "But I just get this sense from the few things he did say that he's never grieved them. I don't think

240

he knows how."

I take this in. Is there a proper way to grieve? Step-by-step instructions? I thought you just cried a bit and got on with it. My mind flashes to the day I came home from school as a kid and my gerbil, Alvin, was lying in his cage, unmoving. "Chin up," my mom said. "Life goes on." I just remember thinking: *Not for Alvin.*

"Do you talk about his parents?" she asks, breaking my reverie. "Reminisce with him? Tell him stories?"

I mull this over. Surely I do. I think about Dinesh so often. What he would do in my shoes. How he was a far superior dad, husband, *everything* than I ever was. How he wouldn't bungle things the way I often do. But do I talk about him? With Aja?

"I'm not sure," I say.

"Hmm," she says, but that one short syllable carries a world of judgment.

"What's that mean?"

"Nothing," she says. "I'd just like you to try it this week. Tell him something about his father — what was his name?"

"Dinesh," I say. My voice cracks on the "nesh" and it surprises me. I clear my throat.

"Or his mother."

"Kate." Her image flashes before me. The

241

dark, elfish locks framing plump cheeks and a smile too large for her face. I can almost hear her pinging laugh in response to Dinesh's antics. It sounded like wind chimes on a blustery day. Or maybe that's just my memory of it.

I swallow.

"Can you do that?"

"Yeah," I say. "I can do that." I gather my things and stand up for the final time. "Thank you, Dr. . . ." I look around for a nameplate, having already forgotten her last name.

"Oh, please. It's Janet."

On the way home, Aja is still entrenched in his game. I tap him on the shoulder. "Can you please take those out?"

"Huh?"

"Your earbuds. Take them out," I say, louder.

He hooks a finger around each wire and tugs.

"We need to talk," I say.

He stares at the dashboard.

"I'm going back to work tomorrow," I say. "And you are going back to school."

Silence.

"But the social worker at the hospital says I can't leave you alone in the afternoon

242

anymore, so that nice woman that came over on Tuesday, Mrs. Holgerson, will be there when you get off the bus. She'll stay and pick up the apartment some and make dinner for us. Apparently she's very good at Swedish food."

When I realized I needed after-school care for Aja, Connie asked around her office and a paralegal knew of a retired nanny who was looking for something part-time. Glenda Holgerson smelled a little like cooked onions, but she had an impressive résumé and a firm but kind demeanor, and didn't flinch when I told her about Aja's recent troubles. I hired her on the spot and added it to the very long list of things I owe my sister for.

"Aja," I say.

He doesn't respond, so I keep talking. "Remember those meatballs you had at IKEA? I think she can make those. She mentioned some kind of dessert, too. Fila? Fika? Something like that. Anyway, it'll be good for us to try some new things."

Aja mumbles something.

"What?"

"I said, I don't need a babysitter."

"I know. She's not really a babysitter. Just someone who will be there in case you need something."

"She's a stranger," he says. "I don't like strangers."

"She's not really a stranger. I mean, you met her on Tuesday."

"Why can't it just be like it was?"

"Because it can't, OK?" I say, my voice louder than I intend.

At that, Aja picks up the earbuds and replaces them in his ears.

I sigh and flick the turn signal as I drive into the apartment complex parking lot. My phone buzzes in my pocket for the third time since we've gotten in the car, and when I park, I pull it out to scroll through the work calls and texts I know I've missed.

Five are from my boss, as I suspected.

But the sixth? Oh, the sweet sixth. It's from Ellie.

Fourteen

JUBILEE

Sitting at the desk in my study Friday night, I clutch the crumpled piece of paper in my fist and stare at my handwriting. Madison called twice this week to remind me we couldn't go on our first "adventure" (her word, not mine) until I got an EpiPen. *I'm not going to be responsible for your untimely death,* she said in what I now recognize as her very Madison H. dramatic fashion.

But that's not what's compelling me to contact Dr. Zhang. Not the only thing, anyway.

The rash — the one on my stomach — has crawled up from my belly button and spread like kudzu all over my chest, my shoulders, my back. I've tried all the home remedies my mother became expert at to help relieve the itching, to help soothe the angry, scaly patches of red — oatmeal baths, teaspoons of Benadryl, antihistamine creams slathered on as thick as frosting on a cupcake. Nothing is working. And I know only Dr. Zhang can help me.

I punch out the email that I've been trying to compose for the better part of the past two days. I have to email her directly because when I called on Friday to make an appointment, the chirpy receptionist informed me that Dr. Zhang has a seven-month waiting list for new patients. I tried to explain I wasn't exactly a new patient, but she only chuckled: "You last saw her twelve *years* ago? Uh, you're a new patient, hon."

I read back over what I've written. It sounds plaintive, oversimplistic, and a little desperate, but I *am* desperate and it's the best I can do.

I hit "send."

And then I wait.

Four minutes later, my email pings.

Jubilee! Of course I remember you. Can you be here Tuesday at 10 am?

I pad to the kitchen, my heart beating excessively for the minimal effort, and dial Madison. She doesn't answer, so I leave a message. Then, though it's not even eight o'clock, I go upstairs and get in bed.

Thump. Thump. Thump.

I open my eyes and scan the room, blinking. My pillow is damp where I've apparently been drooling in my sleep. I wipe my chin with the back of my hand. The light filtering in through the windows informs me it's morning, but I have no idea what time it is. Or if that rapping noise was real or just part of some dream.

Thump. Thump. Thump.

Well, that answers one question. I sit up and wonder who it could be. Probably a salesman or a Jehovah's Witness — I've had a few of each knock on the door the past nine years. I'd always wait silently in the kitchen for them to move on.

Now curiosity propels me out of bed and I creep to the window and carefully move the blue curtain panel so I can peer out. I can't see the porch from this angle, but I can see —

Eric's car. In my driveway. I quickly back away from the window, my heart knocking against my chest. I completely forgot he said he was going to come today — but more important, why on *earth* did I agree to it? I don't even care if the Pontiac runs — it's not like I'd drive it, anyway. My bike gets me to and from the library just fine. I was just caught off guard, I think. He was being so . . . so *un*-Eric. More than just routinely polite, he was being kind and warm and even a little bit funny. But now, in the stark light of day, I feel like some pathetic charity case whom he feels some obligation to because I saved his son, and I wish I had just said no.

Thump. Thump. Thump.

I stand stock-still, hoping maybe he'll just leave if I wait long enough.

Thump. Thump. Thump.

I count slowly and right when I reach one hundred and think he might be giving up —

Thump. Thump. Thump.

Guess not. I pull on a pair of worn leggings that I left on my chair. I head downstairs and open the door just as he's raising his fist to knock again. A blast of cold air hits me in the face.

"Sorry, I . . . uh . . . just woke up," I say, looking from Eric to Aja and then back again. Eric's hand is frozen in midair and I wonder why he's not moving. I know my hair is a tangled disaster, but I don't think I look *too* crazy. At least not crazy enough for the wide-eyed stare on Eric's face.

He clears his throat and — finally — slowly lowers his fist. "Good morning, Jubilee." At my name, Aja's eyes pop open, as round as quarters, grabbing my attention. Then I look back at Eric, but he's not looking at me. Not in my eyes anyway. He's looking, I think, directly at my chest. *Not much to look at,* I hear my mom's voice saying in my ear, followed by her smoker's cackle. It was something she said to me often. Mean, yes, but true — I didn't inherit my mom's particular assets — and I can't imagine what's drawn his attention.

Wondering if I'm in some bizarre dream and I'm just going to find myself topless and vulnerable and desperate to wake up, I glance down. What I see is worse. I fight off the wild urge to slam the door shut in his and Aja's faces run back upstairs, and crawl into the bed, never to get out of it again.

I'm wearing his sweatshirt. The Wharton one. The one I've been sleeping in every single night since he brought me home from the hospital. Not because it's *his,* of course, it's just . . . comfortable. And smells good. But all he sees is that I'm wearing it and all I want to do is die a little bit.

Heat creeps up my face, until it is positively on fire. "Well, thank you for coming," I say, trying to keep my voice steady and composed. "The car is . . . well, you know where the car is. Let me know if you need anything."

I go to close the door, but Eric reaches his hand out, stopping it. "Wait." I stare at his fingers splayed against the grain of the wood. I remember the dream, his fingers touching mine, and my breath comes quicker. One of my online Harvard classes was an art intro: How to Draw the Human Form. The professor said hands were the hardest part of the body to draw, not only because of the complexity of their joints and lines and getting the proportions correct, but because hands are equally as expressive as the face in gesture and emotion. I thought that was stupid. Until now. I swallow with difficulty.

"I'm actually waiting for my sister, Connie. She said she'd help with the car. Do you mind if we come in for a minute?"

I take a step back, trying to put distance between myself and Eric's hands, but he takes it as an invitation. Left with no choice, I step back farther. "Sure," I say. "Um . . . come in."

I close the door behind them and then we're standing there, at the base of the stairs, in an awkward silence. I know I should say something, tell them to make themselves at home, or some other genial expression, but I can't stop thinking about the basic fact that there are two additional people standing inside my house. Guests. That I didn't really invite in, but here they are. The sound of Eric's hands rubbing together in an attempt to warm them up brings me back to the moment. I open my mouth to say something — anything to break the silence — but then his hands catch my attention again, this time because I'm wondering why he doesn't have gloves on in this weather — and that's when it hits me. I forgot to put on *my* gloves. I clasp my hands behind me. "Um . . . I'll be right back," I say, finding the bottom stair with my foot. "You can sit down." I nod toward the living room. "I mean, if you want to."

Upstairs, I strip off Eric's sweatshirt and toss it in the laundry bin, the humiliation of being caught in it inflaming my cheeks once more. The air at once feels cool on my bare skin but also causes a prickly sensation that intensifies the itching. I know scratching will cause more pain than relief, so I resist the urge, quickly apply some more useless cream to my bumpy skin, and then pull a clean T-shirt and cable-knit sweater over my head. I hope the cowl neck will cover the tail end of the rash that's threatening to creep up my collarbone.

I stick my hands in my gloves, take a deep

breath, and walk back downstairs.

When I get to the bottom step, I stop. Aja is engrossed in an iPad and sitting in the velvet-covered easy chair. My chair. Eric is sitting on the couch, on the far left cushion. My mother's seat.

I didn't know it was my mother's seat — or more accurately, that I still think of it as my mother's seat — until I see him sitting there, and a kind of uncomfortable awareness washes over me.

And then I start to notice other things:

The way that the cushion of the velvet chair sags down, offering no support to Aja's tiny frame and giving him the appearance of a limp marionette, draped in the seat.

The ashtray in the center of the coffee table. I removed my mother's half-smoked cigarette from it years ago but never got around to emptying it of its now-stale ashes.

And the books. Good god, the books. Stacks of them cover nearly every surface. Two or three here to the fifteen or so growing from the floor beside my chair and stopping at the perfect height to hold a coffee mug. It's not that I don't put them away, but more that I have nowhere to put them. The shelves are filled to busting, each nook and cranny stuffed with a book, creating a jigsaw puzzle of spines. And I'm suddenly embarrassed to think how much money I've spent over the years on *reading*. And I discover the irony — if I had just gone to the library to check them out, maybe I wouldn't have to work there now to pay my bills.

I wonder if Eric thinks I'm a hoarder of sorts. Like those brothers who were found dead in their New York City apartment among their 140 tons of stuff.

The books and ashtray aside, at least my house is clean — I'm momentarily grateful for my meticulous efforts in keeping dust mites and cobwebs at bay.

I clear my throat and Eric looks up.

"Sorry about the, um . . . mess," I say, sweeping my hand in the general direction of all the books.

"Occupational hazard?"

"Yeah," I say, grinning before I can stop myself. It's the new Eric, the warm one with witticisms that catch me by surprise.

And then my smile disappears and I just stand there, because Aja's in my seat and I've never had two people in my living room before — not since my mother left — and I'm not sure what to do.

A knock at the door causes me to start.

"That'll be Con," Eric says, standing, and

a ludicrous sense of relief fills my belly that my mother's seat is empty once again.

I turn and open the door to a woman holding a tool kit. "You must be Jubilee," she says, walking right in, even though I didn't invite her, and the mental count of people in my house that aren't me goes up by one. I wonder — has the ceiling always been so low? The walls always felt so imposing? Even though frigid air follows her in, my skin starts to prick with sweat.

"You're lucky Eric told me about your car," Connie says, as if we're picking up a conversation we let go just the night before. "He would've only made it worse."

I stare at her eyes — exact replicas of the olives in Eric's head. "Can it get worse than not starting?"

"You have no idea," she says, then turns to Eric. "I've got to head up to the office in a few hours. Shall we get started?"

"Keys are on that table," I say pointing them out. Eric grabs them and follows Connie out the door. Exhaling, I shut it behind them. It's only when I look up that I realize Aja hasn't moved from my chair. His attention is so thoroughly on his video game, he doesn't seem to even realize that his dad and Connie have left.

I stand there, wondering if I should say

254

something, but after a minute, my grumbling stomach propels me into the kitchen for breakfast. It's only as I'm making coffee that I realize I should have offered some to Eric. Should have offered him anything, really. That's what they always do in the movies when someone visits: tea, water, a snack. I remember Aja and wonder if he's hungry. I stick my head into the living room.

"Hey, Aja," I say. He drags his eyes from his video game to me.

"Eggs?"

He blinks. "What?"

"I'm making breakfast. Do you want some?"

He pulls a face, and I realize maybe eggs aren't appealing to a kid's palate. But I don't have any cereal or . . . what else do kids eat? "Er . . . cookies?"

He shakes his head no and looks back down, which I'm glad about, because right after I said it, I realized I finished the last three Chips Ahoys in the pack on Thursday.

After breakfast, I wash my pot, plate, fork, and mug and wander back into the living room. It's making me out of sorts, not being alone in my house. I feel self-conscious, like someone is bearing witness to every single one of my actions, even though Aja hasn't looked up from his game since I asked him about breakfast.

I pick up a few books from the table behind the sofa, as if I mean to put them away, but I'm not sure where exactly to take them to, so I start to rearrange them in the stack, putting the largest ones on the bottom.

"Is your name really Jubilee?"

I jerk my head toward Aja's tiny voice, surprised at the sound, and then tilt my chin. "Ah, yes," I say. "I guess I didn't really get to introduce myself the other day."

He holds his head steady; behind his glasses, his large eyes stay trained on mine.

Then he gives a slight nod and I notice his focus travels to my hands. Studying them, really, his dark eyebrows furrowed. "Why do you wear gloves?" he asks.

I look down, my fingers clasping one another, fiddling with the material of the gloves. I look back up. "Well, um . . . it's kind of hard to explain," I say.

He sucks in his breath, his eyes finding mine again. When he speaks, it comes out as a reverent whisper. "It's because you can't touch people, isn't it?"

My stomach drops down to my feet. *"What?"* How could he possibly . . .

"You can't control it, can you?" His eyes are dancing now, shiny blots of ink.

I narrow my eyes at him. Did one of the nurses tell him? At the hospital? So much for patient confidentiality. Oh god — does that mean *Eric* knows? My mouth goes dry.

"It's OK. You can tell me," he says, leaning forward in the chair. "I swear I won't tell anyone."

I glance at the door, hoping Eric will barge through it, but then not wanting him to be privy to this conversation. And then I wonder why I care so much about what he thinks.

"Can you show me?" Aja asks, and I jerk my head back to him.

"Show you?" Now I'm confused. He wants to see my hands?

"Yeah, a fireball! How big are they? Do they go where you want them to?"

Fireball? I narrow my eyes, my mind a jumble. "Aja," I say, interrupting his flow of questions. "What are you talking about?"

"Your pyrotechnic energy!" he says, so excited now, he's bouncing a little in the chair, and I get concerned that the sagging cushion won't hold.

"My pyro-*what*?"

"And you pretended you hadn't even heard about the X-Men," he says. "I should have known. Right when I saw you. You even look a little like her."

"Like who?"

"Jubilee!" he says. "You're Jubilee!"

I nod, but more because he's finally said something that is in fact a true statement. Something I can agree with. "Well, yes. That's my name, but —"

"From the X-Men! And you can shoot plasmoids from your fingertips" — he starts pointing at things, making little zinging noises — "which is why you have to wear the gloves." I walk around the sofa and sit down on the opposite end from my mother's seat.

"Aja." He continues mock zapping things, his excitement at a near fever pitch.

"Aja!" He stops and looks at me.

"I don't have any . . . powers," I say. "I can't, um . . . zap things. That's just in the movies."

He opens his mouth, right as I remember our conversation from the library. I know he's going to correct me, so I beat him to it.

"I mean, the comic books. Sorry."

He closes his mouth and scrunches his nose, absorbing this. The light in his eyes dims a bit and it's like they're attached to a string on my heart. And it's being tugged. Ludicrously, I find myself wishing I could shoot fireballs from my fingertips, if only not to disappoint him.

"But . . . why do you wear the gloves?" he asks.

I look at him and find myself compelled to tell the truth. "I have an allergy," I say.

At this, his shoulders fall. "An allergy? Like, to peanut butter?"

"Kind of," I say. "But mine's a lot more rare than that."

He tilts his head. "How rare?"

"Very," I say, leaning a little closer to him. "But if I tell you, you can't tell anyone."

He leans a little closer, too, and it feels as if the room is holding its breath.

"I'm allergic to other humans."

His eyes go wide and shiny and bright again, and I don't understand why this pleases me so. But it does.

"That's why I ended up in the hospital after pulling you out of the river." I hold up my gloved fingers and wiggle them. "I can't touch people."

His eyebrows are so high, they're nearly hidden beneath the fringe of thick black hair on his forehead, and then, in an instant, they fall and go crinkly as he ponders this new information. I can almost see the gears turning in his brain. When he finally speaks, it's in a whisper. "So, you kind of *are* a mutant?"

I consider this. And how that's what I've

259

felt like for my entire life. Like a curiosity. A monster. A total freak of nature. But somehow, coming from his mouth, this possibility doesn't seem nearly so bad.

An hour later, Connie and Eric appear in the foyer. They don't knock, but then I don't know why they should. They are doing me a favor.

"How long has your car not been starting for?" Connie asks.

"Um . . . I'm not sure."

"Let me rephrase — when's the last time you drove it?"

I glance at Eric and mumble a response.

"What?"

I clear my throat. "Nine years ago."

Eyebrows shoot up on Connie and Eric's faces like a succession of fireworks.

"Wow. OK," says Connie, bobbing her head a little. "That, um . . . that really makes sense. The fuel tank is completely rusted. I don't think vinegar's going to touch it. I gotta drain that, put in new gas and an additive. Plus, you need a new battery, all new fluids, spark plugs. Oh, and new tires, too. They're just not safe after six years or so — especially since they've been exposed to weather conditions all this time."

Overwhelmed by this influx of information, I look from Connie to Eric. He shrugs, as if in apology.

Connie continues. "I could do the fluids, spark plugs, all the basic stuff. I might even be able to change out the fuel pump, although those can be a bear, depending. But the rest? It's exceeding my mechanical talents. I think it's better in the hands of a professional. I'm sorry, wish I had better news." She glances at her watch. "I gotta get to the office."

Eric walks her to the door and I manage to squeak out a thank-you before she's gone.

"I'm happy to call a tow truck for you. Get it to a mechanic," he says when he comes back in the room.

"Oh, gosh, I'll take care of it," I say, with no intention of doing so.

"I don't mind," he says. "I'll do some research this afternoon, figure out the best place —"

"No," I say, with more force this time.

This pulls him up short.

"I'm just . . . I'm fine with my bike. It's no big deal."

"Let me just do this for you," he says, not skipping a beat. "Really. I owe you."

"You don't owe me!" I say, recognizing the irony that on the way home from the hospital I didn't feel like he was grateful

261

enough, but now it's just too much. And I wish he'd leave it alone. "I didn't do anything."

"You saved —"

"No!" I say, a little louder than I intend. Even Aja glances up from his iPad, and then looks back down. "I did what any other warm-blooded person would do in that situation."

He doesn't immediately respond, giving me a hard stare. Neither one of us blinks for a few moments, and I start to squirm under his scrutiny. It's like we're locked in some kind of battle now, but I don't understand what he's fighting for. He did what he came to do — look at my car — and now we're even. He's out of his obligation.

He breaks the silence. "What if I just give you a ride home from the library, just until you get enough money to fix your car?"

My eyes fly open. This is getting ridiculous. "No, really —" I start.

But he keeps talking like I haven't even spoken. "It's close to the train station so it's not even out of my way. Plus, it's bad enough that you're riding your bike in the cold, but the dark, too? You don't even have any reflectors on it. And what if it snows?"

Why do you even care? I want to shout. I cross my arms in front of me. I hate the

262

way he's talking to me — it's patronizing, like he knows better. And I hate even more that he's a little bit right — I hadn't thought about snow. "I've just ordered reflectors *and* a headlamp," I fire at him. "Not that it's any of your business."

He takes a step back and I think I've won, but then he opens his mouth again and says quietly: "Just let me help you. Please."

"I don't need your help," I say firmly. "You've done more than enough. Thank you." I gesture toward the door with my left hand. I know it's rude, but I'm beyond caring. I just want him out of my house.

He takes another step back and nods, slowly, his eyes never leaving my face. "OK," he says, reaching in his pocket for his knitted hat. The fight has left him and I know I've won. He turns to Aja. "You ready, bud?" he says loud enough for Aja to hear over his earbuds.

Aja gets up, tucks his iPad under his arm, and shuffles out the door. Eric turns to go after him but then fixes me with one last look. "Good-bye, Jubilee," he says.

I stare at him, hard, trying to hold on to the anger that was just coursing through me. But I can't. There's something in his eyes I haven't seen before — a quiet anguish, maybe? — that softens me, and all I

Fifteen

ERIC

I'm an idiot. Stephanie always said I didn't know when to leave well enough alone. That when I lock onto something, I push too hard. And I did it just now with Jubilee. But what I'm trying to figure out while driving home is *why.* Yes, she saved Aja's life. And I do feel indebted to her in some way. But she made it clear she doesn't want my help — doesn't need it. So why couldn't I just leave it alone? It occurs to me that it may very well be ego driven, some deep-seated desire to feel needed by someone — *anyone* — to stem the now quite regular feeling of being so utterly useless to everyone else in my life.

I glance over at Aja in the passenger seat, where he's tapping at that ridiculous screen with his thumbs. I look back at the road, trying to clear my mind, concentrate on the street signs and other traffic, but it seems the more I try not to think about Jubilee, the more I find myself thinking about her.

She was wearing my sweatshirt when she opened the door. The Wharton one. The one I lent her when I took her home from the hospital. And I know it probably doesn't mean anything — it was probably the shirt nearest to her on the floor when I so rudely woke her up with my banging, and she threw it on to come greet me.

And yet. For some reason, I can't stop thinking about that sweatshirt. And the places where the material met her skin.

"Eric," Aja says beside me in his usual monotone, interrupting my thoughts.

"Yeah?" I jerk my head to him.

"You just ran that red light."

"What?" I glance in the rearview mirror. Sure enough, the light is red. "I did?"

But Aja is looking back down at his screen and he doesn't respond. I run my hands through my hair and exhale, wondering what in the hell has gotten into me.

Work is so crazy on Monday that I only have time for a quick call in the afternoon to make sure Aja got home OK and Mrs. Holgerson is there. When I finally get on the train at six fifteen, I pull *The Notebook* out of my bag. I only have about fifteen more pages, but instead of opening it, I close my eyes and lean my head back against the chair. And I wonder, not for the first time, if I really want to be partner.

Is it worth all of this? It's what I've been working toward my entire career. The canned response I gave Stephanie every time she complained about my long hours, about my absence from the family, about my level of engagement with her, with Ellie, with home. "It'll get better," I always promised her. "When I make partner." What I didn't point out was that I was a better parent than so many of my colleagues. I actually left work early once in a while for a teacher conference or a softball game or for the regional science fair where Ellie placed second as a sixth grader against all other middle schoolers. I couldn't understand, then, why she got a D on her progress report for science in the eighth grade.

"It's your favorite subject," I said to her on one of the too-few weekends I got to spend with her post-divorce.

She rolled her eyes, a new habit that I couldn't stand. "Not anymore."

"Since when?"

"Since now," she said. That was right before she told me she was going to Darcy's to spend the night — our first blowout argument. At least the first one I remember, not only because it was the first time she told me she hated me, when I forbid her from going, but because she also said: *I totally get why Mom divorced you.*

Now I wonder if I just should have let her go. If maybe that was the beginning of the end.

But of course I know that relationships don't dissolve over one event, one fight. It's a thousand blows delivered over time — uppercuts, jabs, crosses — some you barely even feel. And then before you know it, you're on the ground seeing stars and wondering what the hell happened.

I think of the text she sent me Thursday.

What are you trying to do? Just stop already.

A response! My daughter, my Ellie, acknowledged me. The first nine words I'd heard from her in more than four months. Not exactly the overwhelming emotional reunion I was hoping for, but I'd take it.

I spent two hours trying to craft the perfect reply. I racked my brain for other *The Virgin Suicides* and *The Bell Jar* quotes with which to impress her while I was pan-frying hot dogs for dinner. I invented lengthy explanations while loading the dishwasher and wiping down counters. I concocted witticisms while checking the front-door lock, turning out lights, and stopping at Aja's door to tell him and The Dog good night.

But when I got in bed later that night, I had discarded every possibility — too cheesy, not funny enough, too obtuse, too long-winded — and the only thing that remained was the truth, which I tapped out one letter at a time with my index finger:

I can't. You're my daughter. Love, Dad

When I step off the train into the dark night, the wind hits me square in the chest and I dip my head lower so that my ears can find shelter under my collar. I think again of Jubilee on her bike in this weather and fervently wish she had accepted my offer to give her a ride.

I stride briskly across the parking lot toward my car. I slide into the front seat and turn the heat up full blast, rubbing my hands together to warm them. I glance at the clock. It's 6:56. The library closes at 7:00. And I'm suddenly compelled to drive there, even though I know I shouldn't. To try one last time.

A block away, it occurs to me she might not be there. It's 7:04 now and she very well could have already locked up, gotten on her bike, started on her way home. But no. When I pull into the parking lot, she's there, standing at the door, her back to me. My blood starts to pump faster at the sight of her and I realize I'm nervous. I hear her voice in my head: *I don't need your help.* I swallow. Why did I come here?

I should leave. But it's too late. My headlights, illuminating her silhouette, have gotten her attention and she turns, holding a set of keys in her right hand, using her left to shield her eyes from the brightness. With a flick of my wrist, I turn off the lights, so as not to blind her. She blinks, staring into the car, and then her eyes widen in recognition. I swallow once more and then lift my hands, palms up, and shrug, hoping to convey the very nonthreatening manner in which I've come, rather than the creepy, stalkerish behavior it just now occurs to me I'm most likely expressing.

I hold my breath as she stares, motionless. And then she slowly shakes her head from side to side. And then I see it, the corner of her mouth slowly turning up. It's all I need.

270

I open the door and stand up.

"What are you doing here?" she says, but her tone is full of wonder, not anger. Relief floods through me.

"I told you it was on the way home," I say. "Just thought I'd drop by. See if anyone needed a lift. I mean, not *you,* of course — you've got your bike."

She smiles now — a full one that stretches her lips and lights her eyes. "I do," she says. "Have my bike."

I nod, thinking quickly. "You know, I was wondering, though, if you could help *me* out."

She cocks her head at me, curious. Waiting.

"I need help deciphering the hidden meaning in all these books I'm reading that are hopelessly over my head. And you happen to understand them," I say. "I was thinking, maybe, we could make a deal — you tutor, while I drive."

At this, she throws her head back and laughs — a full sound that takes me by surprise. And I know I've got her. Warmth fills my belly.

When she stops laughing, she fixes me with a look. "Has anyone ever told you that you're annoyingly persistent?"

I nod. "Once or twice," I say. "So we've

271

got a deal?" I step out from behind the car door and move toward her, my hand out in front of me. But when I see the look on her face, I stop moving. Her relaxed smile has turned into what looks like sheer terror. Her body is tense and she's staring at my hand like it's a snake coming to bite her. I drop it and clear my throat. She looks up at me, her face changing again just as quickly. "I just, um . . . I gotta go get my bike," she says, sticking out her thumb and gesturing to the bike rack.

"Uh . . . OK," I say, following her a few steps behind, but keeping my distance. I don't know what that was, but I don't want to freak her out again. When we reach the bike, she walks around to the left of it, so I go right, putting my hands on the frame to hoist it up at the same time that she grabs the handlebars.

"Oh, I didn't mean . . . I can get it," she says, not letting go.

"I know," I say. "But I'd like to do it."

Her eyes meet mine. "Aren't you doing enough?" There's a smile on her lips but her gaze is strong, unyielding. Jesus, she's stubborn.

"Just let me get it," I say through clenched teeth, picking up the bike more forcefully than I need to in my frustration, giving her no choice but to drop her grip on the handlebars.

She takes a step back, eyeing me, and then trails me as I walk to the car, bike in hand.

"So what's the next book?" she says, standing at the passenger door as I put the bike in the trunk.

I raise my brow at her. "Huh?"

"That we're discussing. I tutor, you drive — remember?"

"Oh, right," I say. "Uh, it's *The Notebook.*"

"*The Notebook*?"

"Yeah."

She lets out a cackle. "If you need help understanding *The Notebook,* we're in trouble."

I pause, my eyes meeting hers. "I'd say we're in trouble, then."

I'm not sure what happens, but when we get in the car, the relative ease with which we bantered in the parking lot vanishes and an awkward silence hangs between us. As I ease the car out of the parking lot, the tick-tock of my blinker fills the air, suddenly sounding as loud and threatening as a nuclear bomb set to explode. I glance over at her and see her gloved hands clenched in her lap. She looks as uncomfortable and tense as I suddenly feel, and I wonder if this was a bad idea. She's clearly independent, but I've been surrounded by strong-willed women my entire life, and it seems like it's more than that. She's hard to read — not that I've ever been good at reading people. But she runs hot and cold like a bipolar faucet, and I never know what I'm going to get. Like at her house on Saturday, it almost felt like she didn't even want us to be there. But then when I came in from working on the car, she and Aja were laughing together. I was stunned, and not just because I hadn't heard Aja laugh like that in, well, forever, but god — her smile. It took up the entire room, and I was actually jealous — *jealous!* — of a ten-year-old. My own son. That he was the one she was beaming at like that.

I massage the stubble on my face. What am I doing? I just came out here for a temporary work gig and to give my daughter some space and now I'm acting like a schoolboy with a foolish crush on the librarian.

"Are you OK?"

"Huh?" I turn my head. Jubilee's staring at me.

"You made a noise. Like a groan."

"Oh . . . right. I'm fine," I say, embarrassed. "Er . . . just a rough day at work."

"Ah," she says.

Before she can ask about it, I clear my throat and change the subject. "So, um . . . *The Notebook,*" I say. "I just finished it on the train."

"You did?" she says, and I don't know if it's my imagination or if her body relaxes a little. "Did you cry?"

"What? No," I say. The light in front of us turns yellow. I press the brakes. "Why would I cry? Did *you* cry?"

"Yeah. I cry every time I read it."

"Every —" I narrow my eyes at her. "Wait, how many times have you read *The Notebook*?"

"I don't know. Six or seven. I haven't read it in a few years though."

I look over at her, gobsmacked. "Why on earth would you read a book six or seven times? It's not like you don't know what happens."

She shoots a look at me — one I'm familiar with from Ellie — conveying it's hopeless to explain if I don't already know.

"OK, but *this* book?" I continue. "It's so cheesy." I reach into the backseat and snag my copy out of my open bag on the floorboard. With one hand on the wheel I use the other to flip to the example I want to offer.

"What are you doing? You can't read and drive."

"We're at a red light," I say, scanning the pages for what I'm looking for.

"Not anymore," she says. I look up and sure enough, the light is green. I glance over at her and she's grinning. A car honks behind us, and I toss the book down.

"Well, it's the part where in the war, he had *Leaves of Grass* in his shirt pocket and it took a bullet for him. Do you remember?"

She nods. "Yeah."

"C'mon, a book of poetry saved his life?" I say, laughing. "It doesn't get cornier than that."

She chuckles. "OK, yes, maybe it's clichéd in some of the details — but it's also an amazing love story. It's like the *Romeo and Juliet* of our time."

"Now Nicholas Sparks is *Shakespeare*? Oh god, I think that's blasphemy. He's got to be rolling over in his grave somewhere."

Though I'm meant to be paying attention to the road, I steal a glance at Jubilee. She's unguarded, smiling, her lips stretched across her face, and a small buzz travels up my spine. The same buzz I got when she was smiling at Aja, except now it's directed at me.

My phone hums where I left it in the

console. I assume it's work and ignore it. When it falls silent, I pick it up and am surprised to see Mrs. Holgerson's name pop up on the screen. I know I'm a little late, but I told her that would be the case sometimes. No, this must be something more. My heart revs as I tap her name. It rings and rings, even though she just called me.

"Shit." I jerk the wheel, making a U-turn in the middle of the street. Jubilee grabs the door to steady herself, but to her credit barely makes a sound. "What —"

"It's Aja," I say, cutting her off, my panic rising by the second.

I speed toward home, my mind conjuring worst-case scenarios as fast as I used to calculate square roots of numbers for fun as a kid. Did he run away again? Jump out of a window? Or something worse? When I pull into the apartment's parking lot, I'm only slightly relieved to not see any police car, fire engine, or emergency vehicle flashing lights.

Without waiting for Jubilee, I run up the stairs two at a time and unlock the door, throwing it open to Mrs. Holgerson on her hands and knees scrubbing the carpet. The pungent scent of carpet cleaner and something else — burned dinner? — fills my nostrils. The apartment is otherwise quiet.

Her face contours itself into squished wrinkles of anger upon seeing me. "No!" she says. "No, no, no." She struggles getting to her feet and I go over to her, extending my hand out for support. "I did *not* sign up for this."

"Did The Dog have an accident?" I ask.

"Try *four*," she says, holding a damp rag. My heart slows as I realize it's just the puppy she's mad about. "But that's nothing compared to the fire!"

"Fire?" And that's when I smell it. The acrid smoke lingering in the air that I mistook for burned food. I feel, rather than see, Jubilee step in the door behind me.

"Your boy! Almost burned down the whole apartment building," she says. "Good thing I checked on him. Then has nothing to say for himself. Nothing!" She shakes her head. "You said a little trouble — not a *delinquent*!"

I pause and narrow my eyes. "He's not a delinquent," I say.

"Whatever," she says.

"No, not whatever. He's not a delinquent," I repeat, firmer this time. "I'm sorry for the trouble, but I think it's best if you just go."

I reach in my wallet for enough bills to cover the amount we agreed on and hold it out to her, not taking my eyes from her face.

She exchanges the damp rag she's holding for the money and lifts her bag off the coffee table. "Good-bye," she says curtly, and then mumbles something that doesn't even sound like English. She huffs past Jubilee out the door, letting it slam with a thud behind her.

Jubilee's eyes meet mine and there's a hint of pride on her face, matching the same satisfied feeling I had in telling Mrs. Holgerson off, standing up for Aja, for my son. But that feeling is quickly replaced by something else.

"Shit," I say, holding the pee-soaked rag. "I think I just ran off the best — the only — babysitter I had for Aja."

Jubilee mutters something under her breath. It sounds like: "I'd hate to see the worst." I smile.

"I gotta —" I stick out my thumb toward Aja's room.

"Go." She waves me off, bending at the knees to lower herself onto the couch. "I'm OK here."

I take the rag to the kitchen sink and then head down the hall, the lingering scent of burning growing stronger with each step. "Aja?" I say, and peek my head around the corner, unsure what I'll find. He's sitting on his bed with The Dog on his lap. His wide eyes take me in when I enter.

"Bud?"

He's like stone, except for the small tremors I can see rippling through his body, and my mind jumps back to the hammer-in-the-table incident. I need to handle this better than that. I sit on the edge of the bed and wait.

We stare at each other, the silence growing, until The Dog emits a whimper, as if he too is getting tired of the game.

Aja blinks. "Are the police going to come get me?" he whispers. And his voice sounds so young, so helpless — nothing like the adult way he typically speaks — that my whole body feels like it's liquefying. The anger that was edging its way into my limbs dissolves, and I move my hand toward him on the bed, as close as he'll let me. I yearn to enfold him into my arms.

"No," I say, and then repeat it for emphasis. "*No.* Is that what Mrs. Holgerson said?" Wow. I really did a bang-up job picking a babysitter. "Tell me what happened."

"It was an accident."

"OK. Were you trying to set something on fire? Telekinetically or something?"

He shakes his head. "It was stupid," he says.

I wait, scared to say anything for fear of

shutting him down. The silence draws out, until Aja finally breaks it.

"Me and Iggy? We were Skyping."

"Iggy," I say, remembering the IM exchange I read between the two of them, and wondering if this Iggy is a bad influence and someone I should be more concerned about. For now, I decide to just listen. "OK." I move my fingers closer until they're brushing his kneecap. I try to give him a comforting squeeze, but he moves his leg. The Dog stands up, unhappy to have been disturbed, and repositions himself on Aja's pillow with a sigh.

"We were playing a game."

"What game?"

"The match game." He ends every sentence as if it's his final one. As if no further explanation is needed. I keep prodding.

"How do you play?"

"You each light a match at the same time and whoever drops theirs first loses."

I take this in. "And you dropped yours?"

He nods. "Yes. It was burning my fingertips. And the trash can was right there."

The tin trash can beside his desk finally catches my eye and I can see the blackened streaks running up the inside of it, along with some droplets of water from where I assume Mrs. Holgerson doused the flames.

All I can think is: *Thank god it wasn't plastic.*

"It was Iggy's idea."

I massage my face with both hands.

"I see," I say. Because I really do. He was playing a game. A stupid game. And when the trash can ignited, he probably just froze in fear.

And even though I know I should be mad — not about just the fire, but the fact that Aja has run off the only option I was able to conjure up on such short notice for his after-school care — a smile starts to creep its way onto my face. My lips twitch. And then a sound burps from between them. And then another. And before I know it, I'm full-on laughing, like I haven't laughed in years. I don't know what's funnier to me, picturing the look on Mrs. Holgerson's face when she discovered the fire or the surprise on Aja's when he realized a lit match was capable of burning him and looked for the closest receptacle, but I cannot get control of the guffaws that keep erupting from my belly. Tears are streaming down my cheeks and just when I think I can finally take a breath, Aja says: "At least it got rid of her old onion smell."

And then I'm off again, my shoulders shaking from the effort. When I finally start to peter out, Aja is smiling at me, and even though I know he hates it, I reach up to palm his shoulder with my hand. Aja maneuvers away before I can touch him. I drop my hand and just stare at him. And in that moment, even though he has Dinesh's thick straight hair, down to the cowlick at the crown of his head, and his crater of a dimple on his right cheek and charmingly large nose, his eyes — and the way they're looking at me — are Kate's incarnate. And I'm so glad I have him, to remind me of my two favorite people no longer on Earth. "God, I love you," I say. His smile disappears and he looks down at his lap, clearly uncomfortable from the affection.

I clear my throat, sitting up a little straighter. And then I remember what Janet suggested, and realize this is the perfect opportunity to tell Aja about Dinesh and the time he almost burned a fraternity house down in college with his infamous flaming lips shot.

"You know, guys do a lot of stupid things," I begin, smiling a little at the memory. "And your dad actually had his own little obsession with fire." At the word "dad," Aja's eyes pop open even wider, almost in a panic. As I open my mouth to continue the story, Aja claps his hands over his ears and starts shaking his head, a moan emitting from his lips:

283

"Noooooooooooooo-noooooooooooo."

"Aja," I say, standing up. I stare at him, unsure how to respond. "It's OK! Calm down. It's OK, bud."

But he won't stop. The moans get louder and he squeezes his eyes shut as if the offending sound is coming from someone else and he wants to block it out. I'm standing there, useless, wondering what Janet would advise I do next, when Aja takes a hand off his ear and points at the door. "Get ooooooouuuuuuut!" he screams. And so I do.

I leave the room and shut the door behind me, my heart pounding in my eardrums, trying, but unable to erase the sound of Aja's tortured moans from my memory. Maybe that's why I haven't shared any stories about his parents, I think, wanting to direct all my anger at Janet and her awful advice.

But I know the truth is far harder to swallow.

Jubilee stands up when she sees me walk into the den. I start, having almost forgotten she was here. She's taken off her coat but left her gloves on, like she's about to handle rare jewels or something.

"Is he . . . OK?" she asks, drawing my eyes

to her face. The wailing has subsided, but it's still ringing in my ears.

"Yeah," I say, but I know it's as unconvincing as it sounds. "Listen, let's . . . uh . . . is it OK if we give him a minute and then I'll drive you home?"

"How about I call a cab?" she says, and relief tinged with guilt floods me. I feel bad that I got her mixed up in my problems.

"Yeah. That's probably the best option."

After I call the taxi, we both sit on the couch, an entire length of cushion between us. The silence seems to stretch past us, from one side of the room to the other, until Jubilee breaks it.

"What's the dog's name?" she asks.

I chuckle. "We don't really have one for him. We've just been calling him The Dog."

"The Dog," she repeats.

"Yep."

"That's a terrible name."

I widen my eyes at her candor. "No more terrible than Rufus or Petey."

"No, actually it is," she says. "*Come here, Rufus.* That sounds right. *Come here, The Dog.* That doesn't even make grammatical sense."

I laugh, and the release feels good. "I guess you're right. Would you be OK with just Dog?"

"I don't know," she says. "I kind of like Rufus now."

"I'll have to run that by Aja," I say.

She nods, content, and we sit in the silence for a few more minutes.

And then: "What are you going to do?"

I rub my hand over my face. "About Rufus?" I ask, even though I know that's not what she's talking about. It's just that I have no answer. What *am* I going to do about Aja, his *grief,* about Ellie, about my seeming inability to parent with any kind of real know-how or acumen?

She smiles. "No, about Aja. Um . . . his babysitter?"

Oh. Right. Mrs. Holgerson. "I don't know." And as I say the words, panic begins to take hold. What *am* I going to do? I suddenly regret shooing her out, even though it felt good at the time. I can't take off work tomorrow, not with this huge acquisition going on. Or any other day this week. As much as I hate it, I kind of need her. "I might have to call and beg her to come back, at least until I can find someone else."

"Uh . . . I don't think that's going to work."

"Why not?"

"When she left? She muttered something in Swedish: *Fan ta dig, din jävel.*"

I look at her, not understanding.

"The first part basically means 'May the devil take you' — or, as we would say: 'Go to hell.'"

"And the second?"

She pauses, and then says quietly: "'You fucker.'"

My jaw drops at the idea of those words coming from that little old lady, and then I start laughing. Jubilee joins in, and the release feels good.

"Wait," I say when we calm down. "You know Swedish?"

"No." She shrugs. "Just the curse words."

I smile, reveling in this unexpected detail.

She looks down and then raises her head again. "He could come to the library."

I focus my eyes on her. "What do you mean?"

"Like, after school. If you need a place for him to go."

I narrow my eyes at her and then give my head a shake. "No. No, I couldn't do that. You don't need . . . you've got plenty going on." Although I don't really know if that's true. What *do* librarians do all day?

She shrugs. "I just thought . . . I mean, you're picking me up this week anyway." She looks down at her feet. "If, um . . . if you still were planning to, I mean."

"Of course. Yes," I say.

"So it just kind of makes sense. At least for a few days, and then you can figure out what to do."

I stare at her. This woman. This confounding, beautiful woman who apparently wears gloves twenty-four hours a day (does she *sleep* in them?) and can translate Swedish curse words. And I know she's right. It does make sense. I sit back, pushing my shoulder blades into the cushion behind me, and delight in the rare feeling of something just falling into place. Instead of just falling.

And then it occurs to me quite suddenly — that out of the two of us, maybe she's not the one who needs help.

When the cab honks its horn from the parking lot, we stand up and walk to the door. From behind me, she says: "What happened to your coffee table?"

We both look back at it. I haven't gotten around to replacing the glass top, so if you put a drink or your feet on it they would drop right through to the ground, meaning it's not so much a coffee table at this point as just a metal frame.

I wipe my hand over my face again and sigh. "Long story."

She follows me down the stairs and I get her bike out of the trunk, despite her now-expected protestations that she can get it herself.

As she's climbing in the back of the cab, she stops and turns to me. "See you tomorrow?"

I nod. "Tomorrow," I say, and I'm not sure if I imagine it or if her lips turn up in a grin. And then she ducks in the car and is gone, leaving me on the cold sidewalk, staring at the crimson taillights of the cab, and then nothing at all.

Sixteen

Jubilee

When I get in Madison's car Tuesday morning, she's holding her hands out toward me, palms up. In one, she's got a doughnut. In the other, a blue pill.

"What is this, *The Matrix*?"

"Huh?"

I nod at the tablet.

"Oh! No. That's funny." She narrows her eyes at me. "Wait — how do you know about *The Matrix*?"

"I was in my house for nine years, not *underground*. I do have TV."

"Huh," she says, and then she lifts up her right hand an inch. "Anyway, *this* is Xanax."

"For me?" I tilt my head at her. "Isn't that a prescription?"

"Yeeeees, and lucky for you, I'm sharing."

I purse my lips together, unsure of this gift.

"Look, you couldn't even go into

TeaCakes the other day. How are you going to make it through New York City?"

I know she's right. It's the reason I didn't sleep last night, thinking of the buildings, the traffic, the streets crowded with all those *people.* Drugs, however, didn't occur to me as the solution.

"Is it strong?"

"Meh." She shrugs. "It'll take the edge off."

I pinch the pill between my gloved index finger and thumb, pop it in my mouth, and swallow. Then I nod at the pastry.

"What's that for?"

"This is your first adventure."

I stare at her. "Um, I've had *doughnuts.*" Seriously, does she think I've been living in a cave?

"Yes. But not a hot, fresh-off-the-line apple cider doughnut from McClellan's bakery down on Forsyth Street. They don't deliver. And trust me when I say it's an adventure for your mouth."

I gently pluck it from her hand, a mix of cinnamon sugar instantly coating the finger-tips of my glove. She watches me as I take a bite. I chew quietly, not wanting to give her the satisfaction of a big production, but it does take every ounce of self-control in me not to moan out loud. She's right. The doughnut is that good.

A smug smile appears on her face, and I know I haven't completely concealed my enjoyment.

"Right?" she says.

"Mm-hmm," I mumble, my mouth already full of the next bite. I give her a big smile, a mix of warm dough and cinnamon caking my teeth, and she laughs.

"Now, let's get you to the doctor."

On the drive into the city, I try to distract myself by letting my thoughts wander — and they make a beeline to Eric, like they've been doing off and on since I left his apartment last night. I was shocked when he showed up at the library as I was locking up — but also a little relieved. I had been feeling guilty since Saturday about how I treated him. Yes, he was pushy — curiously so — but as I thought about it, it did seem like he just genuinely wanted to help me, and it was hard to be angry at that.

But then, when he came toward me, hand out, wanting to shake on our "deal," I froze. Technically it was safe — I had my gloves on — but I haven't willingly touched anyone, or let anyone touch me, in years. I stared at his fingers — those fingers that I've weirdly thought so much about ever since I dreamed about them. That I've re-

imagined in more detail than any Renais-
sance painter. But it wasn't a dream, and
faced with the reality of them — of what
they could do to me — I was terrified. He
dropped his hand and didn't make a thing
of it at all, even as I flushed with embarrassment.

And maybe it was that or maybe it's the
way he was last night with Mrs. Holgerson,
defending Aja like that, or the way he went
to him after, so clearly worried about his
son — I don't know. But he just seems so
genuine. Kind. And not very much like the
asshole Louise and I originally thought he
was.

But there's something else — another
reason I can't stop thinking about him, a
reason I haven't even wanted to admit to
myself until now: I like the way he looks at
me. Not like I'm an oddity, but like I'm just
a normal girl, a woman. And I can't remember the last time I felt normal.

Out the front windshield, the Manhattan
skyline looms into view and I realize the
Xanax is starting to take effect as the
muscles in my shoulders and my arms begin
to relax. But then, I notice, it doesn't touch
the growing pit in my stomach — the one
that's reminding me that I'm *not* normal,
and it's only a matter of time before Eric

realizes that, too.

When we pull into the parking deck in lower Manhattan, I press a finger into my cheek, and then two fingers. I massage the skin around, pushing and stretching it in different directions.

I can't feel my face.

I know I should be alarmed by this, but the opposite occurs — a gentle wave of relaxation washes over me. I giggle.

"What's funny?"

"Nothing." The word kind of floats out of my mouth, making my lips vibrate, which is even more amusing. Another laugh follows, and I change my mind. "Everything."

I giggle some more.

Madison puts the car in park and frowns. "Hmmm . . . maybe I should have cut that pill in half."

I poke her on the forehead with my gloved index finger that's still got remnants of cinnamon sugar. "Don't worry," I say. And then the song immediately bounces into my head, and I'm compelled to add: "Be happy!"

I form an O with my lips and sing: "Doooo-do-do-doodee-do-doodee-do-dee-do-dee-do. Don't worry. Do-dee-doo-dee-dodee-doooooooooo."

Madison rolls her eyes and opens her car door. "Come on, Bobby McFerrin, let's get you inside."

The song stays in my head for the next hour while we walk the two blocks to the Allergy & Asthma Center, while I get checked in, while I change into a paper gown and get all my vitals taken by a nurse in rubber gloves and a face mask who takes great care not to touch me (she must have been prepped). But then I'm left alone on the exam table, waiting for Dr. Zhang, and a soberness kicks in.

I'm suddenly a child again, sitting in one of the hundred doctors' offices I was schlepped to while my mother tried to figure out what was wrong with me. It's all a big blur to me, really. I was so young. But then, a memory, clear as day, hits me. It's my mother, screaming at the top of her lungs. *Don't tell me you* don't know*! That's my* baby *in there. You have to help us. You* have *to.* It pangs my heart, the plaintive desperation in her scratchy tone. Referring to me as her baby. And I just remember how I felt in that moment. Scared, yes. But also loved, protected, defended. And I wonder if maybe I tend to only remember the worst of her, and not the moments like that one.

The door opens, interrupting my

thoughts. Dr. Zhang is smaller than I remember, less intimidating. She offers a warm smile. "Jubilee. How *are* you?"

I consider this. "Still allergic to people."

She nods and smiles. "Got it."

For the next hour, we delve into the twelve years since I saw her last, including the Incident in high school, my housebound years, and my most recent brush with death and hospital visit. She takes meticulous notes on a legal pad, piping up with questions as they come to her, but she doesn't flinch — at any of it — which makes me like her more. Although when I tell her the Aja story, she says, "Maybe let's leave CPR to the EMT next time?"

Finally, she takes a look underneath the paper gown at my rash.

"Have you changed anything recently? Your laundry soap? Lotion? New sheets?"

"No," I say, "everything is the same."

"What about new people? Has anyone been in your home recently?"

I think of Eric and Aja. "Yeah. I had some . . . friends" — is that what they are? — "over."

"So they were sitting on your furniture, I assume." She pauses. "Did they sleep over?"

I jerk my head to her. "No!" I say, but my face flushes at the automatic thought of Eric

296

in my room. My bed. I try to compose myself. "I mean, yes, they sat on my furniture, of course. No to spending the night."

She nods. "Just trying to understand if and how any indirect contact might have occurred. People slough skin cells all the time, and though it hasn't been a problem for you in your past — your allergy has always been caused by direct skin-to-skin touch — my thinking is that your years of reclusiveness have caused your body to become even more sensitive, and maybe even sloughed skin cells are a problem for you now. Think — is there anything that could be coming in contact with your torso like that? You're not sleeping on sheets that someone else has slept on. Are you borrowing clothes or anything?"

At that question, my heart jumps. Eric's sweatshirt.

"I have been wearing a shirt," I say. "Um . . . that doesn't belong to me."

"Hmm." She taps her lips with her pen. "That could be it. Especially if the person wore it before giving it to you."

I think of the way it smells — not like laundry detergent, but woodsy, like him, and when she says it, I'm sure that's exactly right.

"When did you wear it last?"

297

"Um . . . last night."

"But the rash started before that, correct?" She glances back at her notes. "A week ago?"

A flush creeps up my neck. "I, uh . . . have kind of been wearing it every night. But I've never reacted to that before — other people's clothes or sheets or anything," I say, thinking of my childhood romps in mom's warm bed and playing dress-up in her closet.

Dr. Zhang nods. "Allergies can be strange like that. I once had a patient that had been eating shrimp for his entire life and then suddenly, at the age of twenty-six, nearly died at a seafood buffet. It's a mystery. That's extreme, but you see what I mean. Allergies — and their triggers — can change without rhyme or reason." She puts her notepad on the counter. "So, how about this — you don't borrow clothes anymore unless they're clean," she says, turning on the sink. "And maybe think about washing that sweatshirt?"

I do. Think about it. And I'm surprised to find the thought kind of devastates me.

Dr. Zhang scrubs her hands under the stream of water and snaps rubber gloves onto her hands. "Now, let's do a thorough examination, get you a prescription-strength hydrocortisone along with the EpiPens, and go from there. Shall we?"

After the exam, I get dressed and go sit in Dr. Zhang's office, waiting for her. I try to remember the visit twelve years ago, my mom sitting in the molded-plastic seat beside me. I'm sure she was wearing something low-cut, revealing, but I can't picture the exact outfit. And then, more alarmingly, I realize I can't picture her. I can hear her voice, plain as day, but her face is kind of blurred.

Dr. Zhang comes in and sits at the desk across from me. "So," she says. "Jubilee. I don't want to cause unneeded anxiety, but it really does concern me if your skin is reacting to indirect contact now."

I look at her.

"From wearing another person's sweatshirt," she clarifies. "You need to be extraordinarily careful until we can sort this out," she says. "That means absolutely no touching at all. I know you know that, but I can't stress it enough. We have no idea how your body will react."

"OK," I say, but all I really am hearing is "until we can sort this out," and I know this is the part where she's going to ask to study me. To make me one of her research projects. And this is also the part where I walk

299

out. Again.

"So, I don't know if you've read any of my research —"

I shake my head no. Here we go.

"I've been running some clinical trials the past five years on a Chinese herbal treatment to cure severe food allergies. We've had about a sixty percent success rate."

I know I should be impressed by this. Allergies are a confounding ailment in the medical community. They don't make sense evolutionarily speaking, especially mine. Why would my body fight the very thing that is its only chance of procreating? And no one knows the root cause of them — is it environment? Genetics? When the origins of a problem aren't clear, it's near impossible to find a solution. But I leave my face blank, unsure of where she's going with this.

She continues. "I don't think you'd be a good candidate. At least not yet. Your allergy being so . . . rare. I have no idea if it would respond in the same way as food allergies."

I nod, waiting.

"But have you heard of immunotherapy?"

I shake my head.

She clasps her hands in front of her. "It's a common treatment for allergies like rhinitis or bee pollen. Patients are injected with small amounts of the substance they're allergic to, in theory building up a tolerance over time, in order to reduce the immune system response to the allergen. It often leads to relief of the allergy symptoms long after the treatment is stopped."

"Like a cure?" I ask.

She pauses. "I hesitate to call it that," she says, hedging. "It's more of a management system — a way to keep the allergy under control, desensitize someone enough that they can tolerate whatever they're allergic to." She looks to make sure I'm clear on the difference. I nod. "Now they're doing it for food allergies — things like peanut butter and eggs. It's an oral therapy, where they give the patient a small amount of peanut butter or whatever they're allergic to daily, building up their tolerance over time. Early studies have shown some promise."

"OK. What does that have to do with me?"

"Well, Dr. Benefield believed — and I agree with him — that you have some sort of genetic mutation" — at the word "mutation," I'm surprised to find I don't cringe, like I used to; I think of Aja, and my lips turn up — "causing you to be absent one of the millions of proteins all humans have, which is the one you're likely allergic to."

"Right — but you said there was no way

to tell which one it was."

"Well, that wasn't exactly true. Genetic sequencing *could* tell us, but twelve years ago it would have cost millions of dollars and taken several years, if not decades, to try and sequester a single protein."

My heart starts thumping against my rib cage. "And now?"

"It's cheaper. A little faster."

"How much faster?"

"I think we could find it in a year. Or less."

"And when you find it —"

"We'd isolate the protein. Make a solution containing very minute amounts of it, and give it to you every day, in the hopes that you build up a tolerance. That your body stops fighting it."

I sit back in the chair, my heart thundering in my ears. A cure. OK, a "management system." But still. I shake my head a little, not fully believing it. "What's the catch?"

She sticks her pen behind her ear like my mom used to do with a single cigarette. "No catch. But you need to be aware it may not work. And it is still expensive. You'd have to agree to be part of my ongoing research. I'd need to clear it with the department, write a paper on it for a journal. Unless you've got hundreds of thousands of dollars lying around."

I grunt. "Not exactly."

"I didn't think so," she says, but not un-kindly.

We stare at each other as I consider her offer. This is the moment I dreamed of so often in my childhood. A doctor saying there was a treatment — at least a chance at one anyway — instead of looking at me like they wanted to slice me up and put me in a petri dish for further study to assuage their selfish curiosity. So then, why am I not thrilled? Beside myself with excitement? Why does the heartbeat thudding in my ears feel more like fear than elation? "Thank you, Dr. Zhang," I say, looking her squarely in the eyes. "But I believe I'm going to need to think about it."

At the library that afternoon, while I'm sort-ing returns, my body feels numb, like it's just going through the motions. I wonder if this is a symptom of shock. I can't believe there's a treatment — an honest-to-god treatment — that might help me. I feel a buzz in my stomach just thinking of it — a hint of excitement blossoming.

But it's overshadowed by a stronger emo-tion — fear, which seems to have morphed from just run-of-the-mill anxiety in Dr. Zhang's office to downright terror. And I have to ask myself the question I've been dancing around since I left the doctor's office: do I really *want* to be cured? Sure, I used to dream of it as a child, what it would be like to be *normal,* to be hugged, to play on the playground with others at recess. But what do children know? Maybe sitting on the sidelines kept me from breaking my neck on the monkey bars. Maybe this allergy has actually spared me this whole time. Maybe it's the thing — the only thing — that's kept me from getting hurt.

I stop sorting when I come to a book that's obviously been dropped in a bathtub. Its pages are swollen and rippled, and to add insult to injury, the cover is punctured with teeth marks. I can't believe someone just dropped it in the return box without saying anything. I look around for Louise to show her and ask what I should do about it, but she's nowhere to be seen. When my gaze passes over the children's section, Roger looks up and makes eye contact.

"Where's Louise?" I mouth, and he extends the index finger on his raised hand toward the stacks — specifically, a row behind the computer carrels. I look in that direction but don't see her. The computer seats themselves are nearly empty, save for Michael, the pillow golfer, who's always there (I thought Louise was exaggerating, but he really does come every day), and an older woman with thick glasses and a thicker turkey jowl sitting just inches from her screen.

I walk toward the stack Roger pointed at, and when I turn the corner, Louise is there, bent at the waist, her head poked in the shelf between two rows of books. "Louise?" I say. She jerks and smacks her head on the ceiling of the shelf. "Ouch," she says, and then, still bent over, cuts her eyes toward me, putting her pointer finger to her lips. She motions me over with the same hand. I move toward her.

"What are you doing?" I whisper.

"Look," she mouths, pointing to the space on the shelf between the books. I bend over and peer through it, taking in the back of the older woman's head at the computer carrel. Up close, her hair is thin, large swaths of her scalp apparent through the wisps of dull white locks, which have carefully been curled and teased in what I imagine was an attempt to create a fuller appearance.

I look back at Louise, not understanding.

"Look at her *screen,*" she whispers, emphasizing her words by stabbing her finger back at the hole on each syllable.

I turn back and shift my head so that I can see past the woman's bouffant.

"Oh!" The exclamation inadvertently escapes my lips when I realize what I'm seeing is a close-up of a naked male. Specifically, his pelvic region.

Louise's pursed lips are set in a self-satisfied I-told-you-so line. "It's porn, right?" she whispers.

"How should *I* know?" I whisper back. My gaze returns to the screen, like it's a gruesome car wreck and I'm unable to resist staring. I tilt my head for a better angle. "I don't know," I say. "Are those *labels*? It looks kind of clinical."

"Well. It's against the rules, anyway. We can't have private parts up on the computers. What if a child walks by?"

I see her point. "I've got a book I need you to look at," I whisper. "Totally damaged."

She waves me away. "I'll look at it when I get back to the desk."

I stand there a minute longer, something else niggling me. "Listen, remember what you said a while back? About the city council cutting funding?"

"What about it?" she says, not taking her eyes off the screen.

I swallow and then get straight to the

point. "Am I going to get fired?"

She turns to look at me, her eyes glistening with sympathy. "The truth?"

"Yeah."

"Probably," she says, scrunching her nose in apology. "Last one hired, first one fired and all that. Honestly, I was surprised Maryann hired you. That position has been open for four months. I figured we couldn't afford to fill it. And if they cut funding again, we definitely can't afford it."

I pause, taking this in — why *did* they hire me? It's not like I was overwhelmingly qualified.

"What can we do? What can *I* do? I can't lose this job," I say, trying to keep my voice still hushed to match hers.

She shrugs. "I don't know. Figure out a way to fill this place wall-to-wall with bodies every day? Prove to Frank Stafford that this library is wanted — is *needed* — by the people of Lincoln."

"But it is! Every town needs a library."

"Well *we* know that. But our circulation numbers tell a different story," she whispers. And then adds an octave lower: "Although I doubt he even knows how to read them, to tell you the truth."

I ignore that and mull over the two most important bits she's said: we need more books being checked out, and we need more bodies coming in. I'm glad that I had the forward thinking to invite Aja to come to the library every day. But he's just one body. How am I going to get more?

The door opens and we both turn to look. A man shuffles in. A Tuesday regular, Louise calls him the TP Thief, as she once caught him trying to steal toilet paper out of the men's room. She thinks he's homeless — and from the looks of his dirty threadbare coat and the god-awful stench emanating off it, I think she's right. He heads straight for the bathroom.

Right behind him is Aja. He takes a few steps forward and stands on the brown runner at the entryway, as if he's waiting for an invitation to come in farther. A sort of silent acknowledgment passes between us, and then he breaks the gaze, lopes off toward a computer carrel on the other side of the aisle I'm standing in, and dumps his book bag to the ground beside an empty seat.

"Anyway, look, you have to go tell her," Louise says, still whispering.

"Tell who what?"

"This lady," she says, nodding through the stacks. "She can't be looking at that stuff."

"Why *me*?" I squeak, failing to moderate my voice.

Louise's brows jerk up. "Shh," she says.

"You're the one that found her," I whisper, but Louise is already halfway back down the aisle, her hips swiveling with the speed of her gait.

Crap.

As I walk up to the woman and try to gently explain library policy, my face growing red, I feel someone's eyes on me. I turn and my gaze meets Michael's. His mouth cracks into a smile, which he tries to cover with his hand, before he turns back to his computer screen. Great — even the pillow golfer is laughing at me.

At six forty-five, Louise appears beside me, coat on, keys in hand. "I know it's my turn, but can you lock up tonight?" she asks.

I dip my head toward where Aja is still sitting. "Yeah, I've got to wait for his dad to get here anyway. I told him I'd watch him."

"Oh. I didn't realize anyone was still . . . wait . . . you did what?" She narrows her eyes.

"You said we need more bodies," I say, offering her my most charming smile.

"Yeah, but we're not a babysitting service."

"Well, no. But we're not a homeless shelter or a video game arcade either," I say, nodding in the direction of the TP Thief, who's currently browsing the DVD section, and then toward Michael, the pillow golfer at his standard computer carrel. "You said yourself, the job's books *and* community service."

Her eyebrows disappear beneath the gray-ish curtain of fringe on her forehead. "True," she says. "I guess as long as you don't mind." She glances at her watch. "I've got to go. My oldest granddaughter's got bingo night at school and I promised I'd be there. Ends in thirty minutes."

I look at her, wondering how many grand-kids she's got. And then I wonder why I've never thought to ask.

After she leaves, I clean the circulation desk, rehoming the stray pencils, paper clips, rubber bands, and other office sup-plies, and then sit there, glancing at the clock. Six fifty-one. I drum my fingers on the laminate surface and then stand up.

I mosey over near the computer carrels and pretend to be looking for a book on the shelf next to Aja.

"So why'd your mom name you Jubilee?"

I jump, his voice startling me, and turn to look at him.

"Do you think she was a big X-Men fan?"

"Ah, no. Definitely not," I say. Every year on my birthday, my mom told the story of her labor with me. *Thirty-five hours. It was hell. You fought and fought and then at the end when it was time to push — long after that damned epidural wore off — you were trying to come out forehead first, and the cord was wrapped around your neck and the doctor had to go in and grab and pull. Like there was enough room in there for his hands, too! Most pain I've ever experienced. I was so goddamned glad when you were finally out and it was over. Pure joy. That's what I was going to name you. Joy. But then one of the nurses said it was like a jubilee, a reason to celebrate, or something like that. And I thought it sounded fancier. If Joy's on a wedding invitation, you might get a Kmart gift, but Jubilee? That's a Neiman Marcus name. High-end.*

That's how I got my name. She was so joyful to be rid of me. So happy I wasn't causing her problems anymore. But I don't want to tell Aja that.

So I lie.

"Mom was so happy I was finally there. In her arms. And 'jubilee' means 'a joyful celebration.' "

Aja nods. "That makes sense."

"What about you? Why'd your parents name you Aja?"

He's quiet for so long that I wonder if he's

311

heard me. And then softly, he says: "They didn't."

"What?"

"That's not my real name."

"What's your real name?"

He shakes his head.

"Come on, it can't be that bad."

He mutters something.

"What?"

"Clarence," he says, fixing his eyes on me. "It's Clarence."

I try not to laugh, but a small giggle falls out. Aja narrows his eyes at me and I try to compose myself. "Why on earth did they name you Clarence?"

"My dad wanted me to have an American name," he says. "To fit in."

At that, the laughter bubbles over. "With *Clarence*?"

"Yeah," he says, the left side of his mouth turning up. "Terrible, huh?"

"The worst!" I say, still laughing. "I'm sorry. But that is pretty bad."

When I finally calm down, I say: "So how'd you end up with Aja?"

He shrugs. "It's a nickname. From my mom. When I was born, she was trying to learn Sanskrit. My dad's parents are Hindu —"

"Wait, so Eric isn't your —"

312

He shakes his head. "He adopted me, when . . ." But he doesn't finish the sentence. He just looks down at the carpet, shoulders hunched. When I first saw them, I suspected that Eric wasn't his biological dad, what with Aja's slight British accent that Eric doesn't share — not to mention the difference in their appearance: Aja's bronze skin and dark eyes versus Eric's sandy complexion and green eyes — but I didn't know for sure. It was possible Eric's ex-wife was responsible for passing along those characteristics. But at the revelation, my heart breaks a little for Aja, at the same time that it swells a little for Eric. At this further affirmation of his genuine goodness in character.

"I'm sorry," I say, not wanting Aja to dwell on the obviously devastating event, whatever it was that happened to his parents. "So your mom — she was learning Sanskrit?"

He's quiet for a moment longer and I wonder if I've lost him. But then his small voice continues. "She was hoping it would make them like her more. She wanted to be able to talk to them, to show she was putting in such an effort to learn about their culture, or something."

"She was learning to speak it? I thought Sanskrit was just a written language."

"It is mostly, but I think actually some Hindu priests still use it and it's the official language of Uttarakhand in India, where my grandparents were born. Anyway, she said I used to make this noise when I was a baby — not a cry but like this high-pitched mewing sound. Like a baby goat. And the word for 'goat' in Sanskrit is —"

" '*Aja,*' " I say.

"Yep." He looks down again, kicking an invisible wall with his toe. "So my name is really Goat."

I chuckle. "It's better than Clarence."

"Quite," he says formally, eliciting another smile from me. He turns back to his comic book and I take it as a signal our conversation is over. I start to walk back to the desk, find something else to do until Eric arrives.

"I Googled you."

I stop. Turn back to him. "You did?"

"Yeah."

I cock my head. "How'd you know my last name?"

He shrugs. "It's on the library website."

"It is?"

He nods. "I can't believe you were in the *New York Times,*" he says, his eyes wide. "That's like the biggest newspaper ever."

It's my turn to shrug.

"You're lucky," he says.

314

"It's not really that big a deal. It was just one article."

"No, I mean, to not have to touch anybody. I hate being touched. Especially by strangers. You know, like when someone coughs and then they want to shake your hand afterward?" He pulls a face. "No, thank you. But you don't have to deal with that."

"Yeah, I guess not."

He looks back down, like he said all he wanted to say and *that's* the end of our conversation. I glance over his shoulder.

"Is that a comic book?"

"Yes," he says, without taking his eyes off it.

"X-Men?"

"Of course."

I wait a few beats, not wanting to bother him, but I don't have any other work to do, and I'm curious. Not about the comic book, really. But about him. He's different. So matter-of-fact. Always says what he's thinking. I like that.

"What's it about?"

But before he can answer, the door opens and Eric rushes in. "I'm here! I'm here," he says. "I'm sorry I'm late." Flushed pink from the cold, his cheeks have a ruddy, almost boyish quality.

I glance at the clock. It's only 7:05.

"S'ok," I say, still smiling from my conversation. "We were just" — I look back at Aja, but he's reabsorbed in the comic book — "ah, talking." I straighten up from where I've been leaning against a stack and start walking toward the break room to get my coat. I'm not sure if I'm imagining it or if I can actually feel Eric's eyes on me. And if I'm warm because I'm self-conscious or because his gaze feels like the sun.

"Aja, you ready, bud?" he says as I reach the break room.

When I come out a few minutes later, they're both standing by the front door. Aja's got his coat on, his head hanging down, but Eric is looking at me.

I pick the keys up from the desk and walk toward them.

"Thank you," he says. "For doing this."

"It's really no trouble."

He nods. "Still." He turns to the door and opens it, allowing a blast of cold air to rush in. I click off the lights, turn to make sure I haven't missed any, and then scoot through the door that Eric is holding into the dark night. I step to the side while he lets it fall closed and then move to lock it under his watchful eye, while Aja heads to the car.

"So," I say, trying to shake off the feeling

that I'm under a spotlight. "Did we finish? With the *Notebook* discussion?"

He laughs. "I think I was done when you compared it to Shakespeare," he says. "Seriously, though, people don't really talk that way to each other."

"It's based on a true story," I say lamely. His left eyebrow is an arrow pointing to his hairline.

He sighs as we walk to get my bike from the rack. "I guess I'm worried that Ellie loved it so much — that it sets up this crazy standard for love and relationships that doesn't really exist."

I consider this. I don't know anything about love and relationships, but I do know that books and movies can create unrealistic expectations. After reading *Pippi Longstocking* as a child, I became convinced my dad would just show up at the front door one day with some plausible explanation of why he'd been gone my entire life — maybe marooned on a South Seas island like Captain Longstocking. And yes, it was depressing when I was old enough to accept the truth. But then I think what life would be like without these fantasies. These hopes.

"I don't know," I say. "Isn't childhood the time to be idealistic? The time to dream? She'll have plenty of time to be a cynic when she grows up."

He lifts his chin. "How do you do that?"

"What?"

"Take everything I think and turn it on its ear."

My throat tightens at the compliment — at least, I think it's a compliment, because of the way he's looking at me. And I realize it's not just like I'm normal, the way he's looking at me. It's like I'm reciting five hundred decimal points of pi from memory. Like I'm a marvel. Just for saying what I think. My gut clenches and then flips, and I look down at the black tar of the parking lot. Specks of it twinkle like diamonds under the street lamp. And I wonder if this is what people mean when they say they're falling for somebody. That it feels like your stomach is actually falling out of your body. I mean, not that I am. Falling for him.

The moon is bright tonight, like a perfectly round lightbulb framed by the car window. Aja notices it too, and because I'm still having trouble looking directly at Eric, I'm relieved when Aja and I fall into a conversation about space travel.

"Did you know the original tapes of the 1969 moon landing were accidentally erased by NASA?" I'm pleased when he says he didn't, and then our discussion devolves into conspiracy theories, mostly about aliens and the Montauk Project, a purported government research project in Long Island similar to Area 51, which he seems to know a lot about for a ten-year-old.

When Eric pulls into the driveway, I finally garner the courage to turn to him. "What's next?"

My question interrupts his thoughts and he looks at me blankly for a second before responding.

"Oh, um . . . some Stephen King book," he says.

I pause. "Which one? I don't do horror."

He laughs. "Well, my daughter does. She's read three of his — *Carrie, Misery* . . . and another one. I think it's a woman's name."

"*Dolores Claiborne*?"

"Yeah, that sounds right."

"Let's do that one. It's more of a psychological thriller."

"There's a difference?"

I laugh at his confused look. "Yes."

"OK, do you have a copy at the library? I'll check it out tomorrow." We get out of the car at the same time, and he walks to the trunk to get my bike out.

"I'm sure we do," I say. "And I think I've got a copy somewhere. I'll look tonight."

"In those massive piles in there?" he asks,

nodding toward my house. "You're actually going to attempt to *move* them? You'll get buried alive."

"Ha-ha," I say. "Very funny."

"I'm serious," he calls over his shoulder as he walks my bike up to the gate. "Those stacks could topple over at any time." He sets it down and walks back toward me. "If you're not at work tomorrow, I'm calling a search party."

I smile up at him, aware of the two feet of space between us and my conflicting feelings regarding it — how it feels like not nearly enough and entirely too much at the same time. "Thanks for the ride," I say, and turn to walk up the path toward the front porch. My stomach flips again and I put my hand on it to steady it. And then I remind myself, as I'm fitting the key in the lock, that it's the exact same way I felt when Donovan leaned in to kiss me so many years ago.

Right before I almost died.

Seventeen

Eric

The dynamics of the ride home have changed, now that Aja is with us. And I remember why a threesome of children never worked on the playground — someone is always left out. In the car, that person is me. When Aja isn't plugged into his iPad, he and Jubilee talk. Constantly. About strange things, things that I've never heard of, and I don't even know if they're real, like anatidaephobia, the irrational fear that no matter where you are, you're being watched by a duck. Aja laughed so hard at that in the backseat, he was doubled over, clutching his belly in pain.

They talk so much, our conversations have dwindled to hello, yes-or-no questions, and her reply of "Tomorrow" every time I drop her and the bike off and say, "See you tomorrow?"

So it doesn't make sense then that I find

myself eager for the day to end. That my limbs feel lighter the closer I get to the library. That with her — even when she's talking about ducks — is where I most want to be.

Friday is no different. The entire ride home, they're on the topic of inventions, although it's more trading facts than a conversation.

"The lady who invented chocolate chip cookies sold the idea to Nestlé for a dollar."

"Bubble wrap was an accident. They were trying to make three-D wallpaper."

"The inventor of the Fender Stratocaster didn't even know how to play guitar."

It's like there's an extra pocket in their brains where they tuck away useless facts like someone keeping a snotty tissue up their sleeve in the event they may need it again.

By the time we reach Jubilee's house, it occurs to me I won't see her again until Monday, and the thought tugs at me. She reaches for the door handle. "I finished *Dolores Claiborne*," I blurt out. It's not exactly true, I'm only halfway done.

Her hand pauses. "What'd you think?"

"I wouldn't want to be the one to piss her off."

She laughs.

"So, do you wanna —" My lips are dry, and I dampen the bottom one with a quick flick of my tongue. "I know it's the weekend, but maybe we could — I don't know. Get together. Talk about it."

She directs her gaze at the darkened windows of her house, as if the answer will be taped on one of the panes. "Um . . . yeah," she says. "Sure. Do you want to come over tomorrow? I don't — I'm off work."

"Yeah, great," I say. "That's great. I'll bring lunch. It's a date."

"OK," she says, then slips out of the car. In what has now become routine, I get out, collect her bike from the trunk, deposit it behind the gate, and then make sure she's securely in the house before I get back in the car and put it in reverse.

"Did you just ask her on a *date*?" Aja pipes up from the backseat.

"No. No, of course not. She's just helping me with . . . something."

"Oh," Aja says, and turns his attention back to his game.

As soon as we get to Jubilee's on Saturday, Aja slinks over to the armchair, slips his earbuds in, and starts tapping on the screen of his iPad, leaving Jubilee and me to stand awkwardly staring at each other. For once,

I'm thankful for that stupid machine and the opportunity it's affording me to talk to her alone.

"Want some tea? Coffee?" she asks.

"Yeah, coffee would be great," I say, even though I've already had two cups this morning and really shouldn't have more. But I'm leaning closer to just admitting defeat on my cutting-back plan. I swipe my wool beanie off with my free hand. In the other, I'm carrying a paper sack of hoagies. I go to offer it to her, but she turns and walks out of the back doorway of the room. I watch her leave, wondering if I should just sit and wait, when she calls out: "You can come back here."

I follow her voice through the den into an outdated kitchen with eighties appliances and yellowed wallpaper lined with cherries. Jubilee's standing at the counter, her back to me. I try not to notice the way the sun coming through the window highlights the reddish gold in her hair. Or how the locks fall down her back, reaching nearly to the dip of her waist. The way she's got all her weight on one foot, causing her rounded hip to jut out, the curve of her . . .

"How do you take it?" she asks over her shoulder.

I clear my throat. "Um . . . black is fine."

She turns with the mug in her hand and gestures for me to sit at the small table. I set the sack down in front of me and she places the mug in front of that. I stare at her gloves, as they seem to be the safest place to train my gaze. Why in God's name does she always have those blasted things on?

"So." She slides into the seat across from me. "*Dolores Claiborne.*"

"*Dolores Claiborne*," I echo. The table is small — a two-foot-wide circle. A sweetheart table, I think they call them, and now I know why. Because you're sitting so close to the person you're with. So close that if you reach out, just a few inches, you could be touching.

"What'd your daughter think of it?"

"I don't know," I say. "She liked this one line."

"Let me guess — the one about how being a bitch is sometimes the only thing a woman has to hold on to?"

"No," I say, reaching in my back pocket for the notebook that I folded over and stuck there, and flip to the right entry. "*I understood something else, too — that one kiss didn't change a thing. Anyone can give a kiss, after all.*"

"Hmm," Jubilee says, sitting back.

"Yeah, that was my reaction, too. I mean, do you think she's already kissing people? Boys?"

"Well, she's fourteen."

"*Only* fourteen," I say. "Were you kissing people at fourteen?"

"No," she says quietly, looking down at the table. She's blushing so fiercely, I immediately feel bad for asking the question.

After a few seconds of silence, I grab the paper sack. "I brought hoagies," I say.

She stands up and retrieves plates and napkins from the cabinet. I take a sandwich out to Aja and put it on the coffee table in front of him. He doesn't even look up.

When I return to the kitchen, Jubilee says: "That quote's pretty derisive. Doesn't sound like you need to be so worried about her romanticizing love."

Her words hit me in the gut and I realize Jubilee was right — I would rather Ellie be an idealist when it comes to love than a cynic. And I'm worried that if she already is a cynic, that it's my fault. How can a kid believe in love when her own parents ran out of it?

"So which one are you reading next?" Jubilee asks while we eat. "*Carrie* or *Misery*?"

"I don't know."

"You should ask her. See what she thinks."

I let out a small, sad chuckle. "Yeah. I don't think that — I'm not sure that will work." Jubilee cocks her head beside me. I know I need to tell her the truth.

"Ellie's not talking to me. She hasn't, for, oh" — I do the math in my head and cringe — "six months now. Except for one text, essentially telling me to leave her alone."

"Oh," she says, and I wonder what she's thinking. Or rather, I know what she's thinking, what she has to be thinking, and I hate it. "Why?"

The million-dollar question. I don't know how I'm going to answer it until my mouth opens and the words fall out.

"I called her a slut." As painful as it is to admit, it's such a relief to say it, to unburden myself of the terrible secret. To confess. I have a sudden and unexpected flash of insight into Stephanie's weekly visits to her priest for her own admissions of guilt.

"You *what?*" Jubilee's eyes go wide. "Your daughter?"

"Yeah, it wasn't my finest moment." I take another bite of my sandwich and chew, carefully, as if I'm counting the bites until I get the requisite thirty before swallowing. Jubilee just stares at me, waiting.

I turn my ear toward the den, but all I hear is Aja's faint tapping on the screen. I let out a puff of breath. "About a year ago, Ellie started hanging out with this girl, Darcy. She was just one of those kids, a troublemaker, broken home, the whole bit — the kind you hope your child never aligns themselves with." Although saying it out loud, I now see the irony — Ellie's from a broken home, too. "Anyway, in our small town, the rumor mill was rife with accusations about Darcy — she hit on male teachers, was into drugs — not just weed, but harder stuff, like oxy and Ritalin. I mean, I know that kids can be cruel and that rumors are just that . . . rumors. But there were so many — there had to be some truth behind them. So on my weekends with Ellie, I wouldn't let her hang out with Darcy. It's something Stephanie and I didn't see eye to eye on — she took this whole 'kids will be kids' approach, 'you have to give them room to experiment.' I think it was a backlash to Stephanie's own strict upbringing. It infuriated me. We'd have these massive fights about it.

"One weekend when Ellie was with me, I thought she was in her room, listening to her headphones — she always had them on. And I was fighting with Stephanie about not letting Ellie go to Darcy's birthday party. She had apparently already said yes without discussing it with me, which pissed me off. Then she asked me why I had to be so controlling all the time. I got carried away and yelled: *Because our only daughter is becoming a drug-addled slut just like Darcy, and you don't seem to care about it.*"

Jubilee sucks in her breath. "Ouch."

"And when I turned around —"

"Ellie was there."

I nod. "She heard the entire thing. Well, enough, anyway." I shake my head. I'll never forget the look in her eyes. It was pain, not the familiar flare of anger I was used to seeing. Anger I could handle, but hurt — and knowing I was responsible for it — was gut-wrenching. "I apologized immediately, of course, but she wouldn't listen. Told me she was going to pack her things and wanted to go back to her mother's. I wouldn't drive her, I couldn't let her go without her understanding, or at least forgiving me. But finally, on Saturday, when I realized it was hopeless and keeping her there was making her even more angry at me, I drove her back to Stephanie's. She hasn't talked to me since."

"But don't you have some kind of custody agreement?"

I sit back in my seat and swipe my hand down my face before answering. "Every other weekend. I gave Stephanie full custody, because I didn't want Ellie to be shuffled around. I knew stability was more important for her. But after I said . . . what I said, she didn't want to come anymore, and I felt like forcing her would only make it worse. And honestly, I thought she'd come around. I know what I said was horrible, but she's a kid. I'm her dad." I shrug. "I guess too much damage was done. She already hated me for the divorce."

I pick up the hoagie again, and Jubilee does the same. We sit there, listening to each other chew, until the silence becomes unbearable. Part of me wants to know what she's thinking, but part of me is terrified to hear the truth.

"That really sucks," she says, finally. "But if it makes you feel any better, you've still got my father beat."

I try to recall if I'd seen any pictures of a man that could possibly be him on the walls or among her stacks of books. I can't. "Where is your dad?"

She shrugs. "I don't even know *who* he was. My mom never told me."

I take this in. "Oh, good," I say, trying to lighten the mood. "So I'm not the *worst* father in the world, just the second worst."

"Exactly. See? Chin up."

330

I chuckle and pick up my mug. While I take a sip of coffee, I watch Jubilee out of the corner of my eye, my gaze traveling to her lips. I follow the curve of them, my eyes the wheeled cart on a roller coaster, rising in the peaks, dipping in the valley between. They're beautiful. Her lips. And I wonder at the thought that she gets to see them every day, every time she looks in a mirror, a car window reflection. How does she tear her eyes away?

It's then that I notice the mayonnaise — a little glob clinging to the corner of her mouth.

I reach my hand out, thumb extended to wipe it for her, puerilely excited at this unexpected opportunity to touch her. Jubilee freezes, eyeing me.

"You've got a —"

At the last second, she jerks her head back just out of my reach and puts her own hand up to her mouth, leaving my thumb hanging in midair, dejected. "A little mayo," I say, bringing my hand back to my own lip, mirroring for her where she should wipe.

Her cheeks turn pink, flushed, making my breath catch in my throat, as she dabs at the greasy glob with a napkin.

"Did I get it?" she asks.

I nod.

We sit there for a minute, staring at each other.

And then, because I can't stop myself — or because I don't want to anymore — I reach out again, overcome with the need to close the distance between us, to connect with her somehow. She freezes again, the muscles in her shoulders tensing, but this time, I don't care. My hand finds a lock of her hair. I gently wind my fingers around it, in it, swaddling them in the soft hammock of curls, my gaze now lost in the endless auburn currents.

I hear a sharp intake of breath, and it brings me back to myself. I'm invading her space, being too bold. Suddenly embarrassed by my lack of control, my ragged breath, I drop her hair like it's on fire and straighten my spine. But before I can apologize, before I can find the words in my muddled brain to explain my bizarre actions, she catches my wrist with her hand. Her grip is strong and I swear I can feel the heat of her fingers through the material of her gloves. I meet her gaze again. And out of my peripheral vision, I see her chest heaving, inhales and exhales as ragged as my own.

And then her lips part. And it's the only invitation I need.

My left hand captive, I lean toward her, bringing my free hand up to palm her cheek, already imagining the sweet relief of my mouth on —

"*Stop!*" The high screech does just that. Stops me cold. I turn — my hand inches from her face, my head a jumble of confused desire — and I see Aja standing in the door frame, eyes wide, his mouth forming words I'm trying to follow.

"You can't touch her! Move your hand, move your hand!" He's pulling at my arm now, shrieking. Is he having some kind of episode? I stand up, grabbing him by the shoulders, trying to get him to look at me, to calm down. But he doesn't. He just keeps screaming, his panic mounting on itself, until he finally reaches what appears to be the chilling climax of his confusing, delusional rant: "You'll *kill* her!"

EIGHTEEN

JUBILEE

I sit there, too stunned to move. He was going to kiss me. At least I think he was, the way he was reaching for me like that. Admittedly, I'm lacking experience in these matters. But his hand was halfway to my face and he was leaning toward me, just like they do in the movies — even though I grabbed his hand, was trying to stop him from touching me. And then Aja screaming . . . I try to focus on what's happening in front of me.

"I'm not making it up! I swear! Ask her," Aja says.

They both turn to me. I realize I've missed most of the conversation, but I can fill in the spaces. Aja's eyes drop when I look at him. "Sorry," he mumbles. "I know I wasn't supposed to tell anyone."

Eric looks from him back to me, a quizzical expression on his face. "Jubilee — what is he talking about?"

I feel hot all over and I suddenly wish I could disappear. Or that they would. What was I *thinking*? Letting them into my life like this. My *house*. Letting Eric nearly kiss me? Like I'm just some normal person.

My face burns with humiliation and it's like I've been transported back to the high school courtyard where Donovan kissed me and all I can hear is the laughter of what feels like a hundred gleeful teens shrieking in my ear.

I can't believe you kissed her!

You earned *this fifty bucks, dude.*

What a total freak show.

Ugh. What's happening to her face?

"Jubilee?" Eric's face comes back into view and I hate how he's looking at me. With a mixture of confusion and pity and . . . I don't know — like he doesn't know me at all. And my humiliation from then and now is getting all mixed up and my face is on fire and my heart is thumping in my ears and I just want it all to be over.

I stand up, my knees knocking into the chair behind me, sending it crashing to the ground.

"You should leave."

"What?" Eric's eyebrows knit together, and then his face morphs from concern to absolute bewilderment. "Why?"

"I want you to go!" I yell it this time, hoping the volume will conceal any other emotion coming through. I cross my arms, trying to swallow past a lump the size of a golf ball in my throat.

He stands there for a second more, eyes burning into me, questioning.

"Jubilee," he says, his voice quiet but insistent.

I don't respond. I don't waver.

"OK," he says, finally. "OK. We'll go. Come on, Aja." He tries to put a hand on Aja's shoulder, to guide him out of the kitchen, but Aja jerks him off. They shuffle out single file, and when I finally hear the door open and then close with a thudding click, I bend over the table, grasping the edge of it, my chest heaving, hot tears rimming my eyes.

I stand there like that — relieved that they're gone, yet hoping they'll come back — until my knuckles start to ache and my knees feel like they're going to buckle. Then I slowly right the chair that tipped over and sit in it, shoulders slumped, surveying the scene in front of me. The two plates. Two coffee mugs. Two crumpled napkins. To anyone else, it would be a normal sight — the aftermath of two people having lunch at a kitchen table. But for me, it's a peculiar and painful reminder that for the first time in nine years, someone was here — and now he's gone.

Sometime while the afternoon morphed into evening, my humiliation morphed into a vague sense of anger. But I can't pinpoint just what it is that I'm angry at. Donovan? Those heartless kids? Eric for leaving, even though that's exactly what I told him to do? Me for telling him to leave?

Lying in bed, I picture Eric's face as it leaned toward me and focus on another question: was he really going to kiss me? I keep rolling the moment over in my mind, replaying the look on his face, the leaning, Aja's scream, until the realization of what's bothering me about it materializes. I sit straight up. I wanted him to kiss me — in the split second where I thought that's what he was trying to do. And what does that say about me? That I have some kind of bizarre death wish?

I turn toward the nightstand, where Eric's coffee mug sits. When I was cleaning up earlier, I couldn't bring myself to wash it. Or put it down. So I brought it into my room, like a souvenir from an airport gift shop. Now I stare at the rim where Eric's mouth was touching it just hours before and resist the urge to bring it to my lips. What is *wrong* with me? I tear my eyes from it, turn off the lamp, and lie down in the dark. But as sleep overtakes me, the truth slips into my brain. That maybe some things are bigger than a fear of death. Like the fear of never again being looked at the way Eric was looking at me. Like for that entire second in time, I was the only person who mattered.

"Why aren't you dressed?" It's Sunday evening and Madison is on my front porch. Though I figured she'd give up if I let her knock long enough, she didn't and I reluctantly opened the door.

"I'm not going," I say, my mortification from the day before still so fresh, I'm positive she'll be able to see it on my face.

She doesn't.

"Back up, I'm coming in," she says. With no other choice, I jump out of the way, and Madison charges into the den. Then she looks around, taking it in. I expect her to make some smart-alecky comment about all the books but instead she says, "When did you guys move here again?"

"About twelve years ago."

"And how much did your mom pay for

this place?"

"I don't know — like two thirty, I think. Why?"

"Because it's probably worth like three times that now."

"Oh," I say, because I don't care about this house right now, or her real estate interests; all I care about is getting back in my bed and pretending the day before didn't happen.

"So, what's your problem?" she says, dropping her bag on the ground. "And don't tell me it's a long story. You know I'll get it out of you."

"Come on in," I mutter, shutting the door behind her. I follow her into the living room and, not wanting to slip my gloves on, I perch myself as far away from her as I can on the armchair while she gets situated on the couch.

"Go on. Spill it," she says.

So I do. I tell her about Eric and the mayo on my lip and the almost-kiss and Aja screaming and —

"Wait, wait, wait," she says, holding up a hand. "He was going to kiss you? And you were going to *let* him?"

"That doesn't — It's all beside the point. What matters is that Aja was totally freaking out. And then I kind of freaked out —

and I basically kicked them out of my house. I guess."

"Um, it's not 'beside the point.' It kind of seems like the whole point, actually. Are you into this guy?"

"What? No!" I say. "Why would you — That's ridiculous."

She narrows her eyes and I can tell she doesn't believe me.

"OK — I think he's . . ." What *do* I think about Eric? That he's sometimes solemn and earnest, but then surprisingly funny when you least expect it. He's smart, in a terribly logical way. And he's also caring, endearingly so, especially when it comes to his kids. I just like being around him. Maybe more than I'll even admit to myself. "I think he's . . . neat," I say, finally.

" 'Neat'?" she shrieks. "What — is he a tailored suit? A reorganized closet? Are you eleven?" She dissolves into laughter.

"Stop it," I say, although I can't help but chuckle along with her. "OK, fine, I like him. I don't know — he makes me feel . . . warm."

"Oh good, we've upgraded him to a coat. A winter furnace."

The sun, I think. But I don't want to give Madison any more ammunition. "Can you just be serious for a minute?" I say.

"Yes, yes, sorry." She swipes her hand in front of her face as if magically changing her upturned lips into a straight line. "Serious now." But then she says "neat" again under her breath and throws herself back onto the couch cackling.

"Madison!"

"Jube! I'm sorry. It's just — OK, seriously now." She snickers on and off for a few more seconds and then tries again. "Why didn't you just tell him about your condition? Before now?"

"Yeah, because that's *such* an easy conversation to have."

"Well I think it's an important one — so he doesn't go wiping mayonnaise off your face and accidentally put you in the hospital."

"That's dramatic."

"Well you don't know. You said yourself you never know how your body will react." She fixes me with a serious look. "Come on, why didn't you just tell him?"

"I don't know." I start studying and then picking at a hangnail that's been getting caught on my gloves. "I guess I was afraid he would think I was a freak or something, or not want to be around me anymore."

"Well that's ridiculous. Who wouldn't want to be around you? You're the funniest person I know. Especially when you're on drugs."

"Ha-ha," I say.

"Seriously, though. If you like him — if you *want* to kiss him — don't you think you should at least try out this treatment the doctor was telling you about? Maybe you'd be able to —"

"No," I cut her off. "It's just a shot in the dark. If they can even find the protein — *if* their theory is even right to begin with — there's no guarantee it would even work. And it would take months, if not years, to find out. Anyway, it doesn't even matter. The way I acted yesterday, I'm sure I won't be seeing Eric again anytime soon."

"Yeah, but —"

"Madison, no," I say again, more firmly this time.

After a few minutes of silence, she stands up. "Go. Get dressed," she says, shooing me with her hands. "We're going on our adventure, because I dropped all the kids at Donovan's, even though it's not even his night to take them and I had to listen to him bitch at me for a full twenty minutes about it."

I throw my head back. "Ugh. I really don't want to. Can you at least tell me what it is?"

"The movies."

"The movies? That doesn't sound like much of an adventure."

"But it is! It's a three-D one. With dinosaurs. Did they even *have* three-D movies the last time you went to the theater?"

I stare at her.

"Oh, and the snacks! When's the last time you had movie theater popcorn? It's been at least nine years, I know, which is completely unacceptable."

I sigh. "You are not going to leave unless I do this, are you?"

"No," she says. "It's part of my charm."

At the library Monday afternoon, Louise is in a heightened state of steady panic.

"My son-in-law is gluten-free, my granddaughter hates anything green, and my daughter is now, apparently, a vegetarian — what am I going to make for Thanksgiving? Air?"

She clacks away at the computer, searching for various recipes and muttering under her breath. I add a concerned "Mm-hmm" here and there, but I'm not really paying attention. Aja didn't come today. At four thirty, I told myself his bus was running late. At five thirty, I thought maybe he was sick and stayed home. But now it's almost seven, and I have to accept reality — that I told

Eric and Aja to get out, and they did. And they're not coming back. I know it's for the best, that it's what I wanted, but still.

"Oh great, it's the Cat Sisters," I hear Louise say under her breath, and when I look up, she's already out of her chair and halfway to the back room. I turn my head toward the door. Stalking to the circulation desk are two of the largest women I've ever seen, in height and weight. My eyes widen, not just in surprise, but to take the whole of them in. And then, when they're still about five paces away, it hits me. An unholy stench that smells like a mix between raw sewage and ammonia. I close my mouth to keep from tasting it.

One of the women slams a stack of books onto the desk in front of me, and a flurry of animal hair flies up from the force and settles back down on the counter. Cat hair. Cat Sisters. The nickname is starting to make sense. "You new?" she says in a voice so deep, I look up at her wondering if I mistook their gender. Save for a few coarse whiskers on one's chin and their linebacker statures, they definitely appear to be female. As I study them, I notice their outer clothing — a worn tan overcoat on one and a very large sweater on the other — is covered in cat hair.

"I am," I say, still trying not to breathe.

"Our books come in?" the other woman says, her voice as gruff as her sister's.

"Um, what books are those?" I ask.

"The Winged Dragon series. Special-ordered 'em from Ling Ling."

I continue to stare at her, perplexed.

"You know, that Oriental girl."

I pause, wondering if I should point out how rude it is to call a person of Asian descent Oriental, and then deduce that if they are in the habit of calling Shayna "Ling Ling" — either to her face or behind her back — they probably won't care. I push my chair back, grateful to put space between us. "I'll just go check," I say. The woman's frown deepens and her sister's does too, as if they're of one grumpy mind.

When I enter the back room, I see Louise standing over a box of pastries on the counter leftover from the morning. She has a blueberry scone up to her mouth. Her eyes widen when she sees me and she freezes midbite. "Sorry to leave you so suddenly," she says, crumbs falling to her blouse. "I just needed to, um . . . deal with a library emergency."

"Ha-ha," I say, heading over to the shelf where we keep the books on hold.

"How are the Cat Sisters today?" she asks.

I stare at her. "Um . . . rude."

"Yep. That's them."

"And smelly," I add.

"Isn't it the worst?" She smiles, revealing bits of pastry stuck between her teeth.

Irritated, I don't reply, grabbing three large books that have been rubber-banded together. The cover of the first one has a large fantastical dragon breathing fire over a modern cityscape. I take them back out front and hold them up for the Cat Sisters.

"Found 'em," I say.

"Took you long enough," the one with the overcoat mutters.

I clench my gloved fist and sit down, then take the proffered library card from the sweater-garbed one and start the checkout process. When I hand the books and card back over and they finally leave, I take a deep breath of unpolluted air and stare at the blank computer screen in front of me, trying to part the haze of self-pity that's done nothing but build on itself since the movies.

An ear-piercing screech jerks my head like a marionette to the children's section. A little girl, her head wrapped in neat rows of braids and beads, sits on the floor, howling and clutching her knee. "IT HORTS! IT HORTS!" she says in her childlike speech.

346

"Shh," says her mom, standing over her. "I told you not to run in here. Get up, sweetie, you're fine." That only causes the girl to cry harder. Trying another tactic, the woman's body collapses accordion-style, until she's eye-level with her daughter. "Let Mommy kiss it," she says, gently bringing the girl's leg up to her mouth. The girl whimpers, her hysterics subsiding, and she crawls into her mother's arms. The two of them join like they're playing a child's game of chance: paper covers rock.

Other children in the section carry on, pulling books from shelves. Roger pecks away at his computer keyboard, oblivious to the pair, but I can't tear my eyes away from them. Their flagrant display of affection. The palpable love that courses from mother to child as natural as a river flowing downstream.

My lungs contract in my chest, the giant's fist back to exact his revenge, and I can't —

"Jubilee?"

I look up into Eric's olive eyes and wonder how long he's been standing there.

"Are you OK?" he asks, his face a mask of concern.

And it's the sight of him, the warmth in his voice, that causes water to spring to my lashes, my vision to blur. And I realize that no, I'm not OK. I'm not OK at all.

"My mom died," I say, my voice cracking on the word "died." And then, I feel my face crumple like a poorly made sand castle and I start to sob.

Sitting in the front seat of Eric's car, I blow my nose loudly on a tissue he gave me. We're still in the library parking lot, but I'm not sure exactly how I got here, except that he said he was there to drive me home and it struck me as such an unexpected kindness that I began crying even harder, drawing Louise out of the back room. I assume they exchanged some looks and then someone handed me my coat and bag and I followed Eric out the front door, barely keeping my eyes trained on the back of his coat through my tears.

He's silent for what feels like a record amount of time as I honk and blubber and wail. When I finally begin to calm down, I dab at the flow of snot with the tissue and take a few deep breaths, my shoulders shuddering. Only then does it occur to me to be embarrassed at the spectacle I certainly am.

I glance over at him, sitting stoically in the driver's seat, his left hand clenching and unclenching the steering wheel, his right hand resting calmly on his thigh. I take another deep breath.

"Sorry . . . about . . . um . . . all that," I say, my voice still wobbly.

He turns his head toward me. "No, it's fine," he says. "I'm sorry about your mother."

"Well, it was a couple of months ago." I sniffle and wipe my nose again. "I guess it all just kind of hit me at once. That probably sounds ridiculous."

"No," Eric says. "It doesn't."

We sit in silence for a little longer.

"Were you guys close?" Eric asks.

"Not really. I hadn't seen her in nine years. I kind of hated her, to be honest."

Eric narrows his eyes at me, and I know he's listening, waiting for more.

But how to explain my mom? *She smoked and wore tight blouses and was obsessed with men and money. She made fun of me for sport. She treated me like I was her room-mate.* And that's when I finally put voice to what's been bothering me for so many years.

"It's just . . . she left me." I swallow, trying to soothe my raw throat. "Left me right when I needed her most. Right when —" I think of Donovan and the humiliation, but I know that's not all. It's not what's causing my hands to tremble and my bones to feel hollow. And then the woman and child from the library flash in my mind and my chest splits wide open like a skull hitting pavement. "She never touched me. Ever. Not after I got diagnosed. I mean, I know she couldn't give me regular hugs and kisses. But she could have — I don't know — put on gloves and rubbed my back or patted my head, for Christ's sake! Or . . . or . . . I don't know — wrapped me in a blanket and squeezed me tight."

I know I'm rambling, but I'm a burst pipe now, with no control over my words gushing out. "She acted like I was a pariah. I mean, I was used to that, the kids at school treated me like one, too. But my own *mom.*" Rivulets of tears are falling from my eyes, mixing with the blobs of snot coming from my nose, but I don't care. I wipe my face with my gloved hand and lean my head back on the seat, letting the tears fall, until it doesn't feel like I have any left. I sniff.

"I'm sorry," I say. "I don't know why I'm telling you all this."

He doesn't respond. I glance over at him again, but he's just sitting there, like he's made of bronze or something. Why *am* I telling him all of this? I'm suddenly so embarrassed by my admissions, I want to jump out of the car and pedal my bike far away.

"Will you say something?" I ask.

Eric shifts in his seat and massages his jaw, as if, with a little elbow grease, he could rub the prickly black hair that's sprouted right off his face.

"Soooo . . ." He stops rubbing and turns to me. "You wanted your mom to *suffocate* you?"

I stare at him. I know my thoughts were all over the place, but seriously? That's what he latched on to? But then, a small grin cracks the side of his face. I try to narrow my eyebrows — how could he *joke* about this? But his smile is contagious and I'm powerless to stop myself. A giggle escapes my lips, and then another one. And then I'm full-on laughing and I wonder if I look as manic as I feel.

I try to catch my breath, but my body's on autopilot now, alternating between laughing fits and light sobs, and I have to let it run its course. When I finally start to calm down, I expect Eric to say something else or start the car or do something, but he just sits there, staring out the windshield.

So I sit there too, the silence in the car building until it becomes so deafening, I squirm in my seat, searching for something — anything — to say to break the weird tension that's settled in the air around us. Then

Eric clears his throat.

"You know, one time when Ellie was little — like six months old — I took her over to Dinesh's apartment."

I stare at him. "Dinesh?"

He glances in my direction, as if he's just realized I'm there. "Aja's dad," he says. "My best friend. Well, he *was* my best friend." He turns his gaze back out the windshield.

"Anyway, we were still in college and I wanted to prove to him that fatherhood hadn't changed me — wasn't *going* to change me — so I packed all her stuff in a diaper bag and went over there to watch soccer, like we always did, maybe have a beer or two.

"About halfway through the match, Ellie has this massive blowout. I mean huge. Poop was everywhere. All up her back, over her legs, it was getting all on Dinesh's bedspread where I was trying to change her." Eric chuckles. "I remember he was standing behind me yelling, 'Mate! Mate! Get her off! That's where the magic happens!'

"So I need to wash her off, right? That's the only way I'm getting her clean at this point. I take her into Dinesh's bathroom, sit her in the sink, and turn on the water. It's freezing cold and she starts screaming. I

352

mean, she's so loud and I just want to make it stop and the poop is everywhere, so without really thinking I just turn off the cold and turn on the warm. But I didn't remember that Dinesh's water got hot, like scalding hot, really fast. And then Ellie starts screaming again. And when I realized what I'd done, I snatched her out of the sink, but her skin was already burned. Not third degree or anything, but it turned bright red. I wrapped her, poop and all, in a towel and just held her, telling her over and over again how sorry I was, until she finally started to calm down."

He turns to me again. "What I'm trying to say is, there is nothing worse — I mean nothing — than seeing your child in pain. And knowing you caused it? I still feel the guilt for burning her like that. And I can hear her screams plain as day."

"But she was OK," I say.

Eric nods. "Yeah, thank God. Listen, I don't know your mom. But I do know, if doing something that minor to Ellie made me feel like that, I can't imagine what it would be like to know your actions could cause something worse to happen to your child. And to know that she *did* hurt you, for years, before you got diagnosed. That her just loving you was causing you pain."

He shakes his head.

I stare at him, feeling like Mary when she sees the secret garden for the first time. Eric has given me a perspective I've never considered before — maybe she was so scared of hurting me again that she couldn't bring herself to touch me at all. It sounds so nice, like such a plausible explanation, and I want to believe it with all my might. But I can't get Mr. Walcott out of my head: "If it sounds too good to be true, it probably is."

And then something else occurs to me. I narrow my eyes. "How did you know that? That it took years to get a diagnosis?"

"I, ah . . . Aja showed me that article about you. In the *Times.*"

I look down at my lap, my face getting hot. He starts the car and puts the gearshift in reverse. "He thinks you're famous."

I clear my throat. "Yeah, well, he also thought I was an X-woman or whatever you call them," I say. "He's got quite an imagination."

"Tell me about it," Eric says, pulling out of the library parking lot.

We ride in silence for a minute, until I muster the courage to tell him what I've been thinking. "I, uh, I didn't really expect you to come today."

"Why not?"

"The way I acted on Saturday? I wasn't exactly . . . kind."

He shrugs. "I told you I'd give you a ride home until you get your car fixed. I keep my word."

I nod, unsure how to respond. What did I expect him to say — *I couldn't stay away from you,* like some cheesy line from a movie?

He takes a deep breath and runs his hand through his hair, mussing it even more. "Listen, I'm so sorry. I can't believe I almost . . . well . . ."

I lean forward an inch, my breath held tight. Almost *kissed* me. Say it.

He doesn't.

The awkwardness sits between us — the proverbial elephant in the car.

"Well, I won't . . . I promise I'll keep my distance from now on. You don't have to worry about me."

I sit back, wondering why I'm not relieved by his assurance. "So where's Aja?" I ask, changing the subject. "Why didn't he come today?"

"He had therapy. It's usually on Thursday, but it got changed." Eric glances over at me and sees my raised eyebrows. "It was mandated, from the near-drowning-incident thing. Connie took him. I had a meeting I couldn't get out of."

"Ah."

"I was going to tell you on Saturday, but then . . ."

"Right."

A pause, and then Eric says: "You know, you're really good with him."

"He's a good kid. Smart. And funny! God, that story about how he got his name?"

"The goat thing?" Eric smiles. "Yeah. I couldn't believe Dinesh and Kate named him Clarence. I gave him such a hard time for —" He stops talking abruptly. Turns to me. "Wait. How do you know that story?"

I shift in my seat under his gaze. "He told me."

"He did?"

"Yeah."

He massages the side of his face again and exhales.

"Eric, what's the —"

"He won't talk to me. I mean, really about much of anything, but definitely not about his parents. The one time I tried — well, it didn't go well. I don't know how you do it." He says the last sentence more to himself than to me.

I shrug, wishing I had the answer he's looking for. "I just talk to him."

"No. It's not that." He turns the wheel

356

and exhales again, puffing out his cheeks. "Believe me. I've tried that."

A few minutes later, he pulls the car into my driveway and turns off the ignition. He looks at me, and I wonder if he feels the tension between us. "Are you going to be OK? About your mom, I mean."

"Yeah," I say, nodding. "I will."

He nods. "Well, same time tomorrow?"

"Tomorrow," I agree, opening the door and stepping out into the cold night.

"Hey, Jubilee?"

I still my hand from shutting the door. "Yeah?"

"So we're, um . . . we can be friends?"

My gaze travels from his olive-green eyes to the stubble on his cheeks to his dry lips, and then back up to his eyes.

"Friends," I say, and shut the car door behind me.

I know I should be happy. It's a good thing: I can still have Eric and Aja in my life, and they know about me, so it's safe. But as I unlock the door to my house and walk into the dark den, dropping my bag on the ground, I can't understand why I'm not relieved. Why it feels like each heartbeat is pulsing one specific emotion through my thrumming veins, and it's not happiness. It's disappointment.

Nineteen

Eric

An allergy to people. To *people*! Peanut butter, I've heard of. Bees? Absolutely. I even have a cousin who's allergic to cilantro. But *people*? Even though Aja explained it to me on the way home from her house Saturday, I wouldn't believe it until I saw it in print in that *Times* article. It did explain a lot of things, though. The gloves, for starters. Her sometimes skittish nature. Why she ended up in the hospital after fishing Aja out of the river. She literally risked her life — more than I even knew — to save him. And then . . . god, I can't believe I tried to kiss her.

But what I really can't believe, as I watch her walk up to her front door after dropping her off Monday night, is how much I still want to.

When I get home, Connie's sitting on the couch flipping through a magazine. It's the first time I've had a chance to talk to her in a few days — she was at her office all day Sunday and only had time to answer my text asking if she could take Aja to therapy. Her reply: *Yes. But you owe me. Again.*

"How's it going, baby bro?" she asks, looking up at me.

I sit down beside her and run my hands through my hair. "It's been . . . interesting," I say. "You're probably not going to believe this." And then I fill her in on Jubilee, her condition, the almost-kiss.

I'm not sure how I expected her to react — maybe shock, like me? But when I'm finished, Connie laughs.

No, she doesn't *just* laugh.

She hoots.

She guffaws.

She literally cannot catch her breath.

"It's not funny," I say. "I could've killed her!"

She laughs some more and then attempts some slow breaths. "No, no. You're right. That part is not funny. But the rest? Ooh boy." She's off again and I stand there, waiting for her to get ahold of herself.

"Connie! Seriously," I say, sitting on the opposite end of the couch from her. "What's so damn funny?"

"Only you," she says between giggles.

359

"Only *you.*"

"What's that supposed to mean?"

"Oh c'mon, like you don't know."

I don't, so I sit in silence waiting for her to illuminate me.

"Eric! You're the poster boy for going after unavailable women."

"*What?* I am not."

"Yes. You are."

I roll my eyes. "Stephanie is the only relationship I've had. Since I was seventeen, if you recall."

"What about Teresa Falcone?"

"Teresa Fal— That was *middle school.* Does that really count?"

"It does. Her mom had just died and she wasn't interested in going with anybody. But you followed her around mooning over her like some wounded puppy."

"Oh, nice image. Glad you thought so highly of me."

"And then Penny Giovanni?"

"What about her?"

"You asked her to homecoming sophomore year."

"So?"

"She was a lesbian! Well, still is, I guess. But everyone knew it, except you."

Huh. I do remember her snatching her hand away when I finally gathered up enough courage to hold it toward the end of the night.

"Really?"

"Yes!"

"And Stephanie —"

"Wait. I married her. So she was hardly unavailable."

"Do you remember how long it took you to get a date with her? Her father was this crazy controlling Catholic that swore his virginal daughter would keep her legs closed until the end of time or something. And he hated you especially, WASP that you were."

I laugh. I had forgotten the elaborate lengths I had to go to to get her to go out with me, including being interrogated by her dad for an hour in their stuffy, hot living room.

"Anyway," Connie says. "I'm just saying, this is your track record when it comes to women. So, hitting on someone with an allergy to *people*? Well, you can see why I'm amused."

"Well, thank you, kind sister, both for your empathy and that walk down memory lane."

"No problem," she says, then slaps her hands on her knees. "But as much fun as this has been, I need to get going. Long day tomorrow — especially since I missed so much work this afternoon bailing you out

361

— again."

"Yes, yes. Thank you, you're amazing, I don't know what I'd do without you. Et cetera."

Standing up, she pulls her coat on and then wraps a scarf around her neck, pulls a knit hat on top of her head. When she reaches for the front door knob, she pauses. "Are you going to call Ellie on Thursday?"

I look down. "I don't know," I say lamely.

"Eric, it's her birthday."

"I know," I say. It lands on Thanksgiving this year. As a kid, Ellie loved when that happened, because Stephanie would let her choose all the desserts for the meal, so we'd have cake along with two or three different kinds of pie and brownies and snicker-doodles. Her favorite. "I sent her something in the mail. A new journal."

"You should call her."

"Why? So Steph can tell me she doesn't want to talk? Again?"

"No. So she knows her dad called her on her birthday. That at least you tried."

"All I've been doing is trying."

"I know," Connie says, her voice softening. She puts her hand on my arm, squeezes it. "Oh, and one more thing."

"Yeah?"

"Mom and Dad are coming for Christmas

dinner and I told them we'd do it here. At your place."

"You *what?*"

She removes her hand from the knob and puts it on her hip, looking at me. "You should be thanking me. They wanted to come for Thanksgiving, but I told them I was working. Anyway, you know I don't cook."

That's true. When Aja and I moved to town, she brought over a sack of White Castle burgers as a housewarming dinner.

"Honestly, I just can't stand to hear Mom pick apart every detail of my house. *You* do *know a linen closet is for* linens, *don't you, dear?*" She does a dead-on impersonation of our mom's voice.

"That's scary."

"So is she."

"No she's not."

"Whatever. You're the son who can do no wrong, even after you get divorced, adopt a mixed-race child, and alienate your daughter."

I suck in my breath.

"Sorry, too far?"

"Yeah. Listen, I don't even have a dining room table."

"I'll bring a folding one and some chairs. It will be fine."

363

"Great. Mom'll love that."

"She'll be fine with it, Golden Boy. At your house, she'll probably think it's charming."

When Connie leaves, I walk down the hall to Aja's room. After the river and fire incidents, I instituted a strict open-door policy, so I stick my head in without knocking. "Hey, bud."

He doesn't take his eyes off the computer. "Hey."

"How was therapy?"

"Fine."

"Did you talk about anything . . . interesting?" I think of how he talked to Jubilee about his parents and wonder if I should try again. I haven't had the nerve to bring up Dinesh and Kate after the terrible reception last time.

"No."

OK, then. I rap the door frame with my knuckles.

"Well, good night," I say. It's been a long day, I reason. Not the best time for a big conversation. But instead of taking a step back and heading to my room, on a whim, I take a step in and look over his shoulder. He quickly clicks the X to close the tab on the screen with his mouse.

"Uh, no," I say. "No secrets on the computer." His shoulders drop. "Bring it back up, please."

Begrudgingly he does and I scan the page. The headline alone — "How to Do Telekinesis: Advanced Techniques" — stops me cold. The rest is by some man named Arthur who discusses his "abilities" and touts his educational programs for different skill levels — each for the low price of $39.95, of course, as well as a supplement made of monoatomic gold and liquid chi, whatever the hell those things are, that helps enhance psychic powers.

"Aja, I thought we were done with all this."

He doesn't say anything.

"Listen to me. This isn't real. Telekinesis doesn't exist. This guy is a scam. A phony. He's just trying to make money."

"You don't know that," he says, his voice low.

"I do, bud. I do know that."

"No, you don't!" he screams, and jumps up, his chair falling over. "It's not a scam! It's *real*!" He starts crying, big, fat tears falling from his eyes.

I put my hands up. "OK. OK, bud. Let's calm down."

"No! You don't believe me! Just get out.

Get out!"

He throws himself on the bed and buries his face in the pillow, crying in earnest now. I'm torn between going to wrap him up in my arms (which I know he hates) and leaving, so I just stand there, dumbly, watching him. I wait for him to yell at me again to get out, but he doesn't. So I right the chair that fell over, sit down in it, and watch him some more, while the minutes on the digital clock beside his bed tick by one by one. And I wish for the hundredth time that Dinesh were here. Not only because he'd know what to do, but also because Aja wasn't like this when his parents were alive. Sure, he was super smart and a little socially awkward — OK, a lot. But he didn't have serious emotional issues, at least none that Dinesh talked about. And even though I didn't necessarily notice that he hadn't grieved properly, as the therapist pointed out, it doesn't take a rocket scientist to realize that his parents' death has changed him in some profound way — and that I haven't helped him deal with it at all. I've got to figure this out. I've got to do better. And I'm going to start by not leaving when he wants me to.

I cross my arms, determined, and sit there, feet firmly planted on the ground, until Aja's crying stops, his breathing slows, and finally, finally, he falls asleep.

Thanksgiving arrives without much fanfare. Being from England, Dinesh and Kate didn't really celebrate the holiday, so it's no big deal to Aja either. I bought a cooked turkey breast and mashed potatoes from Whole Foods and we ate in the living room while watching reruns of *Star Trek*.

When Aja drifts off to his room to play video games on the computer, I take a deep breath and pick up my phone to call Ellie. She doesn't answer her cell, so I dial the house phone.

Stephanie picks up on the third ring.

"Happy Thanksgiving," I say as amiably as I can.

"You, too," she says.

"Is the birthday girl home?"

"She is."

"Can I talk to her?"

"Eric —"

"Please?" I say, cutting her off. "Will you try?"

Stephanie sighs and I hold my breath as I hear her talking to Ellie. She must have the receiver covered, because I can only make out a few of the words, but I have to give her credit — it does sound like she's doing her best to cajole our daughter. And it works.

"Hello."

My knees nearly buckle when I hear her voice. She's fifteen today, but over the phone she sounds so much younger. So much more like my sweet girl, even though her greeting has her now-perfected edge of anger to it. I don't even care. I'm just so relieved to be speaking with her.

"Ellie," I breathe. "Happy birthday! Fifteen, god, I can't believe it. It feels like you were just born." I know I'm overdoing it, that I need to pull back. I grip my phone tighter, as if that will keep her on the line. "Did you get my gift? The journal."

"Yep," she says.

"Good, good. I thought you might like it, since you did such a great job with your book journal assignment for school. And it will be great for you to write in, you know, good practice for being a magazine editor."

"What?"

"You know, how you said you wanted to be a magazine editor after reading *The Bell Jar.*"

She scoffs. "That was, like, a year ago."

"Oh, well, yeah. Things can change. Sure. You have plenty of time to figure out what you want to do."

"Whatever."

"You know, I'm reading *Carrie* now, and —"

"You said two minutes," she says, cutting me off. Although it doesn't sound like she's talking to me. I hear Stephanie in the background. It sounds something like "Just a few more. It won't kill you."

"No," Ellie says. I hear a clatter, then Stephanie's voice in the receiver.

"Eric, are you there?"

"Yeah."

"I'm sorry," she says. "She just . . . you know."

"Yeah," I say. "Well, listen, give her a big hug for me, OK? Will you do that?"

"Yeah, of course," Stephanie says.

"OK, well, good night."

"Good night."

I hang up and stare at the phone. How did I get here? I look around my apartment. Not just this place, not just New Jersey, but to the point of not knowing what to say to my own daughter. I wish I could be there with her now. Somehow force her to talk to me, to go back to the way things were. But I know I can't.

At least I'm halfway done with my contract here. In three months I'll be back in the same town with her, and maybe then —

maybe I'll figure out what to say, what to do. How to get my daughter back.

After turning off Aja's light and pulling the covers over him, I climb into my own bed and crack open the spine of the Stephen King novel. It's clear Ellie doesn't care that I'm reading these books, but I won't give up. Right now, even if it's a bad plan, it's the only plan I have to connect with her.

I start reading, getting lost in the disturbing mind of this teenage girl, but when I get to the scene where Carrie stops her mother's heart, I put the book down, my own heart hammering in my chest.

I walk out to the kitchen for a glass of water, and tired of dissecting my broken relationship with Ellie, my mind travels to Jubilee. I wonder what she's doing. Impulsively I grab the phone book that's been on the kitchen counter since we moved in and flip through it, wondering when the last time I even opened one was.

I slide my finger over the newsprint page of Js until I reach Jenkins. There are four, but no Jubilee. I'm disappointed she's unlisted, until the name Victoria catches my eye. And it clicks — I remember it's her mom's name from the *Times* article. I rip the page out of the phone book, take it back to my room, and dial the number on my cell.

Jubilee picks up on the fourth ring.

"You were right. This book is terrifying," I say.

"Huh?" Her voice is croaky, tired.

"*Carrie,* the book. I'm reading it. Sorry, did I wake you up?"

"I think so," she says, yawning. "I was reading on the couch. I must have fallen asleep." She yawns again. "How'd you get my number?"

"The phone book," I say.

"Wait — seriously? Do people still use those?"

"Well, I can attest that at least one person has used it this year."

She laughs, and I'm glad I called.

"What are you reading?"

A pause, and then: "*Carrie.*"

I grin. "I thought you didn't do horror."

"I made an exception."

"How on earth did you fall asleep while reading it? I don't think I'll sleep for years."

She laughs. "I don't know. I don't think it's all that scary."

"It's horrifying," I say. "I can't believe my daughter read this."

Jubilee chuckles and makes a noncommittal sound, and then the pace of our conversation slows to a halt. After a few beats of silence, I say: "It's her birthday today. Ellie, that is. I called her."

"How did that go?"

"She said a total of four words, I think? So, you know, better."

"I'm sorry," she says.

"Yeah. Me, too."

The silence grows again and I find myself trying to picture her — if she's sitting or standing, what she's wearing, if she's alone. I strain to see if I can hear anybody in the background. Although, I don't know who'd be with her, since her parents are both out of the picture. I suddenly hate that she spent Thanksgiving alone. I wish I had thought to invite her over.

"So," I say, changing the subject. "If *Carrie* doesn't scare you, what does?"

"What?"

"Tell me something," I say, "something that scares you."

She pauses. "Well, being touched obviously."

"Yeah," I say, "I guess that would." I shift in bed, putting my arm behind my head and leaning back. "Tell me something not obvious."

The silence between us grows serious. When she speaks again, her voice is so low,

I press the phone tighter to my ear, so I don't miss anything. "I'm scared that I've forgotten what it feels like."

"Being touched?"

"Yeah," she says.

I suck in my breath. I don't know what I expected her to say. And I don't know how to respond.

"I guess, I'm afraid I've built it up in my mind," she continues.

"How so?" I match the tone of my voice to hers.

"I don't know. Like, there's this YouTube video I watched once for one of my online classes, World Religions, I think. It was a group of Tibetan monks chanting and meditating together. It was an hour-long clip, and though you get the idea after a minute or two, I watched the entire thing. I don't know why — I was transfixed or something. I could literally feel the vibration of their humming throughout my body. It started in my chest and blossomed out to my head, my limbs, my fingertips. And I've got in my mind that's what it would feel like to be touched again. Like electricity. And even though I'm terrified of it, at the same time I crave it. I know that doesn't make sense."

"No. No, it does. It makes perfect sense."

She falls quiet again. And then, just when I think I need to say something, to change the subject maybe, she speaks. "So is that what it feels like?"

"To be touched?"

"Yeah."

I think for a minute. "I guess, yeah — sometimes it does," I say, and then crack a smile. "Depends on where you're doing the touching." I regret the joke as soon as it's out of my mouth, scared that I've spoiled the moment, or that she'll think I'm making fun of her or trying to embarrass her — make her blush, as she so frequently does. But when I open my mouth to apologize, I hear something. It sounds like sniffling. My heart stops. Dear god, I've made her cry. I palm my face, cringing, trying to figure out what I can say to make it better.

And then a cackle bursts into my ear, and another one, and another. She's laughing. And the sound is all at once shocking and familiar, like a songbird that's back after a long winter, and it loosens something in my chest.

The rest of the month is cold but mild. A few snow flurries, but nothing sticks. I'm glad for Jubilee's sake, since even though I pick her up every night, she still has to ride her bike *to* work. I offered again to take her car to a mechanic and even pay for it, but she wouldn't hear of it. And I think maybe Connie is right. There is a common characteristic shared by the women in my life — they're maddeningly stubborn.

But as I sit next to Jubilee in the front seat of the car, night after night, I'm forced to consider Connie's other theory as well. It's true that the lure of Jubilee has only grown since I found out about her condition. But surely, that's in spite of it, and not because of it. I was drawn to her before I even knew, but now — since our phone conversation on Thanksgiving — I can't stop thinking about her.

About touching her.

Not just the obvious parts. But her collarbone. The parting of her hair. The exposed inside of her wrist where her glove doesn't quite meet her shirtsleeve. I'm overwhelmed by my desire for it.

And I don't think it's because I haven't had sex in so long or felt desire. I am a man, after all, and a model seductively eating a hamburger on TV is enough to spark interest. It's that I haven't felt desire like *this.*

Part of me wants to bring it up with Aja's therapist, to talk to *someone* about it, but I know I'm not here to talk about me.

Sitting, I rest my elbows on the wooden arms of the chair in front of Janet's desk, ready for our monthly check-in. "So, how's he doing?"

She cocks her head. "How do *you* think he's doing?"

Jesus. Should have known better than to expect a straight answer from a shrink.

"Good." Then I say, hedging, "Well, better, I think."

There haven't been any major episodes since the telekinetic website breakdown, and I'm scoring that as a win.

"Have you talked to him about his parents?"

I shift in the seat. You'd think they could at least put a cushion in it. "I tried."

"How'd that go?"

"Not well."

"Hmm."

It's so silent, I can literally hear the seconds tick by on the wall clock to my right.

"Who's Jubilee?"

My eyes dart up to hers. "What?"

"He talks about her a lot."

I clear my throat. "She's a librarian," I say. "She's the one who saved his life. From the river."

"He seems to be fond of her."

376

"Yeah, yeah." I scratch the back of my head with my hand. "I think they get each other or something."

She nods thoughtfully. "Though, I'm concerned that he's harboring some delusions where she's concerned as well."

"What do you mean?"

"He seems to think she's allergic to people."

"Huh." I feel a surge of defensiveness, like I want to protect Jubilee. Her life, her condition, is none of Janet's business. But I also don't want Aja to seem more peculiar than he is. And my loyalty as a father wins out. "Well, she is, actually."

It's Janet's turn to lift her brow. I take some pleasure in unsteadying her. "Really?"

"Yeah, it's some genetic condition, like a mutation. It's rare." I read the *New York Times* article. Twice. First, astounded, as if I were reading about a stranger. And then again with Jubilee in mind, trying to comprehend what her life must have been like. What it's still like.

Janet rearranges her face back into its pleasant expression. "But she doesn't have any psychic . . . abilities that you're aware of, correct?" She offers a small smile, as if we're in on the same joke.

I don't return it. "No. Not that I'm aware of."

She nods. "Aja seems to think that the mutation causing her allergy — which I admittedly didn't think was real — marks her as some kind of evolutionary wonder, and that she perhaps has tapped or untapped supernatural powers."

Even though I know this is the serious part, what I'm supposed to be concerned about, I can't help but smile, picturing Jubilee as some superhero out to save the world. And my gut is back to wondering just how much therapy Aja really needs. Yes, I know he has some . . . issues, stemming from his parents' death. But isn't this just the overactive imagination of a ten-year-old boy at work?

I say as much to Janet, ending with: "He reads a lot of *X-Men.* It's his favorite comic book — and that's exactly what they are, genetic mutants with extraordinary capabilities."

"Fair enough," she says, revealing the palm of her hand. "I just don't want to leave any stone unturned or miss something given some of the choices Aja's made in the past. I want to make sure we're doing everything we can for him."

My guard lowers a tad. "I know, I understand. Me, too."

I stand and pick my coat up off the back of the chair where I draped it. As I'm shrugging it on and walking toward the door, Janet calls out. "Eric?"

I turn. "Yeah."

She fixes me with a kind but stern look. "Talk to him. You've got to keep trying. With kids it often takes multiple attempts."

I nod, thinking of Ellie. Don't I know it.

TWENTY

JUBILEE

December is full of surprises. The first week, Madison forced me to get a cell phone. "It's weird that you don't have one," she said. "They're practically mandatory." Half a Xanax and an hour later I was excited to be in possession of one. But now it feels kind of pointless because the only person who ever calls me on it is Madison.

The second week, Eric invited me over for Christmas. I don't think he really meant to — it was more that he was trapped into it and didn't really have a choice.

"What are you doing for Christmas?" he asked, conversationally, on the drive home one night.

"When is it, next Friday?"

He laughed, and then realized I was serious.

"Uh, yeah," he said. "Do you not celebrate or something?"

I gave my head a small shake. "No. I hate Christmas." I didn't intend to say it, but it just fell out.

"You *hate* Christmas?"

I nodded.

"Why?"

The first few years after Mom left, I made an effort. Put on the *Now This Is Christmas!* CD of terrible holiday pop tunes she used to bop around the house to. Got out the box of drugstore decorations that were half falling apart and put a few here and there. But when the day actually arrived, looking at them — especially the plastic Santa figurine missing half of his cottony beard — just made me sad. I never minded living alone — not really — except for that one day. That inescapable day where every show and commercial on TV and every song reminds you that you're meant to be with someone. Because really, what's the point of celebrating a holiday that's all about giving gifts when you've got no one to give a gift to? My birthday's not much better, to be honest, but at least there aren't a thousand reminders I'm alone on that day.

Anyway, all of that sounds kind of pathetic, even to me, so I tried to explain it away with: "I don't know — the commercialism. All the forced cheer. Oh, and

381

the lights! Dear god, the lights. Look at this neighborhood," I said, waving my hand toward the window. "It looks like an airport runway! Like they're expecting a seven thirty-seven to land at any minute."

Eric barked with laughter. "A real live Grinch. I never would have guessed. Are you going to sneak in all the homes and steal the children's presents next?"

"Maybe," I said, giving him a side grin.

"You should come over to our house," Aja said. "Eric's cooking."

And that's when Eric shifted in his seat and cleared his throat. "Yes, you should come. You're welcome to come. I mean, if you want to. No pressure."

So, see? I don't think he really wanted to invite me, which is why I demurred before getting out of the car. "Offer's open," he shouted after me. "Unless your heart is two sizes too small!"

The biggest surprise happens the third week of the month, when I walk into the library Monday morning and find Roger standing at the circulation desk, looking forlorn. Or confused. I can't tell. "Louise got fired," he says.

"What?"

"Happened first thing this morning. She

came in. Maryann called her back and that was it."

I can't find words. *Louise?* I thought she was like a permanent fixture at the library. "How long has she worked here?"

"Since before I started. And that was eight years ago. I want to say, like, fifteen, at least." He shakes his head. "It was awful — you should have seen her. And on a Monday, too. She was crying. Then *I* started crying." He chokes up a little now as he talks and puts a finger over his mouth. Tears pooling in his eyes, he holds my gaze for a second and walks into the back room.

Stunned, I just stand there, coat and bag still on, behind the circulation desk. I'm not sure what to do next. How did Louise get fired? *Why?* If the city council cut funding it should have been me that they let go. *Last one hired, first one fired,* like Louise said.

Maryann comes out of the back room and she stops when she sees me. Her shoulders tense. "Hello," she says. It's oddly formal, but then she just fired a woman who appeared to be not only a coworker but a friend, so it I guess she wouldn't be in a jovial mood.

"Morning," I say.

"You heard, huh?"

I nod. "It's awful."

She gives a quick nod back and bites her lip, as if to keep from crying. "Well, we're all going to have to step it up a bit more around here, seeing as we'll be short-handed."

"Of course," I say. "Anything."

She clears her throat and moves toward the desk to pick up a folder, then returns to the back room without another word.

The day passes in a blur, and even though Louise and I didn't always have the same work schedule, it's weird to not have her there. Weird to know she won't be back. It's emotionally exhausting, and when Aja walks in at four, I give him my now-customary nod and then let him be for the afternoon. I don't have the energy for our usual conversations.

"What's wrong?" Eric asks on the ride home.

"Huh?" I say, still thinking about Louise.

"You just seem a little . . . not yourself." And I wonder how I am to him. Who I am. What he thinks of me when I am being "myself."

I tell him about the library and the lack of funding, and how Louise was the last person anyone expected to get fired.

Eric listens intently and then says: "Better her than you, right?"

I shift in the passenger seat but don't respond.

"Sorry, that was insensitive."

I nod.

"If it helps, I had a shit day, too."

"You're not supposed to say 'shit,' " Aja pipes up from the backseat.

"You, neither," Eric says.

"What happened?" I ask.

"One of our clients is acquiring an S & P One Hundred and the due diligence is a b—" He glances at the backseat at Aja and clears his throat. "It's a pain," he says. "I don't know my team, since I'm new in the office, so I don't completely trust them to get the EBITDA or the forecasted cash flows right, or anything else for that matter, and ugh, it's just a lot — a lot of oversight. A lot of pressure."

I stare at him. "Was that English?"

He laughs and waves his hand. "It doesn't matter. Enough work talk," he says. But after he makes the pronouncement, there doesn't seem to be anything else to talk about and the car falls silent for the remainder of the drive.

On Thursday that week, Madison sends me my first-ever text message.

Left you a little something on your front porch.

I open the front door and find a dozen apple cider doughnuts in a white box, an envelope with a Xanax, and a card that reads: *I know I'll need one on Christmas — thought you might, too. PS: Only take half a pill at a time, Bobby McFerrin.*

I get into bed with the doughnuts, eat four of them while rereading *Jurassic Park,* and fall asleep in a sea of crumbs.

The next morning I wake up and glance at the clock. Nine fifteen a.m. I groan and stretch and eye my nightstand where I left the pill, and pick up my book, opening it to the page I stopped on last night. At noon, I glance at the pill again. I don't really need it — I'm not going anywhere today. But then again, why not? If it could help tame my anxiety in the city, maybe it could help me hate Christmas a little less. I pop it in my mouth and swallow, only then remembering Madison's instruction to cut it in half. Oops.

I lie back and wait for the relaxing sensation to take effect. It doesn't take long. By three, I'm starving and realize I haven't eaten yet today. Tired of apple cider doughnuts, I go downstairs and rummage through

the fridge. Running low on provisions —
I'm not due for a grocery delivery until
Monday — I stand at the counter eating a
piece of plain bread, doughy and bland in
my dry mouth. That's when I remember
what Aja said when he invited me over:
Eric's cooking! My stomach rumbles.

I find Eric's business card on my desk and
dial him. He answers on the third ring.

"Is the offer still open?" I realize — too
late, maybe — that it's bold, and borderline
rude, and very much unlike me, but I don't
really care. "Don't Worry, Be Happy" is running on a loop in my head.

"Uh, Jubilee?"

"Yes. Sorry. It's me."

"Have you been . . . uh . . . are you all
right? It sounds like you're slurring a bit."

"Oh. I took some drugs. I'm hungry."

"Drugs?"

"Yep."

"What kind?"

"Oh. Just Xanax. To help me relax. I think
it's working."

"OK . . . ," he says. I immediately visual-
ize his ruffling the back of his hair with his
hand. He does that when he thinks. It
sounds like he's thinking. "Well, we just
finished eating, but there's plenty. Do you
want me to come pick you up?"

"No, I can ride my bike over. What's your . . . what's your . . ." I start laughing. "I can't remember the word I want. Where do you live?"

"Uh, I'll come get you."

Thirty minutes later, I've managed to change and brush my teeth. And then I realize I should get him and Aja something. It's Christmas! As I'm wondering if I have time to bike to the Wawa, I hear Eric's car pull up out front. That's when I remember the doughnuts. I bolt up the stairs two at a time and grab the box from the foot of my bed. There are only eight left and they look kind of sad in the box, so I take a minute to fan them out a bit and fill up the empty space.

After I slip on my gloves and coat, I open the door downstairs just as Eric is knocking.

"Hi," I say, a little out of breath.

"Hi yourself," he says back, smiling. I like his smile.

I shove the box of doughnuts at him.

"Merry Christmas."

"Oh! Thanks." He takes the box from me.

"I ate four of them already. Last night." I don't know why I feel compelled to tell him the truth about everything now, but I do.

He laughs and shakes his head. "OK. You

ready to go?"

"I am."

When we get to Eric's apartment, I follow him in the door, expecting to see Aja. I did not expect to see the roomful of faces that greets me.

I freeze. "Oh, God," I say under my breath. "You have company . . . I should have . . ." The floaty, relaxed sensation I was still enjoying on the car ride over is gone and I find myself wishing Madison had put a second pill in that envelope.

Eric turns back and looks me in the eye. "It's fine," he says warmly. "You know Rufus." He gestures to the dog, who's nipping at his heels, and smiles at me. I feel a little buzz.

"You renamed him."

He winks at me. "And you remember Connie, of course."

"Hi!" She gives a little wave from where she's sitting on the couch. I nod.

"And these are my parents, Gary" — he gestures to the man sitting on a folding chair in the dining room — "and Deborah." His mom is standing near the TV. She starts walking toward me, her arms open.

"Oh, it's Christmas," she says. "We can hug hello."

A chorus of "No!" stops her in her tracks.

Bewildered, she looks at Eric and Connie. Then they both start speaking at once.

"She has a terrible cold!"

"She doesn't like to be touched!"

"She's a mutant!" Aja chimes in gleefully. He's just appeared from the hallway.

Eric's mother's eyes widen with each explanation and she places her hand over her chest, as if the commotion is causing her heart to race and she needs to slow it. Feeling awkward, I offer her a smile and wave the gloved fingers on my right hand at her.

She cocks her head in rightful confusion at me, as if to ask: *which is it?*

I clear my throat. "Ah, mostly what Aja said. I have a rare allergy. To um, other people. I can't be touched."

"Oh!" Eric's dad, who's been mostly silent, roars from his seat. "Just like my wife! Eh, Deborah?" He laughs at his own joke, his rotund belly literally quivering from the effort.

"Gary!" She rebukes him sharply. And then lightens her tone. "I think we've had enough Glenlivet, don't you?"

"Ah, no such thing, my love." He looks at me and raises his hand in a waving motion. "Come on over. We were just about to dig into dessert."

I glance at Connie, who's rolling her eyes, and then at Eric, who puffs out his cheeks and blows a slow breath. He sidles up near me and whispers: "I forgot to tell you — I hate Christmas, too."

When we're all seated on the metal folding chairs, Deborah dishes out slices of apple pie onto paper plates. The dog sits at my feet like a statue, looking up at me with his big puppy eyes.

"This is delicious, Eric," says Deborah, patting her mouth with a napkin.

"Connie brought it."

"Oh," she says, turning to her daughter. "What are these apples — Pink Ladies?"

"Yeah, I think so," Connie says, brightening.

"Next time, try Honeycrisp or Granny Smith. They really are the best for baking."

"Ah. Noted," Connie says, shooting Eric a look. He chuckles.

"Can I go to my room now?" Aja asks. My eyes widen at his empty plate. I'm still on my first bite.

"No." Eric says. "Grandma and Grandpa are only here for the afternoon. They haven't seen you in months."

"They're not my grandparents," Aja says evenly. "And Iggy got the new King's Quest, too. He's waiting on me to play it."

"Oh, it's fine, Eric," Deborah says. "Let him go. It's Christmas!"

Eric sighs for a third time. "Fine." Aja jumps up from the table and rushes off. "Does everyone have everything they need?" He glances at me and says in a lower voice: "You good?"

I nod.

"So, Jubilee, I don't mean to pry, but I've never heard of your allergy before," says Deborah. "You really can't be touched?"

"Like the Bubble Boy," Gary declares, a few decibels louder than everyone else at the table. He goes to reach for his glass of scotch and Deborah gently puts her hand on his arm.

The table goes quiet and I feel everyone's eyes on me. "Um. Not exactly. He had some kind of immune disease or deficiency, so he was really susceptible to germs in the environment and from other people. Mine is just an allergy, like to peanut butter or eggs. It just happens to be to the skin cells of other humans."

"Fascinating," Deborah says, taking a sip of her coffee. "So what does it mean exactly?"

"Just what you said, really. I can't have skin-to-skin contact with anyone." I glance at Eric. My face is getting hot and I hope he can't tell. "I get pretty severe rashes, and there's a risk of anaphylactic shock."

"Oh my God." Deborah puts her hand to her chest, and I take a bite of my pie, hoping she won't ask any more questions. "Your poor mother."

I inhale at her words and a piece of crust flies into my throat, causing me to cough violently. My eyes water, and I take a sip of coffee.

Eric speaks up. "So, Mom, um . . . Jubilee loves Emily Dickinson. Isn't she your favorite poet as well?" I look at him, hoping to convey gratitude at the change in subject, weird though it may be.

"Yes, one of them."

"Mom was an English major at Smith."

"She's brilliant, actually," adds Connie. Then under her breath: "Shame she never did anything with it."

Deborah cuts her eyes at her daughter. "Well fortunately, a woman can live a fulfilled life in many different ways, Connie."

I slip the dog a piece of crust under the table.

"Jubilee's a librarian," Eric says.

I clear my throat. "Circulation assistant."

"Marvelous!" says Deborah. "You must

love reading as much as I do."

"You should see her house," Eric laughs. "You can't throw a stone without hitting a book."

"Who are some of your other favorites?" asks Deborah. "I've been on a T. S. Eliot kick lately. He was an interesting man."

" 'The Love Song of J. Alfred Prufrock,' " I say, remembering the poem from an 1800s American literature class I took online. The professor lectured passionately on it, clenching his fist to emphasize words. *This isn't a love* [clenched fist] *poem, but rather a poem about longing* [clenched fist]. *Eliot wants romantic love, yes. But more than that he wants to connect* [clenched fist]. *He wants to find meaning* [clenched fist] *in his stultifying, tea-drinking routine.*

"I like that one."

Deborah tilts her head, studying me. "Yes," she says, kindness pooling in them. "I do, too."

The table falls quiet, the only sound forks scraping bits off plates. An ease settles over the room and it occurs to me that this must be what it's like. Family. Togetherness. Though I'm an intruder, I allow myself an indulgent moment and pretend that they're mine, looking slowly from face to face to face, until I land on Eric.

Eric.

A booming voice knocks me out of my reverie. " 'Let us go then, you and I. When the evening is spread against the sky.' "

Connie looks at her father, bewildered. "Dad?"

"Oh, Gary," Deborah titters. "Honestly." She turns to Connie. "He's just reciting the poem. The Eliot one."

"We really should head out, though," Gary says. "Got a long drive ahead of us."

A fuss is made over clearing the table, who's going to do what, and then Deborah and Gary have their coats and hats on and are ready to leave.

"Aja!" Eric yells.

"Oh, don't disturb him," Deborah says. "We'll just pop in and say bye."

When they get back to the front door, Connie announces that she'll be leaving, too, and a mix-and-match of hugging ensues. I stand back, near the coffee table with no glass, the dog sitting at my heels, so as not to get in anyone's way. Deborah fills the spaces between the good-byes and Merry Christmases and love-yous with banal chatter, like "Did you hear about that blizzard coming next week?" and "That folding table and chairs set worked perfectly for our little holiday, Eric. So charming!" At that, Connie lets out a sharp laugh and elbows Eric in the side.

Then Deborah walks toward me and holds up her hands. "No hugs this time, I swear," she says.

I smile.

"It was so lovely to meet you. Perhaps we'll see each other again?"

"I'd like that," I say.

When everyone's gone, Eric turns to me and shrugs as if to say: *Family. What are you gonna do?* I just smile, but my insides are tumbling, an ocean wave of unexpected feeling. We're alone in the room, and though we've been alone before, somehow this feels different. Like the air is charged. I wonder if he feels it, too. If so, he doesn't let on. "Are you still hungry? I've got some turkey in there. There's more pie."

"Yeah, I actually am," I say, my stomach rumbling. The pie didn't do much to fill me up. "Turkey sounds great."

I follow him into the kitchen, the dog still at my heels, and Eric starts pulling things out of the fridge.

"Your mom seems really nice," I say as he transfers some turkey onto a plate with two forks.

"Yeah. Don't tell Connie that, though."

"They don't get along?"

"You know, just typical mother-daughter stuff." He freezes, the forks suspended in the air. "I'm sorry. I'm such an asshole. Here, your mother just . . . and I . . ."

"It's fine," I say. "Really." Even though a lump has started to form in my throat. I blink back tears. I've been thinking more about her, ever since my talk with Eric, and I wonder if maybe my ire at her was partly typical teenage hatred. And I never had the chance to grow out of it with her. Or I never gave her the chance. I think of all the times she invited me out to Long Island over the years, and the disappointment in her voice when I would say no. But god, everything was always about *her.* And it was just so irritating.

But maybe in person it would have been different, or maybe as we got older, we could have gotten along better, and I just never gave her the chance. Or — after watching Connie and Deborah tonight — I wonder if maybe mothers are always irritating, no matter how old you are. And maybe you love them anyway.

I eat my food in silence as Eric pulls on a pair of rubber gloves and starts on the mountain of dishes piled on his counter and in the sink. I slip Rufus a few pieces of turkey whenever Eric's back is turned.

When I'm finished, I take the plate, scrape the bits leftover into the trash, and set it on the counter with the rest of the dirty dishes.

"Thanks," Eric says.

I grab a kitchen towel from where it's hanging on the oven door and pick up a pan that he's just finished washing. The water droplets left on it immediately soak into my gloves, so I peel them off to keep them dry. Eric eyes me. "Is that safe?"

"I don't know. Are you going to be able to resist touching my very sexy hands?" I wiggle my fingers, teasing him. I'm not sure where this surge of bold confidence has come from, but I'm glad when he chuckles — sending a jolt of electricity up my spine. I pick the pan back up and start drying it. We work in silence, a comfortable assembly line, until I give voice to something that's been bothering me.

"You know a lot about me from reading that *New York Times* article."

"Yeah." Eric cuts his eyes at me, as if waiting to see where I'm going with this.

"It's not fair," I say. "Tell me something I don't know about you."

He continues washing dishes, vigorously scrubbing a Pyrex. He's at it for so long that I start to think maybe he didn't hear my question. Suddenly, he stops scrubbing and the room falls still.

"I killed my best friend," he says.

I stand there, a little stunned. "Well," I say, recovering a little. "I was kind of expecting something along the lines of 'My favorite color is purple.' Or 'I have six toes on my left foot.'"

He doesn't laugh.

I pick up a clean wooden spoon and start wiping it down, then ask softly: "What happened?"

He rinses the glass dish, sets it on the counter for me to dry, and then turns off the water. "I had a client, Bilbrun & Co., acquiring an aluminum factory in Kentucky. Just a little five-hundred-person plant. My team was responsible for due diligence, and I thought the plant was overvaluing their property. I had to hire a Realtor I didn't know in Kentucky, so I wanted to go myself and walk through it with her, make sure everything was on the up-and-up." He pauses and puts his hands on the counter between himself and the sink for support. "Ellie had a soccer championship game that weekend, and I had already missed a lot of her games that season. So I asked Dinesh if he would go to Kentucky in my place."

"So you two worked together?"

"Yeah. Not the same team, but we were always doing little favors like that for each other. 'Always wanted to see the Bluegrass State,' he said when I asked him. 'Maybe I'll take the wife, go horseback riding while we're there.' " The side of Eric's mouth turns up in a little half smile at the memory. "Bilbrun chartered a plane. I didn't even know he took Kate until . . . until I got the call that the plane had gone down on the way there. Engine failure or something."

"Oh, God," I say under my breath. I want to say more, but a shriek so primal fills the air and steals my breath. Aja is suddenly in the room, his mouth emitting the sound like a banshee, his little fists clenched by his sides, eyes squeezed shut, his tan face turning a muted red. And then the screaming starts to turn into words. "YOU KILLED THEM! YOU *KILLED* THEM! HOW COULD YOU?" Tears drip from his eyes like coffee percolating into a pot, and his words start to run together, as if they're tired of being words and want to return to just being sounds. "YOUKILLEDTHEM-YOUKILLEDTHEMYOUKILLEDTHEM-YOUKILLEDTHEM."

"Oh my god. Aja," I hear Eric breathe. He steps toward him, but Aja sees him and is off like a shot, slamming his door with so much force the sound reverberates down the hall.

Eric goes after him, and I hear gentle knocking and mumbled words, but a minute later he's back, grabbing the back of the kitchen chair with both hands and leaning into it. "Fuck," he says, drawing out the word.

"Is he OK?" I ask.

He shakes his head. "I don't know. He won't talk to me. Won't open the door."

"Want me to try?"

Pressing his lips together in a straight line, he says: "I don't think so. Let's give him a minute to cool off."

He straightens his back up abruptly, standing to his full height. "I need a drink," he says. He walks into the dining room and grabs the bottle of Glenlivet from the table and brings it into the kitchen, where he divides what's left into two small glasses.

"Oh, I don't . . . I've never . . ."

"Drank scotch?" he says.

"Drank at all," I say.

He raises his eyebrows at me. "Just into hard drugs, huh?"

I duck my head. "They were *prescription*."

We both smile, and the tension dissipates a little.

He opens the freezer, puts a few cubes of ice in one of the glasses, and hands it to me. "Let the ice melt a little bit before you try it."

I take the glass and put it to my mouth anyway. How bad can it be? I take a sip.

Bad. The answer is very bad. I sputter and spit, the small amount of liquid that made it down my throat burning as if I downed gasoline and someone put a lit match to it.

He shakes his head and mutters, "Stubborn," then moves into action, getting me a glass of water, which I gratefully accept. Once I recover, he joins me at the kitchen table, and we sit there, sipping our drinks. I stick with the water.

"Aaaaaahhhhh." A noise comes out of his mouth — a mix between a groan and a sigh. "Man, I am parenting to beat the band this year."

I look at him — and even though I'm worried about him, the seriousness of what just happened with Aja, I can't help it. I giggle.

"What?" he asks.

" 'To beat the band'?" I ask.

"What? It means —"

"I know what it means," I say, cutting him off. "It's just — is this the nineteen fifties? Or are you just that old?"

His lips turn up, a genuine smile, and I'm

glad. "Oh, excuse me. I'm sorry my idioms aren't modern and trendy enough for you."

I grin back at him. As we sit in comfortable silence, I replay what Eric was telling me. I take another sip of my water and then clear my throat.

"So that's how Aja came to be your son, then? He told me you adopted him after . . . but I didn't know exactly what happened."

He takes a deep breath. "Yeah," he says, exhaling. "Stephanie didn't think we should. Adopt him, that is. It was our last big fight. Well, as a married couple, anyway."

"What — why?" I say. "I can't imagine anyone not wanting Aja."

He studies me for a minute, gives a little grin, and then takes another sip of his scotch. "She thought he should be with his relatives. In England. But that wasn't what Dinesh wanted. Also . . ." He pauses and glances at the hallway to make sure Aja hasn't magically reappeared. "She was worried about Ellie. How it would affect her. I was concerned about that too, of course, but kids adapt. I thought it would be good for her — a lesson that life can change in a big way sometimes. And that we have to be there for the people that we love. Take them in."

He reaches his right hand up to ruffle his

hair, forgetting that he still has his rubber gloves on from dishwashing. When he realizes it, he drops it back on the table. "Stephanie didn't agree. Said she just couldn't go through with it. And I couldn't not go through with it."

"Wow," I say.

He drains his glass. "Anyway," he says, "that was kind of the end of the end for us — me and Stephanie. We filed for divorce shortly after they died."

I wrap my hands around my cold glass, letting everything Eric just told me sink in. Everything he's been through. My heart hurts for him in a way that it's never even hurt for myself. I look at him. Really take him in, not just his "good bone structure" and olive eyes, but the tiny lines around his mouth; the way his hair sticks up like he just got out of bed, no matter how many times he tries to flatten it; his unbuttoned collar, revealing the vulnerable divot of skin at the base of his neck; the ridiculous yellow rubber gloves still on his hands.

And that's when I notice it.

One of the rubber gloves is moving. Toward me. On the table.

I hold my breath, watching it. Waiting.

It stops millimeters from my hand, still cupping the glass.

"I can't, you know," he says, his voice husky, barely a whisper.

"Can't what?" I ask, sure the earth has stopped spinning, that time is standing still.

"Resist your very sexy hands."

He gently tugs at my wrist, compelling my hand to release the cup. I watch as his fingers travel up from the base of my thumb to my palm to my own naked fingers, until our digits become intertwined like the roots of a very old tree.

He sighs. "God, I've really fucked things up with Aja, haven't I?" he breathes. He has, but he doesn't need me to tell him that, so I don't respond. And we just sit there, holding hands at the kitchen table like we're some regular couple and it's some regular Tuesday or Wednesday night in our regular apartment.

But it's not. It's Christmas.

My very favorite holiday.

Shayna's sitting at the circulation desk when I get to work on Monday. Her head is bowed, a dark satin curtain of hair hiding her face, and as I get closer I see that she's intently painting her fingernails. Black, it looks like. I don't think she even notices me walk past her until I hear her say: "D'you hear about that blizzard coming?" She

405

doesn't look up. Doesn't break the short brushstroke rhythm of her painting. "Supposed to dump like two feet of snow on us."

"Yeah," I say, remembering Eric's mother said something about it.

"But it probably won't be anything," she says, blowing on the nails of her right hand. "Remember last year? They said the same thing — we were supposed to get, like, thirty-eight inches and we got seven." She rolls her eyes.

"Yeah," I say, even though I don't remember. I go to the back room to drop my coat and bag. Maryann is sitting in her office, the door open. I give her a little wave. "How was Christmas?"

She looks at me and drops her eyes back to whatever she's working on. "Just fine," she says.

"Good," I say, not expecting her to ask in return. She's been short and irritable ever since she fired Louise, and I've been trying to give her a wide berth and some understanding. It can't be easy to fire a friend — especially one you've been working with for so long.

The snow starts falling right after Shayna's shift is over at three. Just tiny flurries at first, like flecks of white rice being thrown by overzealous wedding-goers from the clouds.

Around four, I find myself staring at a snow-covered Aja. The flakes have grown exponentially — from bits of rice into fat, wet cross-sections of marshmallows — and they cling to his hair and puffy winter coat.

I nod at him, and he goes over to his computer carrel, dropping his bag.

Eric calls at five. "Hey," he says. "The trains are a mess. Everyone's trying to get out of the city. I'll be there as soon as I can."

"No problem," I say. "It's fine here. I don't think it's as bad as everyone says."

Eric says something back, but the line is staticky and he gets cut off.

I hang up and look around, surprised when I realize Aja and I are the only two people left in the library. Even the pillow golfer has left.

"Hey," I say, walking over to him. "Wanna play a game?"

He looks at me, unsure.

"C'mon," I say. "It'll be fun. Go get a stack of books from the shelves. Like five or ten. Any books."

I grab some, too, and we sit on the floor in front of the circulation desk, surrounded by our selections. I pick up one of them. "OK, now I'm going to give you three sentences. Two will be ones that I made up, while one of them will be the real first sentence of the book. You have to guess which one."

Aja gets into it, and we play for over an hour. We're laughing so hard that I don't even notice the door open until I hear a muffled voice shout: "Mm here! Mm here."

I look behind me, and Eric is half bent over just inside the door and seems to be breathing heavily. It's hard to tell, though, because he has a scarf wrapped around the lower half of his face and a hat covering the top half. In fact, his eyes are the only visible part of his body. I stand up and rush toward him, taking in his wild eyes, his heaving chest, and wonder if he might be having a heart attack.

"Are you OK? What happened?"

He straightens up and steps in a little farther, unwrapping his snowflake-covered scarf as he walks. He stops a few feet in front of me and answers my questions with his own. "Have you looked outside? It's an honest-to-god blizzard. I had to leave my car three blocks over on Prince Street." The lights flicker, as if punctuating his account. "Couldn't see two inches in front of me. I'm lucky I didn't get lost coming here."

Curiosity propels my body toward the door. I haven't looked outside since darkness overtook the windows an hour earlier. I peer out into the night and gasp. I can't see the streetlight at the end of the parking lot, but the soft glow it emits is just enough to reveal a world that is bathed in white. It's impossible to distinguish sky from snow-flakes from pavement.

I narrow my eyes, trying to find the outline of my bike on the rack, not five yards from the door. "Where's your car? We're going to have to walk to it. In this!" I say, as if that thought hasn't occurred to him.

He stills, eyebrows raised, the collar of his coat suspended in air midway down his back. "Uh . . . we're not going anywhere," he says. "Not tonight, anyway."

It's so ominous, like a scene straight out of a slasher flick, that a gurgle of laughter strangles my vocal cords.

Aja pipes up: "I bet the electricity is going to —"

And then it does. The lights go out, quiet-ing Aja as if the power also controls his voice. I don't move. It's black as pitch, and I can't see a thing. "Eric?" I say as I wait for my eyes to hopefully adjust and at least give me shapes and figures.

In response, a scream cuts through the darkness, so piercing, so chilling, the hair

TWENTY-ONE

ERIC

"Aja!" I yell, fumbling for my cell phone. I get it out of my pocket, but it slips from my grasp and falls to the floor. The wailing continues. It sounds just like the night I tried to tell that story about Dinesh. "Are you OK? Are you hurt?"

I get on my hands and knees and feel around for it. A squeal breaks through from right above me, adding to the cacophony.

"Sorry, that's your foot," I say to Jubilee, moving my hand. "I'm looking for my phone."

But I don't know if she can hear me; Aja's plaintive crying is so loud, it sounds like a heavy metal singer screaming directly into a microphone. In my ear.

"There!" My hand lands on the phone. Right when I pick it up and find the flashlight setting, the room falls silent.

"Aja?" I call out, swiping the flashlight

mode on and shining my phone in what I think is the direction the noise was coming from. He's not there. I sweep my phone in a slow circle, passing over Jubilee. Her eyes are wide, concerned.

"Just stay there," I say, holding my hand up.

"I think there's a real flashlight in the back. I'll go look," she says.

Well, yes, that's probably a better idea. Except — "You won't be able to see anything!"

"My cell phone's on my desk," she says.

"OK," I say, shining the light from my phone so she can make it to the desk. Once she's there and I've seen her turn on the light on her phone, I turn back to the rows of books in front of me.

"Aja, where are you? Come out right now," I say in my best stern voice, trying to conceal the panic in it. I hear a whimper and walk forward to the stacks. I shine the light down each one, until finally, in the fourth row, I spot him, curled in a ball, his back to the books. He looks up at me, squinting into the light. His cheeks are wet. "I'm sorry, I'm sorry," he's saying over and over. "It's my fault."

I rush to close the gap between us and kneel down. "What's your fault, bud?"

"The lights! I made them go off."

"No, no. That was the storm, the blizzard. I'm sure it downed a power line somewhere. That wasn't you."

I put my hand on his shoulder, but he shrugs it off, so I sit opposite him, setting the phone down so the light shines directly up toward the ceiling like a beacon in the middle of the sea. Aja's shaking his head.

"It *was* me!" he yells. "It was *me.*" And then he starts crying again, in earnest now. "I've been . . . practicing . . . the wrong . . . thing," he says, in between hiccupping sobs.

"What? Take a deep breath now, so I can understand you."

"Where's Jubilee?" he asks. "I want to talk to her."

"No," I say, scratching the day-old stubble on my chin. "No. You have to talk to me, Aja. You *have* to talk to me."

He looks down but doesn't say anything. I wait. I have no idea how much time passes, but he finally — finally — speaks. "This whole time . . . I thought . . . I was telekinetic. That's what . . . I've been practicing, trying to . . . harness. But that's not it. I control electricity . . . just like . . . Bolt."

I squint my eyes, trying to make sense of what he's saying, but I can't. "Who's Bolt?"

"One of the X-Men," he says, and even in his state, there's an edge of annoyance in his voice that sounds like: *Seriously, you don't know who Bolt is?*

I smile, comforted by this. There's the Aja I know.

"His real name's Bradley and he works for Stryker."

"Who's Stryk—"

"The villain!" he says, cutting me off. Then he lowers his voice, as if he's talking to himself instead of me. "Which makes sense, really. I knew I was bad. I know I'm bad. I'm the bad guy." He starts hitting himself in the head with clenched fists.

I grab his arms. "Aja! Aja, stop it. You are *not* bad. You are not a bad guy. Why do you think that? Stop it! Calm down, bud."

Aja stills his fists, but tears are falling from his eyes like a dripping faucet. I move over next to him. "You've got to talk to me, Aja. I'm worried about you. You have to tell me what's going on."

He squeezes his eyes shut and shakes his head. "No, I can't. I can't, I can't, I can't."

"Please. *Please.* I want to help you."

He stops moving his head and curls in an even tighter ball, his fists tight against his cheeks. I'm worried he's going to start hitting himself again and I reach out for his arms, but then he whispers something.

I lean closer. "What?"

"It's not your fault. It's not your fault. It's mine."

"What — the lights? No, I told you, bud, that's from the snow. You didn't —"

"My *parents*!" he shouts, causing my head to jerk an inch or two back. "It's my fault they're dead!"

"Your parents? No. No, Aja. How could that be your fault?"

The tears are falling faster now and I wait, my mind reeling.

"I didn't want them to go," he says finally. He sniffs. "Dad —" His voice cracks on the word and he tries again. "Dad . . . had promised we'd go see the new X-Men movie. It was coming out that weekend. But then he had to go on this work trip."

"OK," I say, encouraging him.

"So when they left, I kept thinking maybe something would happen. Maybe the plane wouldn't be able to fly, or the weather could keep them grounded. And I kept thinking it! I didn't stop. I kept thinking and thinking and thinking and then — and then —"

He collapses, his head hanging over his knees, his shoulders shaking. I put my arm around him tentatively, but he shrugs me off.

"I thought I must be telekinetic," he says in a small voice, "and that I needed to learn how to control it so I didn't hurt anyone else."

"So that's why you've been practicing this whole time?"

He nods.

"But now I think it's electricity. I must have shut down the engine control on the plane, just like I accidentally turned off the lights tonight."

"Aja," I say, grabbing both his shoulders and squaring him toward me.

"Don't touch me!" he screams.

"Sorry!" I say. "I'm sorry."

I wait for him to calm down, to look at me, and then I continue: "I hate to be the one to tell you this, but . . . you don't have any superpowers. What happened on that plane —"

"You don't believe me! You *never* believe me! My dad . . . he always believed me." His fists clench again.

"No, I don't believe you," I say, and his head jerks up at me, anger flashing in his eyes.

"But," I say, more gently, "I do believe *in* you. And I believe — no, I *know* — you didn't cause that plane to crash. Nobody did. It's just something that happened. A really shitty, terrible thing that happened, but it's nobody's fault."

He looks at me skeptically. I know he's not completely convinced, that he still probably hates me a little for being the reason they were on the plane in the first place. But I still hate me a little for that too, so we're even.

Aja's wet eyes glisten in the light of the iPhone. "You said 'shitty,' " he says, sniffling.

I nod. "I did."

"We're not supposed to say that word."

"I know. But honestly? Sometimes it's the only word that works."

Jubilee didn't find a flashlight, but she did find two blankets in her boss's office. We set up camp in the children's section, using my phone's flashlight setting as a campfire of sorts. I folded one of the blankets over itself as a mattress for Aja and draped the other on top of him, even though I thought Jubilee should keep it for herself. "I'll be fine," she said, waving me away. "I'm wearing thermal underwear."

I smiled at her, even though she couldn't really see me in the dark. "Are you trying to seduce me?" I asked, under my breath, so Aja couldn't hear.

A round laugh erupted from her.

Now I tuck the blanket all around him, grateful Jubilee was so selfless, as his tiny body is already shivering a little. I hope it will be enough to keep him warm through the night.

Jubilee and I sit close to the iPhone, but not to each other. There are a few feet of space between us and I long to close the gap, my mind conjuring excuses, plausible reasons I need to be nearer to her. We talk softly about the blizzard, trying to predict how much snow will fall before it's all said and done. We keep it light so as not to scare Aja, though I can tell Jubilee is worried.

When we sense his steady breathing and I'm sure he's asleep, I turn to Jubilee. "Did you hear everything?" I ask.

She nods. "Most of it. So he's thought for the past two years that he was responsible for his parents' death?"

"Yeah," I say, hanging my head. I feel guilty for not trying to talk to him about his parents sooner, for not asking the right questions. But it's all out now, and for that I'm relieved.

She brings her hand up to her heart. "That sweet boy."

"I know."

We both stare at the light. "I wish that

was a real campfire. It's freezing in here." She rubs her gloved hands together.

I nod. "We could do jumping jacks. Doesn't getting your blood circulating help or something?"

"It's better to get naked."

My head jerks toward her, not sure I heard her right. "What?"

She shrugs. "If two people are stuck out in cold weather — say camping or something — you're supposed to take all your clothes off and hold each other under a blanket or sleeping bag. The more skin-to-skin contact, the better, so you can transfer body heat to each other."

My lips feel dry and I realize my mouth is hanging open. I try to push the picture of an unclothed Jubilee out of my mind but find it's a difficult task. Then another thought hits me and I start laughing.

"What's funny?"

"It's just ironic," I say. "The one thing that could keep you from dying if you ever get hypothermia could kill you."

She chuckles.

"Better never go camping," I say. I mean it as a joke, but as the silence stretches out, I wish I hadn't said it. I'm just reminding her of one more thing she can't do, as if she doesn't know. And then I wonder if she knows what I want to do but can't. If she knows that just being near her steals my breath, that I dream of my hands in her hair, that touching her skin with my bare hand — even just the crease of her elbow — would be the definition of joy. And then I can't keep it inside any longer.

"I want to touch you," I breathe. She doesn't respond. We both stare at the light, as if it is a campfire. Minutes tick past, and I wonder if I actually said it out loud, or if I should try saying it again.

And then she speaks. "There might be a . . . treatment."

I suck in my breath. "Really?"

She nods but still won't make eye contact. I wait for her to say more, everything suddenly slowing down. My motions feel sluggish, my heart the pace of a ninety-four-year-old's footsteps.

"Dr. Zhang — my doctor — the allergy expert in New York. She wants to try immunotherapy."

She briefly explains what it is and how it could take a year, if not more, just to isolate the protein she's allergic to.

I take this in, my heart nearly coming to a full stop when I open my mouth to ask this question. I don't know why it feels like the entire balance of life hangs on it, but it does.

I swallow. "Are you going to do it?"

She doesn't answer right away. The air is so still, I can hear the quiet inhale and exhale of her breathing. My phone chimes, making us both jump.

I pick it up. It's Connie.

You OK? I'm still at your apartment. Staying here for the night.

When the trains were a mess, I'm so glad I had the forethought to ask her to go let Rufus out, in case I was late getting home. It didn't occur to me I wouldn't be getting home at all. I quickly tap out an explanation of where I am. As I hit "send," I hear Jubilee exhale, but this time it contains two words.

"I'm scared."

I turn to her. "We'll be OK." I move a little closer to try to offer comfort with proximity — that's what I tell myself I'm doing, anyway. "I'm sure once the snow stops, they'll get the streets plowed. Maybe even by the morning."

"No," she whispers.

And that's when it hits me what she's saying. What she's scared of.

"Why?"

She nibbles her bottom lip. "I don't know.

421

When I was a kid it's all I ever wanted. To be normal." She scoffs a little. "Whatever that means. But now . . ." She pauses, searching for the right words. "You know how in *The Virgin Suicides* the boys have this idea of who the Lisbon sisters are? But they don't really *know* them. They only admire them from a distance, so they end up glorifying them, reinventing them as these fascinating creatures — images that the girls could never really live up to."

I tilt my head, trying to piece together her metaphor. "You've been imagining what your life would be like without the allergy, and you're worried it won't live up to your expectation? Like you were talking about with the Tibetan monks?"

She slowly nods, blinking back tears. "And what if I go through with it and it doesn't even work? What if it's all for nothing?"

I lean closer to her now, trying to catch her eyes with mine in the light of the iPhone. "But what if it does?" I ask.

She starts to shake her head, and before I can stop myself, I reach up my hand and grab her cheek to still it. Luckily, I'm wearing my gloves. She won't look at me.

"What if it's everything?" I whisper.

Finally, in the glow of the iPhone light, her eyes meet mine.

She stares at me, searching, questioning, but I won't break the gaze. And then, the library, the rug we're sitting on — time itself — falls away and I get lost. In my thoughts, in her eyes. In her. I want to kiss her. No, that's not true. I want to devour her. And just when I think I can't — when I know I *won't* — be able to control myself a second longer, she jerks her face away from my hand, breaking the trance. I sit there, my arm frozen in the air, embarrassed by what I was about to do, by my lack of restraint. My chest is heaving like I've just run three miles, and I sit back on my haunches, trying to slow my racing pulse. And that's when I notice she's out of breath, too. Her fingers clutch her heart, rising and falling with the rapid ascent and descent of her own chest. And I think for the first time, maybe this is as hard for her as it is for me. And that makes it just a little bit easier to bear.

The silence draws out as I slowly retreat, putting feet instead of mere inches between us. And then, when I'm pretty sure my voice won't betray my weakness around her, I break the stillness of the air.

"Hey, Jubilee?"

"Yeah?"

"Next time you want to have some deep

discussion, you can skip all that literary metaphor crap. You know that stuff's way over my head."

She laughs softly, and it sounds like wind chimes on a blustery day. And it reminds me of someone — Dinesh's wife, Kate. The way her laughter would fill up a room. But it's even better.

"We should get some sleep," I say.

"Yeah."

We both lie down where we sit, our coats rustling until we get settled. I stare out the window, surprised that the sky looks lighter — and then I realize that the snow has stopped and the moon is shining. It's a good thing — the snowplows will start up, we should be able to leave in the morning — so I'm not sure why a ping of disappointment accompanies the thought. Or why, like a child, I'm longing for time to stop. To stay in this moment, where Aja is peaceful and I'm with Jubilee and for at least a few hours, all feels right, like everything's going to be OK.

"I can't sleep," Jubilee whispers.

I look over at her, the light barely kissing her cheek. I'm jealous of the moon. "Me either," I admit.

"Will you read to me?"

I raise my eyebrows, trying to remember

the last time someone requested that of me. Had to be Ellie, when she was little. I picture her big eyes, her three-year-old lisp. "Um . . . yeah, sure," I say. "I can read to you. What do you want to hear?"

"I don't know. I don't care. There's a stack of books right next to you that Aja and I were looking at."

I reach over in the direction she's pointing and grab the top one. It's got a ponytailed girl in a red dress on the cover. "*Charlotte's Web*," I say, reading the title. "Oh Jesus. Isn't this that depressing movie where the pig gets slaughtered at the end or something?"

"No! The pig doesn't die," she says.

I chuck it down. "Oh great, now you've gone and spoiled it."

"No!" she whispers, laughing. "Read that one. I love that one."

I pick it back up, turn to the first page, and cup my head with one hand. Then I clear my throat and quietly read to Jubilee by the light of the moon streaming through the window, until I hear her breathing deepen and stretch. And then I keep reading, anyway — but not just because I like the story. I like knowing that I'm touching her with my words. That they're crawling in her ears as she sleeps.

Twenty-Two

Jubilee

The lights snap back on with a loud buzz, waking us all up abruptly the next morning. My back is stiff from the hard floor. "What time is it?" I ask, stretching.

Eric moans, and I can tell his back is feeling as bad as mine. He grabs his phone. "I don't know," he says. "It's dead."

"I'm hungry," Aja says.

"Me, too," Eric and I say at the same time. We look at each other and smile. Even though the heat hasn't kicked in yet, I feel warm under his gaze. I think back to the previous night and am a little embarrassed at how much I said. What is it about darkness that compels one to reveal so much? But then I remember his hand on my cheek. His words. A little buzz grows in my stomach.

"I'll check the back room," I say. "See if we have any doughnuts."

"OK," Eric says, plugging his phone charger into a wall socket. "I'm going to head out to the car, see if the snowplows have been through."

While he's gone, and Aja's eating the day-old muffins I found, I clean up our camp, folding up the blankets and putting all the books back on the shelves where they belong. When I get to *Charlotte's Web,* I hold it a second longer, as if I can feel the imprint from Eric's hand, still hear his words in my ears.

And then he's back. The door jangles and I look up. "You should see some of the snowdrifts out there," he says, breathing hard. "Took me forever to trudge through it."

"How's your car?" I ask, ashamed to realize I'm secretly hoping it's stuck, that the snowplows haven't made any progress. I just want to have him to myself, in this library utopia, a little longer.

"Nearly covered, but the plows are close. One street over," he says.

I nod. "Good," I say, trying to hide my disappointment.

He grabs a muffin from the box on the circulation desk and I pretend to busy myself with the computers, making sure they all come back on and boot up correctly.

"Hey," he says, after inhaling a muffin and going back for a second one. "What are you doing for New Year's Eve?"

I look up. "Nothing," I say, blinking.

"Want to spend it with us? Connie said they do fireworks off the bridge downtown. We could find a place to watch them."

I open my mouth to say something about the crowds, but he interjects: "Away from too many people."

I've never been asked on a date before, and I wonder if this is it. The first time. Even if a ten-year-old will be joining us. I bite my lip to keep my smile from growing too large. "Yeah," I say, my lips stretching farther across my face anyway. I duck my head. "Yeah. That sounds good."

Two days later, Madison arrives at my house with an armload of clothing in plastic dry-cleaning bags. "Oh god," she says when I let her in. "You look terrible."

"I'm sick," I say, wiping a tissue beneath my red, runny nose for what feels like the hundredth time that day.

"You can't be sick. It's New Year's Eve! You have a date."

I instantly regretted calling Madison and telling her about Eric's asking me out after he left the library that morning. She immediately began talking about what I was going to wear and doing my makeup, and it all started to feel like too much. Too overwhelming. And maybe Eric didn't even mean for it to be a date.

"I'm not going," I say, my head pounding. "I've got the flu or the worst head cold ever or something."

"Of course you're going. Take some Day-Quil."

"Are drugs your answer for everything?"

She pretends to ponder this and then nods. "Most things."

"Well, I already took some medicine and I still feel like this," I say. "I just need to sleep."

She pouts. "Fine. Ruin my fun. But I'm leaving this black little number here, because it's the one I was going to make you wear anyway." She pulls a garment out of its clear plastic bag encasement and holds up a sweater that has sequins on the front, some kind of leather material on the sides, and wisps of fur around the wrists and hem.

"That looks like a dead cat. With glitter."

"It does not! It's super sexy. Trust me."

"Where are the pants?"

She cocks her head at me. "It's a dress."

I laugh, even though it makes my head hurt worse. "That is *not* a dress."

"Whatever," she says, tossing it on the couch. "I've got to go get the kids from Donovan before his latest whore — oops! I mean date — gets there." She gives a little good-bye salute. "Feel better," she says. "And wear the dress." She points at it where it's draped on the back of the sofa for emphasis. Then she turns to leave.

"I'm not going," I call after her, but she's already shut the door behind herself and I don't know if she hears me.

I wipe my nose again and plop down on the couch. My head feels like it's going to explode. I need to call Eric and cancel, but I'm exhausted and I just want to go to sleep. Besides, I reason, maybe I will feel better after a nap and be up to going. I stretch out, lay my head on a throw pillow, and close my eyes.

"Jubilee?"

I open my eyes and look up, directly into Eric's upside-down face. Am I dreaming? I blink again and take in his freshly shaven cheeks his tousled hair. He looks exceptionally good in my dream.

"Um, the door was unlocked." He points back at it with his thumb. Oh my god. New Year's Eve. This is not a dream. I sit straight up.

"I knocked a few times but you didn't answer, so I just . . . we did say seven, didn't we?"

"It's seven?" I croak, my throat dry and now noticeably sore, as if the cold moved its way from my head to my neck while I slept. I rub my hand over my face and feel some drool on my cheek. I hastily wipe it away and hope Eric didn't notice. "I'm sorry, I should have called you," I say, sniffling. "I'm sick."

"Yeah, I can tell," he says, a flash of concern crossing his face. "Is this . . . is it something to do with your allergy?"

"Oh no," I say. "Just a bad cold or something."

"So I guess the fireworks are out."

"Yeah," I say. "I don't think I'm up for it. But you guys should go. Is Aja in the car?"

"No," Eric says, giving his head a small shake. "He, ah . . . he wanted to spend some time with Connie, so they're hanging together at her place."

My stomach flips. Something about the way he says it makes me think maybe he orchestrated it. That he wanted to be alone with me. But then, that's stupid. It's not like we can *do* anything.

A little tickle in my throat forces me to cough, and then I can't stop. Eric moves a step closer and then freezes as if he just realized there's nothing he can do. He walks past me and into the kitchen. When he comes back with a glass of water in his gloved hand, the hacking has subsided. I take it from him gratefully. After a few sips, I say: "You know, you probably shouldn't be here. I don't want to get you sick, too."

"I think I can chance it," he says. "I promise not to get too close." He winks, and I feel myself growing warm.

As I nurse the water, he peels off his scarf and coat and throws them on the armchair, but I notice he leaves his gloves on. "Now," he says. "What do you need? Hot tea? Chicken soup?"

As he stands there looking at me, I study him. Why is he here? Why is he doing this for *me*? I can't understand it. And I think maybe, I don't want to. I don't want to analyze it anymore. I just want to give in to everything I'm feeling, even if I can't give in to *everything*. I flush, hoping my thoughts aren't written on my face.

"Tea would be nice," I say. "I have some in the cabinet to the top right of the stove."

He nods and points at the TV. "You turn on the New Year's countdown so we don't miss whatever terrible pop band is playing. I'll be right back."

432

I stand up to grab the remote from where it's resting next to the TV and click buttons until Ryan Seacrest's plastic smile and coiffed hair fill the screen. When I settle back into the couch, something brushes the back of my neck and I jump, startled, and reach up, half-scared my hand is about to come in contact with a spider. Instead, I find myself touching the crazy fur part on Madison's sweater dress. I pull it into my lap.

"Do you take sugar?" I look up at Eric where he fills the frame of the doorway between the den and the kitchen.

"Just a little," I say. "Thanks."

He eyes the sweater. "What is that?"

"A dress. Allegedly. Madison brought it over," I say.

"A dress?" he says, cracking a smile. "Looks like a dead raccoon or something."

"I know!" I hold it up so he can take in the leather and sequins.

"Oh dear god," he laughs. "It's hideous. Why did she give it to you?"

"She wanted me to wear it tonight."

His eyes go big. "What? *Nooo.* That's amazing. Were you going to?"

"Of course not," I say.

"Well now you have to put it on," he says. "Obviously."

"What? No." I start laughing, and it turns into a cough. "I am not doing that."

"I'm afraid I insist," he says, crossing his arms. "If only to prove that it is, in fact, an article of clothing and not a deceased animal. Go." He waves his hand toward the stairs. "While I finish making the tea."

He leaves the room and I sit there clutching the dress, a smile on my face. This is so ridiculous. But I am curious to see what it actually looks like on. I climb the stairs and, in my bedroom, peel off my T-shirt and sweatpants. Then I catch sight of myself in the mirror and cringe a little at my appearance. My hair is a tangled disaster and my face looks pale, the circles beneath my eyes pronounced. I test my breath by breathing out into my cupped hand and inhale a combination of sickness and morning breath. I head to the bathroom to brush my teeth and then I wash my face and pinch my cheeks to try to add a little color to them.

Back in my room I put on fresh underwear and a bra and pull Madison's dress over my head. At first I think it's far too small — even though Madison and I are roughly the same size — but after pulling and tugging on it, I finally get it down over my body. I look in the mirror and see that some of the weird fur-feather-like trimmings have stuck to my mouth. I peel them off, spitting a little to get a piece off my tongue, and then take in the rest of my reflection. The dress clings to me like Saran wrap, showing off every curve, which I'm sure *is* sexy on someone like Madison, whose breasts are noticeably larger than mine, but on me it just accentuates everything I don't have. And then the fur and the sequins, well — I can't help it. I giggle. It is truly terrible.

"Jubilee?" Eric calls from downstairs.

"Yeah?"

"You coming down?"

"No!" I shout back. "It's worse than we thought."

"You have to!" he says. "You promised."

I laugh. "I did not."

He doesn't respond. And then I hear a creaking sound and I know he's coming up the stairs.

"Don't you dare come up here!" I say, looking around the room in a tiny panic, wondering where I can hide. And then, barring that option, what I can put on over the dress. Nothing's in arm's reach.

"Couldn't hear you. What did you say?" He grins at me from the door and then his eyes drop to the dress and he sucks in his breath.

"Awful, right?"

He doesn't say anything. Just stands there looking, his jaw a little slack, his chest heaving from his jaunt up the stairs. My body starts heating up under his scrutiny and I'm afraid I'm turning a thousand shades of red, which seems to be my default setting around him.

"Eric?" I say, my throat dry.

"You," he says, taking a step toward me, "are so . . ." He takes another step. He drops his head, shakes it. Mumbles something under his breath. Then he meets my gaze again and takes three more slow, pensive steps until he's right in front of me.

I lift my eyebrows in surprise, at both his half declaration and his close proximity. "You like it?" I say, my voice a whisper.

"No. God no," he whispers back. "The dress is dreadful."

I laugh and he grins at me. And then he reaches his gloved hand tentatively up to my face. "But you . . ."

I don't know what comes over me in that moment, but instead of dodging his hand, jerking away, I lean toward it, putting my cheek in his palm like a desperate, feral cat in need of petting. He spreads his fingers like a starfish, threading them in my hair, his thumb stretching under my chin, and I wish more than anything I could feel the warmth of his skin on mine, but I know the knit of the glove is as good as it's going to get. I close my eyes, willing my rapid heart-beat to slow. I swallow, the action burning my raw throat.

"Jubilee," Eric says.

"Yes?"

"Open your eyes."

I look at him. Into his olive-green eyes that are moving closer with each suspended second. He's going to kiss me. I know he is and I'm powerless to stop it. Because I want it, more than I've ever wanted anything in my ridiculous, lonely life. I want to feel his chapped lips on mine, his tongue in my mouth, the heat of his breath. I know it would kill me. I'm as sure of it as I am my own name. But in this moment, I'm sure of something else — I would gladly die.

But then, at the last second, he stops, his face inches from mine. And he holds my gaze as his gloved thumb brushes over my bottom lip. I fight the urge to close my eyes, to give in to the sensation of the thousands of nerve endings firing in rapid succession, as he slowly rubs the pad of his thumb back and forth. And then it's gone, and my lip feels bare, exposed, as his hand travels down from my cheek to my neck, his fingers trailblazing a path on my skin.

He gently traces my exposed collarbone, his thumb resting in the hollow just above my chest. And all I can hear are the suddenly audible inhales and exhales of breath — but I can no longer tell if they're his or mine. And then his hand leaves my neck, slowly journeying lower, over the fabric of the dress, his fingers outlining the edge of my bra until — finally, as if I was always aware that this was the destination — his hand is on my breast, cupping it in his palm. His thumb brushes the two layers of fabric covering my nipple and I suck in my breath. That's when I know with utter confidence the heavy exhales are his, because I've stopped breathing altogether. My head feels light, like it may float off my body at any second, and my kneecaps are feathers, incapable of bearing the weight of my body.

"Eric," I whisper. Or maybe I'm just thinking it. Rolling his name around in my mind like a hard candy on the tongue. Savoring it.

And then a muffled chiming tone floats up through the air. It starts like the buzzing of a mosquito and then gets incessantly louder. We both freeze. "I, uh . . . I should probably get that," he says, his voice husky.

I swallow and force my head to give a little

438

nod. "Yeah," I say.

He moves his hand from my breast and takes a step back, digging into his pocket for his phone.

He talks for a minute, but I'm not paying attention to his words. I can't process anything except what just happened. And I can't even process that.

When he brings the phone back down, ending the call, I look at him.

"That was Connie," he says. "Aja's ready to go home. Apparently his iPad died and he forgot the charger. Connie offered to go get it for him, but he said he wanted to play on his computer anyway, and there was no talking him out of it. She said she'd be happy to take him and hang with him there, but I should probably . . . I think I should —"

"No, of course," I say, suddenly self-conscious. "You should go. Be with him."

But he doesn't move. He just stands there, gloved hands hanging by his sides innocently, as if they weren't just changing my entire worldview a few moments earlier.

He clears his throat. "Come with me," he says.

"To your house?"

"Yeah. I mean, if you're feeling up to it." He grins and adds: "I think I've got a pack of ramen in the cupboard I could make for you."

I consider this, how I'm feeling. There's my sore throat and cough, of course, and then there's the fact that my entire body is ever-so-slightly trembling — but I know that has nothing to do with my cold. And I also know that the only place I want to be tonight is wherever he is.

"OK," I say. "Just let me change."

"Yes," he says with a soft chuckle. "You should definitely change. I'll wait downstairs."

On the way to Connie's, I find myself staring at Eric's profile — his square jaw, his arms, his hands on the steering wheel — and playing the short event in my room over and over again like a skipping record. I wonder what else would have happened if the phone hadn't rung. And I wonder if Eric's thinking that, too.

When we get to his sister's house, he leaves the car running. "I'll just grab him," he says. "You can sit tight. I won't be but a minute."

"OK," I say. He shuts the door and I watch him walk toward her front porch another flush of heat coursing through my body. Once he's inside, his cell lights up in the console where he left it, blaring that obnoxious ringtone.

"Damn phone," I mutter.

It's silent for a few seconds and then it's off again, lighting up and buzzing and ringing. By the time Eric gets back to the car with Aja, whoever is calling him has tried six times.

"Your phone is blowing up," I say as he eases into the driver's seat.

"What?" He turns to me.

"Your phone," I say as it takes off ringing again. He picks it up, punches a button, and holds it to his ear.

"Hey, Aja." I turn toward the backseat to look at him.

"Hey," he says. I'm about to ask him if he knows that more cars are stolen on New Year's Eve than any other holiday, when the panic in Eric's voice catches my attention.

"What's going on? Slow down . . . slow down! When? . . . How? Oh my god . . . OK, OK . . . Jesus . . ."

His face grows paler with each word and there's a tremor to his voice I've never heard before. I stare at him, a pit growing in my stomach, and then his eyes meet mine.

I raise my eyebrows and he mouths one word: "Ellie."

■ ■ ■ ■

PART III

■ ■ ■ ■

We should meet in another life, we should
meet in air, me and you.

Sylvia Plath

(Twenty Years Ago)

THE NEW YORK TIMES

(continued from page 19B) It begs the question: what does the future look like for a girl who can't have human contact?

"No contact sports, for starters," says Dr. Benefield. "And yes, Ms. Jenkins must be very careful about hugging her daughter or touching her anywhere that's not covered by a protective layer of clothing. Allergies are unpredictable and you just can't take the chance. One day it's a severe rash and then the next it's anaphylaxis — life or death."

A frightening prospect for any child, but what about as she gets older? I mention boys, the normal rites of passage that teenagers go through: hand-holding, first kisses — and eventually, sex.

Dr. Benefield shifts in his seat.

"Sometimes science can advance at a rapid pace," he says. "It's entirely possible that, with the right attention and research, a cure of some sort could be conceived for Jubilee's condition in the next five or ten years."

And if it isn't?

He clears his throat. "Then yes, Jubilee will remain unable to have skin-to-skin contact."

"So, no kissing," I clarify. "No sex."

Dr. Benefield offers a curt nod. "Correct."

It's a difficult condition to fathom, and many draw comparisons between Jubilee's case and *The Boy in the Plastic Bubble,* a 1976 made-for-TV movie starring John Travolta. The plot was loosely based on the real lives of David Vetter and Ted DeVita, two boys born with extremely compromised immune systems — any contact with water, food, or clothing that had not been highly sterilized could kill them. The boys were both confined to sterile, germ-free rooms for the entirety of their short lives (Vetter survived 13 years, while DeVita lived to see his eighteenth birthday).

When I mention the "bubble boys" to Dr. Benefield, he nods, as if it's not the first time he's heard the association. "It's just an entirely different circumstance," he says. "Jubilee can be out in the world — she just can't connect with anyone in it."

He means "connect" in the physical sense

of course, but one has to wonder if it's a Freudian slip. After all, if you can't touch, hug, or kiss anyone — how much connecting are you doing?

For now, Jubilee doesn't let those overarching life questions about her future get to her. When our little interview comes to a close and she's done with her homework at the kitchen table, she looks from me to her mom. "Can I go read now?"

This story is part of a special health series of articles on the sharp rise of childhood allergies in the world, including a look at some of the rarest conditions. Look for next week's article: "The Boy Who Couldn't See the Sun."

TWENTY-THREE

JUBILEE

If you'd told me six months ago that shortly in the future I'd be on Interstate 95 speeding north in the dead of night on New Year's Eve in a car with a man and a ten-year-old boy, I'd have laughed and laughed and laughed (after panicking a bit at the mere thought of leaving my house). But I guess nobody could have told me that, because six months ago I was alone.

And now? Decidedly not alone, but wishing with each passing road sign that I had been more parsimonious with that Xanax Madison gave me for Christmas.

I glance over at Eric, who's had the same intense look on his face since he got the phone call. When he hung up, he immediately started the car, floored it out of Connie's driveway, and began driving through the streets of Lincoln like a man possessed. It wasn't until we were passing the dark,

449

overgrown, abandoned golf course on the outskirts of town that I realized he wasn't taking me home, and the panic started to set in. Just when I thought I had gotten used to being in the few places outside of my house that I had ventured — when I was starting to think I had conquered most of my agoraphobia — I was now stuck in a tin can hurtling outside the city limits and learning that I am not in fact over my fear of the unknown.

"So, um . . . ," I say in a small voice. "I guess I'm coming with you?" Eric's elbow is lodged on the door frame, propping his fist up to clench tufts of his hair. Lost in thought, he barely glances at me when I speak, and then his eyes go wide.

"Shit!" he says, but he doesn't slow the car. "I didn't even — All I was thinking about was getting to her. Do you want me to turn around?"

I do, but I also know that he doesn't really want to. "No, it's OK."

"Are you sure? I could stop at the next exit. Call you a cab?"

Being alone in a place I've never been before strikes even more fear than driving somewhere I've never been with Eric and Aja.

"No, no, it's fine."

Eric nods, squeezing his hair again.

"What happened?" I ask quietly.

He sighs before he speaks. "Drug over-dose. Ellie had a seizure."

"Oh my god. From what?"

"I don't know. I knew Ellie was into pot, but I didn't think — I thought that was all. *Goddamn it!* I told Stephanie . . ." He trails off into his own thoughts.

I wait a few minutes and then ask: "Is she OK . . . is she going to be?"

"I don't know."

We stop for gas and snacks after about an hour, but the rest of the five-hour drive is mostly silent. When we cross the New Hampshire border around three a.m., Aja says: "Did you know it takes Venus two hundred forty-three Earth days to make a full rotation on its axis, but only two hundred twenty-five to orbit the sun? So a day on Venus is longer than a year."

I try to remember what I learned about Venus in school, and all I can think of is that awful Ray Bradbury story where the girl gets locked in the closet.

When we get to the hospital, Eric pulls right up in front, where it clearly states *Emergency Vehicles Only,* and jumps out. Since he took the keys, Aja and I are left with no choice but to follow him out into the cold air. We catch up to him at the elevator. There are a few other people in the small square box and I suck in my breath, trying to make myself as tiny as possible. Just when it feels like the walls are closing in, the elevator dings on the fifth floor and Eric gets out. He looks both ways and nods his head, like he's spotted something familiar on his left, and starts walking. Halfway down the hall, a woman stands up from her seated position in a molded plastic chair, like she's been waiting for us.

"How is she?" Eric asks before we even reach her.

"She's fine. She'll be fine," the woman says.

Eric nods, but I can feel the anxiety coming off him in waves. "Why are you out here? Can I see her?"

"She's sleeping right now. I'm letting her rest."

"Steph, what *happened*?"

"I don't know," she says, and then her face drops and she just looks tired. Exhausted, really. They both lower themselves into the chairs in front of the door. "Apparently, they thought they were smoking regular weed, but one of the kids had got this synthetic stuff instead. The police said it was K2, but

one of the girls called it Spice. I Googled it
— looks pretty bad. But she didn't know,
Eric. She didn't know." Fat tears drop from
her eyes. And then, as if she's finally allowing herself to understand the events of the
day, she says: "Oh, God — she could have
died."

Eric wraps his arms around her and lets
her cry, murmuring in her hair. "It's OK . . .
She didn't . . . She's OK." She collapses
against him.

The scene is so private, so intimate, I turn
away and find myself looking at a large
framed drawing on the wall. It's a crayon
picture of a tree with *Edna, age 7* signed in
a childish scrawl at the bottom. I stare at it
like it's the *Mona Lisa* and I've never seen
anything so fascinating, all while blinking
rapidly. My eyes have started to burn, and I
know it has nothing to do with Ellie.

I'm embarrassed to even admit to myself
that I'm jealous. I'm in a hospital where
Eric's daughter nearly died, and all I can
think about is the warmth of his arms and
how I want them wrapped around *me.*
Touching *me.* How I want his breath in *my*
hair. And how unfair it is that I will never
be able to feel his cheek on mine, his skin
on my skin. Unless . . .

"Who are you?"

The question jolts me around and my eyes lock with Stephanie's. "Oh, hi, I'm . . ."

"She's a friend," Eric says. "A librarian."

I jolt at the classification.

"She was in the car when you called, and I didn't even — I just panicked."

"Oh," Stephanie says, but her forehead remains wrinkled in confusion over my presence. "Hi, Aja." She moves her gaze to him. "You've gotten taller."

He doesn't look up at her.

Stephanie nods, as if she expected that. She turns to Eric. "Well, Ellie was up until about thirty minutes ago, so I imagine she'll be sleeping for most of the morning. The doctor said they'll most likely release her late tonight or first thing tomorrow morning. He just wants to make sure the seizure . . . that it was an isolated event. Why don't you guys go home, get something to eat, some rest. I know that was a long drive."

"Longer than Venus orbiting the sun," Aja mutters.

I bite back a smile.

"No. I'm not leaving," says Eric. "Not until I can see her."

Stephanie sighs. "At least take them home, Eric. Aja looks exhausted."

It's the second time she's said it, but it only occurs to me now to be curious. *Home.*

Surely we're not going to Stephanie's house. I mean, it appears their divorce is amicable, but that would still be awkward.

But I don't say anything as we ride the elevator back down and walk out to the car (which has fortunately not been towed in the fifteen minutes we were gone). The car ride is silent, too, Eric's thoughts no doubt on his daughter.

Just as the first rays of sun start to lighten the night sky, we pull up to a small, yellow-slatted Cape Cod, a brick chimney peeking over the back of the roof like bunny ears in a class picture. Though the roads have been clear, the driveway and walk up to the house are caked in half a foot of snow. Eric parks on the street and we crunch our way single file to the front door.

I expect to be greeted by warmth when we step into the foyer, but it's not much better than being outside. "Gotta turn up the heat," Eric mumbles. "Turn the water on, plug the fridge in." He's making a running list in his head, while I'm busy trying to catch up to the fact that no one lives here.

Eric busies himself throughout the house while Aja and I walk into the kitchen. He plugs his iPad into a wall socket and sets it on the counter.

"Aja," I whisper.

455

He looks up at me.

"Whose house is this?"

He juts his head toward me, nose wrinkled, jaw slack, as if I've gone completely mental.

"Eric's," he says, and then: "Mine, too, I suppose."

"But you live in New Jersey. Is he trying to sell this one?"

"No," he says, as if that's the end of the conversation. As if that explains everything.

"Aja," I say, my voice a little firmer. "Why does Eric still have this house?"

His eyebrows are horizontal parentheses. "Because we live in it? New Jersey is just temporary. Six months. For his job."

He takes off down the hall, presumably toward his room, and I'm left standing there, mouth agape at this revelation. Eric lives in New Hampshire, which means . . . Eric will be leaving.

My knees, no longer interested in holding me upright, bend. There's no kitchen table, so I just lower myself to the tile I'm standing on.

"I don't have much for breakfast, but you both probably want to just sleep right now anyway. Pizza or Chinese OK for later? They deliver —" Eric's voice breaks through the fog of my thoughts. "Jubilee?" he says when he sees me. "You OK?"

I lift my head to look at him, my arms propped on my knees. He looks so solid, so sturdy. Not at all like a phantom. But now I know that's exactly what he is. "Yeah," I say. "Just tired."

"God, of course you are," he says sincerely. "I'm so sorry. I can't believe I brought you here. Into all my problems."

"It's fine," I say, lowering my head back on my forearms. I feel like I'm going to be sick.

"You're not fine," he says, coming closer. "You're sick, and I dragged you all the way out here. God, I'm an idiot. What can I get for you? What do you need?"

You, I want to respond. *I need you.*

But I don't. I've lived twenty-seven years without him. I can live twenty-seven more.

"Really, I'm OK," I say, forcing myself to stand up.

"You sure?" he says.

I nod.

He scrutinizes my face, and I can tell he doesn't believe me, but he doesn't push further. "OK," he says. "Well, ah . . . make yourself at home. The takeout menus are in the top drawer to the left of the sink. I turned the water back on, but you might want to give it a while to heat up, if you want to take a shower. There are towels in my bathroom. Clean sheets in the closet. You can have my bed tonight."

I nod again but don't raise my eyes to him. And then, just like that, he's gone.

There are two couches in the den where Aja and I lie down after Eric leaves. Aja turns on the TV but he passes out within minutes and I'm left to my thoughts, my mind still reeling about what he said.

At first I was mad — how could Eric not have told me he was leaving? How could he have allowed me to get so comfortable with him, to feel so close? But then reality sets in and I have to acknowledge the truth: Why *would* he tell me? It's not like he owes me anything. I'm just some girl he's been giving a ride home for a few months. His words to Stephanie ring in my ears. I'm just a *librarian. A friend.* And I'm suddenly embarrassed that I ever thought it was anything more. But then another part of my brain chimes in: He tried to kiss me. And last night — his hands. His hands were . . . where they were. I shake my head to rid myself of the memory. No — what does any of that even mean? I'm old enough to know that kisses aren't contracts. And almost-kisses, well, they mean even less. And a hand on my breast, over my shirt? Well, more happens to fifteen-year-olds under the bleachers at football games. I can't believe that I thought so much of it. People get caught in the moment, but that's all they are — moments. They don't mean anything. I realize with Eric, I've just been seeing what I wanted to see this whole time, what I hoped was happening. But I can't be touched — not *under* my shirt, not anywhere, really. And he knows that — so how *could* we be anything more?

And really, I should have known he was leaving. And not just because he's a good dad and he would obviously choose to be near his daughter, but because Mr. Walcott used to say: "Look for the pattern." Of course, he was talking about solving math problems, but it's a strategy that works for life, too. The pattern is: everyone leaves. Or more specifically: everyone leaves me. And I don't mean it in the pathetic, sad, self-pitying way it sounds (although I acknowledge that it is, in fact, pathetic, sad, and self-pitying). It's just facts, the pattern of my life. My father. Mom. Hell, even Louise. If I remotely find myself caring about someone, they will not stick around. I'm sure it's just a matter of time before Madison takes off.

At some point in my meanderings, I must have fallen asleep, because I wake later on the couch, groggy, with the TV still on. Aja's awake and watching it.

"What time is it?" I ask, noticing my throat feels a little better. Small favors.

"Five," he says.

"P.m.?" I ask, a little stunned I slept that long.

"Yeah. I'm starved."

"Me too," I say.

I get up to find the takeout menus and about thirty minutes later Aja and I are eating greasy noodles and chicken in some kind of thick, overly sweet sauce on the floor of the den. There's a dining room table and chairs in the room adjacent to the kitchen, but you can't see the TV from there and Aja wanted me to watch *X-Men.* He points out the character Jubilee when she's on-screen.

"She's not a main character in this one," he says, his mouth full of rice. "Or the next two. But you're going to have a bigger part in *Apocalypse.* Well, not *you.* But you know."

"*Apocalypse,* huh? That doesn't sound too promising."

After *X-Men* is over, Aja flips channels, stopping on Discovery. It's some ocean-mysteries show and an underwater camera is focusing up close on a blue whale as he filters plankton through his big grille of a mouth.

Seeing the whale reminds me of something. "Did you know there's this whale scientists discovered that sings at a higher tone than any other whale in the world?" I say to Aja. "They measure the sounds in hertzes or something like that. Anyway, he just swims around the ocean by himself, unable to communicate with any other whales."

"Really?" he asks.

"Yep. Read it online a few years ago." I pause, and then add: "It was one of the saddest things I think I've ever read about an animal."

Aja's quiet for a minute and then says: "I don't think that's the saddest thing."

"No?"

He sits up straighter on the couch. "Do you know how koalas die?"

I narrow my eyes, trying to recall any vague information I may have accumulated over the years about koala bears. "No. I don't."

"Their teeth are built for eating eucalyptus leaves, right? But after years and years of eating it, their teeth get worn down to these

461

little nubs and they can't chew it anymore, so they starve to death."

"Really?"

"Yeah," he says. "I think that's the saddest thing."

I think for a minute. "Did you know that chimpanzees don't swim?"

"That's actually not true," he says.

"Wait — what?"

"Yeah. It's a commonly believed falsehood, but a couple scientists documented chimps swimming a few years ago," he says. "So, they *can* swim. They just generally choose not to."

"Huh," I say, genuinely surprised by this new information. "Well, anyway, I read that if one of them falls in a river or something, another one will go in after it to try and save it, even though it means they'll both die. It's happened at a couple zoos — chimps drowning in the moats surrounding their enclosures."

Aja nods, taking this in.

"I've always thought that was really sad, too. And also, kind of sweet."

Aja's quiet for another minute. And then: "I still think the koala one wins."

I smile at the way his mind works and turn back to the show.

And then a fresh wave of anguish flows

through me, as I realize when Eric leaves, Aja will be leaving, too.

I don't believe in séances, but standing in Eric's room at midnight, I understand why mediums in movies always want you to bring artifacts of the person's life — shirts, a wallet, jewelry. It's like a piece of them is still attached to it. It's why I can feel my mom every time I go into her room. And now, it's why I half expect to see Eric materialize in front of me at any minute, even though I know he's still at the hospital. I get undressed and take a shower in his bathroom, trying but failing to ignore that this is the same place Eric stands, the same water that arcs and bends and flows around his sharp edges and soft curves, the same towels that get to touch him in places I've never seen.

What am I *doing* here? In New Hampshire? In his house? With fresh reminders of everything I'll never have at every turn. I suddenly want to be home. Such a strong yearning emanates from my gut that I think about calling a cab, with no regard to how much a five-hour drive might cost or how uncomfortable I'd be in the backseat of a strange car, a stranger navigating it. I just want to get out of here.

But then I remember Aja in the next room. And I know I can't leave him alone.

I towel off and hurriedly get dressed, in a T-shirt and track pants from Eric's drawer (sniffing them first to make sure they're clean, so I don't have a reaction; they smell like laundry soap). I cover the bare mattress in clean sheets, crawl in, and close my eyes, but I can't sleep. Eric is everywhere. His scent, his possessions, the indent where his body lies night after night — his presence is palpable. But it's like the air — all around me, but impossible to touch.

TWENTY-FOUR

ERIC

Ellie looks older and younger at the same time, if that's possible. Her flat-ironed hair now has streaks of cerulean, the same color her lips used to turn when she devoured those artificial ice pops in the summer. Raspberry, her favorite, was inexplicably blue.

But she's tiny, impossibly tiny in the hospital bed, as if she's Alice in Wonderland and just drank the shrinking potion, her shoulders turning in on themselves, her body being eaten by the thin mattress.

I turn my attention to her nose, where a tiny diamond rests in the curve above her nostril, and try not to have a coronary about Stephanie's letting her get a piercing. At least it's not a tattoo.

While I study her, breathing in the relief that her body is still full of life, no matter how she's decorated it, she stares right back

at me, her eyes cold and unflinching. I wait
— does she still hate me? I'm afraid to say
anything — afraid to say the wrong thing.

And then she says: "Daddy," and I think
my knees might buckle from relief.

"Ellie."

"Daddy, I'm so sorry." Her face crumples
in segments like an accordion, starting with
her forehead. Tears leak down her cheeks.

"Oh, honey," I say, scooping her into my
arms. I sit on the edge of her hospital bed,
letting her drench my shoulder. I stroke her
blue hair until her ragged breathing slowly
regains an even cadence.

She extricates herself from my arms and
sits back, wiping her nose with the back of
her bare arm. I reach over for a tissue from
the counter and hand it to her.

"What were you thinking?" I ask, reaching
up to her face and tucking an errant lock
behind her ear.

"I don't know," she says, looking down.
"Darcy said it was just like regular weed."

"But even the weed, Ellie. This isn't you,"
I say, flicking the blue strands grazing her
shoulder to emphasize my point.

She jerks away, anger flashing in her eyes.
"You don't know who I am."

I drop my hand. Look at her. Let her
words sink in. "You're right. I don't know

who you are. Not anymore. But, Ellie, I'm trying. I really want to know."

"What, by reading some stupid books?" she snaps.

I flinch.

"Yeah, by reading some books," I say, mindful to keep my tone calm, steady. "Reading your journal. I didn't have much choice, did I? You wouldn't exactly speak to me."

"I wonder why." She rolls her eyes and crosses her arms in front of her chest.

"Ellie, I know what I said was awful, but I'm sorry. I've apologized a hundred times. You know, people say things, sometimes, that they don't mean. It happens. People make mistakes. *I* made a mistake."

"You think this is all because of what you *said*?"

"Well, yeah." I sit up a little straighter. "Isn't it?"

She scoffs. "Oh my God. Mom was right. You are so emotionally clueless."

I try to ignore this dig and wait for her to continue. She doesn't. She just turns her head and looks out the window, as if the street lamp is a completely fascinating piece of technology she's never seen before.

"Are you going to —"

"You *left* me!" she screams, startling me.

467

"You left! You said when you were divorcing Mom that you would still always be there. Just not in the same house. But you weren't!"

Jubilee flashes in my mind. Her rumpled body in the passenger seat of my car, shoulders heaving at her mother's betrayal. Is that how Ellie has felt this whole time? The thought levels me.

"And you took *him* with you."

"Aja?"

"It's what you always wanted, isn't it? A son. Someone that's not complicated and emotional. A kid that's easy to understand. And you got him and then you had your chance to leave. To have some easy life without me and you took it."

My eyes grow bigger with each thought that tumbles from her mouth. I don't even know where to begin when it's my turn to speak. "Aja," I start, "is anything but uncomplicated and unemotional. And I think I'm doing a worse job with him than I ever did with you, if that helps at all. And this job, what I moved for? It's just a temporary assignment. Six months. Didn't your mother tell you that?"

"Yeah," she says. "But that's what they all start out as, and then you do a good job and they want you to stay."

"Why do you think that?"

"That's what Darcy said. Her dad moved them here on a 'temporary' one-year assignment." She makes finger quotes around the word "temporary" and it strikes me as very adult. I wonder if Darcy taught her that, too. "And they've been here for two years now with no sign of leaving."

Oh, if only it had been temporary, I think, but I bite my tongue.

"Well, this *is* temporary. I'm filling in for the VP's maternity leave and she is coming back. We're working on the transition now. Besides, even if they did ask me to stay, I never would. I would *never* leave you. Not for good."

She sniffs. "Even if they asked you to be partner?"

I look at her sad eyes. Her nose stud glints in the fluorescent light. And I say with utter confidence: "Even if they asked me to be partner."

She gives a little nod and looks down at her hands. I'm not sure where to go from here. I'm not sure if she believes me. I'm not sure if I can undo all the damage I've unwittingly done. But I am sure that I'm moving back, as soon as I can. And that I'll never leave her again.

And then, for the second time in that

hospital room, I think of Jubilee.

I get home around three a.m., bone tired despite a quick, uncomfortable nap sitting up in a hospital chair that afternoon. The house is dark, but thankfully warmer than when I left it. I walk down the hall, peeking into Aja's dark room, his dark figure a restful mound on the bed. I continue to my room, the old floorboards creaking beneath my feet. I unbutton the top of my shirt as I go. A sour tang wafts up, reminding me I haven't showered in nearly forty-eight hours, but I'm too exhausted to deal with that now.

I come to the foot of my bed and stand there. Jubilee, like Aja, is a waifish shapeless heap under the sheets, but I feel pulled toward her, like she's on the winning side in a game of tug-of-war. I would give anything to surrender. To crawl in bed beside her, feel the length of her body against mine, the heat of her skin, the drumming of her heart. I wonder if she thinks about it, too.

And then suddenly, I'm overcome with the desire to find out. To know if I'm alone in my longing, a lighthouse signaling to an empty sea.

"Jubilee," I breathe. My veins thrum as I wait for her response. She doesn't stir. I try

470

one more time.

"Jubilee." I peer at her in the dark and can just make out her face, the outline of her upside-down pout against my pillow. I walk to the opposite side of the king-size bed and hesitate. In theory, two people can sleep in this bed and never find each other during the night. I should know — Stephanie and I successfully avoided each other for months in a bed this size.

But the thought of Jubilee just an arm's length away — the waves of her hair beckoning me like the ocean to the shore — proves too tempting to bear. I pick up the extra pillow, reach for a blanket from the top of the open closet, and stretch out on the carpet below her feet, listening to her breathe and waiting for sleep to overtake me. But it doesn't come for a long, long time.

The next morning, I get up before the house is awake and run to the corner market for coffee and bagels. When I get back, Jubilee is in the kitchen filling a glass at the sink.

"Morning," I say, setting the sack on the counter. She's wearing one of my white undershirts and a pair of track pants. Even with the waistband folded over three or four times they still hang on her hips.

"Morning," she replies, and then gulps the water.

"Um, I've got to go back to the hospital this morning. Help Ellie get checked out and settled at home. And then we can leave. Is that OK?"

"Sure," she says, but the word has a chill. It's a tone I haven't heard from her before and it gives me pause. "Can I use your washing machine?" she asks.

"Of course. Anything you need. Oh, and I bought bagels." I pat the bag for emphasis. "Will you let Aja know?"

"Yep," she says, putting her glass under the faucet again.

I turn to go, not knowing what to say next. After all, I just dragged this woman across many state lines to my house in New Hampshire with no warning in the middle of the night — I'd probably be a little miffed, too.

With a stiff hug and the promise that I'll return every other weekend before I move for good in February, I leave Ellie at Stephanie's house.

"Answer my texts," I say, fixing her with my best dad look.

"Only if you stop sending stupid ones."

"Not much chance of that."

She offers a half smile, and though I want

to shout, *No more drugs! No more Darcy! No more leaving the house!* I decide it's best to leave on a high note. Besides, Stephanie surprisingly agreed with me that Ellie should be grounded for a month, so at least I can rest in the knowledge that she won't be leaving home for anything but school for the foreseeable future.

On the way back to New Jersey, Aja taps at his video game, while I let the last few days sink in, along with a bone-weary exhaustion. It's not until we're halfway through the drive that I realize Jubilee isn't speaking. Hasn't since I picked them up at the house and loaded everyone into the car.

"Did you call in to the library?" I ask, realizing that it's probably open today — the day after New Year's — and that she's missing work.

"Yeah. Shayna's covering for me," she says, and turns to watch the passing trees and snow-covered hills out the passenger window.

"Hey, I'm really sorry again, about bringing you into all this. But I'm glad — I'm glad you were here." I clear my throat.

"It's fine," she says, cutting me off. "It was no big deal."

"Yeah, but . . ." I search for words, the right ones, but they don't come.

"Really. It's fine," she repeats with finality.

And I wonder if I've been misreading her this entire time. The glances, the flushed cheeks, the palpable tension in the air between us. Did I make it all up? Have I been so blinded by my own attraction that I imagined Jubilee's? And then I remember Ellie's words in the hospital, stuck in my mind like a pebble in a shoe: "emotionally clueless." But, being in her room, touching her cheek with my gloved hand, her collarbone, her perfectly round breast — I know, I *know* she felt it, too.

But then what? We've never talked about it. About any of those moments, except for that night in the library when she referenced some abstract treatment that she may or may not get. And I think of what Connie said — how I always want what I can't have. And maybe I need to face the reality of this situation — I want Jubilee and I can't have her. And maybe Jubilee's just a step ahead of me and has already figured that out.

When we finally get back to Lincoln, I offer to swing by a drugstore, get her some soup or medicine — it seems like her cold is better, but I feel guilty for not even asking. "I just want to get home," she says.

I nod. "It's just that I promised you ramen," I say, hoping for a smile. "I don't like to go back on my promises."

She doesn't respond. The rest of the ride we pass in silence.

I pull into her driveway and put the gearshift in park. She reaches for the door handle and before I know what I'm doing, I touch her coat sleeve. She jerks her arm like my hand is the mouth of a king cobra.

"What are you doing?" she asks, her eyes on me for the first time since we left New Hampshire.

"Nothing. I don't — I'm sorry. It's just . . ." I take a deep breath, trying to rein in the desperation encircling me like a vine. I exhale. "See you tomorrow?"

"No," she says.

"What?" My brow rises, then drops, as directionless and confused as I feel.

"I don't need a ride anymore."

"Sure you do. It's still co—"

"I'm not some damsel in distress that you have to save!" she says, and it's like all air suddenly leaves the car in a whoosh. "I don't need you to get me soup, I don't need you to fix my car, I don't need you to drive me home! I was fine before you came and I'll be fine now."

I sit there, my body suspended in time, too stunned to move, to respond.

She looks down at her gloved hands in

her lap and when she speaks again her voice is small. "You've done more than enough. Thank you."

And then, the door opens, and just like that, she's gone.

I remain still, unaware of how much time is passing, until I hear Aja's voice from the backseat. "Eric?"

I glance in the rearview mirror, meeting his eyes, which are as round and wide as mine.

"Can I still go to the library?" he asks, his voice trembly.

"I don't know, bud," I say, putting the car in reverse and slowly backing out of Jubilee's driveway. "I don't think so."

Twenty-Five

Jubilee

I didn't sleep at all that night — or the next. How could I, when all I could hear were my words replaying like a scratched record in my head and all I could see was Eric's hurt face just staring at me from the front seat of his car?

Exhausted, I slowly move through my Monday morning routine, washing my face, pulling on my thermal underwear. I get a pang in my heart remembering Eric's response that night in the library when I told him I was wearing it: *Are you trying to seduce me?* And I wonder how many more moments I'll have to go through like this; how many memories I've created of him; how completely he's invaded my life in such a short time.

I contemplate calling in sick to work, but I need the distraction.

The day is long and feels as though the

world is conspiring to remind me of all that has gone wrong. The pillow golfer, Michael, who has never said four words to me, suddenly wants to know where Louise is. "She on some kind of sabbatical? I haven't seen her for a while," he says. I notice that standing up, instead of hunched over a computer screen, he's not unattractive. If you passed him on the street, you'd have no idea he spends his entire day in the library sitting on a pillow.

"Fired," I reply. "City council cut funding." He stares at me, his brown eyes searching mine, and I'm convinced he's wondering what everyone else is: why it wasn't me.

"Well that's a bummer," he says. I make a noncommittal sound and look back down at the books I'm sorting, hoping he'll take the hint.

"Ah, that's a great book," he says, pointing to the one in my right hand. I look down at it. *On the Road* by Jack Kerouac. I've never read it.

"Really?" I ask, raising my eyebrows at him, surprised that he reads. Surprised that he does anything but play that stupid golf computer game.

"Really," he says, a sadness in his eyes. "It was my dad's favorite." I look down at it again, and when I look back up, he's gone.

478

At four thirty, the door opens and out of the corner of my eye I see Aja. I turn toward him, but realize it's just a boy, same small frame, but with dull brown curly hair instead of Aja's shiny jet black. And that's what almost breaks me. I was so mad at Eric, so eager to disentangle him from my life, I wasn't thinking about Aja. What must he think of me? I almost call Eric, tell him it's fine for Aja to still come to the library, but in the end, I can't bring myself to do it. As much as I'll miss Aja, it's better this way. A clean break.

But if that's really true, I can't explain why, for the next week, every time the door opens, my heart quickens in my chest, thumping with hope that it's one of them coming in. Eric or Aja.

By the end of January, I've finally given up, resigned myself to the fact that it's really over — whatever it was — and I finally stop watching the door, stop hoping that Eric will burst in like some kind of Hollywood paramour.

And that's when he comes in.

Not Eric.

But Donovan.

I blink three times when I see him, trying to make sense of him in this space, of him in a suit, of him at all. Donovan only exists to me as a boy in a courtyard, wearing an obnoxious sideways trucker hat and a pair of lips that gave me my first and only kiss, an arrogant teen who nearly killed me, all for a bet.

Time slows as he walks toward me, and I wonder in quick succession first if he'll recognize me, and then if I have time to run off to the back room and hide. A plan that might work if only my feet would just move.

"Jubilee," he says, answering my first question in his maple-syrup voice. It's deeper, but I'd recognize it anywhere. He stops in front of the desk, and I feel his eyes crawling from the top of my head down to the gloves on my hands. It takes every ounce of willpower to remain still and unbothered by his inspection.

"Madison told me you were working here," he says, a slow smile spreading across his face. "I had to come see it for myself. Sorry it took me so long to stop by."

Only Donovan would think that after all this time, I was waiting to see him, that his presence is desired by everyone.

"You look good," he says, and the remark catches me off guard, especially because he's dropped the theatrics. It's not slick and slimy, the way he says it, although remembering what Madison said about his extracurricular activities, I'm sure he's got complimenting women down to a science.

"Thank you," I say, although I realize with great relief that even though the heart fluttering in my throat suggests otherwise, I don't care what he thinks. Not anymore.

I want to return the compliment, but really, he looks the same. Just an older, more filled-out version of the boy in the courtyard. And his pants are properly fitted to his waist, rather than slung low to advertise the Hollister logo on the boxers he wore in high school.

"Anyway, I won't keep you. Just wanted to say I'm so glad she could do all this for you," he says.

"Who?" I ask, wondering if I've missed part of the conversation we're apparently having.

"Madison," he says.

Oh, right. I guess he knows she helped me get the job.

"God, for years, she felt so guilty."

I tilt my head, now sure I've missed something. "Wait — what are you talking about?"

"The bet," he says, as if that clarifies everything. "You know, how it was all her idea. Man, when she heard you had actually *died* — I don't know who started that crazy

481

rumor — I thought she was going to lose it." He laughs. "Anyway, that was all so long ago. Water under the bridge, right?"

My body goes cold. *Madison?* That doesn't even make sense — Donovan was her boyfriend. Why would she want him to kiss me? But then, other things start to click into place. Like how eager she was to help me when I ran into her at the gas station. And how easily I got this job, when Louise said it had been sitting open for four months — wait, *Louise.*

My eyes jerk up to Donovan. "Why did Louise get fired?"

"Who's Louise?"

"She was a librarian here. They fired her a few weeks ago."

"Oh. Right. That might technically be my fault. I didn't know her name, though. Madison called me all in a tizzy saying the funds were low and the director was going to fire you, but she couldn't let that happen, that you really needed the job. The bank donates ten grand to the library foundation every year, so I just made a call and said if you got fired, we would be withholding the check. I wasn't sure if it would work — I mean, ten Gs isn't that much money, you know? But it did." He shrugs. "Was the least I could do."

I stare at him, unable to conceal my shock. "You . . . are really . . . something," I say slowly.

"Well, thank you." He flashes a smile and tugs on his jacket lapel.

"I mean Madison said you were an asshole, but you really, really are."

His smile vanishes. "Hey, no need for name-calling. I was trying to do you a favor."

"Yeah? Just like kissing the high school pariah was such a *favor*? Listen, next time you want to perform one of your amazing grand gestures, leave me out of it."

"Jubilee." His voice softens. "I'm sorry. Look, I was a little shit back then. I know that. But I never meant — I didn't know."

His eyelashes point toward the ground and he puts on a convincing show of looking chagrined. "You were never a pariah," he says, his voice so quiet I have to lean forward to make out what he's saying. "Not to me." He takes a breath. Exhales. "Madison overheard me saying that I thought you were . . . hot, or whatever. Beautiful. And she was pissed. Jealous. I think that was her idea of revenge or something. I never should have gone along with it."

"No. You shouldn't have." I try to infuse force into my words but find I can only lace

483

their outer edges with anger, like a lazy crocheter. I suddenly have no fight left. My head is swirling with all this new information and old memories, but mostly sorrow at how cruel high schoolers — and adults — can be. Or no, maybe adults are even crueler. The acts of a flippant, immature twelfth grader, I can forgive — but this? The knowledge that she's befriended me out of some obligation, that she's been lying to me this entire time, is somehow more painful than her original sin.

Donovan bobs his head and then leaves it hanging as if it's connected to the ground by an invisible thread. "If there's anything I can do for you . . ."

"I think you've done enough," I say, but not unkindly. Our eyes meet, and even though he's probably still a shit, I forgive him. I realize he just doesn't matter. Not anymore.

One of the benefits of living alone is not having any witnesses to your most pathetic behavior. That evening, I ignore Madison's three phone calls — two on my cell and one on my home phone (which I assume is her, though I suppose it could be a telemarketer wanting to discuss ice-cream flavors) — and have a full-on pity party. The attire? Eric's

Wharton sweatshirt, which no longer smells like him since I washed it, but I put the collar of it up to my nose anyway, inhaling the memory of him. Then I go to the kitchen and fry up a batch of French toast like I'm feeding a family of six, and take it to the couch. I turn on the TV, mushing bread into my mouth with one hand and flipping channels with the other, until I land on a documentary on the Montauk Project. I stop midchew, the aliens reminding me of Aja, and then I'm sobbing and snotting all over the place, my tears mixing with the cinnamon sugar coating my lips.

I miss him, more than I expected to. And I miss Eric, even though I hate myself for it. It's so pitiful, so girlish, like I'm back in high school mooning over Donovan. And look what a waste that turned out to be. But mostly I hate that I feel more alone than I ever did in the nine years that I was actually alone.

I wish I had never left the house. Just let the money run out and starved to death when the food went too. They would have found me when the eviction became final — maybe I would have even made the *New York Times* again: "Girl Who Couldn't Be Touched Dies Atop Obscene Number of Books."

Depleted, I stretch out on the couch and pull Eric's shirt collar up around my slimy nose again, taking comfort in the one small silver lining in this whole mess: at least I found out about Eric before I attempted the immunotherapy. I can't believe I even thought about it. What if it *had* worked? Of course, it wouldn't have in time for him. He'd have been long gone to New Hampshire. But in theory, if we *had* been able to touch, if I had felt the strength of his arms around me, the sharp stubble of his chin against my cheek, his dry, chapped lips on mine — instead of just imagined it — this would be so much worse. Wouldn't it?

I clutch the sweatshirt material in my fist and squeeze, tighter and tighter, hoping the throbbing tension in my hand will lessen the searing pain of the illusive gaping hole in my chest.

But it doesn't.

On Sunday, I'm roused from sleep by a sharp rapping at the door. I know it's Madison. I've been ignoring her calls for four days now and she came by the library yesterday while I was in the back room. I told Roger to tell her I wasn't there.

"But I've just said, 'She's in the back room. I'll go get her,' " he said.

486

"Tell her you were wrong."

He rolled his eyes, but he did it.

I know I need to face her sometime, and I figure now's as good a time as any. Better than making some scene in the library anyway.

I shuffle down the stairs and fling open the door to . . .

Eric. He takes me in, starting with my wide eyes, my jaw hanging from its hinges, and then lower.

"Nice shirt," he says.

Crap. Please don't let me be wearing his sweatshirt again. I look down and exhale with relief. It's my MC Hammer hoodie that I bought off eBay a few years ago when I was in an ironic mood. It says, in big block letters: CAN'T TOUCH THIS.

"What are you doing here?"

He swipes his beanie off his head and holds it in front of him, so that he's literally standing on my porch hat in hand. I don't know why I find this funny.

"Aja and I . . . we're moving back to New Hampshire. Next week."

"I know."

"You do?"

I shrug. "I figured."

"Listen, I just . . . can I come in? I need to say some things."

487

I stare at him, knowing it will be harder if I let him in, but also that not only do I want him to come in more than anything in this world, I want him to stay. I take my shoulder off the door and open it wider. "Fine," I say, walking into the den. He follows me, each step behind me increasing the speed of my heartbeat.

I sit in the armchair, leaving the couch as his only option. He sits. He studies the ashtray on the coffee table for a minute before he speaks. "Why are you so mad at me?"

The way he so calmly asks it bursts something wide open in me.

"You lied to me!"

His brow pops up at my outburst. "What? How?"

"You never told me! That you were leaving. I didn't know! All these weeks — how could you not have told me?"

"I don't know. I guess I didn't think about it."

I open my mouth, enraged, but he holds up a hand. "No. That's not — I didn't mean it like that. I guess I didn't want to think about it." And then he peers at me, as if he's just now seeing me since I opened the door. "Wait — why do you even care?"

"What do you mean 'why do I care?' "

"Exactly what I said." I'm a bull's-eye in his sights now. He's not backing down.

I fidget under his stare. "I've just gotten really close to . . . Aja."

"Mm," he says, dropping his gaze. His shoulders follow suit. "That's what I figured."

I stifle a scream. "You're so . . . impossible!"

His head jerks up. "Me? *Me?!* I'm . . ." He scoffs. "I don't even —"

"What do you want me to say?" I yell, cutting him off. "That every time you look at me, touch me with those stupid gloves, it's like I can't catch my breath? That I'm desperate to feel your skin on mine, even if it kills me — literally? Is that what you want to hear?" I take a deep breath, an instant relief washing over me at the release, even though I simultaneously want to throw myself under the couch and hide. But it's out there now, and I can't take it back.

"Yes," he says. "Because even though you're quite possibly the most stubborn woman I've ever met, and have obviously never learned how to use a comb on that crazy mane of yours, and you possess excessive amounts of inane and useless trivia, inexplicably all I want to do is touch you with my stupid gloves."

I stare at him. "Was that supposed to be a compliment?"

"No," he says. "But this is: Driving you home from the library is easily the best part of my day. Of any day. And despite your wild hair — or maybe because of it, hell if I know — you're more beautiful than anyone has a right to be. But more than that, you have somehow become the light shining into the dark and narrow tunnel that has been my life these past few years. And I don't want to let you go."

My breath catches in my throat. "You don't?"

"No."

Tears spring to my eyes as we stare at each other, a heavy silence settling over us, fraught with tension. I sit there waiting for the euphoria — the great joy at knowing it wasn't all in my head, that he feels the same way I do — but it doesn't come.

"Well, I don't see what any of it matters," I say, the anger at his leaving blooming fresh again.

"But what about the treatment?"

"What about it?" I snap.

"Don't you want to at least try it?"

"What's the *point*?" I say, though not even a month ago, when the thought of not being able to ever touch Eric became unbearable, I was almost convinced to do it. Almost. "What — are you going to wait around in New Hampshire to see if it works?"

"Yeah, why not? It's just five hours. We could still see each other."

Though I'm flattered, I know he's still just holding on to the fantasy that I've been living in the past few months. It's time to face reality. "Eric, listen to yourself! Your whole life is there, your daughter. Mine is here. But even forgetting all that, Dr. Zhang said it could take up to a year to even find the protein, never mind the time it will take to do the therapy. And what if it never works? You'd just wait *forever* — not move on with your life?" I sigh, some of the anger dissipating. "I wouldn't expect you to wait — I could never let you do that."

"Then don't do it for me!" he explodes. "Do it for yourself. Stop living your life like you're terrified of it, squirreled away in your house with all your *books.* You deserve more, Jubilee! God, you deserve so much more."

I stare at him, stunned. I open my mouth to shout back at him — how *dare* he tell me how to live my life? But then I see his olive-green eyes, the passion in them, the same pain that mirrors mine — and the last bit of fight left in me drains away.

A lump forms in my throat. "I'm going to miss you," I say, my eyes filling, blurring my vision.

"But you don't have to, you know," he says. "We can keep in touch. I'll call. Email. I want to know how you're doing. What you're doing." Then he smiles and adds: "What you're reading."

I stare at him, taking this in. It sounds so tempting, staying in his life. Hearing his voice on the phone. But I realize I don't want just his voice. I don't want just a piece of him. Maybe it's greedy, but I want all of him. And I can't have him. And inevitably someone else will. What happens when he starts dating someone? Am I supposed to grin and bear it like I'm just another friend in his life? The thought alone guts me.

I shake my head at him slowly. "I can't," I say. "It's just . . . I can't." I want to tell him why, to explain that it's not fair to me — or to him, really — but what does *fair* have to do with anything? The world is unfair. Merciless and punishing. And looking at the pain in his eyes, I realize that's something he already knows.

He bobs his head slowly like a boat rocking on gentle waves. And then rubs both hands over his face. I stare at them, the

492

knobby knuckles, the strong veins coursing from his fingers to his wrists, and I feel a last pang in my heart, knowing with utter, devastating confidence that I'll never feel their touch on my skin.

"So this is it," he says with a finality that I knew was coming — that was inevitable — but that I wasn't really ready for. An ache starts in my core and radiates throughout my bones, my limbs, like the reverberation of a gong that's been struck by a giant. And I realize then that I have never known pain. Not really. Not when the kids taunted me on my bench at recess, not when Donovan kissed me and set fire to my throat, constricting my airway, not even when my mother died. Not until this moment, staring into Eric's eyes and feeling the full unfairness of this being the end, when we never even got to have a beginning.

"What do we do now?" I ask, my voice cracking with emotion. I'm barely aware of water dropping to the floor from my eyes.

Eric stands up, and I know this is it. This is good-bye. And I almost wish he had never come at all. Almost.

"Now," he says, his eyes growing dark as he grabs the blanket draped over the back of the couch. He starts unfolding it, bit by bit. He holds an end in each hand, stretching is out as far as his arms will reach. "I am going to suffocate you."

My body involuntarily pulls back, confused, and then I remember our conversation in the car. Me blubbering on and on about my mom. And a chuckle escapes my throat, and then I'm full-on laughing.

"C'mere, you," he says.

I stand on shaky legs and fall into the blanket, into him. He wraps me up like a burrito, holding me tight. My shoulders shudder from laughing, but he doesn't let go.

Not even when his shoulders start to match the movement of mine. Not even when neither one of us is laughing anymore.

TWENTY-SIX

ERIC

In the tenth grade, when I got home from my date with Penny Giovanni, my mom was waiting up for me at the kitchen table with a cup of coffee. In all her infinite wisdom, she sensed that something was wrong. I confessed my disappointment at not getting to hold Penny's hand and confided I was worried maybe there was something wrong with me (this, of course, was prior to my realization that there *was* something wrong with me in Penny's eyes — my gender). Mom waved off my concerns. "Love is all about timing," she said, and the logic of that explanation spoke to my rationality. It comforted me. It demystified the frilly feelings and fluttering hearts that girls always talked about in movies and books.

But leaving Jubilee's house, I now realize that what she should have said is: "Relationships are all about timing." Because love —

it'll show up when you least expect it, when you're not at all looking for it, in the middle of a small-town library with a wild-haired woman wearing a nightgown. When it comes to timing, love doesn't give a flying fuck.

"I've found A therapist in New Hampshire that I think would be great for Aja," says Janet, sliding a card across the table to me. "He's made a lot of progress, and I don't want him to backslide."

I take the card and sit up a little, so I can stuff it into my back pocket. "No, of course," I say. "I'll call as soon as we get settled."

Aja has made progress in that I've been sharing stories about his dad and he lets me tell them. He even laughs at some of them (like the Fourth of July Dinesh ate thirty-six hot dogs on a bet that he could beat the Coney Island champion, and was sick for three days after). He also hasn't been practicing telekinesis as far as I can tell or trying to control electricity (I was worried he might start after the library incident), and I think maybe we've moved past that, which is a relief.

But his big, brown eyes are still rimmed with sadness, and some nights, late, I've even heard him cry. Though, to be honest, since leaving Jubilee's, I've not exactly been a paragon of joy. We're what my mom would call a couple of sad sacks.

"How long does this . . . grieving process usually take?" I ask, unsure if I'm asking for Aja or myself.

She presses her lips together in a kind smile. "Longer than you'd expect," she says. "It gets better, but it never really goes away."

I nod.

"Keep the lines of communication open. And just keep being there for him," she says. "Just like you've been doing."

I put my hands on my knees and push down, using the leverage to help me stand. "Well, thank you," I say. How do you say good-bye to a therapist? A handshake? Are we supposed to hug? I opt for a little wave. "You've been so helpful. To both of us."

She nods. "Just doing my job."

I walk toward the door and reach for the handle.

"Oh, and Eric," she says from behind me.

"Yeah?" I turn around.

"It's about Jubilee."

I freeze.

"I think Aja would benefit from saying good-bye to her. He seems a little — bereft, when he talks about her, and how their relationship ended so . . . abruptly. I think they grew quite close."

She squints at me and I wonder how much she knows, or suspects, anyway. I nod and hold my hand up at her in acknowledgment. "Thanks," I say.

On the way to the car, I pull out my phone and text Ellie. I've been texting her every day, even though she doesn't always respond. Some are serious and some are like this one:

Been thinking of getting a nose ring.
Should I go hoop or stud? Dad

I slip my phone back into my pocket and turn to Aja. "Pizza for dinner?" I ask as we both get in the car.

"I don't care," he mumbles, pulling on his belt buckle.

We drive for a few minutes in silence. I wish I had escaped from Janet's office before she had the chance to say anything, but I know she's right. I can't just sweep Aja and Jubilee's relationship under the rug, as much as I want to try to put Jubilee behind me. To move on. It's not fair to Aja.

"Hey," I say.

He looks up.

"You know it's not Jubilee's fault you had to stop going to the library."

He raises his eyebrows. "It's not?"

"No," I say. "It's mine."

He doesn't ask why, and I'm glad not to tell him. "I know she misses you. Do you want to try and see her once more before we leave?"

He bites his lip and looks out the window. After a few minutes he says: "Yeah. I do."

"OK," I say, dreading having to say good-bye again, while at the same time dying to see her. "We'll go on Saturday."

My phone buzzes and I pull it out at the next red light.

God, you're such a dork.

I smile.

"What about Rufus?" Aja asks that evening as we're packing up the final boxes in the kitchen. I'm writing COFFEE MUGS in big black letters on the cardboard where I stashed my collection, so I don't lose them again.

The dog barks when he hears his name. "What about him?" I say, folding the flaps of the box over themselves.

"I think we should leave him — with her," he says.

I pause. "Who?" I say, even though I know exactly.

"Jubilee," he says.

"Why?"

He shrugs. "She likes him," he says slowly. And then he drops his head. "I'm afraid she'll be lonely without us."

I nod. My fear is selfishly, jealously the opposite. I'm afraid she won't be lonely for long enough.

"Yeah, bud," I say. "We can give her the dog."

At that, Rufus barks, and the matter is settled.

On Saturday evening, I pull the car up in front of Jubilee's house, but not in the driveway, having decided that as much as I want to, I can't see her again. Not face-to-face.

Aja gets out and opens the back to get Rufus.

I peer out through the darkness as he walks through the yard up to the front door, knocks on it, and waits. The porch light comes on. The door opens. Rufus jumps up on Jubilee, almost knocking her down. I'm surprised, realizing just how much he's grown in the few months since we first got him. She kneels and he's licking her face

500

with his pink tongue, while she giggles. She strokes his fur, calming him, and then her face grows serious as Aja explains why he's there.

She shakes her head, once. Twice. And then Aja says something to convince her and she smiles, nodding.

Then she disappears inside, shutting the door. I wince, like I've been punched in the gut. She didn't even look at me. Didn't wave. And I wonder, though it's only been a week, if maybe she's already over it. Maybe her feelings weren't as intense as mine.

But then I notice Aja hasn't moved. He's not coming back to the car. So I wait along with him, for whatever is about to happen next.

And then, the door opens. And Jubilee is standing there with a blanket open wide. I open my mouth to say something. Shout. Warn her that Aja hates being hugged. But it's too late. She engulfs him in the blanket, squeezing tight. And — miraculously — Aja doesn't move. He stands there, letting himself be loved.

Over his blanket-covered head, I see Jubilee's eyes look toward the car, searching for mine in the darkness. I don't know if she can see me, but I smile at her so hard, my cheeks will be sore for a thousand tomorrows. And I think, how silly of me not to realize that out of all the people in the world, Jubilee would be the only one that could touch him.

Twenty-Seven

JUBILEE

Instead of wallowing in self-pity like I've been doing most evenings this week after work, last night I decided to distract myself by reading *On the Road.* It was so good I stayed up until three a.m., until my eyes wouldn't stay open anymore. I'm just finishing the final few pages when Madison comes barging into the library on Friday morning.

"Where in the world have you been?" she demands.

I lower the book. Look up at her. "Right here," I say calmly.

"Oh, don't give me that. You know what I mean. You haven't answered a single call and you even had Roger *lie* to me. I know you were here that day."

I lean back and sigh. I knew this confrontation was coming — I'm actually surprised it took this long. "Where have *you* been?" I ask, turning the question on her. "That was what — two weeks ago?"

"The kids have been sick."

I instantly feel bad. "Oh god," I say. "Are they OK?"

"Yes, just puking all over me and themselves." She pulls a face. "Hannah got it first, but with kids it's like dominoes and it's one after another."

"I'm sorry," I say.

"Not as sorry as I am," she says, and the way she's looking at me, I know she's no longer talking about her kids. "Donovan told me what he said to you. The jerk."

"Is it true?" I ask, holding on to the sliver of hope that he was lying.

"Yeah," she says, looking down.

"Why'd you do it?" I ask.

"Jealousy."

"Of *me*?" I cackle. "You had *everything* in high school. I just don't understand how that's possible."

"I don't know," she says. "You were so pretty and you had this whole air of mystery about you. And Donovan . . . whatever, it doesn't matter now. It was stupid. *I* was stupid."

"I wish you had told me. Wish I didn't have to find out from him."

"I know," she says. "I should have."

"So was any of it real? Your friendship? Or was it just out of guilt — some pity project for you."

"No! Jube, I . . . I mean, I guess it started out that way —"

I cut her off. It's what I thought, but it stings to have it confirmed. "And god, Louise? I mean, she got *fired.* She's worked her whole life here. What were you *thinking*?"

She looks down, chagrined. "I know, I know," says Madison. "I feel terrible. I'll think of something, I swear." Her eyes meet mine again. "But you have to understand —"

"I think I understand perfectly," I say. "And I think we're done here."

"Jubilee!" She doesn't make any motion to leave, so I abruptly get up from my chair and go into the back room, because it's the only place I can think to go. She doesn't follow.

My head is ringing with anger, and it makes my nose tingle and floods my eyes until it overflows, rolling down my cheeks in the form of water. I feel so stupid. About Madison. About Eric and Aja's leaving. About everything. It's like I was living in some fantasy high school land where the most popular girl wanted to be my friend and I could fall in love and have a boyfriend like a normal person.

"Grow up," I mutter to myself, embarrassed by my naivety. God, things were so much easier when I was alone. But luckily, except for this job, I guess I'm back to where I started. Alone. And that's just fine with me. Safer, even, considering. I straighten my back, wipe my face, and take a deep breath. Then I go back out to the circulation desk.

Madison is gone.

Later, I'm restocking the biography shelves when I notice Michael, the pillow golfer, standing at the printer, muttering to himself. It's weird to see him anywhere but at his carrel staring at that ridiculous green screen and teeing off or whatever he does in that video game.

I move a little closer to investigate. "Damn it!" he says under his breath, then lightly taps the top of the machine with his fist. I jump, startled. He looks up.

"Oh, sorry," he says, looking a little like a schoolboy who's been caught writing on his desk. If I wasn't so miserable, it would be kind of endearing.

"Can I help?"

His eyes go wide, as if it didn't occur to him to ask for assistance. "Yeah," he says.

"If you can — I've been trying to print this thing for thirty minutes and the paper keeps getting stuck. I've wasted, like, four dollars in quarters already. I thought I got it out but now it's telling me it's still jammed or something."

"It's finicky," I say, remembering Louise telling me the trick on my first day. I reach down and pull a drawer out of the bottom of the printer where we store the paper. He's right next to the paper tray so I look up at him. "Can you stand back a little?"

He takes a step back.

"A little more?"

He moves two more steps.

"Thanks," I say, and then fill the tray to the top with paper. I turn to him. "It has to be at least halfway full of paper or it won't work properly. Just one of those things."

"Ah," he says. "Gotta love technology. You should put a sign up or something."

"We have. A few times. People rip it, write on it. One time someone even stole it. So we just stopped trying."

"Wow," he says. "That's kind of crazy."

"Yeah," I say. "Well, listen, I'll go get the key from the desk and get your money back for you."

"No, it's fine," he says. "The money doesn't matter, I just want to get this printed."

"What is it?" I ask, curiosity getting the better of me. "Something to do with your video game?"

He looks down, embarrassed. "No, uh . . . nothing like that. It's just a . . . business plan."

"Really?" I say, surprised that he has any ambitions outside of the video game. "What kind of business?"

"You know that old golf course just outside of town? The run-down one?"

"Yeah," I say. I remember passing it in the dead of night on the way to New Hampshire. With Eric. I swallow and push him out of my mind.

"I want to buy it. Bring it back. It's a great location," he says, looking at me now. His eyes are shining.

"Huh," I say. "Good for you. Well, I'll go get the key now."

I return a few minutes later and he's standing at his carrel straightening a stack of paper — his business plan, I presume. I unlock the coin box at the printer and retrieve $4 worth of quarters for him, putting them in a plastic cup I picked up from the desk.

I set it down next to his computer carrel. "Here you go," I say.

"Thanks," he says, sitting back down and turning his attention back to his game.

I stand there for a minute, until I'm overcome by my nosiness. "Hey, why do you come in here every day? Just to play this game?" I'm embarrassed as soon as it's out of my mouth, not realizing how rude it was going to sound. "I'm sorry. I didn't mean —"

"No, it's OK," he says, but then he just stares at the screen and doesn't respond. After twenty or thirty long seconds, I'm about to walk off when he finally speaks.

"My parents died. Last year. My mom from breast cancer. And then my dad a few months later. Freak accident."

"Car wreck?"

"No, he fell off the ladder while trying to clean the gutters." He chuckles softly. "Mom was always telling him to hire someone."

"My god, I'm so sorry."

"Yeah," he says. "Anyway, my parents were pretty prominent people, and so afterward, people kept calling, dropping by my house and my office unannounced to check on me, sending me things, and I just couldn't take it anymore. The reminders. The pity. So I took a leave of absence from work. And then one day I wandered in here to get away from it all. And then I kept coming. I didn't really think about it, but I guess it was a good distraction. It was easier than being out there, anyway." He waves his hand toward the door. "Guess that sounds a little crazy."

"No," I say. "It doesn't. Not to me."

He looks up, surprised. "Really?"

"Yeah," I say.

He nods. "Cool." He turns back to his computer, and I turn back to my desk, tears in my eyes for the second time that day.

Over the next few weeks, Madison is even more relentless in her calls, texts, and random unannounced visits at the library and my house. I try to ignore her, but she's pretty much impossible. Finally, one day she's waiting on my front porch when I get home. I park my bike behind the fence and walk up to the front steps, stopping at the bottom.

"Please just go away," I say, pulling my keys out of my bag.

"Not until you hear me out."

I cross my arms and look at her.

She takes a deep breath. "When I first saw you at the gas station a few months ago, I was shocked. It brought back so many memories — so many feelings that I tried to forget over the years — especially guilt about that god-awful, stupid bet and what it did to you.

"And then, when you said you needed a job, yes, I wanted to help, I wanted to do anything I could for you, to make up for what I had done. And god, when I found out about your condition and how you'd been spending your life — that Donovan had been telling the truth — I felt even worse. So yeah, maybe it was a little pity project, or whatever you want to call it, just to selfishly lessen my remorse."

At this, I roll my eyes and scoff. She holds up her hand. "I admit that," she says. "But, Jube, the more I got to know you, the more I liked you. And then, I was so excited just to have a friend in my life. You have no idea how hard it's been since Donovan and I split up. They say when things like that happen, you find out who your real friends are, and it's true. Turns out, most people in my life were just there because they thought Donovan and I were some golden couple, or because he was some bigwig at the bank, and when we got divorced I was so alone. And then, there you were. And you needed me. But it turns out, I needed you, too. More than you know."

I stare at her, taking this in. And I realize I always just assumed Madison had a million friends, like she did in high school. It never occurred to me she could ever be just as lonely as I was. As I am.

I bite my lip, wanting to stay angry — knowing I *should* be angry — but when she looks at me, I know I'll forgive her. That I already have. Besides, Mr. Walcott always said beggars can't be choosers, and really, she's the only friend I've got left.

"Jesus, Madison," I say, dropping my arms. "Can you get off my porch?"

She looks at me with sadness. "Yeah," she says, her shoulders sagging. She starts down the steps.

"Don't be so dramatic," I say. "I need you to move so I can unlock the door and let you in."

"Really?" she asks, her head popping up.

"Yes," I say. "Really."

"Oh my gosh! I wish I could hug you."

"Let's not get carried away," I say. "We just made up. And since I'm your only friend, you probably shouldn't chance putting me in the hospital."

Later, when we're settled on the couch catching up over cups of coffee, Rufus lying contentedly at my feet, I fill her in on Eric. "Oh, Jube," she says. "That sucks."

And I sadly laugh at how succinctly that sums it up. Then I ask her the question that

I've been mulling over ever since Eric left my house.

"Do you sometimes wish you had never met Donovan?"

She looks at me, thinking. "Sometimes, yeah," she says. She takes a sip from her mug. Swallows. "And then I look at Sammy and Hannah and Molly and that's when meeting Donovan becomes the best thing that ever happened to me."

I nod. "But what if you didn't have kids? What if you and Donovan had gotten married and then he cheated and you had nothing to show for it?"

"What are you asking? If love is worth the risk?"

I shrug. "I don't know." And then: "Yeah, I guess that is what I'm asking."

She lets out a long breath, chuckling a little on the exhale. "Listen, love can be a real shit-show," she says. "Especially my love life. Had I known that Donovan and I were going to end up the way we did, would I have still gone through with it? I don't know. But that's the thing, isn't it? We never know. Loving people, trusting people. It's always a risk. And there's ever only one way to find out if it's worth it."

I sit back, taking this in. And then out of nowhere, I think of Michael. And what he said in the library — how life is easier when you hole yourself up away from the world, away from the pain. How I did that for nine years. And then when I finally came out of hiding, I met Eric. And even though it hurt — even though it still hurts, every second of every day — would I really rather have never met him? In those nine years alone, I never experienced even an ounce of the pure joy, the exhilaration I felt in those few moments with Eric.

And I wonder, if I hole myself back up, protect myself from the world and the people in it — what other moments will I be missing?

And that's when I know that Madison's right. You have to take risks.

On Sunday, I wake up, let Rufus out, and eat a poached egg on toast, cut into tiny bite-size pieces — though my agoraphobia seems better, I still have a profound fear of choking to death. Then I go stand at the door to my mother's room. I stare at it, as if taking mental pictures of the scalloped bedspread, the knockoff perfume jars on the dresser, the full jewelry boxes — and then I begin.

It takes most of the morning and afternoon, sorting the things in her closet, her drawers, making piles for charity, trash, and to keep, the what-to-keep pile being the smallest of them all. Rufus watches with mild curiosity from his perch just inside the door to the room. I break down the bed, pushing the frame, mattress, and box spring out into the hall, along with the dresser, the nightstand. And then I dive into the first of her three jewelry boxes. I know it's all costume — she took the few good pieces she owned with her to Long Island — but I go through it all, anyhow, if only just to hold each necklace and earring one last time. To conjure the memory of when I last saw her in them.

It's not until the bottom of the third box that I find it — a letter, addressed to Kimberly Yount in Fountain City, Tennessee. The return address is my mother's, mine — from when we lived in Fountain City. A black rubber stamp has been pressed into the front between the two — RETURN TO SENDER. I flip it over to find that it's unopened.

I stare at it. And wonder who it could be. She never mentioned a Kimberly, even when we lived in Tennessee, apparently just a few miles away from this woman.

I sit down on the hardwood floor and slide my thumb under the flap, ripping through the old glue with little effort. I pull a folded piece of lined notebook paper out of the envelope and unbend its creases. I start reading.

Kimmy,

I know you don't want to hear from me, but you won't return my calls. Not that I blame you, I guess. I just need somebody right now. And you're the closest thing to a friend I ever had.

Jubilee — that's my daughter, that's what I named her, maybe you already knew that, I don't know — anyway, the doctors, they're saying she's got something awful. And I'm scared. They're saying I can't touch her. That no one can.

She's always been an anxious girl — long before these problems started. She would wake up in the night screaming bloody murder like you never heard. Night terrors, that's what the doctor said. But I knew it was something more — like she was born scared of the world. Like she always knew what she had before I knew it. And I thought it must have been my fault. You know I don't believe in sinning or God punishing people or whatever, but I also know it's not right, what I did — and maybe Jubilee has to pay for that? Like karma, or something.

And now that she's got this thing, she's even more jittery than before, although I guess I can't blame her. She won't let me anywhere near her. The doctors said if I was safe, if I wore gloves, didn't have any skin-to-skin contact, it would probably be all right. But she's just so frightened.

I bought this nightgown at Belk — this ugly old thing with long sleeves and about eight miles of fabric. (I don't know who sleeps in something like that — although on second thought, I guess it's exactly like something you'd wear. No offense.) And some nights when Juby's sleeping, I sneak into her room and put my arms around her, careful not to wake her, not to touch her skin. And oh, she smells so good. Just like my baby girl, even though she's six now. And it just breaks my heart.

I don't know why I'm telling you all this, except maybe it'll make you feel better to know that I'm in a world of hurt. And I guess I deserve it for ruining your marriage like I did. Or maybe I just want you to feel sorry for me. Lord knows I could use a friend right now, even if it's out of pity.

Anyway, for what it's worth. I'm sorry.

Vicki

When I finish, I read it again. And then a third time. And though it's got clues to who my possible father is and insight to my mother's past that I never dreamed of knowing — and am not even sure that I wanted to know — all I can focus on is that ridiculous nightgown I found in her closet and used as my Halloween costume. And I'm laughing even as my hands shake and tears roll down my face. My mother — who owned far too many too-tight blouses and smoked far too many cigarettes and was far, far from perfect — she held me. She loved me. The only way she knew how.

Eventually, I pick myself up off the floor, put my mom's letter in the what-to-keep pile, and continue with the sorting. A few hours later, muscles aching, I go downstairs, satisfied with the day's work. I sit on the sofa, pick a book off the top of one of my teetering stacks, and decide to spend the rest of the evening reading, Rufus's head in my lap.

Tomorrow, I'll move my furniture in. Right after I call Dr. Zhang.

EPILOGUE:
SEVEN YEARS LATER

"What's miraculous about a spider's
web?" said Mrs. Arable. "I don't see why
you say a web is a miracle —
it's just a web."
"Ever try to spin one?" asked Dr. Dorian.
E. B. White, *Charlotte's Web*

THE NEW YORK TIMES

A RARE CONDITION,
A RADICAL CURE
by William Colton

Every day for the past eighteen months, Jubilee Jenkins drank tea. But not just any tea — a special brew, formulated with a heady mix of Chinese herbs by New York doctor Mei Zhang. The same mix of herbs that Jenkins also applied to her skin as a lotion twice daily and bathed in every night.

No, it's not the latest fountain-of-youth trend,

but a treatment for a rare condition that has left Jenkins, 33, on the sidelines for most of her life. An allergy. To humans.

It may sound like something out of a Michael Crichton novel, but it's all too real for Jenkins, who was first diagnosed at the tender age of six. "It was devastating," she said. "I couldn't have a regular childhood, for fear of being touched."

The affliction (first reported by the *New York Times* 28 years ago) only grew worse as she got older, confining her to her house for most of her twenties. But then she met with Dr. Zhang, who had an idea: to use genetic sequencing to isolate the human protein she was missing — the one (or ones) her body would attack when it was detected on her skin after contact with others — and to slowly introduce it to her system in the form of immunotherapy, a treatment that's had some success with severe food allergies.

Jenkins resisted at first. "I had lived my whole life this way." She shrugs. "I guess I was just scared." But then something changed her mind. "I met someone," she says, ducking her head. "I guess he made me realize I wanted to be a part of this world — with or without my allergy. It would just be easier to live in it without it."

Dr. Zhang's team of geneticists isolated the

protein rather quickly — within five months — but five years of treatment garnered disappointing results. "She could tolerate minuscule amounts, but every time we tried to increase it, she would react. After a few years, we were finally able to up the dose, but we were nowhere near a cure. Nowhere near the realm of her getting a handshake or hug from somebody without a severe reaction. And that, obviously, was the goal."

That's when Dr. Zhang decided to try a novel approach that she's been researching for more than ten years: HFAT-3, or Herbal Food Allergy Treatment. It's a combination of Chinese herbal compounds and extracts that have been found to reduce inflammation, block histamine release — and even alter the molecular biology of immune system cells. In other words, they reduce the body's knee-jerk reaction to a known allergen and can even prevent anaphylactic shock.

"My herbal treatment has worked very successfully — about an 80 percent cure rate — for various food allergies. And I just thought, why not? What did we have to lose?"

As it turns out, nothing — but they had everything to gain.

In February of this year, Jubilee was given the news she'd once only dreamed of. " 'You're cured' — that's what Dr. Zhang said.

I don't think I really believed it. Even when she hugged me," Ms. Jenkins said. "It's a miracle."

But Dr. Zhang disagrees. "It's just science," she said. "And a little bit of really good luck."

JUBILEE

"Oh dear, someone ripped a page of *Charlotte's Web,*" says Louise, reaching in the drawer for the Filmoplast.

I look, and my heart leaps into my throat. It's the book. The same blue hardback binding. The little girl with the red dress. "I'll fix it," I say, taking it from her just so my hands can touch the same place his did seven years ago when he read to me under the cover of darkness in the library. I hold it to my nose, even though I know it will only smell like a musty old book. I inhale anyway. Louise looks at me funny and then grabs her purse. "I'm going to lunch."

Mr. Walcott used to say, "Time heals all wounds." But it's not true. Time doesn't heal anything. All it does is dull the memory, until some reminder — like a classic children's book — sharpens the focus, takes your breath, and all the feelings come rushing back.

I revel in it for a minute, then set the book down on the top of the circulation desk, smooth a piece of Filmoplast on the torn page. When I close the cover, a bark grabs my attention. I look up and see Rufus dragging Madison into the library.

"What are you doing? You're supposed to leave him tied up outside!"

"Oh, like I've ever had any control over him," she says. "Are you ready to go?"

I laugh, marveling at how I can never be mad at her. Even years ago when I felt completely betrayed by her, I caved at her first sincere apology.

It was only a few weeks after that Louise got her job back. Not because of Madison — there was nothing she could really do. But because the library received an anonymous donation for $400,000, a whopping sum that put Maryann in such a good mood, she forgot why she was ever mad at me to begin with. A lot of chatter ensued among the staff on who could have made such a gift. I thought it was Donovan at first, but Madison howled when I shared my suspicions. "I mean, he's doing fine at the bank, but his salary isn't even *close* to that much money," she said.

And then I wondered if maybe Eric had

somehow had a hand in it. I didn't think he had that kind of money either, but maybe he was able to convince one of the many corporations he worked with to make the gift. I reveled in the thought, playing out his generosity like the end of some Lifetime movie, even though I knew it was a remote possibility.

It wasn't until years later that we discovered that Michael, the pillow golfer (though it feels weird to call him that now, considering), was behind it. Turns out, what Michael meant when he said his parents were "prominent citizens" was that they were filthy rich — and he was their sole heir.

"Come on, Jube. Let's go."

"Keep your pants on," I say, scanning *Charlotte's Web* in and making a note of its damage on the computer.

Outside, the sun is a giant orange in the sky, radiating a sweet warmth and happiness into the July day. "Thanks for getting Rufus," I say as we stroll down the sidewalk. "I promise I'll get a new dog walker soon. It's just hard to replace Terry. He loved Rufus so much."

Terry was my mailman (not Earl, as I had dubbed him). I met him while walking Rufus one day and he mentioned — while producing a dog treat out of his pocket that

Rufus snatched with glee — that he was retiring from the post office and would be taking care of dogs as his new hobby. I hired him on the spot and he had been walking Rufus on the days I worked ever since. But now he and his wife are moving down to Florida to live in a condo on the beach.

When we reach TeaCakes, I tie Rufus up to the stand outside, where the owner has left a big bowl of water and a few chew toys for the dogs of his customers.

"Jube, seriously. You're moving like a glacier."

"So? What's the big rush?" I ask as she holds open the door for me and I step inside. And then I see.

"Happy birthday!" a chorus of familiar faces shouts. But the brightest, loudest one of all is Michael. He steps forward, grinning. "Are you surprised?"

I cover my mouth with my hand, taking in all the people in front of me: Louise (how'd she get here so fast?), Roger, Dr. Zhang (I can't believe she drove in from the city), and even Terry and his wife. My eyes return to Michael.

"Did you do this?" I ask him.

"Yeah. Well, with some help from Madison."

I reach my hand out to him and he takes

527

it, squeezing it. My heart swells, and I think how lucky I am. Not just for Michael, but for everyone in this room. For the family I never thought I'd have.

I narrow my eyes at him. "Wait, I thought you were supposed to be in Chicago." Michael had been talking about the National Golf Course Owners Association's annual meeting for a month now. Per his plan, he bought the abandoned course on the outskirts of Lincoln a few years ago and has quickly turned it into a hot spot for NYC businessmen and -women looking to hit the links.

"A little white lie," he says. "It's actually next month."

I laugh. "I guess you're forgiven."

"Did I miss the cake?" a voice behind me says.

I turn around.

"Maryann!" I give her a hug and then step back. "Hold on — if you're here, who's at the library?"

"I closed it," she says, winking. "Just for an hour." She leaves her arm on my shoulder and Louise comes up and puts her hand on my waist, steering me toward a long table in the back groaning under an entirely too-large sheet cake. "Come on," she says. "Let's go eat."

■ ■ ■ ■

Later that night as I sit on the couch in my den, rereading *Northanger Abbey* for the hundredth time, I can't concentrate. Like most evenings the past two weeks, my mind keeps wandering to Michael. Tonight, I'm marveling over the course of our friendship these past seven years. How after I fixed the printer for him that day, we started chatting more regularly — our talks slowly morphing into in-depth conversations about life, where we would stay in the library long after I was supposed to close up for the night. And then, he was just always *there,* like a light fixture in the middle of the ceiling. Stable, dependable, someone I could count on over the years. He stuck by my side through all the failed treatments, letting me feel sorry for myself when I needed, but also knowing when to give me a gentle nudge when it was time to pick myself up. And I was there for him as he truly began to grieve his parents and slowly bring himself back to life, buying the golf course and starting over.

Even though we became close, I never thought I had feelings for him like *that* — not like I had for Eric. That is, until two weeks ago, when he took me out to see the renovated clubhouse on the course. While we were talking about the stain he had chosen for the hardwood floors — a mix of Jacobean and Ebony — he suddenly blurted out: "I love you." It took me a minute to register what he was saying and then his face came into focus, and I was filled with — I don't know — love, I think. Although it's a different love than what I felt for Eric. But then, I wonder if maybe every love is different, unique, like the grains of the wood planks in the floor we were standing on — and all the more beautiful for their distinctions.

I mumbled something about how the stain was very natural looking and left the clubhouse. And Michael, because he's Michael, hasn't brought it up since.

My cell phone rings, jarring me from my thoughts. Madison. I slide my thumb across the screen to answer it.

"Are you ready for next week? The big move?"

After years of Madison's cajoling, I finally gave in to her insistence that I sell the house. "It's a seller's market," she said a few months ago. "Lincoln is so hot, with its small-town feel and close proximity to Manhattan. All those Prospect Park families are leaving their overpriced brownstones by the droves for the yards and schools in towns like this. You would make a killing."

She was right. It sold within two days of hitting the market, for $32,000 above the asking price. I knew I should be ecstatic — and I wanted to be — but something was holding me back. Probably the fact that I've lived in this house for so long. That it was my mother's. That I have so many memories here.

"Yeah," I say. "I think so."

"See you bright and early," she says.

When we hang up, I look around the room, thinking about my mother. Her presence is less palpable, but I don't think it's just because it's been so long, or because I redecorated. I think it's because I've made peace with her, with our relationship. That letter I found so many years ago gave me as many questions as it gave me answers, but the most important thing it gave me was the knowledge that she did love me, she just didn't know how to show it. And then I think about Michael and how he can.

A warmth grows in my belly as I picture his lopsided grin, his lanky frame, and I put my book down, able to finally name the feeling I have when I'm with him: contentment.

The next day, Michael enters the front door

of my new brick loft overlooking the river downtown, carrying a stack of two cardboard boxes in his arms. "That's the last of it," he says. Madison motions for him to set them down by the couch.

"Thank you so much," I say as he stands up, groaning. "You really didn't have to help."

"I wouldn't have, if I had remembered how many books you have," he says.

I laugh, my eyes roving over the length of his body, pausing at the sinewy muscles in his arms that he's now massaging dramatically. And I almost blurt it out right then: *I love you, too.* But the words are caught in my throat.

I look down at the box I'm unpacking and then back up. "Hey, it's such a gorgeous day. Why don't we all take a break and go to that new gelato place by TeaCakes? My treat."

"I think I might need something stronger than gelato," Michael says.

"C'mon," I say, grinning. "We'll hit the wine shop on the way back."

I clip Rufus's leash onto his collar and we all head down the three flights of stairs to the street. It's a Friday afternoon and the streets are mostly empty, the rush hour of lunch over, workers stationed back in their stores and office buildings.

As we stroll through town, Michael's regaling Madison with a story from work that week: a member of a foursome suffered a heart attack on the green, but instead of calling the game when the ambulance came, one of the guys asked the driver to move so he could continue playing because he was shooting so well. "I could get a perfect round!" he shouted as his friend was being loaded into the back of the emergency vehicle.

"Oh my god, that's terrible!" Madison says. I laugh again, even though it's my second time hearing it. Madison's laughing too, but then she abruptly stops. Not just laughing, but moving. I stop, too, and look up at her to make sure she's OK. She's staring straight ahead of us and her face has blanched, as if she's seen a ghost. She grabs my arm, and I pray it's not Donovan out with yet another girl young enough to be his daughter (even though their divorce has become more amicable, he's still kind of a dick) as I follow her gaze down the street. And then when I spot what's got her attention, all air, thought, and feeling leaves me at once.

It's Eric.

Our eyes meet, and though he slows his

gait, he doesn't come to a full stop until he's an arm's length away. I could literally reach out and touch him. But I don't. Rufus gets there first.

"Hey, buddy." Eric's face lights up and he bends down, scratching the dog on his head. When they're done with their reunion, he stands back up and looks at Michael, who sticks out his hand.

"I'm Michael," he says, and it feels like I've crossed into some bizarre world — where there are two suns, Eric and Michael, and they're colliding.

Eric takes his hand, shakes it. "Eric," he says. I can feel a wave of recognition come over Michael. We spoke at length about Eric after we became friends. He knows who he is, even if he didn't know what he looked like.

"Nice to meet you, man," Michael says.

Eric nods and looks at Madison. She gives a little wave. "I'm Madison," she says. "And I just remembered I have a little errand I need to run before we get gelato."

"I'll come with you," Michael pipes up, following her lead, intuiting that I need a moment alone with Eric. He gently squeezes my arm. I give him a look that I hope conveys gratitude. Madison reaches for Rufus's leash. I let it drop into her hands.

I turn my head to watch them go, but I can feel Eric's eyes remain on me. When they reach the corner, I look back at him and he's grinning. "Is that *the* Madison?" he asks.

I tilt my head at him. "What do you mean?"

"The one who gave you that god-awful dress? With the feathers."

I throw my head back and laugh, thinking how that night feels like a million years and just a few days ago at the exact same time.

"Yeah, that's her," I say.

"And Michael?" He raises his eyebrows. Questioning.

"A friend," I say, but I'm afraid my flushing face is suggesting otherwise.

Eric nods, his gaze steady, intense, his expression unreadable. Then he clears his throat and straightens, sticking his hands in his pockets.

I'm not sure what else to say, so I say nothing. And then we just stare at each other, the common courtesies behind us, silence filling the space between us. I take the opportunity to study him. His eyes are still green like olives; his brown hair, though streaked with a little more gray, still sticks out at weird angles, begging to be mussed by a grandmotherly sort. He's grown a beard, but it doesn't look purposeful — more as if his razor is just on strike. I stare at the beard — everything else is too familiar, too heart-wrenchingly congruent with my memory.

Suddenly the silence becomes unbearable and I blurt: "Where's Aja?"

At the same time that he says: "How are you?"

We both laugh, breaking the tension. "You first," I say.

"Aja's at Connie's house. We're helping her move to the city. I just came into town for more boxes, actually."

I nod. "And how is he?" I ask, though it's more a perfunctory question. A few weeks after they moved back to New Hampshire, Aja emailed me. I still don't know how he got my email address, but we kept in touch, sending funny articles, facts, and jokes back and forth every couple of months. I always wanted to ask him about Eric, especially in the beginning, but I knew it wasn't fair to Aja. To put him in the middle like that. And anyway, I wasn't sure I wanted to know — especially if Eric had moved on.

"Good." He grins. "Really good. Starts college this fall."

"Dartmouth, right?"

"Yeah," he says. "I'm glad you were able

to keep in touch. He missed you so much when we left." His face goes solemn and the word "missed" hangs in the air. It's a silly word, not nearly big or grand enough to encompass what it really means. You can *miss* a pitch in baseball, but a person . . .

"I missed him, too," I say, a lump forming in my throat.

His eyes track down from my face, taking me in. I close mine, but it doesn't make a difference. I can still feel his gaze burning into my flesh. I'd be lying if I said I haven't fantasized about this moment — seeing Eric again. Once, years ago, I ran into Connie at the drugstore. We exchanged short pleasantries, but I was shaken for the rest of the day, wondering how I would have felt if Eric had been with her. *If* I would have felt. When you love someone — and it became clear to me, as the months passed after Eric left, that that's exactly how I felt about him — where do those feelings go? I realized the answer that day — they don't go anywhere. Even now, as much as I care for Michael, it's almost as if I have two different hearts, and the one that's been housing my feelings for Eric all these years is now beating loud and clear in my chest.

"Where are your gloves?" he asks, and my eyes snap open.

"I don't . . . I don't wear them anymore." I thought maybe Aja would have told him back in February, but now I wonder if Eric bought into the same philosophy as I did — that it was better not to know.

He searches my face. "Are you . . . does that mean that you . . ." He swallows.

I nod. "Yes." There's something on my cheek, a trickle — and I look up to see if it's started to rain, but the air is dry.

As I reach up to feel what it is, Eric's hand shoots out like a bullet from a gun and he grabs my wrist. A puff of air escapes my lips. He's touching me. Our eyes lock as his fingers encircle my skin, the warmth of them like sunlight on a temperate day. The perfect amount of heat.

And part of me thinks how unfair, how unspeakably cruel, life can be. How this moment — his skin on mine — is all I ever wanted, all I ever thought about for weeks, months, years of my life. But it's been *seven* years. So why now? Why is he standing here, making me feel this way, just when I thought I had everything sorted out?

But then, I think of my mom and of Madison and Donovan, and even of my deepening relationship with Michael, and I know that if I've learned anything, it's that love is messy. It doesn't come to us in a perfect box all wrapped up in a bow. It's more like a gift from a child, crayon-scrawled and crumpled. Imperfect. But always a gift just the same.

It's just that not all gifts are meant to last forever.

Michael's face flashes in my mind and I'm conflicted. He loves me. And I — well, part of me — cares for him, too. But the other part . . .

I look at Eric standing in front of me and I can't help it — I smile at him with abandon. He cocks his head, grinning back. With his other hand, he palms my face, using the pad of his thumb to gently catch the drop of water and then swipe it across my cheekbone.

"Jubilee," he says in wide wonder, as if my name is a secret he's held on his tongue for years and at last, he gets to tell it. "You're crying."

Frozen, we stare at each other, his hand glued to my face, his other still holding my wrist. With my free hand, I grab his arm and we stand there, clutching each other, a bizarre puzzle of limbs.

I lean toward him, until the flats of our foreheads are touching and my eyes are swimming in his and his sweet breath is warm on my face. But it's not close enough.

I reach up and grab the back of his neck, pulling him closer until his lips are firmly on mine.

And we're kissing.

Finally, we're kissing.

We're kissing to make up for the hundreds of kisses we never got to share, and maybe for the hundreds of kisses we never will.

We're kissing to beat the band.

And then, we're laughing. Our mouths open wide, our cackles traveling out into the street. We don't care who hears or how ridiculous we look. We're laughing as hard as I'm crying. And as I concentrate on the heat of his hands on my face, my wrist — his skin on my skin — something bursts free inside me like a wild animal escaping from a cage.

It's the humming of one thousand Tibetan monks.

An electric current.

It's everything.

AUTHOR'S NOTE

While there is no evidence that Jubilee's allergy exists, many of the stories contained within this novel, along with the day-to-day fear that Jubilee endures, are all-too-real scenarios for people and families battling severe and life-threatening food allergies. The immunotherapy and Chinese medicine used to treat Jubilee's affliction are based on the research and lifework of pioneering allergy experts Dr. Kari Nadeau at Stanford University and Dr. Xiu-Min Li at Mount Sinai Hospital, respectively. Their treatments have shown great promise in the still largely mysterious world of food allergies. As part of my research, the *New York Times Magazine* article "Allergy Buster" by Melanie Thernstrom (March 7, 2013) and "Inside the Search for Chinese Herbal Food Allergy Treatments" by Claire Gagne for AllergicLiving.com (February 18, 2015) proved immeasurably helpful.

ACKNOWLEDGMENTS

First and foremost, thank you to the readers who read, loved and championed *Before I Go*. Your emails and messages are what made me think I could write another book, so essentially, this is all your fault.

Many thanks, also, to the following:

My agent, Emma Sweeney, whose brilliant insights helped turn my crazy idea into the beginnings of a novel.

My editor, Karen Kosztolnyik, whose patience, encouragement, and skill are unrivaled in the entire world of publishing.

Also unrivaled — the amazingly enthusiastic and talented team at Gallery Books, especially Jen Bergstrom, Carolyn Reidy, Louise Burke, Meagan Harris, Wendy Sheanin, Liz Psaltis, Abby Zidle, Melanie Mitzman, Diana Velasquez, Becky Prager, and Molly Gregory. I'm so lucky to have you in my corner.

My foreign publishers all over the world,

with special thanks to the incredible team at Allen & Unwin, including Annette Barlow and Sam Redman.

Kira Watson for, somehow, keeping up with all the contracts, emails, and questions, and making everything run smoothly.

The experts that lent their time and expertise on everything from allergies to accounting to social work: Dr. Leo Sage, Dr. Mark Livezey, Mike and Jessica Chamlee, Maribeth Nolan, Johnna Stein (and Katie Garrison for your introductions). Any factual inaccuracies or creative embellishments are mine alone.

Amy Carlan and all the librarians at the Jefferson Public Library, thank you for sharing your time, your library, and your hilarious stories with me.

My sister, Megan Oakley, for reading this book at least one thousand times and then reading it again. Thank you also for being one of my go-to experts in the field of allergies, although I wish with all my heart you didn't have to be.

My parents, Bill and Kathy Oakley (especially you, Mom, for instilling in me the love of words and books and libraries), my grandmother Marion, and the rest of my crazy clan of people (Tulls, Wymans, and Oakleys) for your love and support.

My fellow debs: Karma Brown, Amy Reichert, Sona Charaipotra, and Shelly King. What happens on Flowdock stays on Flowdock.

My friends and beta readers: Karma Brown (yes, I have to thank you twice), Kimberly Belle, Shannon Jones, Caley Bowman, Kelly Marages, Brooke Hight, and Kirsten Palladino. Thank you.

The remarkable bloggers, reviewers, librarians, and booksellers who have not only championed my novels but work endlessly promoting the books and authors they love. You are good people and the world is better with you in it.

My children: Henry, Sorella, Olivia, and Everett, whose stories are far more creative and entertaining than mine. Like the laundry basket in our house, my love for you is constantly overflowing.

And finally, my husband, Fred — without you, it is all meaningless.

ABOUT THE AUTHOR

Colleen Oakley is an Atlanta-based writer and author of the novel *Before I Go*. Her articles, essays, and interviews have been featured in *The New York Times, Ladies' Home Journal, Marie Claire, Women's Health, Redbook, Parade,* and *Martha Stewart Weddings*. Before she was a freelance writer, Colleen was editor in chief of *Women's Health & Fitness* and senior editor at *Marie Claire. Close Enough to Touch* is her second novel.

The employees of Thorndike Press hope you have enjoyed this Large Print book. All our Thorndike, Wheeler, and Kennebec Large Print titles are designed for easy reading, and all our books are made to last. Other Thorndike Press Large Print books are available at your library, through selected bookstores, or directly from us.

For information about titles, please call:
  (800) 223-1244

or visit our website at:
  gale.com/thorndike

To share your comments, please write:
  Publisher
  Thorndike Press
  10 Water St., Suite 310
  Waterville, ME 04901